KIT COPE
RIDES THE HIGH COUNTRY

A NOVEL BY

ALAN ELTRON BARRELL

Published by

MELROSE BOOKS

An Imprint of Melrose Press Limited
St Thomas Place, Ely
Cambridgeshire
CB7 4GG, UK
www.melrosebooks.co.uk

FIRST EDITION

Cover designed by Gerallt D. Hughes

ISBN 978-1-907732-63-8

Printed and bound in Great Britain by:
Mimeo Ltd, Huntingdon, Cambridgeshire

For my Family:
My Mother and Father
Annette Mary and George Peter
My brothers Brett John and Daniel Paul
And my sister
Samantha Lee

He who climbeth on the highest mountains,
laugheth at all tragic plays and tragic realities.

Nietzsche

PART
I

The man who had been scalped by the Indian renegade God Dog was a sight not many a man had seen, and certainly a sight *no* man had seen in Wagon Trail.

Kit Cope, on the other hand, had seen something similar. Back in his buffalo hunting days he had skinned over several hundred hides, and often while working on the last few carcasses in the sweltering prairie heat, had had to stop to catch his breath; usually he would take a seat on a hide that hadn't been skinned yet, and survey his handiwork. Although by then he was an expert with a blade, and could have taken a scalp as quick as any Indian, as yet skinning a buffalo was never anything less than an arduous task. Of course, it wasn't like you skinned *one* buffalo; usually you had twelve to twenty-four hides to get through – thirty-six to sixty when they had first started out.

But their plain success had been their own worst enemy, as most cowpokes put it. The herds petered out and the skinners became trail scouts or cattle herders, or else put in for work as lawmen or peacekeepers, as Kit Cope had done himself.

Some of the oldest buffalo hunters he had worked with back in the day, and from whom he had learnt the most, had even been mountain men before that, skinning beaver. In fact, he had even known an ex-mountain man *called* Skinning Beaver by the Indians he had traded pelts with – early on, before the multitudes came on up the river, so to speak.

But in *that* instance, the demand had petered out, not the supply. People wearing beaver as far as Abilene and Dodge, and even all the way in England, no longer felt beaver to be as popular no sooner than they saw some high-society type step out of a coach wearing a buffalo.

Skinning Beaver – Old Morgan – had told Kit how it all started, and how it all worked, out one day on the prairie pulling and ripping at the hide of a dead buffalo he had drug right up next to Kit's one single-handedly, because the man enjoyed conversation while he worked.

Ripping at the carcass he had said, "Son, you may be young, but if you've got a gun and a good knife in your hands in these lands, you can carve yourself a fine living. If it's sharp or it can shoot, it's as good as money in your hand.

"First time I killed me a beaver I killed it to eat, on account of it was the only thing I could find up there in them mountains. Outside of a squirrel. And, 'I God, if you've ever had to shoot your gun empty at a squirrel, and then outrun a avalanche, you'll know not to twice. At least, with a beaver, it's one or two shots and you either got it licked or you don't–"

Kit had interrupted him, more interested in what he had said before that. Kit asked him if he had really outrun a avalanche.

Old Morgan said, "Son, me and that squirrel both. He was ahead of me all the way."

Kit had chuckled to himself at the thought of Old Morg up in the mountains, firing his gun empty at a tree, and then waiting for the smoke to clear and the echo to fade... only to see the squirrel come flying out of the branches and go rushing on down the mount. And then, in the silence that resumed, Old Morg standing there listening carefully, to an indistinct but distant sound – of an avalanche! Kit imagined Morg's big, bushy buffalo hunter eyebrows hitting his hairline; imagined Old Morg running down after the escaping squirrel, glancing back up the slope over his shoulder every now and again at the oncoming wall of snow, taking down pine trees–

"There you are off again in that head of yours," Old Morgan said. "One day that imagination of yours is gonna be your downfall. I seen the way you look out across the plains. Dreaming of fortune and adventure, huh?"

"Yeh," Kit had said, solemnly. "Somethin' like that."

Anything but my hands in one of these stinking carcasses, he thought, still ripping and sawing with his knife.

"Now now, son," Old Morg had said, "there's plenty of fine adventure in just plain old survival, 'cause that's exactly where the opportunity knocks. See, back then them beaver pelts was just piling up in my cave next to the campfire. I was meanin' to chuck 'em out, on account of the smell was getting a might rank. But then this lone Injun comes along, 'cause he smells me cooking beaver, and he can't speak a word I can make hide nor tail of, so I offer him a bit of beaver straight off the stick: 'Come on in make yourself welcome. I ain't had no company other than a bunch of stinking dead beavers and my own self since I wondered on up here and got stuck.' You know how's I like conversation, or at least some kind of... interaction."

Any mention of Indians – back then even more, but still now – fascinated Kit. Back then he had heard of, but never seen, an Indian. The stories he had heard were each time gripping. It seemed to him there was nothing out there to fear more than an Indian; some kind of strange... *wild* man.

"An Indian?" Kit had said, stopping for a moment. "An Indian came into your cave and ate beaver with you?"

"'I God, he did," Old Morg said; but he carried on cutting, as methodical as only countless skinnings over a lifetime could accustom a man. "That he did," he repeated as he cut.

Kit was dumbstruck. At the time he had reckoned Morg to be spinning his spurs.

Kit said to him, "Ate beaver with you and didn't *kill* you?"

"He didn't at that. I'm still here, ain't I?"

"Yeah, but–"

"Indians was different then," Morg said matter-of-factly. "Or at least they was *there*, up in them mountains."

Kit remained silent. Old Morg spoke with such authority on the subject, as only sheer experience can allow, that he moved a younger, less-experienced man such as himself to silence.

He said, "There was no reason to fear one man up a mountain in a cave, sitting with a pile of dead beavers. He regarded me rather as an oddity. Something new and maybe interesting. As I did him."

Kit considered this silently, while Morg went on.

"Well, I could see soon enough that he was more interested in my pile of dead beaver pelts than ever he was me; started picking and feeling through them and then... piling them neatly up."

"Neatly *up*?"

"That's right, neatly up. Wanted to make a trade."

"What for?"

"This," Morg said, showing him the bloody blade he always worked with.

"That's an *Injun* blade?" Kit said incredulously.

"Well... no."

Kit was confused. Old Morg stuck it back into the bloody buffalo carcass and continued cutting.

He said, "He's got it off some other... mountain man."

"Oh," Kit replied, let down and disappointed on account of his habit to hype up a thing.

"But it's still be*longed* to an Indian," Morg reminded him. "For a whiles, anyway. I traded all my pelts for it and away he went. Seemed a fine trade to me, a bunch of stinking old beaver pelts for a good blade. Much better'n the one I had – which I traded later on down the line.

"So I decided to try my luck at shooting me some more beaver and trading thereabouts. Well, soon I shot myself empty but had more beaver pelts than any one man can carry. So, naturally, I decided to trade what I couldn't carry with the men in the mountains, and then take the rest on down with me and go trade them back up the river for fresh ammo to shoot me even more of 'em."

Again, Kit had been more interested in what Old Morg had said before that, and for more or less the same reason.

"The men in the mountains?" he had said to Morg. "There was more of them? These... tame Injuns?"

"No no," Morg said, "they wasn't tame, they just weren't yet hostile."

"Oh."

"That's right. Had no reason to be. Up there in them mountains is where I got my Indian handle, Skinning Beaver. *From* them, the Injuns.

So I got my Indian knife – what's not Indian – and my Indian name, what is, up there in them mountains."

Old Morg had finished skinning his hide. With one hand he tossed the entire thing over onto the pile, and high up on it, and then dragged the pink carcass away.

But soon he was back. He wiped both sides of his blade clean on the hide Kit was still skinning away at.

Kit became conscious of how far he was behind the old ex-mountain man, who had been here almost before it all began, and he doubled his efforts.

"Here, let me help you with that, son," Old Morg had said.

Kit was mighty surprised. No one had ever helped him with anything. He had never known his father, and only knew *of* his mother. She had been a whore; his father, probably some cowpoke who rode in off the prairie to blow three months' worth of wages in one night's whoring, and who then rode back on out, empty-pocketed once more.

Kit had once thought it something to be ashamed of: that he was the son of a thousand fathers sired by one single whore. But in and around Dodge, if you told a man your mother was a whore, he'd as likely say, "So was mine." Or, "Where'd she work? Maybe my pa rolled with her and we're half-brothers – maybe *I* rolled with her."

Kit had had just such a conversation once with another young buffalo hunter, or skinner, as was more likely. Usually the older hands did the shooting and the young pokes like Kit and his half-brothers skinned for wages. Usually men like Old Morgan didn't even talk to them, usually just scowled and spat tobacco juice.

So Kit was mighty taken aback by Morg offering to help him. So much so that he felt compelled to ask the man, "*Why?*"

Morg said, "Because I can see you're struggling's why."

In fact, he had seemed somewhat annoyed by the absurdity of such a question, as he pulled one end of the buffalo carcass toward himself, sunk his knife into it and began slicing and chopping just as if it was one of his own.

"Son," he said to Kit, "maybe I'm the last of my kind left or else

I went crazy up in them mountains, but I still think when a good man sees another good man who's struggling, especially if that man's a younger man, then he oughta help."

Kit was even more stupefied. "You do?" he said.

"Yeah. Or maybe I went mad up in them mountains. Maybe I never really come down out of 'em, and a part of me's still up there trying to find them beavers."

Kit stopped.

"Keep cutting, son," Old Morg said. "Just because I'm helpin' you don't mean I'm gonna skin the whole gosh dern thing for ya!"

Kit rapidly resumed.

"Hell! I wanta see those skinny bare arms bloody right up to them armpits, like mine. Take a look at that!"

Old Morg lifted an arm to the heavenly blue sky, exposing the rustiest red armpit Kit had ever wished he'd never seen. But thankfully not for long.

Both of them were shirtless out on the prairie, streaked and smeared with a mixture of both fresh and dried blood. But Kit was bloody only to his elbows, although at some point he had made the mistake of wiping his sweaty forehead with a backhand.

"That's right," Morg said, as Kit cut. "Them elbows being bloody as they are just ain't gonna cut it. Look at you, you've done wiped blood on your face, looks like Injun warpaint."

There was a moment of silence between the two.

Then Morg said, "'I God, I done lost my train of thought. And worse yet I done for*got* that I forgot I done lost it! I was sayin'... sayin'... What was I sayin'?"

Kit ripped a good-sized flap of buffalo hide free from the flesh, at last.

He said to Morg as he tried to twist the flap free from the various sinews that held it to the hide, "You was telling me about how you came down out of them mountains to trade your fur pelts."

"I was?"

"From what I can recall," Kit said, hard at work.

Old Morg spat.

"No I wasn't," he said. "I was talking about relations with them mountain Indians."

"Only once I mentioned tame Indians. The men in the mountains," Kit reminded him.

Old Morg said, "Ahhh, yeah. There you are messing things up with that plumb-eyed imagination of yours. I was saying how I've come down out of them mountains to trade my fur pelts, for ammo and the suchlike. Yeah. That's right!

` "Well," he said to Kit, "what I meaned to tell you, was that all the pelts I could carry, and I mean *all*, I done managed to trade – for provisions. Like beef jerky – more than a packhorse could carry. I had to stuff beef jerky in my boots – the new ones I traded for. Although, I'll tell ya, I had to take a lot less than I'd've liked for the fur pelts on account of all the bullet holes I put in 'em – apparently you're suppose to *trap* furs, I learned."

But Old Morg breathed a sigh of satisfaction all the same.

"So for the next couple of year," he told Kit, "I was an official 'Mountain Man'. When I came down out of the mountains, I was treated like a prince, and was traded with like one. Even had me a canoe, though it almost took me over a waterfall one time and I had to abandon it.

"Eventually I filled that whole gosh derned cave up in them mountains, packed it full of pelts to the soot-stained ceiling, 'I God! Took me a whole year. But by *then* even the Injuns didn't want 'em no more, wanted nothin' to with 'em, wouldn't even accept them as *gifts* – and trade weren't good up the river no more. There was plenty of beaver, but no one wanted any more. *Why?* I'd ask myself. *'I God, why?* And d'you know why?" he asked Kit.

Kit took a moment to consider if he did. "No, I don't believe I do," he concluded.

"Neither did I. When I did just that. What you just did. Wracked my brain to no avail. So I asked some folks comin' off the boat, so to speak. Turns out nobody wants beaver no more, they're fed up with it. *Every*body's wearin' beaver. Beggars are wearin' beaver, they said. A man tells me a bank got *robbed* by a man wearin' beaver. 'I God! Well, what do people wear now? They wear buffalo, he says. Those who can afford it, anyhow. Not the beggars then, I says. No, no, he tells me, they're still wearin' beaver. The rich are wearing buffalo. Buffalo is in."

"So," Old Morg said, almost finished at his end of Kit's buffalo. "The next step was to go where the buffalo was at. Well, cut a long story short as the fella says, I asked directions along the way, got into a few Indian fights, and here I am. Minus two fingers, a toe and a thumb, but here I am – more or less."

"I guess you are at that," Kit said, using the old buffalo hunter and mountain man's happy mode of speech.

"Ayesir."

Old Morg was already finished at his end. "'I God, son," he said. "I could finish that quicker'n two of you, but I'm not gonna. Help a man help himself, as far as he's willing."

Kit looked up at him, frowning again. Old Morg was a confusing man, with strange ideas in his head.

"You just keep cutting," Morg told him. "It won't cut itself," he added, and spat. "I'm outta tabaccy, but I still keep spittin'."

Old Morg had the worst tobacco habit Kit had ever seen – even among buffalo hunters. While sawing at a skin, he would stuff three blood-streaked fingers into his front pocket and pull out his tobacco wedge, then use the same skinning knife to cut off a bit to chew, and stuff it into his mouth with those same bloody fingers. You could even see the blood on his yellow-stained teeth. No wonder he always spat. A man with a mouth like that could spit all his life and still not get it clean. 'I God!

Kit finally did finish his end of the buffalo.

So that was how it all started, and more importantly how it all worked – with everyone wanting to wear the next new thing the rich were wearing, and once they *weren't* wearing it, that was it, there was no more of a demand for it – according to Old Morg, anyhow.

But with buffalo, it hadn't quite worked that way. Unlike the beaver pelts, the supply couldn't even half-meet the demand, which only grew and never dwindled. Soon, there *was* no supply – or there may as well have *been* none, there were so few. Hunter-skinners had to venture further and further to find buffalo, and fewer and fewer were willing. Near the end, the wagons came back empty – if you didn't count the arrows in them. And that is, if they came back at all. Old Morg himself had supposedly been killed by Indians, who had happened to be trying to hunt the same buffalo, and that kind of signalled the end of it for Kit.

It *had* only been one last renegade buffalo, apparently, that Old Morg had gone after even after his own crew had decided to turn back – but outside of beaver, skinning buffalo was the only thing Old Morg knew any more. He was too old to put in for law work and too old to cow – the next big thing, although it had always been around: herding cattle and horses and such.

But that weren't for Old Morg, nosir. He *went out right*, Kit often thought, even now, all these years on down the trail. Went out the way he would have wanted to, The Last Buffalo Hunter. And the last buffalo.

For Old Morg, Kit often thought, it was a world of firsts and lasts. For Kit, a world of seconds and thirds – fatherless son of a whore and what not. Seconds and thirds.

But in a way, Old Morg was perhaps the closest Kit had ever come to feeling what it might be like to have a father, and to be a son.

He taught Kit how to shoot – at bottles, that is – but by the time he was good enough to hit a buffalo, there weren't any. But he had become good with both a pistola, as Old Morg called it, and a rifle – both the newer Winchester and even the big old roaring Henry that was Old Morg's preference.

Morg said he had always wanted a son, and by happenstance had once impregnated a sporting woman – which was just another name for a whore – but that she had died giving birth to it, and it had died trying to get born.

"How'd it die?" Kit had asked one day when the subject had been broached.

Morg spat.

"It was hung," he replied.

"What?" Kit said.

"Yep," the old man scowled. "Hung for the crime of being born."

Kit was high confused all over again. He said to Morg, "How can they hang a baby for being *born*?"

Morg was about to spit, but didn't.

"No, see," he said, "it got hung by the... umby cord."

"Huh?"

"By the... umby cord. You know, the cord what's attached to the baby's belly. You know, to its belly whatsit."

"*Oh*," Kit said.

"Yeah, that's right. It got hung by the... by the... the umby cord. It's come out and, aw heck son, I swear on my life, that umby cord's got somehow wrapped around its neck and pulled tight as a duck's butt, and it's been hung as it's come out."

This time he did spit, a particularly long and nasty streak – right next to the hide he was working on. He was busy peeling off its face.

He said to Kit, "'I God, son, I swear, the floor dropped out under that child's feet and it was hung like an outlaw at the gallows. Never had a chance, born with a noose around its neck as it fell out between its mother's dingus."

"Dingus?"

"Well... thing. Between her legs."

Old Morg became bright red in the face, and fell silent.

In retrospect, it seemed to Kit that Old Morg had given up any further attempt at fruitful courtship between gentleman and sporting lady after that. After that he had gone off into the mountains, away from the towns and the people and the whores and the trouble they could get you in.

"You stay away from them, the whores," he would often say. "Ain't nothin' but trouble up in there."

So he had gone up the mountain and discovered beaver instead, and after that he was up and down and all over for it, until it turned out people were bored with it and wanted to try something new. But that was people for you.

Kit in fact thought a lot about whores, even then – since he knew his mother had been one. But also because he overheard the older buffalo hunters discussing the best whores in town past and present. The whole idea intrigued him, even though he didn't entirely understand what it all amounted to, but at the same time something about it deeply disturbed him.

It didn't help that Morg would catch him daydreaming while ripping into a carcass and say things like, "Dreamin' of a whore somewhere out there over yonder? Course you are," he would say. "Course you are. Son, I knowed a mountain man who traded pelts to sleep with another mountain man's wife, and then his dingus fell off."

Kit had been horrified to hear of this, but Old Morg just spat matter-of-factly and went on.

"And he never did get his pelts back, neither. *Or* his dingus. After it fell off – when next he tried go for a pee-pee – wal... he felt a might short-changed, to say the least. So he decided to go back up into the mountains to get his fur pelts back, try find the mountain man who had short-changed him.

"He found the man, but the man had already sold the pelts, and they were as gone as gone's ever gonna be, you hear? So you know what happened? You *know* what happened? The man gave him his wife, instead. And now I ask you, son, what good is a trade like that?"

It was something Kit pondered many times, especially when he started thinking of whores, and felt his dingus twitch.

He didn't much like his dingus, but it seemed to him he needed it – but it did sound like it could be a lot of trouble.

Also, Old Morg had once made fun of it. Often while skinning they took their clothes off so as to stop them from getting too bloody. One time during a particularly large and timely skinning session, Kit had been getting so bloody Old Morg told him to get his duds off.

"'I God," Morg had said. He looked about to spit, and did. "'I God," he said again, tucking his chin into his neck. "I've seen a prairie chicken with a pecker bigger'n that. Best put those duds back on, son, before the other hands start poking fun."

It seemed that Kit had something very wrong down there, and everything that went with it was likewise very wrong. Best to just leave it alone. Best just to keep his duds back on.

But worst to Kit, was that he was, by way of a few simple calculations in his head, a result of the wrongness. A living, breathing result of the wrongness. Maybe if a baby could be hung for the crime of being born, a man who wasn't hung at birth for the crime of the sex act would be punished; sentenced to roam the earth a fatherless bastard child of no man in no man's land. No man's and every man's, it seemed.

Kit tried his best to keep his mind on other things, but it wasn't easy. There wasn't much else to keep your mind on at his age; everywhere you went in Dodge there were whores and big, red-faced buffalo hunters laughing that big old raucous laugh they all got whenever they drank the whiskey.

On whiskey, which Kit also had an abiding interest in, Old Morg would say, "Now whiskey I got nothing against. Got nothing against whiskey itself. But it messes with a man's senses. How many gunfights have you seen two sober men have? That's right, none. Guns and whiskey and gambling just don't make good bedfellows."

"Bedfellows? What are bedfellows?"

"You, uh... you forget about that. You just remember, that in the end, whiskey will make you weak for whores, and whores'll make your whatsit drop off. Your rodger."

From then on Kit decided to guard himself against whiskey too, which meant there was even less to turn his mind to.

The only thing he could think about were the stinking carcasses, or dream of being a mountain man, alone in the mountains, trapping beaver.

If he was honest with himself, Kit couldn't see any virtue in any one pursuit and not another in life. It was just that there was something about being a mountain man, there at the beginning of it all, coming down the mount and going up the river, welcomed with awe by all those new fish coming up the river, getting to show all the young girls his shiny silky pelts. He could even show a girl his gun, if her father wasn't watching – maybe behind a tree. Perhaps he could even *give* her a pelt, for free, as a gift, and she would... what would she?

He often imagined himself as a mountain man, but in the end it amounted to the same thing every time; it amounted to him giving a girl a look at his gun behind a tree – he imagined himself clicking the chamber for her while holding the pistola low and out of sight of her pa – or giving her a beaver pelt to stroke. And what then? Heading on back off up into the mountains?

Kit didn't even want beaver, no more than he wanted buffalo hides; he wanted... what did he want, when he thought about it? He wanted to give a girl, who'd come up the river, a pelt for free, as a gift, to...

One day Old Morg had cleared things up for him a little, while they were piling skins up on the wagon while the skinned carcasses lay slowly cooking under the naked sun, and flies hummed and vultures wheeled high overhead.

Morg slumped a hide into the wagon. "Son," he said, "nothing's for free in this world, and even what is, comes with a hidden cost. Like once," Morg explained, "while I was trying to find where the buffalos was at, or someone reliable to give me directions... I drank water out of a hoofprint."

"You drank water out of what?" Kit said.

"You heard me right first time, boy. I drank water out of a hoofprint. I knew I had to wait until I crossed a creek or a flowing stream, but I'd been in the desert almost two days and drunk nothing for the last six hours but a handful of piss."

Kit made a face, and slumped another hide into the wagon.

"That's right," said Old Morg, "handful of my own piss. My throat was burning, but I knew that river was coming soon, had to be, and all my hard travelling would pay off. But, 'I God, son, I swear, *there* not more than two horse strides away, smack bang in the middle of the flat, dry desert, was a single mother-lovin' hoofprint."

"Just one?" Kit said.

"That's right. Just one. And no more."

Kit held his face in a frown for quite some time while he worked.

Morg was saying, "And suddenly, as I've come near it, my horse has lowered its head and started to drink. So I've jumped down, pushed her head away, got down on my hands and knees, and drunk. Now in that puddle, was a hidden cost. I knew I should have waited, but didn't – and maybe I never should have drank my own piss. Maybe then a dern hoofprint wouldn't have seemed so dang appetising at the time. But it did and I did, and a done bun can't be undone.

"I got sick, son, awful sick. The world fell outta me arse, like old McAllen the Irish used to say it did him, and what part of it didn't came burping up out of my mouth or squeezing outta my skin's every pore. And you know what's worse?" Morg said to Kit. "The river weren't but twenty minutes away."

"Jee," Kit had said.

"That's right. Twenty minutes – if even that. Now, 'I God, son, it looked like a gift from above, laid down by the hand of God hisself, but that hoofprint was far from free."

It was at this point that Kit realised he didn't want to give away no free beaver pelts, that his free beaver pelt contained its very own hidden cost and wasn't for free at all; he wanted to trade... wanted to trade it for... for...

For a friend?

But that weren't quite right now, was it? He wouldn't give another mountain 'boy' a free beaver pelt he had had to hunt and catch and take the pains to skin.

Kit had overheard many a buffalo hunter discussing the cost of whoring; some sporting women cost as much as two or three hides, and could separate a man from a month's wages in under five minutes, which Old Morg quite rightly pointed out was a poor trade.

"I wouldn't trade a hide for no whore," Old Morg had said. "Ever again."

In the end, Kit thought, was giving a pretty young girl a fur pelt as a 'free' gift, any different than giving her a hide or two – or, heck, now that he thought of it, a month's wages straight up – for the exact same reason the buffalo hunters did? And were you not just concealing, in the end, with it, your own, as it were, hidden cost?

Morg had once said, "Most men who go with a whore get more'n they trade for, have their ting-tings come clean off in their hands while they go for a pee-pee, or have a ball drop off of a sudden."

"A *ball* drop off?" Kit had said.

"Yep," Old Morg confirmed. "I knowed a old skinner who traded everything he ever managed to get his hands on whoring, who only had one ball left in the end. Showed it to me one time. It was one ball alright. Poorest sight I ever saw."

Kit thought he would keep his wages *and* his hides – and *both* his balls, to boot. Kit mostly saved his money anyhow, put it in the bank – but banks back then weren't always so safe in Dodge, until the Earps came to town, but that was another story.

Kit used to keep three-quarters of his wages in the bank, and the rest tucked in his boot or blanket. He was saving to buy a big second-hand saddle in the window of the *Dodge City Store of Conveniences and General Provisions.*

Thing was, he couldn't even afford a horse – but he one day dreamed of being able to buy one. But then he would need to put it up in a livery stable, and rates was high, *and* would have to pay to have it shoed – and he didn't know an anvil from a hammer when it came to Black Smithery.

"You're aimin' too high," Old Morg once said, lowering his big old smoking Henry rifle. "If I was you, I'd go get me a mule."

"I don't want no mule," Kit said back to that, a little testily.

"Or a packhorse," Old Morg said. He set his rifle's hindsight. "I had me a packhorse once. I took it up into the mountains to see if I couldn't come back down with even *more* beaver to trade, but I made the mistake of trying to take an old goat trail, and, well, unfortunately... it fell down into a gully."

Old Morg closed one eye and thumbed some muck out of the fore-sight. That had been Kit's fault, he remembered. He had handed Kit the rifle and Kit had rested it barrel-down in the grass. For that, Old Morg had fetched him a slap.

Aiming down the sights, he said out of his mouth-corner, "But out here on the flat prairie a packhorse'll do just fine. And I reckon it'll carry you."

Kit was just saying, "Don't *want* no packhorse–" when the great Henry rifle roared and gave out a huge acrid gust of smoke. Kit had been downwind of it and got a lungful – boy, did he! He started coughing and choking and waving the thick smoke out from in front of his eyes.

They were watering, and quite heavily. "What'd you hit?" Kit asked him.

Morg said, "What I been aiming at all this time, I 'spect."

Kit couldn't see anything lying in the prairie grass, nearby or distant – nor had he seen anything while Old Morg had been adjusting his sights, for that matter.

"What'd you shoot at?" Kit asked again.

"There. See? The sun."

"The sun?"

"That's right, son. The sun."

"Well," Kit said after a moment, "did you get it?"

"We'll see tonight."

"What'll we see?" Kit asked.

"Well, we'll see when the fire goes off it whether I hit it or not," Morg said. "See, son, at night's when you can see all the bullet holes. Lot of cowboys have shot at her over the years, as any man can see for himself. None of 'em've brought her down, that's for sure. I aim to be the first."

It seemed to Kit that Old Morg believed the sun and the moon to be one and the same, as if when the sun went down it was doused in some distant sea, only to rise again as a cold and fireless orb.

They waited on the prairie until nightfall. Kit looked at the moon sceptically.

"I think there's a new one in it," Morg said. "Matter of fact, I could swear to it."

There was a long moment of silence. Crickets chirped all around them in the long prairie grass.

It was Old Morg who broke the silence at last. "One day I'm gonna be the one to shoot it down and ride on over and jump up on it."

But Old Morg never did manage to shoot down the moon, or ride on over and jump up onto it, Kit often thought somewhat sadly to himself. Sometimes Kit imagined to himself that Old Morg was still out there somewhere, alive and well, instead of killed by a bunch of Injuns in a scarce buffalo hunt, as was the rumour. Well, the 'fact', according to Smith Allen, a scraggly old buffalo hunter turned saloon-owner who said he saw the whole thing; saw the very arrow that took down Old Morgan's horse – said the arrow hit the sorrel straight in the chest – and then the great Indian who reigned in over Morg and lanced him in the heart, took his scalp and held it high over his head and hollered triumphantly, apparently.

But, well, Kit guessed even if it weren't true, Old Morg would have probably passed long ago, from rickety old age alone. On the other ankle, no one, not even Old Morg himself, knew how old he was. Old Morg just used to say, "Old enough to know I ain't gettin' any younger." Whatever that had meant.

In the end, Old Morg had been a peculiar customer, Kit often reflected. You could think what you wanted to about the man but you couldn't help but be overwhelmed by the extent of the man's wisdom and knowledge – *and* experience. And not the kind comes from any book, since Old Morg couldn't read, *not a word* – or, for that matter, write (although, mind you, Morg had traded fur for many a good book in his time; used to say, "Son, a good pocket-sized book about your person is about the handiest criterion of civilization on God's creation. Can help start a fire in near any weather *and*, by God, d'you know how much a goddamn box of those Therapeutic Papers costs in your average general store? It's goddamned daylight robbery is what it is! Costs a man his arm to wipe his ass! Although I'll allow it really does seem man just ain't cut out to use leaves and grass and what not even when he *is* out in the wild. There's just somethin' about leaves weren't made for it.").

Yep, Old Morg had even been around to witness the very first boxes of Therapeutic Papers to be delivered into western civilization. One of the most overlooked criterions of the settling of the west, he used to say.

"Came in to Dodge off the train and were in all the general stores you walked into," he had once told Kit. "At first folks was embarrassed to buy 'em. I was myself. Truth to it is I'd get one of the younger skinners to run in and buy me a box or two if I knew I was riding out into the sticks for a few days. Beat the hell out of wiping your ass with thistles and thorns, but it cost ya. But now, like I said, a good book..."

Hell, Old Morg had seen the west before *towns* were even built. Kit sometimes wondered what Old Morg *hadn't* been the first to see. He had seen the buffalo herds free on the earth, herds more than a million strong, every *one* with its skin still intact; had even seen wild horses, spread out across the valleys so's you couldn't even see the grass they was grazing on, before the wagons came on up the trail and riled up the Indians, as he put it, done messed everything up.

Yep, Old Morg had seen it all. The before and the after.

Well, that was it, and it was that, and there weren't much more to tell. Several hundred carcasses later, Kit had put in for law work. Morg had gone off after the last buffalo with a small posse and never returned, and Kit was once again on his own.

But by then he was a seasoned plainsman, as good as Morg had taught him to be – which was as good as Morg. But being a seasoned plainsman and being a lawman with any kind of life expectancy in Dodge City were two very different things. In fact, Kit had left Dodge City only shortly after signing up.

No sooner had he done so than he had almost been killed's why.

Kit had almost been killed while trying to enforce the City Firearms Ordinance, which was that no firearms were to be carried within the city limits. No sooner had he told a bunch of rowdy cowboys precisely that than a shootout had ensued, in which Kit had been shot in the back of the shoulder, and once in the ass while diving over a water barrel. Fortunately Kit had high-tailed it out of there and that was all that came of it; although the wounds *had* become infected and Kit had rode a high fever for a week, right to the very heights of delirium. At the time, he had thought himself to be dying. But when the fever subsided, and he came back down to earth, so to speak, he swore to himself there and then that he would leave Dodge.

Although he had lived and worked around there all his life – and rumour had it his mother had whored there before leaving for Abilene – it just didn't feel right no more; and plain truth of it was Morg was gone, and he saw no more reason to stay.

Dodge City was also just altogether too violent – a simple dispute over a game of cards could end in death by gut-shot or worse. Or even *eye*ballin' a man the wrong way could get you killed. Happened all the time. It seemed as any kind of lawman or peacekeeper in Dodge City you had about the estimated life expectancy of a rabbit dropped into a den of rattlesnakes, if even that. Probably it was *called* Dodge on account of all the bullets that had to be dodged.

Kit figured there just weren't much future in Dodge – or chances of survival. Although, Kit heard things were much better there nowadays, since Wyatt Earp and his brothers had arrived. He didn't know exactly what their secret was, but whatever it was, it sure did work good – although they *did* say, with regards to enforcing the firearms ordinance, if Mr Wyatt Earp or any of his brothers saw a man walking in town with a firearm he would remind him of the ordinance by clubbing him over the back of the head with a Colt, before reading him his rights.

Sounded effective to Kit – he had seen first-hand if not ass-over-heels what happened when you simply asked.

Kit, in fact, had heard rumour that Wyatt had once been a buffalo hunter himself – a man of his own enterprise, they said. Had hired on his own skinners and done the shooting himself, and that those skinners now worked with him as lawmen too. A great man. A man whose name was known in many places.

Kit imagined one day he might be such a man, but doubted it, although reminded himself he had started out a skinner – before becoming a lawman, much like Mr Earp.

But anyhow, at the time he left Dodge, it was as lawless a place as it was ever gonna be – worse even than Abilene, they said; much worse. Kit took his money out of the bank, and what little he had tucked up in his blanket, of course, and finally bought that saddle and horse he had always wanted – although by then it was a somewhat different saddle sitting in the window, Mexican, although to his mind it looked just as good, if not even better on account of the silver finishings on it. He even managed to procure for himself a decent saddlebag, and won a finely weighted pistol and leather holster belt in a poker game, much to the annoyance of the man who had owned it and been dumb enough to take it off and lay it down on the table. Pure luck to Kit, of course, since he seldom gambled. Kit wasn't the gambling type, although sometimes he had played cards with a few of the young skinners out on the prairies at night, round the campfires, using stones as money, the cards always covered with bloody thumbprints.

He liked the gun just fine but the belt was a little too big for his waist, and hung to one side. But that side was the drawing side, and it just so happened that Kit's hand reached the pistol perfectly. All in all, he saw it as a good omen – and it was time to leave, to find some lighter-hearted town to keep the peace in.

And like that, he rode on out of Dodge and never looked back, roamed the land, hunted and camped and slept under the starlight beside a fire, learned that the silver finishings on his saddle were a foolish addition since during the day the sun bounced right off them and revealed your position for countless miles around to anyone who cared to see, but fortunately encountered no trouble. The Indians in these parts were said to be whipped in any case – apart from a few holdouts, they said. Although he didn't see any.

He enjoyed being out on the open prairie and living off the land; it gave him a lot of time to think, but after a while it grew dull, and Kit got to thinking about, well, women, or even whores – or sporting women, he preferred to think of them. Kit figured on any cold night out on the open prairie a woman would have been a lot better choice than a hot brick at the bottom of a blanket to keep a man warm, and he saddled up at last, tired of aimless wandering and in search of a place to settle.

His aim had always been to find some halfway town cattlemen and travellers on their way up the trail to Dodge or Abilene would perhaps use as a sort of way station; a stopping point for awhile, to wet their throats and settle their stomachs, or perhaps have a horse shod or a saddle repaired, not to mention re-provision, before moving on.

And find it he did. Young Kit ended up in a little pisswater of a place by the name of Wagon Trail. Where, to the present day, he remained a fully commissioned peacekeeper. And where, thanks to its smaller size and absence of a railroad, things were nothing like Dodge at all...

And where, today, he had been leaning up against a post under the boardwalk outside Ned's Three-Chair early in the morning, freshly shaved and trimmed behind the ears, when the scalped man came riding in to town, slumped over and looking just about half-alive in the saddle, on a horse so gaunt it looked like it had almost been rode straight to death.

For once in Kit's life, it was a first; the first time in his life he had ever seen, much less *expected* to see, a man alive and at the same time with his entire head of hair scalped clean off from his ears up. And sure, *sure*, he had seen something similar all right. Several hundred somethings, back in his buffalo hunting days.

Because, plain truth of it was – by Kit's reckoning, anyhow – the backside of any one of those several hundred stripped buffalo hides he and Old Morg had worked on every day for a coon's age, looked like that there unfortunate fella's head.

"'I God," he said to himself.

Mister McLoughlin, as it later turned out was his last name, had lost his scalp (as it also later turned out) while lying face down on the ground next to a wagon wheel pretending to be stone dead, after having taken an arrow in the back.

There was no arrow in there now; he had somehow broken that part of it which would have still been protruding off or pulled it out, but the wound looked to be infected, and badly, as quickly tended to be the case with almost all wounds sustained while out on the open plains. Kit had once seen an ingrown toenail turn a buffalo hunter's big toe twice its size and so sore he had had to cut a hole in his boot – which hadn't helped; the toe had only swollen further, to Kit's recollection, necessitating an even larger hole. And all in a matter of days.

But nothing looked to be infected more of this man's than his head. Kit was about the only one who could look at it without feeling his gorge rise – Doc Benton even looked away once or twice as he examined the wound – but after seeing and smelling as many countless decaying carcasses as Kit had, he could have stomached the sight and smell of just about anything. A fact he in fact took pride in.

The man's horse had been taken to one of the town's livery stables, to be fed and watered. Kit had seen the animal up close and had been shocked at the sight of it. The man had near ridden the animal to damnation, and had driven his spurs so deep and hard into its flanks it had a pair of nasty infected wounds of its own.

Apparently the ride from wherever the man had come from to Wagon Trail had taken everything he had out of him; he fell sideways out of the saddle and into Kit's arms like a bride. The ugliest damned bride Kit'd ever seen.

For a moment he hadn't known what to do with him, standing there in the main street, and had looked around for someone else more qualified – but soon realized no one else *was* more qualified, and came to his senses.

The only logical thing to do was take the man to Doc Benton – who fortunately was in town – and get Percy Parker, a fellow peacekeeper but a lazy and unwilling one at that, to see the man's horse to a livery stable before the poor thing keeled over and died there and then. Which is what he had done.

And, 'I God, there had been plenty of gawkers! Just about the whole town of Wagon Trail had turned out to see the scene or tried to catch a glimpse of it; come to shop windows or stepped out of blacksmiths and saloons to see what all the ruckus was about. Even Ned, the town barber, had left a customer heavily lathered but unshaven and stepped out onto the porch to watch Kit try to handle the situation – for such a time that his neglected customer had come out on the porch too, self-righteous and irritated at first but soon just as intrigued by the whole affair himself.

Kit had not forgotten the strange remark made by Mister Ned Lowe then. He had said it from behind his forearm, which he had held up protectively over his mouth, as if to prevent himself from suddenly retching at the sight of the man. He had said, "Kit, kindly get that man away from my 'stablishment quick as you can now; I wouldn't want folk in this town thinkin' it was me'd give him that haircut."

It confused Kit because Ned Lowe was not the kind of man to make that kind of joke, if any joke at all, much less at a time like that; although he *was* known to be extremely paranoid and nervous at times, and often wanted to know if anyone had made any recent comments about any haircuts he had given, just about every time you sat down in one of his chairs to get one yourself, in fact – which was just as confusing, because he was as fine a barber as Kit had known and he had often told him so. Dodge City had no finer, Kit often told him – even though he had never had a haircut in Dodge City.

In fact, just this morning, while peeling back one of Kit's ears and trimming behind it with a fine pair of small scissors, Ned Lowe had asked Kit if Percy Parker thought poorly of his practice, since he never came in.

"Why, no," Kit had told him, after a moment's reflection, "I don't think so, Mister Lowe. It's just he's too gosh dern bone idle and lazy to, I reckon. If it was much more of an effort for Percy to breathe I 'spect he'd keel over and die," he added. "Truth is he likely won't come in for a cut till his hat won't fit his head. And I doubt you'll even see him in here for a shave until the sheriff him*self* orders it."

"So it wasn't him said I give a haircut like a Comanche Indun then?" Ned asked.

Kit struggled to keep a straight face, as it was an amusing notion.

"No, Mister Lowe," he said, but less sympathetically this time, and for good reason. "If I'm to be a hunnert percent honest with you, Mister Lowe, it was Ed Lister said it. And in all fairness, you *did* cut his earlobe – some say *near off*."

"Certainly he does himself," Kit added quickly.

"Oh, everyone knows the man's got a nervous twitch," Ned said nervously. "That's why he got his ear cut! Had nothin' to do with me. *Or* my scissors."

"Well, that may be true," Kit admitted, "but Doc Benton had to sew it back to, all the same. And... and a done bun can't be undone, as the fella says."

"I'm telling you, it was his nervous twitch did it!" Ned Lowe maintained.

Kit wasn't going to get drawn any further into the argument, *or* take sides, for that matter. Edward Lister was a hired ranch hand – and a rowdy one at that – for O'Neil Masterson, a reputable businessman who had established a big homestead less than a mile from town and who relied extensively upon its stores for his provisions and those amenities that were beyond himself. To a greater extent than any of Wagon Trail's inhabitants would have liked to admit, even to themselves, the entire town (more or less) relied to no small extent on its continued good relations with the Mastersons – and that included his hired help. Truth be told, Ed Lister *did* have a nervous twitch, and one on the exact same side where you could still see the black stitch marks the doc had left in his 'lobe, but Kit decided it best to remain neutral in opinion.

That discussion had been just this morning, shortly before the man came loping along into town without his scalp on.

So maybe that was it then. Maybe the peculiar remark he had made had merely been an extension of Ned's normal nervousness, further perpetuated by the fairly recent incident concerning the near cutting-off of Ed Lister's earlobe and the accusation going about town as much as the dispute as to whose fault it had been.

Anyway, there were far more important things to think about – and matters to attend to.

Now they were at Doc Benton's, a small, white-framed clapboard house on the outskirts of town with a pretty little white picket fence around it. It was fortunate Doc Benton had been in town this morning, since often he was required out at the Masterson residence to treat O'Neil Masterson's older brother, who was bed-bound and dying of tuberculosis. Sometimes during a bad spell the treatment went overnight and late into the next day, and the doc arrived again only in the evening.

Doc Benton was presently hard at work on the man's festering scalp, wiping it down with cotton wads dabbed and soaked with the contents of various bottles and potions Kit knew nothing about – although most of them seemed by smell to be alcohol-based.

While the doc was cleaning the head wound – meticulously over and over, it seemed – Percy Parker returned to tell Kit the man's horse was being fed and watered and was in good hands at Dim Bill's Livery.

"Well that took long enough," Kit remarked.

Percy ignored the remark and nodded instead, at the man being treated on the table. He said, "Got a name, does he?"

"He hasn't come conscious yet," Kit told him. "Once he does I 'spect he'll be the first to tell us."

Doc Benton said, "Now, that he hasn't's just as well, boys, because I expect he'd have had to be held down like a carpenter's plank for me to clean this scalp. Cleaning it with these here solvents while awake would have stung him like crazy.

"I imagine," he added, "it would feel like he suddenly had a... had a beehive on his head."

Kit winced at the mere idea. Percy's face was already screwed up and had been since he walked in anyway.

The doc said, "Now would you boys mind helping me get him turned over. I understand he's got another wound in his back. I'd like to take a look at it."

"Yessir," Kit and Percy said, almost simultaneously.

They helped turn him over. The doc started to cut away at the man's shirt where he had sustained the wound, evinced by the tattered hole in the cloth and the blood soaked into the fabric – now more of a maroon-brown colour.

"Percy," Kit said suddenly, "go on and get Sheriff Cotton."

He had become irritated, as he often did, by the man's continued idle presence. Percy had his chin and nose tucked into his shoulder and was looking away anyway.

"Why don't *you* go get him?" Percy protested.

"Because I done carried this man all the way here without an ounce of help from you. You just led his horse to a livery stable. And Dim Bill's one at that.

"Dim Bill's one's closest," Kit added, "and oft ill-provisioned and you know it. The whole dern town does."

Percy looked about to argue, and then reconsidered. "Sure, I'll go get him," he said sulkily, "but I think he's out a ways on the prairie, account of rumour has it there's a freegraze outfit that's turned up. Wants to see if any'll be comin' into town. You know how's they always cause trouble."

"Well, just go get him wherever he is," Kit said impatiently. He had heard the rumour about the freegrazers – another cattle outfit headed up the trail – and wasn't looking forward to any dry-necked rowdy cowhands coming into town. Freegrazers almost always spelt trouble.

Percy left, slamming the doc's pane-glass front door a little harder than he ought to have.

"Sorry about that, Doc," Kit apologised, but the doc had been deeply engrossed examining the wound in the man's back and had paid no attention to it.

"This man's got a arrowhead in his scapula," he said. "His shoulder blade, as you can see. Now I can risk pulling it out, but I doubt it's just a hunting arrow he's been hit with. See, the Injuns, most all of 'em, will make battle-arrows in such a way you've gotta push them out the other side rather than try pull them out. You do that, try pull 'em out, and your whole damned insides come out with 'em. And you don't want that now, do you?"

"Nosir," Kit said. "I'm much obliged to you, by the way. I didn't know that. Although I've been hit in just such a place myself. But by bullet not by bow," he added.

"Oh, is that so?" the doc said, still trimming the cloth.

"Yessir, it is," Kit said. "While trying to enforce a city firearms ordinance."

"Did they shoot you in the back or hit you while you was running?"

"While I was running, sir," Kit said.

"Well I'd just as soon say you was a wise young man, but if I'm to give my honest opinion, I find those very ordinances to be rambunctious and ambitious and liable to give rise to those very occasions in which firearms that wouldn't have been are otherwise drawn and fired.

"I also find them to be bad for business," he added.

"Well, sir," Kit said, "I was just doing my job."

"So am I. But to *do* a job you gotta *have* a job to do."

Kit was about to comment further, but just then, to both he and the doc's surprise, the man coughed, and started to try to turn himself back over onto his front – with all the precision of an overturned turtle, Kit thought.

In the process, he swung an arm out at the doc and fetched him a blow across the elbow, but fortunately Kit was fast to lean over and force the man back onto his back, holding him down by putting both hands on his shoulders and a good deal of his own weight.

"It's okay, mister," he said to him. "It's alright. You're in good hands now. Ain't nobody gonna try hurt you here."

Kit saw that the man's lips were dry, swollen bad and chapped – clearly he had gone without water for quite some time, as had his horse.

"Got a name, do you?" Kit asked him.

The man struggled to speak with his lips the way they were. He said something neither Kit nor the doc quite caught.

Kit said, "Don't worry none that you're held down, mister. It's just you've got a wound in your back and we're tending to it.

"Seems Injun," he added.

"Name's... McLoughlin," the man said, a little louder this time. "I'm... Ellis McLoughlin."

Kit and the doc exchanged looks. The doc's eyes said, "Now that's progress, Kit, carry on making it."

"Well, Mister McLoughlin," Kit said, glancing at the doc again, "I'm Kit Cope and this here's Doctor Benton. The sheriff's on his way over. Just what in hell happened to you?"

But Mister McLoughlin did not respond.

"Mister McLoughlin?" Kit said.

"He's unconscious again, son," Doc Benton said. "Help me sit him up, I'm gonna try push that arrow through while I've got the chance, and it ain't gonna be pretty."

But unfortunately, while the doc was pushing the arrow through, and it was just beginning to start protruding through the other side, Mister Ellis McLoughlin came full awake and screamed his lungs out. Started swinging his arms about and knocking over various bottles and smashing them, crashing surgical equipment to the floor.

Kit tried his best to get him in a bear hug, but it was half a bear hug at best, with one arm still flailing.

Then he went straight out again, as though he had never awoken in the first place, which seemed strange to Kit. The man ought to've made his mind up to come awake or stay asleep.

"Quick," the doc said, "I don't want that happening again."

Whatever the doctor was doing back there, pushing with some tool, Kit saw the arrow point peak the skin again and then split the flesh of

Mister McLoughlin's chest clean open and a stream of blood begin to gush.

Well, that's a familiar sight, Kit thought.

The doctor came around and with some sort of plier-like tool pulled the rest of the arrowhead and the straight bit of stick attached to it clean out. As soon as he did he staunched the flow of blood on both sides, front and back, with wads of cotton, and told Kit to lay Mister McLoughlin down again.

"Phew,' Doc Benton said. "I'm glad that's over."

He held the arrowhead up to the light of the small, clean room's only, although admittedly oblong, window.

He said, "There, just as I suspected, barbed."

Just as with all things Indian, Kit was fascinated, staring at the arrowhead Doc Benton held up like a prospector at a nugget of gold.

"Most likely Comanche," the doc continued. "Yep, a Comanche war arrow. See, the ones they use for hunting they intend to retrieve after, so naturally they don't barb the tips."

"You're a knowledgeable man, Doctor Benton," Kit said earnestly. "Mean to say, it benefits a man to be in your company."

"Well, I do consider myself something of a student of wounds; as such I find it pays to have an understanding of the weapons that make them. And I've seen a fair few Injun one's in my time.

"Now, come on," he said, lowering the arrowhead and turning away from the window, "let's get this fella cleaned and patched up before the sheriff gets here."

By the time the sheriff arrived – with Percy at his tail like a loyal mutt – Kit and the doc had wrapped Mister McLoughlin's chest and shoulder with several turns of clean bandage and even his head.

What had caught Kit's attention most while they had been bandaging Mister McLoughlin's head was the awful way his face had sagged. His eyebrows seemed to droop down over the tops of his eye sockets, and his hanging cheeks added to the awfulness by pulling like two fingers at the skin at the bottom of each one of his eyes, exposing the wet lower orbs of the eyeballs themselves, which were heavily bloodshot. It reminded him slightly of a sooty face he had once seen a young skinner pull over a campfire as he tried to demonstrate the stages of decomposition after death. He couldn't remember the young skinner's name, but he could remember his claim of having come across a human body in the early stages of decomposition vividly, due to his attempts to describe, and then further attempt to display, them over the firelight, pulling down on his face with his fingers. If Kit recalled the account correctly, the young skinner's outfit had discovered an abandoned settlement down by a river, and the decomposing body of the man had been within it. He also recalled that the young skinner had said one of the older buffalo hunters had deduced suicide, since the dead man had a hole in one of his temples and his scalp was intact. But no doubt it had been the result of an Indian raid, for the weapon was nowhere to be seen.

The look of his ears didn't help his appearance any either, Kit reckoned, for they too had sagged – although that wasn't quite the right word, 'sagged'. 'Turned', maybe. Neither ear looked to be at the right angle any longer; the one seemed to be heading for the hinge of his jaw, the other seemed to be almost on the side of his neck.

If there was a more sorry-looking specimen of a man in existence, for all his years of daydreaming Kit could not for the life of himself imagine what he might look like.

Another thing that had bothered Kit as they dressed Mister McLoughlin's wounds was the distressed mutterings he had made every now and then.

"Killed my boy," he had said at one point, and "Magdalena!" at another, muttering names.

Kit recalled the names of at least two ladies. A Magdalena and an Anna. And one of the mutterings Mister McLoughlin made had been, "My daughter, oh God!" So Kit assumed one of the two to be his daughter, the other his wife. Although Old Morg had always said, "An assumption makes an ass out of *you* and me."

Sheriff Rainbow Cotton, 'Bow Cotton to most, a man Kit deeply admired, nodded first at the doc upon entering, saying "Doc," in acknowledgement, and then at Kit.

"Kit."

"Morning, sir," Kit greeted him enthusiastically.

What Kit admired most about Sheriff 'Bow Cotton was that he was clearly an able man and as such appreciated other able men; and although Kit was still young, and the sheriff knew well of his altercation in Dodge in which he was shot in the shoulder and more embarrassingly 'the backside', it seemed that he recognised Kit to be a man who could be relied upon, and treated him with respect.

Of course, Kit himself had told him of the 'altercation' in Dodge when he had been asked if he had any experience in law work, when he had applied for the job.

"Why, yessir," he had said in front of the sheriff's desk in Wagon Trail's tiny jailhouse. "In Dodge City. I was shot in the shoulder and the... the hindquarter, sir."

"The hindquarter?" Sheriff Rainbow Cotton had said. "You mean your horse was shot?"

"Uh, nosir. It was my own hindquarter."

"I see. And this was in Dodge City you say?"

"Yessir."

The Sheriff gave him the once-over, from boot to brow; he seemed to think Kit a healthy specimen from what Kit could make of it, and Kit liked the look he was given.

"Well, son," he said to Kit, "if you've braved to keep the peace in Dodge City, I guess you're good to keep it anywhere. You've got my vote."

A bright smile had lit Kit's face. At such times in his life since then, when similar moments came along to perk his pride, he always felt that same pang of pain – and remembered Old Morg, who had as good as seen and raised him.

After, the sheriff had asked, "What did you do before upholding the law in the Queen of the Cattle Towns, son?" He was clearly impressed with the destination, at any rate.

"I was a buffalo hunter, sir," Kit said proudly.

"Bit young to have been a buffalo hunter, no?"

"Under circumstances normal, yesir; but in this case, no," Kit said. "I had the good fortune to gain the favour of an experienced buffalo hunter who used to be a mountain man. A, uh… a fur trapper – although at first he shot them –who showed me fast how to ply my trade. I'm mighty grateful to him."

"Why, I think I am too," the sheriff said merrily. "I do believe I have me here a catch."

Kit's bright smile had become that much brighter, and his affectionate pang for Old Morg that much more painfully affectionate.

"My, my," the sheriff said now, in Doc Benton's little white treatment room. "My, my, what have we here?" he said.

"Looks to be an Injun attack, sir," Kit told him.

Doc Benton said, "Took an arrow in the back and was scalped – alive, it seems."

"How's that?" the sheriff asked.

"Well, I speculate he must have been playing dead, 'Bow," the doc said. He and the sheriff were on first-name terms, whereas Kit would not have dared call the sheriff 'Bow or even *Rain*bow, which he didn't like being called in any case on account of the biblical implication, apparently. In general, it was said he said, "I figure a rainbow appears *after* a storm instead of before it; I'd like to think, as sheriff, I'd be there *before* as appose to turn up after. I therefore find that handle inappropriate."

"And why'd you speculate that, doc?" he asked now.

"Well, for two reasons," the doc said to him. "The one being he's still alive, and the other being the wound he took was far from fatal. Took it high up in the scapula. A man in such a position could still run or hide or even fight. I therefore suspect he played dead rather than do either of the aforementioned three."

"My, why the doc has a way with words, don't he?" Sheriff Cotton said to Kit – if the comment was intended for Percy he didn't give any evidence of it.

"He's a knowledgeable man," Kit allowed. "There's much to be learned from him," he added.

"Yes, too much," the sheriff said impatiently. "Particularly about the ill effects of alcohol on the stomach. I've always found it settles mine. Not to mention the benefits of *chewing* tobacco over smoking it!"

Kit knew that the sheriff liked a good smoke and detested men who chewed tobacco and spat all over the place – "Everywhere else but in the spittoon," he said – considering the habit to be as uncivilized as eating raw meat over cooked.

He and the doc often argued the point, to no avail. Kit didn't chew *or* smoke tobacco, or even drink, but saw the sheriff's point to favour men smoking it over them chewing it – saw it on just about every boardwalk in town; not to mention all around and indeed anywhere else but *in...* near about every spittoon in town.

"So what we got altogether here then, doc?" the sheriff said. "I mean, what're we dealing with here? A man who played dead and then got hisself scalped?"

Kit felt he had something to add that might enlighten the situation. He said, "Well, while we was tending to him, Sheriff, he mentioned a possible wife and daughter – and son. Or two daughters and a son," he added.

"Is that so?"

"Yessir."

"Got a name, do he?"

"A Mister McLoughlin," Kit said. "Uh... Ellis McLoughlin, I think it was."

"Uh-huh, and what about you, doc?" the sheriff asked. "You also think this was a Injun attack?"

"By my reckoning," the doc said at length, "it looks to have been an ambush. The arrow I took out of him was a Comanche war arrow, barbed. He was probably set upon by about twelve. I suspect they've kidnapped his wife and daughter, if he did have them with him, and from what he muttered, killed his son. And stolen all his horses and whatnot, of course."

"Indians is supposed to be whipped in these parts, all up and down the trail," the sheriff reminded him.

"Holdouts?" Kit suggested.

"Only *one* I know of," the sheriff replied to that. "And he's supposed to be hiding out on the Llano, with his tail tucked between his legs to boot. It could be scalphunters did it, you know. Some bandit outfit trying to make it look Injun. It's been known to happen."

Kit knew Sherriff Cotton didn't want to admit the only other logical alternative within the distance this man could have come: the Indian renegade God Dog. He *had* in fact mentioned him, but not his name; it was God Dog who was supposedly chased out into the Llano, hiding there somewhere amongst the waterless peaks and flats with his tail tucked up between his legs like some scared puppy. That was the rumour coming off the trail from every next cowpoke, anyhow. But everyone knew God Dog was the most fearless, far-reaching and reckless Indian holdout of all time.

Sup*posedly*, some riled up trail boss, after suffering a sizable horse theft at the hands of God Dog, had formed a posse and chased him right out into the Llano – and supposedly further out into the Llano than any whites had ever been previously: the land being utterly waterless and unknown to anyone but the last of the Indian holdouts.

"I don't believe that story," Kit spoke up.

"What story's that?" the sheriff asked.

"The one that keeps coming off the trail. The one about... about God Dog."

The sheriff sighed, looking grimly at the unconscious victim – now possibly of God Dog. As if freegrazers weren't enough trouble to worry about. Now he had a man without a scalp and possibly his whole family attacked within riding distance of Wagon Trail.

He said, "Well, look, if the man ain't conscious there's not much I can do here!"

"He's in and out of it, Sheriff," Kit said.

"Well, so far he's only been out of it!"

Doc Benton said, "Well then we'll just have to wait around until he comes to, won't we? Ain't nothing else we can do."

"Problem is," the sheriff said, "hairless Mister McLoughlin over here ain't the only problem we got right now brewing in Wagon Trail. A sizeable bunch of freegrazers turned up and're camping just over the hill. About ten to fifteen hands with five to ten horses per man. There's a horse wrangler I saw wrangling, a cook, a chuck wagon, the works. Worst of it is, I'd say they're trailing at least one thousand five hundred head of cattle. That's a problem that requires my attention. Now if I cannot do anything here right now, as you can imagine there's other preparations I've to attend to."

There was a moment's pause as the sheriff turned the matter over in his mind.

"I tell you what," he said finally. "Percy, you stay here. Kit, you come with me. If he comes conscious, get Percy to come find me or Kit, who'll know where I am if I ain't with him. Kit?"

"Yessir?"

"I'd like to see the horse this man rode in on."

Kit searched the sheriff's eyes, as if trying to see what the man was thinking in his troubled head – something was obviously troubling him heavily, apart from the freegrazers; from what Kit could see it seemed he had some additional and rather bothersome suspicion to confirm.

"Yessir," Kit said. "It's at Dim Bill's livery."

Sheriff Cotton suddenly looked unimpressed. "Dim Bill's? It'd be better tended to left tied to the hitching rail outside the saloon. Someone might come out and piss in the water trough for it. Which idiot took it there?"

"It weren't me," Kit quickly absolved himself.

"Then I've a mind who it was," the sheriff replied. "Come on, Kit. Let's go. To Dim Bill's," he added regretfully.

Wagon Trail looked like one long grassy rut made by the widest wagon going west on God's Creation, with settlements that had sprung up slowly, but steadily, on either side as other wagons unloaded and then later more pulled up behind those in front, necessitating alleys, side and even back streets.

In fact they said the modest little town came into being when a settler decided he had come far enough up the trail and decided here he was going to stop. Soon others coming up the trail had received assistance from him and it had become a regular rest point and trading post on the way up the trails to the major end points of the cattle drives to Kansas like Abilene, Wichita and Dodge, where railheads shipped them off to stockyards in cities like Chicago and those elsewhere east. They say he had actually turned the lumber of his wagon into a house, and further timber from trees and lumber from trade later on into further establishments like a livery stable and blacksmith, where he stabled, fed, watered and shoed horses, as well as fixed saddles and other leather goods like holsters and saddlebags; dug his own wells, welded and put together water pumps; mended wagons and their wheels by the dozen.

So the town's assumed name, Wagon Trail, was considered by most fairly apt.

It only had one saloon, although a second one was presently being erected right across the street, but compensated for its lack of saloons with several general stores, a rooming house, two livery stables, a doctor's practice and two too many blacksmiths (who would literally fight each other for the right to shoe a horse), Ned Lowe's three-chair barber shop and bath, etcetera.

Kit and Cotton went down the doc's pavestone walk and out through the gap in the low white picket fence surrounding his practice.

"If I was the doc I'd at least have a gate," the sheriff commented a little enviously, looking down around himself. "Picket fence and no gate's about as good as a gate and no picket fence, in my book."

Kit didn't comment and they started up the street, beside other clapboard properties, none with quite so fancy a finish as the doc's – or a picket fence, with or without gate, for that matter. Most were unpainted and opened right out onto the main street, with small areas of garden out back of them at best, usually just big enough to hang a washing line.

As soon as the boardwalk started they stepped up onto it, and no sooner had they done so than the sheriff's worst fears were confirmed.

There were four unfamiliar horses tethered to the hitching rail outside the saloon. They were big horses, well fed and watered, although they must have come far up the trail – to Sheriff Cotton they looked like Texan horses. They had the appearance of having travelled no more than a mile, if even that... which was at least the distance they had come to get into town.

"You ever seen such a fine set of fillies, Sheriff?" Kit asked. He could not take his eyes off the horses blinking away at the flies and twitching their ears and tails at the hitch rail – at flies, unfortunately, because, as the sheriff had said, the odd drunk tended to come out, hold onto the hitch rail and urinate into the trough beneath. Sheriff Cotton hated all forms of uncivilized behaviour. The sheriff had in fact arrested and jailed a man for leaning over the hitching rail one night and vomiting into the trough, and had let him go the next day without charge and confused as to what he had done wrong.

"Not in Wagon Trail," the sheriff replied, taking out his pistol and checking its load. "Let's hope the men who rode in on them are nearly half as fine, and we shouldn't have any trouble here."

They continued to walk on up the boardwalk. Kit would have checked his pistol too, prompted by the sheriff doing so himself, but there was no point: he checked his pistol upon rising every morning first thing, before even taking a wiz, and practised his draw practically whenever he was bored – which was fairly often in Wagon Trail.

"You reckon those horses belong to some of the freegrazers you rode out to check on this morning?" Kit asked.

"I reckon so," the sheriff sighed. "I spoke to the trail boss. *Bosses*. They seemed reasonable enough, although we've seen that before and still had plenty of trouble from their boys. Haven't we?"

Kit hadn't realized the sheriff had actually made contact with the outfit; he had assumed he had merely ridden out to confirm the rumour and ridden back with an affirmative.

"You spoke to 'em?" Kit asked, astonished.

"He said he'd warn his boys not to make trouble. The one I spoke to," the sheriff added.

There was a moment's silence.

Then Sheriff Cotton said, "I'll tell you one thing though: I wasn't given any welcome looks. Although I did ask how long it'd be before they'd be moving on."

"So what do we do?" Kit asked, with the saloon only three or four establishments away.

"We'll just go on in and introduce ourselves," the sheriff told him. "On second thoughts, I'll do the introducin'. And the talking."

That was fine with Kit, an introvert with strangers at best if not with most people he even knew.

They went past Ned Lowe's without looking in, but heard the door open behind them, and stay open.

"Christ that man's nosey," the sheriff said, without looking back. "I suppose he wants us to let him know if we've heard anything about his haircuts."

Kit chuckled, knowing exactly what the sheriff meant. Sheriff Cotton frequented Ned's at least once every two weeks, if not once every week, for some sort of trim or refinery.

They passed Mrs Elmira's general store, which was closed and had a sign saying as much in the window. Nothing was wrong with her that Kit knew of; she had probably closed it as soon as she heard the freegraze rumour, since she had suffered the loss of quite a few items in the past to cow outfits and found the entire enterprise unprofitable at such times as cattle herders were camped nearby.

The last establishment between Mrs Elmira's and the saloon was empty. As they passed the soaped-up windows, the sheriff nodded a 'ready' to Kit. Kit nodded back, but glanced again at the circled streaks of dried soap wiped onto the inside of the windows of the empty store in the hope to see in. Apparently it had been bought out by Mr O'Neil Masterson as a wedding gift for his daughter and her husband and it was going to be a butchers.

Kit looked forward to it; the Mastersons were rearing some fine cattle and shoat up at that huge homestead of theirs. But unfortunately, eating it would probably only make those inhabitants of the town who were embittered by their reliance on the Mastersons to become even more embittered. Maybe they wouldn't even buy any.

On the other boot, people might buy just to keep relations good, or even to improve them.

People were strange.

"Alright," Sheriff Cotton said, as they paused briefly before they would come in sight of the saloon's windows and therefore the riders within it. "Here goes. Keep it casual."

Kit was wired like a spring – about as casual as an uncovered rattler – but nodded just the same.

They stepped into view of the saloon's nearest window, walking at an even pace, neither looking in. It was Sheriff Cotton who went in first, putting his hand on the top of one of the batwing doors and pulling it out, before going in, as was his habit. Kit followed him, grabbing the top of the batwing as it swung back and entering behind.

Three big men were standing at the large bar in back that ran the length of the saloon. Kit wondered where the forth rider was; a wonder soon set to rest. A set of stairs went over the bar at one end and led up to a railing above, where several doors opened on rooms occupied by sporting women. Behind one of the doors came the enthusiastic creaking of bedsprings.

The barkeep stood in front of the men, nervously running an

outright rag of a dishcloth around and around the mouth of a mug. His name was Duncan Mcdowry, and Kit didn't like him, though Sheriff Cotton had no qualms with him. Kit's dislike of the man was mainly because his saloon was what Old Morg had warned him to stay out of in Dodge all his early days: a whorehouse and a gambling den where whiskey could be bought and imbibed and a man's will weakened so that he could be further deprived of his hard-earned livelihood – it also seemed to be the source of most if not almost all of the trouble in Wagon Trail when it came to freegrazers coming in off the prairie.

Old Morg had also warned him of the shaky moral nature that must be inside a man who could earn his living such a way. He and Kit worked hard on the open prairie, he said, hunting, shooting and skinning, piling the wagons, sleeping on the hard ground under the open sky, braving the elements; they could consider themselves good if not even great men, but such a man as that – who stood and waited before his loaded bar, under a dry roof, waiting to depart the thirsty, hungry and hard-working man of his earnings like a spider in its web waits for the insect – how could such a man even call himself a man?

It was Duncan looking up from the mug he was polishing at Sheriff Cotton coming in with Kit close at his heels that first alerted the three big men. They half-turned from the bar to see what had caught the barkeep's attention to such an extent that it in fact stopped him from polishing that mug, other than to serve them, for the first time since they had stepped in.

They looked at the two come in with mild surprise. Each had a beer mug in his hand which rested on the bar. Despite the fresh look of their horses, the men themselves looked tired and fed up – not what Kit had expected at all. Only the man squeaking the bed springs in one of the rooms above must not have been tired – for these men seemed too tired to do even that.

"Howdy, boys," Sheriff Cotton said.

The men's sluggish eyes noted the sheriff's badge on his lapel. One of the men, who was on the end, looked Kit up and down as if he disapproved of him, after seeing the badge he wore. As if such a sprite as himself shouldn't have been wearing one if *he* wasn't – perhaps he had applied for law work at one time and been turned down, Kit thought.

The men nodded to the sheriff, but none acknowledged Kit.

ˋ"You boys wouldn't happen to be with the cow outfit over the hill would ya? I met your trail boss this morning. McMyrtle. Baxter McMyrtle."

"Well, you missed our boss's boss then," the middle man said, largest of the three. "Mister Anderton."

"Well, that's an awful pity," the sheriff replied. "I suppose I might have learned something new. Where you boys from?"

It was the one in the middle again who spoke up. He kept a big walrus moustache, which fascinated Kit – how did a man get his moustache to grow like that? Kit would have liked to ask him, but the reply could well be gunfire.

"Us or our outfit?" the man asked.

The sheriff looked at Kit and smiled, which Kit thought a bad idea – provocative – before turning his attention back to the big man in the middle with the walrus moustache.

"How about your outfit, for starters," he said impatiently.

"We're from Texas, we're tired and we just want to wash the dust out of our necks in peace. Our friend upstairs prefers to wet his rod first, *before* he takes a drink. That good enough for you?"

"I see you boys are packing?"

"Packing what?"

"Colts, by the looks of things," the sheriff said, inspecting their midsections.

"I see you fellas are packing too. What of it? I'd as soon walk into a town naked as without my piece."

"You are aware this town has a firearms ordinance?"

"I didn't know it *was* a town, let alone had an ordinance."

"Well, then you missed both signs, I guess," the sheriff said, and sighed. He seemed to relax. "I'm gonna let you boys keep your guns on you, as long as you promise me not to shoot at each other with 'em. Or more importantly at us or anyone else in this town."

The men were nodding agreeably. Kit didn't actually think they wanted any trouble, or, for that matter, were of a troublesome nature – for now, that was.

Sheriff Cotton stepped up to the bar. "With one exception," he said to them. "I'll allow you can shoot the barkeep if he doesn't keep 'em coming."

All three of the men laughed now. The atmosphere in the saloon seemed to have changed completely in only moments.

"Dunc," Sheriff Cotton said, "give these men another round on me."

Duncan rushed to fill another three mugs, but put the one he had been polishing aside, with the tatty rag still in it, before he rushed to the task.

"There's four of us, Sheriff," one of the men reminded him.

"Yeah, I can hear," the sheriff said, which elicited another hearty laugh from the men. "Dunc, you pour him one when he comes down and tell him it's courtesy of the town sheriff." He listened to the bed springs creaking for a moment, Kit thought somewhat theatrically, and then said, "*If* he comes down."

"Sounds like he's gonna come down through the ceiling," he added.

This had the men really laughing.

"Well, boys, you stay outta trouble now," he said.

"We will, Sheriff. Like I said, we're just tired comin' off the trail. Some of us have been working the drags, just wanna wash out the dust."

"The drags?" the sheriff said. "Workin' the drags with horses like that?" He pointed a thumb over his shoulder, at the door.

"Oh no," walrus said. "Those're our show horses. We just use 'em when we're visiting and want to make a good impression."

Kit thought for a moment the sheriff wanted to say, "Well, your horses did" – in fact, he saw the man hesitate with what he was sure were the very words in his mouth.

"They're nice horses. I'll give you that," the sheriff said. "Where you boys headed? Kansas, of course, on account of the railroads, but whereabouts in Kansas?"

"We've come up from the Rio Grande, in Texas. Well, I have

anyhow," walrus said. "These fine boys with me we hired on in San Antonio. Excepting Coe. He's with me."

"And... Coe is?" the sheriff asked.

"Coe's the one makin' all that noise upstairs. I'm Dwight. This is Lebold and Kiefer. We're much obliged for the beers."

"Good meetin' ya's. I'm Sheriff 'Bow Cotton, this is my deputy Kit Cope." He stepped forward and began to shake the men's hands, Dwight's first, even though he was in the middle and not the closest.

But Kit was still standing there a little stunned when the sheriff stepped back after all the hand-shaking. The sheriff had called him his deputy; Kit knew he was nothing of the kind. The sheriff had never made him deputy of Wagon Trail. Wagon Trail didn't even have a deputy.

He snapped out of it and stepped forward, a little too eagerly – for a deputy sheriff – shaking the men's hands. Walrus – Dwight – had a firm shake (Morg had always said often you can judge a man by his hand-shake), but Lebold, the man on the end who had looked at him with disapproval, added a little additional squeeze to his. Kiefer's handshake was neither of ill intent nor any other that Kit could tell of.

As he stepped back, Lebold looked past him at Sheriff Cotton. He said, "A bit young to be a deputy, ain't he?"

"Or even in law work," he added.

Sheriff Cotton turned from the bar and smiled confidently. He said, "This boy's kept peace and order in Dodge City. And has two bullet holes in him to prove it. I'd want no one else at my side in a gunfight."

Kit couldn't believe his ears: he knew the sheriff approved of him, but he never knew it was that much. Perhaps he was just playing up to impress the freegrazers.

"Dodge City?" Lebold said incredulously. He looked Kit up and down again, as if he must have seen the wrong person the first time he looked. "Is that right?"

"Yes sir," Kit said firmly.

"That's where we're headed," Lebold said.

"We've come up the Chisholm Trail and forked off for the first time. Usually we follow it directly to Abilene," Dwight said. "First time we're headed for Dodge."

Kit said, "Well, I'll give you a piece of advice then, sir. When you enter Dodge, check your weapons at the jailhouse first thing unless you want to wake up in it."

Dwight frowned.

"And why's that?" Lebold said.

Kit said to Lebold, "'Cause otherwise Wyatt Earp'll bash you over the head without even *warn*ing you of the ordinance."

"I've heard the name Wyatt Earp," Dwight said.

"He don't even ask you to hand 'em over," Kit continued. "And he once shot a gun clean out of a man's hand without even hitting one of his fingers, the moment he drew."

"Damn," Dwight said. "Like I said, I been to Abilene before more'n once, but this'll be our first time in Dodge. Nobody pays much mind to the ordinance in Abby and things're fierce. At least, since Bear River Tom was kilt, that is. I guess maybe one'd have some peace of mind if it was truly enforced. They say we can get more for our cattle in Dodge than in Abilene, and anyway Abilene's almost a closed market now."

"Maybe," Kit said, "but just remember, sir, I wouldn't have the same attitude with your firearms as you've displayed here, not in Dodge. Wyatt Earp and his brothers'll open you up. He's also known to carry a sawed-off double barrelled shotgun under his jacket."

"Well I'll be," Dwight said, and finished the last of his beer, picking up the next one as soon as he put the empty glass down. "Well I'm much obliged to you, young man. I'll be sure to pass that news on to the rest of the boys. But I have heard talk of this Wyatt Earp. What's he look like?"

"Uh," Kit blurted. "Uh... he's tall. And dark. With a broader set of shoulders than most buffalo hunters. In fact, he was one." He went on, "Thick moustache, tweaked up at the ends. His nose looks like the beak of an eagle. He has the hair of a hawk. And he has the sharpest green eyes you ever saw."

Dwight tried to picture this figure blown all out of proportion, with difficulty. "Well I'll be," he said.

"Fastest gunhand that ever lived. He'll have his gun out and to your eye before you even have your hand to your hip," Kit said. "Shot at night and day and never been hit once with a single bullet, not even nicked. And of all places, in Dodge City, the cowboy capital of the world. Wyatt Earp don't play around. No man kept a tighter watch."

There was a moment of awed silence. Even the bed springs had stopped. Kit was impressed with the run of his imagination; of course he had never seen, much less heard, all that about the man, but *had* heard he was good.

"I think we'll leave our guns at the camp, at that," Dwight said. "Won't we, boys?"

The creaking of bedsprings started up again, slowly at first but then just as vigorously.

Lebold still had his eye on Kit. He was an envious-looking man, yet he was impressive himself, both in height and stature. His beard was full, and he almost reminded Kit of a buffalo hunter himself.

Was the man perhaps challenged by him, Kit came to wonder.

Lebold said, "Shot twice, huh?"

Sheriff Cotton laughed, but lightly. "Show 'em, Kit."

Kit hesitated uneasily for a moment. He looked at the sheriff, who merely nodded encouragingly.

"Go on, show 'em," he repeated.

Kit would have to undo his buttons to take his shirt off and get his shoulder out, which would have been an effort, so instead he shrugged and began to unbuckle his belt, to the men's immediate interest. Kit raised himself up on his forefeet, turned and pulled his duds down on the one side, revealing the big round twisted scar smack-bang in the middle of his pale white buttock.

"Ouch," Dwight said. "What were you hit with, a gosh dern Henry rifle? I thought all those boys'd switched to the Winchester up there, being more civilized and all."

"Not this outfit," Kit said, seizing the moment: *he* hadn't said anything about a Henry. The reason the scar was so huge was in fact due to the terrible infection he got afterward, and the ineptitude of the drunken doctor or sawbones or whatever he had been who had pried the bullet out – on the seventh or eighth attempt. A painful ordeal Kit would not likely forget for the rest of his life.

He pulled his duds back up and buttoned them. Then he took a broad step back from the bar, as if preparing to run and dive over it. The men watched this with interest.

Kit said, "I got hit in the shoulder while running towards a saloon across the street when a gunfight broke out. Tucked my head into my armpit like this as I dove through the window."

Kit demonstrated by attempting to get his head as far into his armpit as possible.

Sheriff Cotton was impressed. Even Lebold looked somewhat taken aback, if not impressed exactly – unimpressed, was more like it. But not because it was unimpressive. To the contrary, it seemed.

Kit said, "Landed on a card table, which I overturned and returned fire over. Then a couple of 'em surrounded the saloon and I took a dead run for the bar. I heard the big Henry go off just as I dove over it, but I felt it hit me first.

"That's how fast a bullet comes out," he added. "Any of you been shot before?"

"No," Dwight said, as if admittedly disappointed by the fact. "But Lebold's been snakebit."

"Well," Kit said, "it hits you before you hear it. That's how fast it comes out."

"I heard it's that way," the man called Kiefer said, lowering the beer the sheriff had bought him. "A man in our outfit's been hit. But only in the arm. The upper arm. Tolt me near the same thing."

Kit was buckling his belt, but halted. *Heck*, he thought; showing them his shoulder now that he thought about it would be well worth it.

"I'll show you the one I took in the shoulder," he said, and pulled out his shirttails.

He began to work out the buttons, from the top down, figuring to not have to undo them all. Finally, after undoing several, he popped his one side out.

He turned and showed them his shoulder blade, where there was another large round twisted welt. It looked almost as if the bullet had been spinning as it hit him and had twisted the flesh with it as it entered. It was a wound clearly made by a bullet.

"Dang," Dwight said. "How'd you like that? Huh, Lebold? How's that compare with your snakebite?"

"I was *poi*soned," Lebold maintained. "Almost died. Was bit by a deadly rattler."

Kit was tucking his shoulder back into his shirt, thinking to say he was as good as poisoned too, by the infection that followed.

"Who was ever bit by a rattler that weren't?" Sheriff Cotton said absent-mindedly. "I never heard of a rattler that weren't deadly. You sure it was a *rat*tler bit you... and not a rat?"

Lebold took offence.

"Why, yes I do, it made the rattling sound," he said defensively. "Then it bit."

"Oh, why? You one of those fools who hears a snake and freezes still? If a rattler rattles, I git. I don't stand there and wait to be bit."

Dwight and Kiefer had themselves a good chuckle. Kit was closing his top button, struggling with it under his chin.

"I uncover rattlers by the day," the sheriff was saying. "Why, two're permanent residents of my barn and practically pay rent. Well, we have an agreement; they take care of the rats and I hit the black widows with a broom stick so's *they* don't get bit themselves."

The men didn't know what to make of this claimed arrangement between snake and man, but laughed heartily at the absurdity of it.

"Where'd it bite you, anyhow?" the sheriff asked.

"On the foot," Lebold said, sounding very much on the defensive now.

"Only the foot!" the sheriff goaded him. "Why there's not much there to bite but a bit of skin and bone. No wonder you're still alive. Take a rattler bite on the inside thigh or the forearm and you'll likely lose that limb, courtesy of a sawbones and only if he's a quick one at that. It's that, lose a limb, or your life. You're a lucky man, Mister Lebold. Why, next to Kit, you're practically Wyatt Earp himself."

Lebold took an aggressive step forward, but Dwight stopped him with a firm hand.

"Alright," he said, "let's not get too riled up here." He looked at the sheriff. "We'll be mindful in Dodge, much obliged to Kit. And you needn't mind us, Sheriff. I give you my word there won't be trouble. Least not from us."

"Uh, Mister Dwight, sir?" Kit interrupted respectfully.

Dwight seemed pleased and even mildly surprised to be addressed as sir.

"What is it, son?" he asked.

"What are drags?" Kit asked. "You said you were working the drags."

"Oh," Dwight said, drawing himself up to his full height and placing his hands on his hips, where a fine leather belt and holster with a large Colt pistol in it creaked. "Workin' the drags," he said, "is driving the herd at the rear. As you can imagine, all those hooves kicking up dust all day don't make for pleasant work. That's why we take turns and rotate."

"Oh," Kit said. Now he understood what Dwight had meant by not using the horses hitched to the rail outside 'on the drags' – they would be ruint. Still, he was confused about the whole process of cattle herding, and Dwight saw it.

He said, "We got two men always on the drags, one man on point – that's leading the herd – two twos on either side watching the flanks and a scout who rides ahead looking for a place to bed down for the night or for good grazing ground or... say for instance, a good place in a river to cross."

"In a river?" Kit said, impressed. "Have you crossed many rivers?"

"I've almost drownded twice," Dwight said. "I've lost count the amount of creeks and rivers I've crossed. I've crossed all the rivers on the Chisholm Trail both ways more'n once."

Kit was impressed by a man who had lost count of the amount of rivers he had crossed. Most men kept count, or boasted the number. Kit himself couldn't swim too well, and had crossed a few rivers of his own when he had left Dodge – but on horseback of course. He knew how scary it was to cross even a small river, and he had heard tell of unimaginably large ones crossed by the cowboys on the well-known cattle trails. He had heard many tales of drownings, and of plenty of cowboys on the trail who would turn back more than three quarters of the way through a drive, rather than cross a river.

Crossing a river was no joke, and not to be taken lightly.

Kit said, "Well, that's mighty impressive, sir. Coming down from Dodge I crossed a few myself. Actually I was born in Dodge."

"Well I'll be," Dwight said again, giving him a once-over himself. "You better stop bein' so impressive before Lebold just gets all et up inside."

He flipped Kit a wink.

Lebold had had it. "I'm going upstairs and poke a whore," he said. "I've had it with this idle talk."

He laid a few bits down on the bar top and then walked the length of the bar, passing Kit a might close.

"Just be careful of the rats," Sheriff Cotton called after him once he was at the stairs. "They've got bites like rattlesnakes around here on account of the size of the 'roaches."

He chuckled.

"Well," he said as the man started up the stairs, "I wish you boys luck on the trail. I'd be mighty obliged to you if you'd advise your friends when you get back that they're welcome in town if they behave, which means no firing of guns, even into the air, and that you've met me and I'm a reasonable man."

"I will do, Sheriff," Dwight said. 'We've been allowed into town in shifts so I'll be sure to do that; try save you some trouble."

"Like I said," Sheriff Cotton said, "I'd be much obliged to you. Good day, gentlemen."

"Uh, Mister Dwight?" Kit said urgently, as they were evidently wrapping up.

"What is it, son?" Dwight had been about to take a sip of beer, but lowered his mug.

"Uh... how do you get your moustache to grow like that?" he asked.

Kit thought the man was going to take offence as he had feared, but instead he seemed to appreciate Kit's fondness of it – or rather outright recognition of it as a superior moustache.

He was just about to open his mouth and say something when the man called Kiefer chuckled and said, "He drank a cure-all tonic an Irishman sold him off the back of a chuck wagon in Abilene, and it's growed that way ever since."

Dwight closed his mouth, and shrugged. Looking at his horseshoe-shaped moustache, Kit guessed it was as good an explanation as any.

“That went better than I thought,” the sheriff said to Kit once they were outside the saloon, both feeling the relief. “I thought you goaded them some,” Kit admitted.

The batwing doors were still swinging. On their way out they had just shouldered on through them.

“Oh, I don't think so,” said the sheriff. “I was just making sure we was on the same page, is all.”

“Think we'll have trouble?”

“Maybe from some of the others. But it's good to know they're only allowed into town in shifts. Let's hope it stays that way.”

The sheriff looked down the length of the boardwalk, towards where it ended for a while in bare earth and a few patches of trampled green grass to allow for a blacksmiths and none other than Dim Bill's Livery Stable.

Kit was looking at the four fillies. They were beautiful horses all right.

“Alright,” Sheriff Cotton sighed, “let's proceed to Dim Bill's livery and take a look at that horse.”

They went up the boardwalk a ways and then dropped off the end of it onto the ground. Why the carpenter who had built steps at the one end hadn't at the other was a mystery to Kit, but unfortunately the man could not be called to account – Bill Cooper was two years underground in Wagon Trail's only cemetery on account of some kind of seizure he had on the back of a horse. Although some said it was the fall, not the seizure, that had killed him, and that he had had those kinds of seizures before and lived. Just never on the back of a horse.

Kit didn't know what to make of it; that had been well before Kit had been here.

As soon as their boots touched the moist earth they were spotted by the blacksmith, who was sitting on a tree stump outside his smithy, smoking a cigar. He was the cleanest-looking blacksmith Kit had ever seen, and no less hardworking. He did a lot of work for the Mastersons and sometimes even rode out to the homestead.

"Howdy, Burt," the sheriff said.

"Why, hello there, Sheriff," Burt replied. "Just havin' me a cee-gar before I get to workin' on my next shoe."

"Don't let us stop you."

The sheriff tipped his hat.

"Oh, I won't," Burt said. He took a big draw on the cigar, until the end was alive as a campfire ember. Then he near coughed hisself to death.

Taking it away from his lips he said, "My wife's mighty thankful to you, Sheriff. For showing me the error of my tobacco-chewing ways." He coughed. Then he spat between his feet and drew on the cigar again.

"How is Nancy?" the sheriff asked.

"Happy as a pig in mud," Burt said. "Now I don't chew it."

"Well, good day to you then," Sheriff Cotton said awkwardly.

Kit nodded at Burt, not knowing what to make of whatever agenda was going on here.

The doors of Dim Bill's Livery were almost completely closed, open just enough to let a man in sideways. Kit and the sheriff had to side-walk in.

A horse whinnied worriedly somewhere in an enclosure. There was barely light enough in the livery to see to the end of your nose after coming in out of the bright of day.

Most people assumed Bill Mutton was referred to as Dim Bill due to being retarded in some way, or a little slow of thought. This was not the case. Bill Mutton was called Dim Bill on account of his apparent dislike of light – or claimed sensitivity to it, Doc Benton had once observed. Apparently he suffered blinding headaches from too much light on the eyes. His house was behind the town's main street and its windows were always curtained. It was also said that Dim Bill left for his livery before light, and only headed home again after dark.

Hence the name Dim Bill.

"I wouldn't stable a goat in here," the sheriff remarked quietly to Kit. "And how'm I suppose to see this horse in here anyway? I can't see a foot in front of my own nose."

Kit shrugged. At least Dim Bill was the one man who depended in absolutely no way on business from the Mastersons. The Mastersons, like many, avoided Dim Bill altogether – since they believed him to be retarded, and never saw otherwise since he only came and went in the dark. If it really was some kind of disease or condition he had, Kit thought it to be a very unfortunate one. The man would never see or feel the world in all its bright lit glory, the open prairie green from horizon to horizon... how a man could live like that, Kit didn't know.

"Billy!" the sheriff shouted. "I say, Bill!"

There was a sudden rasping sound from above, but both Kit and the sheriff looked down. Two white, sand-filled sacks lifted from the floor and began to rise into the air, attached to a thick rope. The movement at their feet had been so sudden and unexpected that Sheriff Cotton had drawn his gun.

As Dim Bill came down from the rafters holding on to the other end of the rope attached to the sandbags that were now swinging overhead, the sheriff uncocked his pistol cautiously.

"You're lucky I didn't shoot a hole in one of your bags," the sheriff said to Bill. "You would have gone back up and had to use a ladder to come down like the rest of us."

Dim Bill shrugged. "It's quicker this way."

The sheriff sighed impatiently; he indeed detested all forms of uncivilized behaviour. He holstered his pistol slowly.

"Who said there was a hurry?" he asked.

"Why, I just like to come down fast is all."

"And how'd you get back up?"

"Why, I use my ladder. It only works down. If I could work it up, I would."

Dim Bill suddenly let go of the rope in his hand. This time the rasping sound from the rafters was lighter but faster. The bags of sand landed heavily near the sheriff's feet.

Kit half expected him to draw his gun again at them, maybe even shoot at one this time – but he didn't.

He said to Bill, "You got that horse in here Percy brought in earlier?"

"Well, depends on what you mean," Bill said.

"What're you talking about?" the sheriff asked him. "You either got it or you don't. Which is it?"

Bill said, "Well it's here, but it ain't. It's died."

The sheriff looked at Kit and rolled his eyes up.

"Is it still in its stable?" Kit asked.

"Well of course it's still in its stable," Bill said. "I'll need a cart and at least two mules to pull it – out into the street if someone don't come to claim it."

"Did you feed and water it?" the sheriff asked.

"Well, I was going to, but didn't."

"Why not?"

"Well," Bill said, "because it... died. Ain't much use tryin' to feed and water a dead horse."

The sheriff sighed. Even Kit sighed.

"Can you show us to its stable, Bill?" Kit asked.

"Well, sure, though I don't know what you'd want with a dead horse. I hope nobody's holding me liable, that horse was dead when Percy rode it in here."

"What?" the sheriff said as Dim Bill led them through the dim light to the stable. "Are you telling me Percy Parker *rode* that horse in here?"

"That's what he did," Bill said.

"Why that lazy little..." the sheriff didn't finish that particular line of thought out loud. "Somebody ought to tan his hide," he said instead. "Or box his ears. I'm gonna have his hide for a carpet, I swear to it. I'll have him on jail-watch night and day to guard an empty cell. I will not abide that kind of laziness. That's just intolerable."

Kit himself intended to have words with the man.

Bill led them to a big wooden stable door, unlocked, and pulled it wide. They could see the dim outline of a horse lying on its side on the uneven hay-scattered floor in there.

"I'd like to be able to see it," the sheriff said.

"I'll fetch a lantern," Bill said.

"Christ Almighty. Do you want Kit to light it?"

"No, I'll look away while I strike the match. It's the flare I can't stand, then I just adjust the flame."

Dim Bill disappeared into the darkness. Soon they heard clanking somewhere in a corner at the back of the livery. Kit thought, as his eyes adjusted slightly to the darkness, that even in such poor light he could see the horse's ribs sticking right out of its side.

There was the scratch and flare of a match, the sound of tinkering, and then a ball of light. It moved through the darkness towards them; Dim Bill floated behind it like a ghost, eerily underlit. Kit saw that he was a gaunt and very pale man, even in the yellow lantern light. Fish-belly white.

He handed the lantern to Kit, and then quickly turned away.

"Kindly turn it down when you're finished with it," Bill said. "Or better yet, blow it out."

"Will do," Kit agreed. He adjusted the flame to its full brightness and then held it out over the horse stable.

The animal was emaciated. The sheriff whistled a low but long whistle. *Dreaded appreciation*, Kit thought it.

"Pass me that lantern, Kit," the sheriff said.

Sheriff Cotton held the lantern closer to the horse, and then stepped over to the other side of it, to examine its head. Kit noticed the saddle was gone.

"You pull the saddle off, Bill?" he called back.

Bill said somewhat at a distance, "Course I did. What kind of question's that to ask? What kind of eejit would stable a saddled horse?"

Kit realised it had been a stupid question; more his thinking aloud than anything else.

"Kit?" the sheriff said.

"Yes, sir?" he replied.

"This isn't that man's horse."

"Well, he rode in on it," Kit said.

There was a moment's silence, then the sheriff said, "Let's say what's-his-name back there—"

"Mister McLoughlin."

"Mister Mcloughlin is a homesteader. Okay? Headed up the trail, lookin' to move. To a new town. Hell, to sodbust for all we know. But let's say he's got his wife and daughter and son with him. Let's assume he's got a wagon or two full of possessions and at least four horses to pull them. Even say it's just one wagon, and he's got two horses.

"He gets ambushed and hit in the back with an arrow, lands on the ground and feigns death. He feigns it so well he gets scalped and keeps feigning it. They take his wife and daughter, kill his son, steal all his stuff... but he manages to get up afterwards, mount and ride a horse safely all the way to Wagon Trail...

"It just don't add up," he said. "Even if he rode this horse three days it shouldn't look this far gone. I think this horse was left behind, after his own ones were taken. Left behind for what it was... near good as dead."

Kit's mind was whirling; the sheriff, also, was a knowledgeable man – though in a different way from the doc.

"Let's take a look at that saddle," the sheriff said.

"Bill," Kit called. "Where'd you put that saddle that was on this horse? The sheriff would like to take a look at it."

"It's on the floor in the stable next to it," Bill called back out of the darkness.

They moved to the next stable along, which had no door and no hay on the floor and was obviously used for storage. A bunch of utilities cluttered it. A saw bench. A broom handle. A broken broom head. A milk pail that looked like someone had given its side a good old kick. A big rusty old hacksaw like the one two men would use to cut a log in half. But no saddle.

The sheriff held the lantern higher up, suddenly revealing the saddle, hung on the side of the stable wall from a big upturned slaughterhouse hook. Even in the fluttering yellow lantern light Kit could see the saddle was worn to a frazzle, the leather belts and buckles tattered at the ends, the saddle horn worn down by a hundred hands like an old bar of soap; even the stirrup ropes were coming apart and the stirrups themselves rusted through from having been through one too many rivers.

Kit was slightly ashamed he hadn't noticed the state of the saddle earlier on, too shocked by the sight of the man without a scalp and the condition of his horse itself to pay much attention to it.

"It's as I suspected," the sheriff said in a grave voice. "And feared," he added.

"What's that, sheriff?" Kit asked.

"Well, a long time ago," he explained to Kit, "an outfit of Texas Rangers came through Wagon Trail. They'd been up and down the trail hanging horse thieves, chasing Indians, the odd bank or stagecoach robber. You name it, they'd done it or were doing it.

"I spoke to their captain who came over to the jailhouse to give me some fliers – ask me to hang up some wanted posters. I spoke to him briefly about Indians, which he had an intense dislike for – on account of one killed his great granddaddy or somethin'. He was chasing God Dog, among others – I forget the names. Some infamous ones who'd 'jumped the reservations', so to speak. He told me something I won't forget, 'cause the stories he told me of Indian atrocities were unimaginable, but this one I won't forget. On account of its peculiarity. This was uncommon practice even among Indians."

The sheriff moved back over to the stable with the dead and emaciated horse lying in it. He held the lantern out and illuminated the starved form of its body, whose own skin had sucked so closely around its ribs it seemed to be an animal with fur bones.

"He told me God Dog had another name," the sheriff said grimly behind the swinging lantern. "A name the other tribes had given him even before the Indian wars. The captain told me the name in the Indian tongue, but I've forgot it. The translation I'll likely not forget as long as I live, and for what comes after, I think I'll keep it just in case."

He held the lantern closer to the dead horse.

"They called him '*Rides His Horse To Death*'."

Perhaps there was some truth to that story about the riled up trail boss suffering a sizeable loss of horses at the hands of God Dog, after all, Kit thought – and leading a murderous posse that chased him further out onto the Llano than any Indian had ever been chased before. Or *followed* him, in any case, before giving up – although Kit knew it wouldn't have been a simple case of giving up but a life-and-death decision to continue pursuit or turn back. Kit had heard many stories of the Llano; almost as many stories of it as he had of perilous river crossings and tales of drownings, including those of cattle and horses.

Kit reckoned if what the sheriff had concluded was true – and it seemed to be on all accounts to Kit – then the dead horse had not only belonged to the dangerous Indian renegade, God Dog, but had perhaps come all the way with him from the Llano, ridden to death.

The sheriff said as much himself, almost at the same time Kit was thinking the same thing. He said he'd bet a month's wages this horse had been on the Llano. He said he'd also bet it had once been almost as healthy a specimen of its kind as any one of those four horses tethered outside Mcdowry's saloon. Maybe even healthier. Which made looking at its now-emaciated corpse all the worse.

It was different than looking at the body of a buffalo, which almost always looked about to burst it was so well grazed. Kit could skin that kind of animal without feeling much for it provided it had been killed quick, slaughter a goat or chop the head off a prairie chicken without a flinch; but a horse was altogether something else.

Kit didn't like to think it, because he knew it was also what the renegade Indian's name meant, but it was an accurate way to describe what a horse was: a God Dog. Which was, of course, what his name meant: Horse.

Kit now preferred to think of him by his other handle: *Rides His Horse To Death*.

Sheriff Cotton suddenly turned the lantern down and then blew it out. Kit smelt the coal oil coming off the wick as the sheriff handed it back to him.

"Give that back to Bill," he said. "I've seen enough of this poor animal's hide." He stepped back and closed the stable door. "And I'll tell you what else," he said. "Percy's not only gonna be on chamber pot duty in the jailhouse for a month, he's gonna dig the hole and bury this horse himself."

Kit handed the lantern back to Dim Bill, who had come over as soon as it had been blown out.

Bill said, "What do you want me to do with it, Sheriff?"

"Hold it for me a day or two. Can you do that for me, Bill?"

"Why... I guess so. But no longer than that. I just don't want it to turn is all."

"It won't."

"I dunno, it looks mighty close to it," Bill said. "And better have your man come clear it out by night."

"How 'bout before sunrise?" the sheriff inquired.

"Even better," said Dim Bill.

★ ★ ★

When Cotton and Kit took a step up onto the boardwalk and started back along it, the first thing they noticed was that there was only one horse left tethered outside the saloon.

"Want to take a guess whose horse that is?" the sheriff asked.

But Kit had caught the comment too late to reply, lost deep in thought about this whole situation.

When they went past the saloon Sheriff Cotton stopped for a moment, inspected the horse and listened, and then walked over to the batwing doors and rested both arms on top of them.

"Howdy," Kit heard him say to someone inside. "I take it you're the one they call Coe?"

Kit heard a low voice inside say, "That's me. I take it you're the one they call Sheriff around here? If you are, much obliged for the beer."

"That'd be me. And you're welcome."

"You the one was shot in the bum by Wyatt Earp?"

"Uh, no," the sheriff said. "I believe you've been misinformed. That would be my deputy."

Kit felt vibrations on the planks under his feet, then heard the hollow bang of boot heels begin at the other end of the boardwalk.

It was Percy Parker, coming at them at a dead run. His hat had blown off his head and was fluttering behind him, the hat string – which Kit thought to be overlong – blown tight against his Adams apple, which Kit thought to be overly large.

"Now what do you suppose he wants?" the sheriff said coolly, leaning back from the batwings.

"I 'spect he has something urgent to tell," Kit observed.

But when Percy came to a stop in front of them, he said nothing; he was breathless and had to double over at the waist instead and take in several deep, hooping breaths.

"Percy," the sheriff said to him bent over, "if you throw up on the boardwalk I'm liable to have you scrub down the whole thing on your hands and knees with a horse brush."

"No... sir..." Percy managed. "It's the man... what's been scalped. He's been awake a straight five minutes this time. The doc tolt me to come fetch youse at once."

The sheriff tipped his hat to the man beyond the saloon doors. "Business calls, if you'll beg my pardon."

"I won't beg it," came the voice from inside, "but I'll give as I'll allow it."

"I s'pose that'll hafta do then."

The three started down to the doc's.

★ ★ ★

Doc Benton motioned them into the little white treatment room as soon as they got there. They stared at the man who had been scalped, who lay motionless on the treatment table in the middle.

There was a long and awkward silence.

Then the doc said, "I'm afraid our patient has shuffled off this mortal coil."

"What?" Sheriff Cotton said.

"He has expired," Doc Benton repeated.

"Well that's mighty inconsiderate of him," the sheriff said. "Considering."

Kit removed his hat respectfully. Percy glanced across at him and then did a double take, looking at him in surprise. Kit never removed his hat. In fact, he was more surprised by the fact that Kit had removed his hat than that the man who had been scalped alive was dead.

Percy realised he couldn't in fact remember a time he had ever seen Kit not wearing it – excepting those few occasions when Kit put his feet up on the jailhouse porch rail and pulled it down over his eyes. But even then he *half*-wore it.

It was a big, wide-brimmed hat with a round crown dimpled in at the front. Percy had once asked if he could try it on, and had been given a look similar to the kind some men might give a man who asked if he could have a look at their gun.

It didn't look new. In fact, it was badly faded and even had a spurt of old dried blood on it.

"A buffalo's," Kit had once said after Percy gave it an inquisitive look.

Nevertheless, there was something impressive about it – or Percy would have never asked to try it on. At some point, it must once have been quite expensive, and come from somewhere far away. To Kit it was his trusted and tried-and-tested roof against the elements; it had withstood wind, rain, sleet and snow – he had even grown into it slowly over the years. Old Morgan had given it to him one day after selling a wagonload of hides to a trader on the outskirts of Dodge. He had bought himself a new one and handed it to Kit, and Kit had treasured it ever since – even if at first it was only his nose that stopped his entire head from disappearing into it, and he had had to wear it at a tilt. No matter how bad it looked, then or now, the thought of buying a new one had never once crossed his mind.

But without his weather-worn, wind-beaten and battered hat, he was a deceptively handsome specimen. His hair was thick and full, unlike Percy's, which was thin and scraggly. It was a handsome, sunburned blonde, compared to his charcoal-coloured greasy strands. His jaw line was solid and his features stood out as if whittled from wood. There was a mild dimple in his lightly-stubbled chin, whereas Percy's chin was home to a fluffy, uneven growth of hair that made him look like a kicked goat.

Percy felt his inferiority. Come to think of it, he always had. He knew all the sporting girls in town speculated why Kit Cope never paid them mind, mainly because Percy had been with all seven of them and he did too. Often he had been asked about Kit, and just as often he had asked himself what exactly they thought was so special about him.

Now, perhaps, he realized. Perhaps it was his rugged handsomeness. Perhaps it was his hat?

He was solidly built for his age – from his days hunting and skinning buffalo on the plains, Percy supposed. His hands were unusually bony and big, compared to Percy's small skeletal appendages. They had once compared palms; Percy's were soft as a piano player's, while Kit's were leathery and heavily marked with calluses, as if he had laid down the railroads as well. He had the confident air of a trail guide and the walk of a skilled woodsman, and that was perhaps what was *most* bothersome about him – since he was far too young to already have attained either of those airs. No sooner had he rode into town and signed up to keep the peace, than Percy had found himself taking orders from two. He had immediately assumed a position of superiority over Percy, as if by some unseen law of nature, and told him what to do. Often, he looked at him with disapproval. But it was disapproval of his actions, or rather lack thereof.

"So... what do we do now?" Sheriff Cotton broke the silence.

"Fortunately," the doctor said, "in the time that he was conscious I took it upon myself to make the necessary inquiries on behalf of you fine gentlemen."

"And?" the sheriff prompted impatiently.

"Well," the doc said, "turns out Mister Ellison McLoughlin was a sodbuster. He come west from Missouri with his family seeking his fortune, staked his claim and built a sod house on it, had to ride ten miles to haul water back in barrels for his wife and livestock while he worked on a well for near two year. Said he dug three hundred feet straight down through hard clay and rock with a pick and shovel. Then he hit a load of spurting black muck instead of water, he said, and the well was ruint. Sold his claim for ten dollars. Up and loaded all his worldly possessions into a wagon, including his wife and two daughters and son, and fed up he headed up the trail for town life in Ellsworth."

"Sounds like he struck oil," the sheriff said.

"He said it was a load of useless black muck that sucked off a fine pair of boots. He wisht he never come west," the doc added.

"Well I'll be goddamed," said the sheriff. "A man who strikes oil and then sells his claim for ten dollars de*serves* to be scalped. Man has to be plumb out of his mind."

"Yeah, but he don't deserve to lose his wife and kin," the doc reminded him.

"No, I guess he don't at that," the sheriff admitted.

Old Morg had once told Kit about oil, a strange and mysterious brown substance that seeped from the earth in sacred places, and could be used by experienced plainsmen to treat wounds and skin diseases. The Indians knew of the sacred places, he had told Kit, and that the brown substance when lit would burn forever.

"For*ever*?" Kit had said.

"That's right, son," Morg had replied. "Burns night and day. The Indians use it to light their tribal ceremonies. But it has many other uses. . . her from the sun, can be used to clean guns – . . . axle. Oh, and it brews into a fine coffee."

. . . he doc, "So what happened to him then?"

"Well, reason he's dead is the arrowhead was poison tipped," the doc said. "Wasn't much on it, but enough to take slow effect. That's what's been wrong with him all this time. I reckon it was the drained venom of a rattler. I've heard they use it; take the rattler and hook a stick under its fangs, pull 'em outwards and the venom begins to drip. They say you can drain an entire snake that way, until its bite's harmless."

Old Morg had told Kit of this too. What Old Morg didn't know!

"Did he say where he was ambushed?" the sheriff asked.

"He wasn't."

"Huh?"

"It was one Indian, he tolt me. One Indian that was everywhere and nowhere. His exact words," the doc added.

Sheriff Cotton glanced at Kit.

"God Dog," Kit said.

Sheriff Cotton nodded slowly.

The doc said, "He was west of the Chisholm Trail, roughly following it. Something spooked his mules in the woods and they ran in different directions, until they tipped the wagon. That's when the Injun appeared and started firing arrows. Mister Ellis McLoughlin over here took one in the back and thought his only chance of survival was to pretend he was dead."

"That ain't a wise thing to do around Indians."

"I lend credence to that notion," the doc said. "The man should have fought, but he said all he had was the head of a blunt pickaxe and a plough, and somewhere in the back of a tipped wagon at that."

"Now that's a man I don't envy," the sheriff said.

Kit put his hat back on. A man would have to be stupid to travel this country without a firearm. For such a man, Kit was willing to go bareheaded only so long.

Doc Benton said, "He told me he saw his son get kilt. Clubbed to death, and his little scalp took as a prize. Apparently the Indian took time to cut it carefully from his head. His wife and two daughters bound and tied, and then he said his hair was pulled hard and next thing he knew he had no hair."

"Did he see which way he went?"

"He said he didn't see much but mud and blood after that. Buried his head in the sand and bit down to keep from screaming."

"Well," the sheriff said, "did he say whereabouts this all was?"

"The best I could get from him is about three miles shy of the Canadian. They were aimin' to bed down on the banks and cross in the morning."

"Time of day?"

"Yesterday noon."

"So he's got just under a day's head start from there?"

"I'd say just about," the doc said. "Oh, and there's this," he added.

Doc Benton dipped his hand into his shirt pocket and pulled out a worn photograph. He handed it to the sheriff, who inspected it closely.

"Well, at least we know what they look like – if they've been sold maybe they can be bought back. I reckon he'll be taking them down to Mexico to sell at the border."

He handed the picture to Kit.

No matter how many times Kit saw a photograph, the absolute inexplicability of them captivated him every time. He could stare at one for hours – and in the past had – marvelling at the moment captured and frozen still. How it was possible to capture the world on a piece of paper with some peculiar device was beyond Kit's wildest imaginings.

Only this time the marvel of the photograph itself was lost on Kit, for in the photo was a young girl of roughly about Kit's age, with long, curly, golden-blond hair catching in the sunlight; he could see the bumps of her breasts at the top of her dress, and felt his dingus twitch.

He swallowed.

The photograph showed a family of five standing together in front of a bare and badly built sod house, all looking miserable – especially the eldest-looking of the women – but the young girl who had caught Kit's eye like no other he had ever seen, in photograph or in flesh, smiled happily, as if unaffected by the evident hardships of the 'poar' sod busting family. She was the dandiest thing he had ever seen; young and fresh – and unspoiled.

Kit squinted closer at the photograph. The rear wall of the sod house was leaning over to one side, and two crooked logs had been propped against it – to stop the entire back wall from collapsing. The roof was also caving in at one corner. It was made of wood rafters covered with hay and mud – too much mud, by the looks of things, and not enough hay. Kit noticed no windows amidst the stacked mud bricks, just an open entry way and the beginnings of a pounded mud floor. He could see the well next to the house, circled unevenly with the same type of mud bricks, and a mule team.

But mainly he couldn't take his eyes off the girl. It was the girl he had always imagined he would one day meet, the daughter of some ambitious homesteader fresh off the boat, pushing west with his family and looking to stake a claim, new to a land he knew well. And to think that right now she was in the hands of a cruel and ruthless renegade Indian...

Would she still have that smile? Would she be able to pull it ever again? Was she even still alive?

Her sister, stood on one side of her father in the photograph, appeared to be a poor alternative, bearing no likeness to her at all: she had bucked teeth poking from a heavily freckled face, short, sheered hair, and a startlingly masculine set to her shoulders – as if she took turns in the traces when the mules got tired.

When Percy held out his hand to have a look at the photograph, Kit paid no notice, and Percy had to crane his neck to get a vague look at it over Kit's broad shoulder.

Kit said, "I'll hang onto this, Sheriff. Could be we need it," and unbuttoned his top pocket. When he looked up, he saw that Sheriff Cotton was looking at the floorboards distantly, pondering something.

"What is it, 'Bow?" Doc Benton asked him. "What you chewin' over?"

Sheriff Cotton said, "It's no use. There's nothing we can do."

The sheriff's disenchanted words spurred Kit like a pair of riding boots to the flanks. They *had* to do something.

"What do you mean?" he said.

"I mean just what I said," Sheriff Cotton replied. "I don't see what we can do here. We've got a freegraze outfit just over the hill sending their boys into town in *shifts*. We can't just up and go after a Indian and leave town. First of all, there's only three of us. Second of all, we don't even have a tracker. We'd never be able to pick up his trail.

"I'm stumped, is what I'm saying," he added.

There was a moment's contemplative silence. Kit thought mostly about the girl in the photograph...

Imagine saving her, he thought to himself. *Coming to her rescue guns ablazing. Saving her from that horrible Indian. Imagine being her saviour...*

Kit wracked his brain for a solution... and soon one came.

"Wait a minute," he said. "What if we ride out to the herd and explain the situation to their trail boss. Surely he could spare a few men. *They've* got a trail scout," he added. "That right there's a tracker."

Sheriff Cotton was staring at him as if that notion would never have occurred to him in a hunnert years. He blinked.

"I know it's a long shot, Sheriff," Kit explained, "but it's worth a try, ain't it?"

The sheriff considered it.

Doc Benton said, "Sounds like a plan he's got, 'Bow. Heck, while you boys are away you can swear Ned Lowe in as sheriff. He'll have half the town locked up by the time you get back, for avoiding his clippers."

"Naw, I couldn't swear in Ned Lowe," Sheriff Cotton said. "He'd be apt to try arrest Ed Lister and then we'd *really* have trouble."

"Ed *Lister*!" Kit said excitedly. "Maybe we could even ride up to the Mastersons' and explain *them* the situation. Maybe they'd borrow us some horses so we could each have a second mount. For hard riding," he added, knowing, as he did, that God Dog would be riding his horse to death – was probably riding it right now, for that matter, to death.

"Now that's pushing it," Sheriff Cotton said. "The Mastersons are a tight-fisted bunch."

"C'mon, Sheriff," Kit pleaded. "Maybe we could ask around town for volunteers, maybe we could even form a posse. Ed Lister might join. Ed Lister's a top hand."

"Ed Lister's just had his ear sewed back on," the sheriff reminded him. "What makes you think he'll want to ride off with us and get his whole head scalped?"

"It's worth a try, Sheriff," Kit pleaded again. "What d'you say?"

Sheriff Cotton looked about to reply, and then hesitated. "We'd need supplies," he said. "Bedrolls, canteens, rifles – maybe even slickers."

"We can borrow 'em," Kit said. "Get all our provisions from the general stores. Why, Dim Bill's got one spare saddle that we know of. I'm good to go; my horse is saddled, fed, watered, rested and ready to ride. It's stabled over at Bill Wilson's."

Sheriff Cotton still looked reluctant. "Yeah, but... still, what about the town?"

"*I'll* stay behind, keep an eye on things," Percy Parker volunteered.

"Oh no you won't," the sheriff told him. "If we're gettin' scalped you're comin' with us."

Percy slumped his shoulders.

"All right," Sheriff Cotton said to Kit. "Let's you and I ride on out to the herd, see if we can't speak to one of the trail bosses."

Kit almost let out a whoop, but managed to contain himself. He was genuinely excited, despite it all. He saw what lay ahead as possibly that very opportunity about which he had always dreamed, mostly while skinning hides on the plains. Old Morg had always thought he was dreaming of whores, but it was adventure Kit dreamed about...

Or was it?

It was Lebold who saw them coming. Two men astride horses. Lebold was a hand with a keen eye, or at least liked to think so, and the first thing he looked for whenever he saw riders approaching was familiarity.

The riders weren't part of the Anderton McMyrtle outfit, but they weren't exactly totally unfamiliar to him, either.

He waited for them to ride up. It seemed he recognized them. Then he placed them. It was the sheriff of the little trail town they had been in not but awhile ago, the one who had bought them all a round of beer, with that kid deputy of his; the one got shot in the ass. Lebold wondered what they wanted, if maybe they'd had trouble from some of the boys.

Another four men had been allowed into town once they got back to the herd, the men resentful because they had had to wait for Coe, who had been late, before they could all depart. Now Coe was back on the other side of the herd. Dwight was getting some coffee from the chuck wagon while Kiefer waited behind him for his own cup to be filled. Lebold stood over the campfire.

When the two riders finally rode up and dismounted, he tossed what remained of his coffee into the fire, which sputtered. He gave them a deadeye, and then walked back to the cook without any urgency, to hand him the tin mug.

He said to Dwight, "Looks like we've got company."

Dwight looked over his shoulder casually, and then did a double take. He turned back to the cook and the coffee pot briefly, and then after a moment walked over to Kit and Cotton carefully with his brimming coffee.

"Did we forget something or something?" he asked slightly insolently.

"Not quite," Sheriff Cotton said to him. "Can you point the way to the trail boss?"

"What's the problem?"

"An Indian," Kit spoke up.

Dwight turned his attention to Kit. "An Indian?"

Kiefer dropped his coffee mug from a suddenly unsteady hand. The cook, a scrawny Mexican wearing a sombrero with a brim near as wide as a wagon wheel, jumped back just in time to save his boots – but his hat fell over his face.

"*Where?*" Kiefer said. "Where's Injuns?"

Dwight said, "Shut up, Kief. What's that you say?"

Sheriff Cotton turned to Kit, figured he might as well finish what he'd started.

Kit said, "There's a Indian's jumped his reservation and set upon a wagon, scalped and killed a man and his son – and stolen his wife and two daughters to boot."

Kiefer said, "Where? *Here?*"

"No no," Sheriff Cotton said, not wanting a misunderstanding. "Back a ways down the trail, 'bout three miles shy of the Canadian."

"We think he's headed to Mexico," Kit added.

Dwight slowly ran his fingers down the sides of his moustache, smoothing it out around his lips. He said, "Why, you boys ain't Texas Rangers too, are ya? What's it to you? The Canadian's about a hundred miles or more from here."

"He rode into our town."

"Who?"

"The man who got hisself scalped," Kit said.

"That just don't make no sense," Dwight said.

"He played dead," the sheriff explained.

Dwight hesitated, and then said, "That's not a wise thing to do around an Indian."

"I think he learnt that," the sheriff agreed.

"Well... I'll be." Dwight sipped his coffee.

"That just don't make no sense," Kiefer muttered.

"I already said that." Dwight was shaking his head.

Lebold now had another cup of coffee too. He sipped and said, "So what you boys want to speak to our bosses for?"

This time it was the sheriff who spoke up. "We're looking for able men, brave and willing, to help go after him. I figure to get the women back and hang him." Nobody said anything so the sheriff went on. "We'll need a man who can track, and some men who can shoot straight. We've got three men of our own," he added. "We're looking to form a posse."

Silence.

Sheriff Cotton said, "Each man will be temporarily sworn in by myself."

Lebold looked challengingly at Kit as he heard this, and a sly look came into his eyes.

Kiefer said, "I ain't going after no Indian, get myself scalped."

"Yeah," Dwight said. "I reckon not. I like my hair on my head, not strung out on the side of some Injun's horse."

"Well," the sheriff said, "like I said, we're looking for able men, brave and willing. Like Kit here."

"Psh," Lebold said under his breath.

"Well, anyhow," the sheriff said, "I'd again appreciate it if you could point me in the direction of one of your bosses."

"Anderton's on the other side of the herd," Lebold said. He pointed across the herd, to where a mounted man was conferring with another. "That's Coe over there with him."

"Which one you reckon it's best I talk to?"

Dwight said, "That's him. Anderton. McMyrtle's more of a... partner. In fact, he's already cost us a wagonload of supplies at the Red."

"Thanking you kindly." Sheriff Cotton tipped his hat. Then he remembered something and said, "Oh, Kit's got a picture of the women we're goin' after. Kit?"

Kit was suddenly hesitant to show the men the picture, but Sheriff Cotton nodded to him impatiently, not understanding the cause of Kit's hesitation.

"Kit?" he repeated.

"Yeah... sure." Kit snapped out of it, unbuttoned his top pocket and handed the photograph over to whoever might take it first.

Lebold stepped forward and snatched it roughly. Kit watched his eyes worriedly as he inspected it. His expression seemed to soften.

"A Indian's got aholt of these here girls?" he asked, looking up.

"That's right," the sheriff said. "And killed and scalped that boy and his father. We're goin' after him. With help or without it."

Lebold snorted insolently and handed it to Dwight, who looked the photograph over himself. "That's a damn shame. Fine lookin' bunch of ladies to lose to a Injin," he said.

Kiefer had a brief look, without much interest – *he* wasn't going after no Indian – and then handed it back to Kit.

Kit was relieved to have it back. He tucked it into his pocket again and buttoned it up quick.

"That don't irk you none?" Sheriff Cotton asked them.

"Sure," Dwight said. "It irks us plenty. But fact is no man in this here outfit's goin' anywhere without permission of the bosses. We got two thousand five hunnert head of cattle to keep here."

Kit looked over the herd, a seemingly endless mass of short and long-horn cattle spread out over the valley for miles. The men on the outskirts of the herd were mere specks, their horses dots. It was the biggest herd Kit had ever seen.

Here and there amidst the herd a bull lowered.

"Well," the sheriff said, "we'll go have a word with this Anderton."

Lebold said, "Make sure you skirt the herd and don't ride in too close. We don't want a stampede. We've already had two, one time from the rattle of a skillet. They must've thought they was all gonna get et. It's a jumpy herd."

Kit tried to imagine that many cattle stampeding, and found he couldn't. The notion itself, however, was terrifying.

"We won't," he managed to say, and he and the sheriff walked back and stepped a foot into their stirrups, remounting. They turned their horses away and gave their flanks a light jolt with their spurs.

They set off into a trot.

★ ★ ★

On the other side of the herd they found the man called Anderton. He sat high in his saddle, on a marvellous mount, and had a militaristic air to him. Another thing Kit noticed was that he was missing a finger on his right hand, where a thin cigar was pinched between a neatly trimmed thumb and forefinger.

"How can I help you gentlemen?" he said. "I trust none of my boys've been giving you trouble?"

"No, sir," Sheriff Cotton reassured him. "We're here on account of a Indian raid."

Anderton's eyebrows perked up. "Nonsense," he said. "All the Indians in these parts are whupped. I whupped 'em myself. Under General Jim Miles."

"It's a renegade's jumped his reservation," Sheriff Cotton said. "Just one. Acting on his own. He scalped a boy and his pa and stole his horse and women."

"Is that so?"

"Yes it is. You may have heard of him. We've reason to believe it's a Comanche by the name of God Dog."

"*God* Dog?" Anderton said incredulously. "Why I've been after that scoundrel myself. For years. Horse thief extraordinaire. Used to stampede cattle all up and down the trail, wreaking havoc. Slippery as a water moccasin."

"Yeah, well, we're goin' after him."

Anderton looked out over the herd and then shifted in his saddle, as if he wished he could suddenly abandon it and join them.

He said, "I wouldn't mind another crack at that scoundrel myself. If it weren't for this herd I might just ride with you. How many men've you got?"

"Well, that's just the problem," Sheriff Cotton said. "Three."

"Three? You'll need more than that if it's God Dog you're after."

"That's why we're here."

"Come again?" Anderton said.

"We'd like to borrow some of your men. With your permission, of course."

Anderton looked at Kit, for the first time it seemed. Then he looked back at the sheriff.

"I'll be moving on in three days," he said. "Due northwest. I can't afford to lose another man. I've already lost one in the Nueces, and another in a night stampede. If I could spare four men and those men were willing, would you furnish the mounts? 'Cause I can't spare no horses."

Kit began to feel his spirits lift. He glanced at Sheriff Cotton.

Sheriff Cotton said, "We'll ride up to the Mastersons' homestead and see if we can't borrow four or five."

"All right then, I'll let you have my drag riders because I can spare them with the herd settled."

"Oh," the sheriff said cheerfully, "I believe I've already met them."

"I always let the men riding drag into towns first. As an incentive," he added.

"We're much obliged, Mister Anderton."

"It's Sergeant."

"Sergeant, then. There's one other thing."

"And that is?"

"We need a tracker."

"Hah," Anderton laughed. "Now *that* I cannot spare. I'm only doing this because I'd sleep better knowing that scoundrel is underground. If I were to lose my scout I'd be high out of sorts." He flicked the end of his cigar away. "Dwight rotates to the drags whenever we get close to a town, thinks I don't notice, but normally rides on point. He has a sufficient degree of scouting skill, a good man, though not my best."

"He the one with the big moustache," the sheriff asked, "looks like a walrus?"

"That'd be him."

"Good. He'll do. Well then... Kit?"

"Sir?"

"Let's take that ride up to the Mastersons'."

"One thing," he added, to Anderton.

"Yes? What is it?"

"You might could sell some stock up there."

"I value the advice, thank you, but these cattle are bred and trailed to order."

"It's a fine herd," Sheriff Cotton said. He nodded to Kit.

They turned and spurred their horses.

★ ★ ★

"Alright, boys," Sheriff Cotton said as he reined in back at the camp. "You got your permission."

This time he didn't bother to dismount.

"What's that?" Lebold said. He was relieving himself against the rear wheel of the chuck wagon. The Mexican cook was folding up the chuckbox and shaking his head disgustedly.

"I said you've got your permission to come along. If you're brave enough, that is."

Lebold shook himself off and hitched up his pants. He walked over casually, looking up at Kit and Cotton. But his eye lingered on Kit.

"Sure," he said, looking at Kit. "Can count me in."

"Good man," the sheriff said. "I have it from your trail boss the herd'll be headed due northwest in three days. How long you reckon it'll take us to get to the Canadian?"

"Oh... about two, three days' hard ride. Without no herd it'll be easy riding for us."

"I expect it will."

Dwight was walking away from a rope remuda full of resting horses. He soon entered camp and joined Lebold's side.

"So you get anywhere?" he asked up at them, as if he expected they hadn't.

"Yep," Sheriff Cotton said. "I understand you possess some scouting skills, Mister Dwight."

"That's correct. Mostly I'm the point man."

"You brave enough? Lebold's in. I'm to take four men. Drag riders. Where'd that Kiefer guy go?"

For once Dwight wished he hadn't switched to the drags just to be the first into town – especially a one-horse town like Wagon Trail.

"God damn it," he said under his breath. Dwight was not a man to shirk from duties, but neither was he a man to needlessly add duties to the ones he already had. He didn't like the thought of having to ride all the way back to the Canadian, which he had already crossed, much less down to Mexico, if that's where this Indian was supposedly headed.

The sheriff said to him, "If you'll round up your drag riders we'll be back in a hour or so. We'll furnish the mounts."

"I don't ride no horse other than my own," Lebold said.

"Very well then."

"If it's a good horse, I'll ride it," Dwight relented, walking back to the rope remuda.

Kit watched from his saddle as Dwight began to swing a lasso into an effortless hoop over his head. Kit himself possessed the skill but had not yet perfected it like that. He tossed it out amidst the horses and roped one around the neck, pulling it towards where he stood hand over hand. Then he tied it to the top rope while he slapped a saddle on it from off the floor. He soon had it out and mounted and rode off.

"All right," the sheriff said, watching him skirt the herd at a gallop. "Bring your guns and ammo and canteens and anything else you think you'll need. Kit and I'll be back shortly. I aim to ride immediately."

★ ★ ★

They rode out to the Mastersons' homestead.

It wasn't often that Kit got to see it. The Mastersons' huge homestead had been built from lumber hauled all the way from Chicago, Kit had heard. A wagon train had brought it down from Dodge, where the Union Pacific had offloaded it. All made to order. Even carpenters had come off the train, recruited from cities in the east, and an architect with a pencil-thin moustache. Many hands in town had also hired on and helped in some way during its construction.

It was centred in a clearing amidst some large cottonwoods on top of a gentle rise in the land. Kit could remember hearing the distant pops and cracks of the whips they had used on the mule teams to get them to pull up the deeply-rooted stumps. To the east of it was a large red barn and stables. A negro was pouring a bag of feed into a trough on one side of a wooden remuda. Several beautiful looking horses were trotting over to feed.

Behind it Kit saw a young man on horseback in a field, droving about a dozen horses, about and to and fro as if doing it for fun or practice. He certainly didn't wear the clothes of your usual drover. His jacket tail was split in two at the back, and he wore a high black hat with a small impractical brim that reminded Kit of Abe Lincoln.

There was a brass-bound hitching rail on the right side of the large house. Too large. What did someone do with a house that large? Kit wondered. It was larger than the entire rooming house down in Wagon Trail.

Kit and the sheriff rode up and dismounted, tying their horses to the rail. No sooner had they done so than the front door opened. A flight of wooden steps led up to it.

"How do you do, Mister Masterson," the sheriff said merrily.

But Mister Masterson, who had heard them riding up and opened the door, looked tired and haggard, although he was dressed well. He wore a pair of brown trousers ironed sharp as a pair of sheers and a white pinstripe shirt. Clothes no doubt from the east. A tight pair of braces ran over his shoulders.

He said, "Not so good, Sheriff. My brother's dying and there's nothing anyone can do. It's beginning to take its toll. On all of us."

Kit looked up at a window and just caught sight of a pale figure looking down at them, before moving away from the curtain disinterestedly.

Sheriff Cotton said, "You want me to send the doc back up?"

"No, no. I'm beginning to believe there's not much he can do either."

"I'm sorry to hear that."

Mister Masterson said, "Yeah. So what brings you up here?"

"I've a favour to ask," the sheriff said.

"Go ahead."

"We'd like to borrow six horses."

"I don't lend horses, they're for sale."

"Everyone's contributing," Kit interrupted.

"Who's this?" Mister Masterson asked. "Contributing to what?"

"That's my deputy," Sheriff Cotton told him. "Contributing to the manhunt," he added.

"The manhunt? What manhunt? Not another horse thief?"

"Well, I'm sure he's that too," Cotton said.

"*Who* is? Are my horses in danger?"

"Mister Masterson, uh... let me explain," the sheriff tried. He told Mister Masterson about the man who had rode into town this morning without his scalp with him, and that he was now dead; that his wagon had been set upon near the Canadian River and his wife and two daughters stolen. Oh, and that he'd died from a poisoned arrow – most likely tipped with rattler venom, according to Doc Benton.

"Good God," Mister Masterson said. "My goodness."

Sheriff Cotton said, "We're goin' after him and we'll need extra mounts if we're ever to catch up with him – he's got about a day's head start on us already. We reckon he's heading down to Mexico to sell them at the border."

"I wouldn't be so sure," Mister Masterson said. "I hear those hold-outs terrorising the trails ride west onto the Llano Estacado. Since you say that's where this God Dog comes from, he might well be headed back there. I wouldn't give my horses much chance out there, or you men either."

Kit looked at Cotton. Kit wondered why they had been so certain that God Dog would be headed down to the border of Mexico; that he would escape west back onto the Llano made much more sense. The Llano Estacado, often marked on the trail maps as The Staked Plains: a flat, semi-arid, dry and treeless expanse of limitless earth and sky, scolded by an unobstructed sun by day and a chilled and bitter moon by night; it was the only land the Indians were more than welcome to keep.

The Canadian river roughly formed the Llano's northern boundary on most maps; to the west it was bounded by the Pecos Valley and on the east by the red Permian Plains. Its most notable feature, though, outside of the frequent mirages to further torment its thirsty victims, was the Caprock Escarpment, a sheer cliff rising three hundred feet into the air seemingly from horizon to horizon – it stood to reason that God Dog would be headed there.

Again Kit wondered why they had been so set on the Mexican border in the first place. The Llano was nearer and near inaccessible – to the whites. Besides, it was a well-known refuge for Comanche and Kiowa holdouts who didn't want to be confined to the sickly reservations in the Indian Territory. It had thus far proved impenetrable to the US Cavalry and even the most seasoned of the Texas Rangers, the Indians fleeing into the draws and the featureless distances or into the labyrinth of waterless canyons like the Palo Duro. Waterless, that is, for the whites. The Indians knew where the water was, somehow. Whites had died trying to find it.

It was the last Indian stronghold, and Kit had heard enough horror stories to know it. Before the Kiowas and the Comanches, it had been home to the Apache, as vicious a breed of Indian as ever lived.

Sheriff Cotton was trying to assure Mister Masterson of his horses' safety, were he to lend them any, that is. "We'll be sure to check for his tracks," he was saying. "If he's too far gone we won't follow – it's not only horses we're borrowing, it's men."

"You want men?"

"Ed Lister's a sturdy sort," the sheriff suggested.

"Bah, he's acting like a girl since his ear got snipped," Mister Masterson said. "Won't stop fiddling with it. I keep tellin' him it's apt to come off again he keeps that up. I could about spare my negro, but that's it," he added. "Though I shouldn't really say 'mine'; he's his own man."

They turned and followed Mister Masterson's gaze. The negro, who had been emptying the bag of feed into the horse trough when they arrived, was now sitting on the top rung of the corral, watching them.

Mister Masterson said, "He's good with horses and cattle, and can fire a rifle."

"What about the horses?" the sheriff asked.

"I'll borrow you them on one condition. Any you injure or kill you pay for."

"I'd say that's a deal," Sheriff Cotton said.

"Mister Masterson?" Kit said.

The man gave him a hard and unappreciative look. "Yes?"

"What's the *name* of your negro?"

"His name's Jebediah. Jebediah Rawlins. Responds best to Jeb. *Jeb!*" he called.

The negro climbed down from the remuda hastily and began to walk towards them.

"He's also a good cook," Mister Masterson said. "I have him operate our chuck wagon during the spring round up. A good *practical* cook, of course," he added.

As Jebediah made his way towards where they stood Kit saw that he kept his eyes downcast, as if not allowed to meet his master's gaze. He was slick and shiny with sweat. Lean muscle showed between the rips and tears in his shirt and trousers. Kit had never spoken to a negro before, though he had seen a fair few and heard much about them. This one wore an old, pale brown hat, which looked like it had been sat on several dozen times and reformed with a fist on many an occasion. He had a face that looked as if it knew many hardships.

"Yes, bass," Jebediah Rawlins said obediently when he reached them. He smelt strongly of lye soap, Kit noticed.

Mister Masterson said, "Saddle up, Jeb. You'll be accompanying these gentlemen on a manhunt. It's a Comanche horse and child thief they're after."

"Yes, bass," he said, without changing expression.

"And let these men select six horses from the corral – but make sure they don't take Melisa's mare."

"Yes, bass."

He turned and headed back to the corral from which he had come.

"If you follow him to the barn and stables he'll see to your mounts," Mister Masterson said. "Good luck to you, gentlemen."

"I'd like to thank you sincerely, Mister Mast–"

"Thank me by bringing my horses and negro back in one piece."

"We'll do that," the sheriff assured him.

Without saying anything more, or looking much convinced for that matter, Mister Masterson went back into his house and closed the door – rather hard.

"That also went a sight better than I thought it would," Sheriff Cotton commented, after a moment. "Come on, Kit, let's go."

★ ★ ★

Lebold squinted and said, "They got a third rider with 'em now."

The men stood up from the campfire to get a better look, dusting off their chaps. Indeed, they saw a third rider approaching in the distance – and the six horses they were trailing. Fine looking fillies.

Dwight said, "How'd we get roped up into this shenanigan again?"

"We should never've volunteered to ride drag for the last leg, that's why – and that was *your* idea," Lebold said to him.

"Yeah, well, it usually goes down without a hitch." Dwight spat.

"Is that a..." Kiefer said absently, and trailed off. "That a negro?"

Coe stood on the points of his boots and craned his neck, being the shorter of the four. "That's a negro," he said, surprised.

"What they brought a negro for?" Lebold asked.

"Dunno," Dwight said. "But seven's better'n six even if one man *is* a nigra."

"Maybe he can shoot," Coe suggested.

Soon the horses galloped up and the riders reined in. The sheriff immediately swung free of his horse, before it had even come to a complete stop.

"You boys ready?" he asked.

"Ready and waitin', Sheriff," Dwight said. The negro, he noticed, would not meet any of their eyes; he stared down at his horse's neck.

"You boys got any food with you?" the sheriff asked.

Dwight said, "Canteens're full, we got beef jerky packed into our saddlebags and Coe's got a hunk of bacon in his."

"Good," the sheriff said. "Guns and ammo?"

"A full load and a extra box each. Each man's been equipped with at least one rifle and pistol."

"Alright, let's saddle up and ride, boys," Sheriff Cotton said. "We're eatin' daylight."

The men picked their saddles up off the floor and began to disperse in the general direction of their grazing mounts.

"Each man'll trail an extra mount behind him," Sheriff Cotton added. "Come get your mount from Jeb. He'll be riding with us. You're to treat him decent. I'm as Texan as you are and I'll be doin' the same."

Kit sat proud in his saddle and watched the men arranging and tightening their gear, each man effectively under the sheriff's command, sheathing their rifles in their saddle scabbards and fastening their canteens and bedrolls to their horses.

On their way back they had stopped in town to gather provisions from several stores, on credit: ammo, jerky, bedrolls and the suchlike. Remembering what Old Morg used to say, Kit had grabbed a box of Therapeutic Papers. Then they had stopped at the doc's to tell Percy to fetch his horse and suit up; slow as he was they weren't prepared to wait for him either, and he was to catch them up south of town on the trail. Kit had reminded him to fetch his rifle from the jailhouse and had given him the key.

Now, sitting on his horse as the men saddled up around him, Kit felt his heart miss a beat. This was it. *It.* The adventure he had waited all his life for: The Hunt for the Indian Renegade God Dog.

Kit couldn't hardly wait.

PART
II

God Dog usually rode twenty hours and rested four, especially after a raid, but hadn't counted on the women slowing him down so much. Especially the eldest.

He soon decided that at the next creek he would kill her.

He was trailing three horses behind him, each with one of the women tied to it. He had fastened their ankles to the steel stirrups, so that if they tried to escape they would be trampled under their horses – or even if they simply fell. He found it far more effective than draping his captives over a horse's back and tying their hands to their feet under the horse's belly – he had once lost a captive that way, a little girl who had managed to work one of her wrists out from the rope and untie her feet. He had not looked back for quite some time after she had, and when he finally did the horse behind him was riderless. He had had to turn and trace his own tracks nearly three miles back, where he found her bare feet going north. He decided not to follow, since he knew a passel of riders were after him and riding almost as hard. There was no time. But he almost had gone after her just to scalp her for the inconvenience she caused him. He was pretty sure that she would likely die anyhow, set upon by coyotes or wolves. He had ridden past a pack about thereabouts – the little bare-footed girl had chosen a poor spot to dismount... So he had turned around and gone back.

After that occurrence he had never done it again, now always tying ankle to stirrup, and so tight it caused the ankles to bleed. All three women had bleeding ankles, a sight which pleased God Dog – for it assured him they were fastened securely.

The creek ought to be about a mile away. He intended to water the horses there and the two girls; then he would deal with the elder. He regretted wasting his time bringing her now, and realized he should have killed her back in the forest near the Canadian.

Surprisingly, the family hadn't been following the well-trodden cattle trail and had been somewhat west of it, which is why God Dog had decided to set upon them. He had picked up their spoor and followed it for many miles, and then, realizing that they were headed to the Canadian, an area he knew well, had ridden ahead and found a suitable spot from which to ambush.

And ambush he had. It had been easy, with not a single shot fired back. In fact, when God Dog had finally righted the wagon and gone through its contents after tying the women, he hadn't come across a single weapon, not even a bowie knife – he had found the head of a pickaxe, however, smeared with a black muck, most likely oil, but had left it due to its bluntness. Besides, it was too heavy to take.

These were stupid whites, and he knew it: carrying no weapons, travelling just off one of the well-known cattle trails and even headed to a point in the Canadian that was not particularly known to be the best place to cross, especially with a wagon.

God Dog had no qualms with what he had done – never had – and was perfectly at peace with himself. The whites were murderers and thieves, cheats; their word could never be trusted, not even their pieces of paper – the signing of which had caused so many of his people to lose their land and their lives during the Indian Wars.

God Dog had once been a great and noble warrior, but those times were past. The white man was remorseless, the white men limitless in number, and their weapons continually improved and increased in quantity, as did their soldiers. It seemed there was no end of white men willing to fight the Indians. It seemed there was no agreement that could be made with any of them; they seemed to have an unquenchable thirst and greed for land. They took and took and took. Even the land they forced the Indians to move onto they later returned to take.

God Dog could remember what happened to the Sioux in the Black Hills. The white man had discovered gold there, under their sacred hunting grounds, and that had been the end of the Black Hill Sioux. They had been massacred, and those that hadn't were driven from their land.

God Dog himself had survived many battles and raids, but finally when his people had been defeated and gone onto the reservations, he had decided to leave them, had decided never to set foot on the white man's reservations, but to rob and terrorize him all of his days.

God Dog's soul was dead, and had returned to the Great Spirit; it was only his flesh that now went forth across the earth to torment men. His soul had died long ago, the day his third and last wife was killed. The Comanches had continued to press north out of Texas, to get away from the whites, ceaselessly pulling up their lodges and relocating them, until finally, one snowy morning in winter while they were encamped on the banks of the Washita, white soldiers had descended upon their village.

God Dog had cut through the back of his tepee as soon as he heard the warning shots, fleeing with his wife across the cold river. But riders had splashed into it behind him and soon his wife had fallen and was no longer at his side, shot in the back. God Dog had dived under the shallow icy water until the rider's horse was on top of him, and then burst out and pulled the rider off, knifing him in the throat and then mounting his horse in one single swift movement and riding away.

It was the last wife he had lost to the whites. His first wife had died as they continued to press further and further north; unused to the travel and the cold she had grown sick and steadily sicker, and died in his arms in his lodge. His second wife had died much like his last; her back had been slashed open by a sabre, as God Dog had fled yet another encampment that had been set upon in the early hours of a winter dawn.

In those days many tribes had joined and united against the white man, and God Dog had been among them. The Comanche and the Kiowa, who had lived for generations in the beautiful Washita Mountains and along the waters of the Red, the Washita and the Canadian rivers, had waged a guerrilla-style war for almost a decade after they had heard of the atrocities committed by the great white warrior Custer upon Black Kettle and their Cheyenne friends. And it would be the Cheyennes in the north, joined with the Sioux and Arapaho, who would finally defeat The Great White Warrior. God Dog had not been at the Battle of Little Big Horn, but he had celebrated the victory all the same when the news came to him: the great white warrior, Custer, had fallen. It had been a great day, as all thought the land would be at last returned and the white man would leave. But no such thing had happened. If anything, even more white men had come. As many as the stars.

God Dog had attended many councils in those times, where many great warriors from many great tribes had spoken: Cheyenne, Arapaho, Sioux, Lakota, Kiowa, Comanche, even Apache. He had heard the wise words of the elders in the early days, but had discarded them – he had followed, instead, the war chants of the young ones, himself young, and taken the fatal first steps.

The white settlers were killing off their sacred buffalo, leaving their carcasses to rot upon the plains, and they began to attack the invaders. The elders had advised against it – not to attack the white man, for his mind was strong and his heart was swift – but still they had attacked.

But in the time when the great tribes had united, attitudes had changed in council – for it was soon evident that peace could not be made with the white man, nor any treaty formed, for he could not be trusted. He made promises and broke them. He declared more and more territory belonging to the Indians to be open for homesteading. He put up telegraph poles and built forts all up and down the trails. And his horrific jutting rail, which carried the great iron horse, began to cut right through the most sacred of their hunting grounds, scaring away the buffalo. He even dynamited the foothills and the mountains, to make way for his rails.

But at that time, well before the battle of the Big Horn – well before he rode with Quanah of the Kwahadi Comanches and Stone Calf of the Cheyenne at the battle of Adobe Walls – God Dog had still been young and had believed firmly in victory; that soon everything would return to the way it was before.

But the years had taught him otherwise: nothing would be as it was, ever again.

For at first the battles had seemed on an even keel, even those raids upon the northern forts – with the whites' single-shot muzzle-loaders being not that much more effective than their own bows and arrows. Soon they had developed an effective strategy, to attack after the volleys while the whites reloaded; they merely waited for the soldiers to deliver their fire, and then attacked, made a wild dash for them when they saw the ramrods frantically going up and down. Many whites fell, and victory seemed perfectly possible.

Then the whites had somehow acquired rifles which seemed to fire endlessly without the need to be reloaded, and thousands of Indians had been killed by mere hundreds. Unbeknownst to them all, the new breech-loading Springfield rifles had been ordered to the northern forts they had been planning to attack that spring, together with hundreds and thousands of rounds of ammunition.

None had been expecting the Springfield rifles, and they had been completely thrown off when the soldiers had not paused between shots to use their ramrods as usual; there had seemed to be no end to the white men's shooting. The same had happened at Adobe Walls.

Many had gone onto the reservations, near the agencies. God Dog had scorned their decision to take the white man's road, and gone west to the Staked Plains to live with his Kiowa and Comanche brothers, for the white man could not bear this land, and seemed to have no interest in it. For indeed, everything there was scarce.

It was where he was headed now, pushing west, with the three women, for his Kiowa brothers would pay a high price for these two fine girls, especially the one with the long golden curls. God Dog thought he would have a go himself, before he traded her, and now he looked very much forward to the upcoming creek, which he could see shimmering in the hot distance.

A big hunchbacked vulture, drinking at the water's trickling edge, saw him coming and took flight.

"Go," he said. "Find your friends and be back with them, for you will find a meal waiting."

After the recent run of his thoughts, which often turned to his hatred for the white man while riding, he also found himself looking forward to killing the old woman. He would take her scalp, to show to the Kiowas; to show them that he had had a third, but that she had been old, her hair more grey than brown, and he had killed her.

God Dog thought with relish of the way he might do it. Perhaps he could hang her upside down from a tree limb, scalp her and then build a slow fire beneath her head and cook her slowly to death. Or he could stake her to the ground, make a small incision in her belly, and pull out several metres of her insides; and leave her alive to watch the coyotes come to feed upon them: a slow and satisfying way to kill a white. Perhaps he could sew her shut between the legs, and force her to drink several canteens of water from the creek – although he knew he did not really have time for that; and that the last time he had done it the woman had managed to urinate between the threads in any case, although it had pained her immensely.

Most of all, he looked forward to doing it in front of the two young girls, for when they watched they would know his pain and the pain of his people.

They would know his pain.

Magdalena had never known such complete bodily ache and pain, and had never expected to know it. Her ankles stung, and blowflies kept lighting on and off them. Every time she jerked her foot in one of the stirrups, to shush away the flies, the string cut deeper into her ankle, and the flies returned. She knew well the dangers of infection, and that if she got one she could lose life or limb. But it seemed no use; the flies were apparently along for the trip.

She wondered where the grotesque-looking Indian was taking them. She had never seen such an ugly and frightening face in all her life – and such a pair of dead, remorseless eyes. His face was dark brown and leathery, as if seared by the sun. The cheek bones under his cruel eyes were bigger than any Magdalena had ever seen, and they lent a skeletal aspect to the Indian. His lower lip was split in the middle, so that his lower teeth showed in a dog-like snarl due to a scar formation that had fused the lip back together unevenly. One eye was milky and apparently damaged, for a scar cut across the top of the eye socket and ran down the full length of the cheek beneath. His hair was long and black and straight and greasy-looking, shining in the sunlight.

He reminded Magdalena of a grubby old tom cat that used to come to their kitchen door back in Missouri, near the river, for mule scraps her ma would throw out. It had had a tattered pair of flaps for ears, one eye and scars all over its face, bald patches on its body, and a stub for a tail: a cat that had been in some tough territorial battles.

The Indian wore an old pair of loose-fitting deer-skin leggings, a soft-looking pair of hand-made buffalo-hide boots, and a loose blue-coloured buckskin shirt. Various charms and Indian oddities appeared to be strung about his person – colourfully painted beads and decorative feathers, an old eagle claw, a pair of coyote ears or some sort of wolf's or dog's, other trophies of the once living – the worst of these being several scalps strung closely together and attached to his hip. Most of them looked old, shrivelled, sandy and dry, but two hanging there were wet with fresh blood. Being directly behind him, she stared at the two scalps, that of her father's and the bright fluffy blond hair of her younger brother, George – who he had killed in cold blood, whose head he had caved in with a club.

She had no more tears to cry for them, for her eyes had dried up, and now she thirsted like never before. She simply did not have any more water to spare. Even back home at the sod house in Texas, when pa had had to ride all day while they busted the sod, returning in the evening with the barrels of water, which they drank lavishly, she had not known such thirst.

But worst of all was the Indian's smell. A putrid, rotting meat-smell mixed with the sour odour of sweat and unclean armpits. It was a nause-ating smell that made her wretch several times when she would suddenly catch full wind of it.

She noticed he wore some sort of bleached bone necklace, possibly human, and had a porcupine quill comb clipped onto the side of his shirt – probably he used it to keep his hair so straight. She noticed a charm tied to his other hip, mainly because it made a sound like a rattler as his horse moved up and down beneath him – well, Papa's horse. It was made from the skin of some animal, maybe a muskrat or deer, and sounded like it had been filled with little stones.

Magdalena looked upwards, forced to squint by the brightness. The sun rode high in the cloudless blue vault of the sky and beat down like a blacksmith's hammer upon a piece of molten iron fresh from the furnace. She could feel it scolding her scalp right through her hair. Such heat made her weak and faint.

And my, but she thirsted so!

She turned slightly in her saddle and looked back, not wanting to alert the Indian with any sudden movement. Her slightly younger sister was on the horse trailing behind her. Magdalena had never seen her look so out of sorts, and felt her heart pang with pain. Tear-tracks ran down her dusty freckled cheeks and her eyes looked bloodshot and red. Her lips were cracked and split, like the spine of a battered book. She looked up at Magdalena, and sheer misery lived in her eyes. Her lips trembled.

Behind the horse she was on, Magdalena could see her ma; she did not seem to be fairing as well as either of her two daughters, slouched exhaustedly in the saddle. Magdalena was worried that her ma would fall or suddenly slide out of the saddle, and end up churned under the horse. Probably the horse would buck wildly if she did, to shake her loose from under it, and stomp and trample her to death with its hooves in the process.

She turned back, too afraid to tell Jenny to try to wake her, for the Indian man would hear, and there was no telling what he would do. When they had set out he had told them not to talk or whisper to one another again – or else he would stop and feed fire ants into their heads by their ears.

She realized, then, that they were dead – or worse. He was leading them further and further into unknown country, for it was featureless – she had not seen a single tree or marker for miles, just brown grass and thorny thickets and bushes. She wondered when he would stop to drink, or to water the horses, but he continued to ride, without looking back.

She wished they had never left the sod house on the plains; Pa had built it, with his own bare hands, and although her mother had hated it and complained continuously about its leaning walls and muddy floor, Magdalena had preferred it there. If only Pa had not dug the well where he had, or if only it had not been spoiled by the mysterious black muck he had found down there. Perhaps they would not have left.

Pa had been tired of riding ten miles every day to the river and hauling back the big barrels of water, but assured them day after day that soon he would reach water down in the well and they could all drink as much fresh water as they could fit in their bellies. Ma had been the most disappointed of all when he had come out of the well covered in the filthy black muck, minus his only pair of boots. She had exploded at him, in a fit of frustration and rage, and the only way Pa had managed to calm her down was to speak of moving to a town. A town called Ellsworth he had heard a cattleman mention.

"Or I reckon I could dig us another well," he had suggested.

To that Ma had said, "You been diggin' that well for almose a year! I tolt you not to dig it so close to the house! Anyway, it's just as far to water horizontally as vertically, so you can fetch it from the river!"

"Without no shoes!" Pa had protested. "Why, there's snappin' turtles in that river!"

"Well then you'll have to fetch it without no toes neither!"

Pa had deliberated that.

"Truth is I reckon we ain't cut out for this, Anna. Reckon you and the girls would fare better in a town."

"Oh, and do what there?" Ma had asked.

"I'll put in for law work."

"Law work? You can't even fire a gun."

"Then I'll get a job in a saloon."

"Doing what? Cleaning out spittoons?"

"If needs be."

"And what about the girls? I don't want them becomin' no whores!"

"Perhaps they'll meet a nice man in Ellsworth. They sure ain't gonna meet nobody out here – besides the odd traveller, some no-good wisp of smoke passin' through."

"I s'pose *that's* true," Ma had conceded.

"There's big cattle barons headed to Ellsworth, they say, and the railroad's there. The girls could go anywhere they want."

Ma had calmed down and had even seemed glad the well had been ruint.

"Then we'll move to Ellsworth," Pa had decided.

And so they had – decided to, that is. And this is where it had got them, lashed upon the backs of their horses and stolen by a dangerous-looking Indian. Magdalena had seen Indians before, but never up close; she had seen them in the distance once – while they were travelling west in a long wagon train – lining a ridge and watching them. But the men had stopped and fired at the ridge with their rifles and the Indians had disappeared. At night they had formed a corral with all the wagons and slept within it.

A scent suddenly caught in her nose. She looked up, and saw a trickling creek not even fifteen yards ahead of them. She swallowed hard as she looked at it and her throat hurt. She hoped he would stop, but even if he did, would he let them down to drink? Or would he just water himself and the horses, for he seemed to Magdalena to be the cruellest man that had ever lived.

She noticed a big, ugly, black vulture take flight from the edge of the creek, and then the Indian muttered something she couldn't quite make out. It was as if he was talking to it, for he followed its flight in the sky.

His horse began to slow down in front to a trot, their own horses adjusting their pace, and once he reached the creek he swung his leg over the horse and stepped down.

He came over to her and began to untie her ankles, causing her to gasp from the stinging pain as he pulled on the tightly knotted strings; then he moved to the horses behind her and untied her sister and mother.

She was free, free to climb down, but should she? She turned in the saddle to see him coming back along the line of horses. Ma was still slumped in her saddle.

He looked up at her, and she immediately averted her gaze.

"Get down and drink," he said in an incredibly deep voice. "While you can," he added.

But Magdalena was too afraid to. She stayed on her horse.

Suddenly he reached up and grabbed her, pulling her off onto the hard, cracked earth. She grazed her elbows and knees, which immediately began to bleed. The horse whinnied and stepped away nervously.

Then he dragged her by the hair along the dirt until she was in the creek. Magdalena began to whimper, but no tears came.

"Drink," he said, and pushed her head into the water. But he did not hold it there; when she pulled her head out it was soaked and dripping. She lowered herself until her lips were level with the water and drank.

"Not too fast," she heard him say, and now he was pulling her head *out* of the water. He pulled her hair so hard she had to stand up, but once she did he let go and pushed her backwards into the creek.

Jenny saw this and quickly got down from the horse she was on. She saw that her ma was looking around, dazed and confused.

"Ma," she said, "you got to get down. N–"

She felt a fist clench in her own hair and then she was being dragged back painfully. The heels of her shoes cut a track along the dirt.

She was pitched into the creek.

The Indian walked back to the last horse, reached up and grabbed their ma's hair.

"Ma!" Magdalena cried.

He pulled her down onto the ground and began to kick her in the stomach, hard, causing her to curl up into a foetal position.

Magdalena rushed out of the creek, her dresses heavy with water, but when she got to the Indian he backhanded her in the face and she fell on her backside. Blood began to pour from her nose into her lap.

"I said you *drink*," he repeated, and drew a knife from a sheath. He crouched in front of her, pulled her head back by the hair and held the blade to her throat. "Back to the creek," he said, "or I'll cut your tongue out." He grabbed her cheeks in a big hard hand and squeezed until her jaws opened and her tongue popped out. "I'll cut it off and feed it to the coyotes. *Go!*"

Magdalena got herself up and went back to the creek. Now she was crying. Jenny was sitting in the creek and watching the Indian. She sat down next to her in the water.

The Indian took hold of their ma's hair as he had done theirs and began to drag her over to a post oak tree on the bank. There he slumped her up against it.

Then he came back to the creek and relieved himself in it, right in front of the two girls. They were looking up at him as he did so, and the look on their faces made him laugh, laugh long and loud.

Magdalena's vision blurred with tears. Jenny was holding onto her shoulder now and crying against her.

Then the big Indian closed his pants and walked to his horse. He threw up the flap of one of his saddlebags and began to rummage through it. Magdalena and Jenny watched, wide-eyed, as he brought out a big needle and a coil of thick thread. It was the same type of needle and thread the cattlemen used to sew the eyes of jumpy animals shut for the first few days of a drive until they were trail broken. He tucked it into a pocket and then closed the flap and went back to the post oak tree, where their ma lay. He took hold of her hair, pulled it up, and then drew his knife. He held its keen edge to her forehead.

"I'm going to give this to Big Bear for a gift," he said. "And leave you to the vultures."

His hand moved in a flash, and suddenly only the hair was held in his hand, like a wig.

She began to scream; he began to laugh.

Two and a half days after starting out, they came to the banks of the Canadian. It had been an eventful two days – and this day was not yet even up.

Crossing the Canadian had come to be a very real fear in Kit's mind. He had never crossed a river as big as the Canadian before, and he had begun to worry about it almost as soon as they let out the first afternoon, for Kiefer had spoken of the man they had lost in the Nueces River in Texas, a river not nearly as big, and the reality that he would in fact have to cross the Canadian River in two or three days had finally hit home. This was not an imagined venture, with him, as usual, making it gallantly across without a hitch. This was the real thing.

According to Kiefer the man who had drowned in the Nueces had even been able to swim, just not with a bull steer on top of him.

They had made camp the first night well into the morning, managing about thirty miles or so, which wasn't bad considering they had let out in the late afternoon. Over a warm meal of bacon, beef biscuit and coffee, the conversation had turned to rivers.

It was Coe who had started it.

He had said in the uncomfortable silence that new acquaintance often makes, "Dern, boys, well I ain't lookin' forward to goin' back across the Canadian. North *and* south. That's twice you could get kilt."

Dwight said, "We got to do the Cimarron first."

"Then that's three rivers we've got to cross?" Kit asked.

"Cimarron shouldn't be a problem. I know a good place to cross," Dwight said. "And the North Canadian crossing is easier than the South."

Kiefer said, "Main problem with the Canadian's quicksand. Suck up a man whole."

"That's nonsense," Dwight said. "At best you can bog."

"I heard a man got sucked up whole," Kiefer maintained.

"That's just a trail tale."

"Yeah, well, I reckon it's a true one."

Lebold was poking at the fire absently with a stick. He said, "Quicksand can't really suck a man up. It can suck a boot off or bog your horse right to the belly, but that's about it."

"What about that time we had to leave a steer in it, account of it got too stuck?" Kiefer asked.

"I 'spect it eventually drownded."

"Yeah, well, *I* reckon it got sucked in."

"Naw," Lebold said. "I'm pretty sure it was drownded."

"I reckon it got drownt," Coe agreed.

"You boys don't know much about quicksand then," Kiefer went on. "I know for a fact it'll slowly suck a man right in, along with the horse he's sat on."

"What kinda man will sit on his horse while it gets sucked under?" Sheriff Cotton asked incredulously.

"A man what can't swim," Kiefer said. "I seen it. I'm tellin' you boys, quicksand'll suck a whole wagon up. Suck them mules right under."

Lebold said, "Yeah, well, I wish some'd suck *you* right under. Maybe then you'd shut up about quicksand and we could worry about a river when we come to it."

Old Morgan had told Kit as much; that quicksand could not really swallow a man totally up. He *had* mentioned, however, how frantic struggling would only get a man further stuck, and that once he had seen a cow outfit using a mule team to unbog a horse at the Red.

Jeb Rawlins, Mister Masterson's negro, did not sit with them at the campfire; once they had roped the horses a remuda he would stay with them, out of the circle of firelight. That night he slept next to the remuda. He neither spoke nor met anyone's gaze. Kit turned back from the fire at one point to squint into the darkness, and thought he saw him chewing on the end of a piece of jerky.

The Cimarron River had not turned out to be much, but then they were fortunate. It hadn't rained for a spell and the water was low. At no point did any of the horses have to swim.

Kiefer had, however, waited for Dwight to cross before crossing himself, following the exact same path in the crisp-blue flowing water. Percy Parker had also tried to follow it, pale in the face, for he had never crossed any rivers that Kit knew about; he held so tightly to the reins that his horse whinnied and shook its head.

Old Morg had once told Kit that a trapper he knew had died somewhere near the Cimarron, killed by Comanche Indians. But that had been long ago, before the Indians had been whipped.

They saw no signs of Indians anywhere.

That day as they rode across the plains Dwight came loping back with an air of urgency. He had been scouting ahead.

"What is it?" Sheriff Cotton asked him.

"Just come have a look-see yourself," he said.

He got into formation with the seven riders, who rode abreast, and they trotted over a rise. As they came over it they saw a large mesquite tree in the distance. To his surprise, Kit saw a man standing beneath it, up on tiptoe. He appeared to be looking up into the branches, as if he had lost something up there. Maybe someone had slung his saddlebag over a branch.

But as they rode closer Kit noticed that the man was *floating* about a foot in the air. As they came closer still he noticed that his down-pointing boots were turned inward and touching at the tips, and he did indeed look as if he were standing up on tiptoe. His hands were bound behind his back, and his neck cranked right upwards.

Kit was now close enough to see the rope that was pulled tight around his neck, and draped over a high branch above.

They rode in under the cool shade of the mesquite tree and reined in. All stared in silence.

"He's bin hung," Percy said nervously.

"You don't say," Lebold said. "Goddamn tenderfoot nuisance," he muttered under his breath. He took a sip from his canteen, rinsed out his mouth and then spat a spurt into his cupped hand, and pattered it over his face and the back of his neck.

"What's that sign say on him?" Kiefer asked.

There was a square piece of canvas strung around the dead man's neck, like a 'closed' sign on a store door.

Dwight said, "It says he's a horse thief – *was*."

"Yep, I reckon he ain't gonna be stealin' no more horses," Coe said.

Kit looked up at the hanging man's stubbled face. It was a pale purple-blue colour and the eyes bulged as if about to burst. His lips were drained of all colour. The hemp noose had cut into his neck, and rusty-looking blood had dried around the rope.

"Waste of a good rope," Lebold said. "Reckon we outghta cut him down and take it."

"*I* don't want no hang rope," Kiefer said.

"Yeah, me neither," Percy remarked.

Lebold looked at him angrily. "Nobody asked you, tenderfoot!"

Dwight said, "Leave him be."

"Naw, that's a good rope."

"Nobody's taking the rope," Sheriff Cotton said. "He's meant to hang there to warn other horse thieves. I don't know 'bout you, but I don't want my horse stolen – I like my horse. I like riding it."

Lebold tried to cool down.

"I scared away some coyotes when I topped the rise," Dwight told them, trying to change the subject. "They was tryin' to pull one of his boots off."

They looked down at the man's boots. Indeed, the right one had dozens of little rips and bite marks in it and looked to have been tugged on by a sharp pair of teeth.

"I ought to cut him down," Lebold insisted.

"You leave him be," Sheriff Cotton said. "Come on, let's go. We're eatin' daylight."

He spurred his horse. One by one they followed.

Kit wondered what it would be like to hang a man. He was the last out from under the tree. The dead man did not spook him as such. It was the grim fate that had befallen the man that kept Kit's attention. Probably they had whipped a horse out from under him...

Not long afterwards there was an accident. Percy rode his horse over a prairie dog hole. Its forefoot stepped into the hole while they were riding pretty fast and Percy was suddenly thrown over its head. He went over holding onto the reins and landed flat on his back.

When they turned their horses and rode back he couldn't speak he was so winded.

"That goddamn tenderfoot," Lebold said. "Now someone's gonna have to shoot that horse."

Percy's horse, Moonlight, had stepped out of the hole and was trying to walk, but each time it placed its hoof on the ground it had to lift it again.

"God damn it," Sheriff Cotton said. "Get him up on his feet. Someone lift him, get that wind out of him."

Dwight and Kit dismounted, but the rest remained in their saddles. Dwight went over and inspected the horse's foot. He bent and tried to manipulate its forefoot, but the horse whinnied and tried to get away from him each time he did.

"We're gonna hafta shoot it," he said.

"I ain't shootin' it," Kiefer said from his mount.

"Who's gonna shoot it?"

"I already shot one in Texas," Coe said. "I done my fair share of horse shootin' for one trip."

It seemed ironic to Kit: earlier they had seen a man hung for *stealing* a horse, and now they were going to kill one in cold blood just because it had an injured foreleg. Of course, it was not the first time he had been in a situation where a horse had to be shot. On several occasions he had seen buffalo hunters shoot their horses due to some injury they had sustained while riding, usually during the chase.

Old Morg had once had to shoot a horse of his after taking it across a creek. It had stepped into a hole under the water and broken its leg.

"If we don't shoot it the coyotes'll eat her alive," he had told Kit. "We'll be doing her a favour."

"Why don't we get the nigger to shoot it," Kiefer suggested.

Kit drew his pistol and placed the barrel against the horse's head; he thumbed back the hammer...

The shot rang out across the plain and echoed back from the distances. There was a moment of ringing silence, then the horse thudded heavily to the earth.

Kit holstered his pistol and climbed back onto his horse.

It was strange, but Kit was glad he had shot it. Mainly because of the way everyone was looking at him, wide-eyed, as if they had suddenly seen something in him they hadn't expected to see. Even Jeb Rawlins, Kit noticed, had for the first time looked him briefly in the eye.

Kit spurred his horse and rode on.

"I would've shot it," Lebold said.

"Well maybe you can shoot it a second time," Sheriff Cotton said contemptuously.

Dwight had Percy up on his feet and was lifting him into the air from behind, to get the wind out of him.

Sheriff Cotton said, "Get his saddle off and put it on one of the extra mounts."

Dwight let Percy alone and began unbuckling the saddle from under the dead horse's belly. Blood was still spurting from the hole in its temple and pooling in the dirt.

Percy had recovered but still looked a bit red in the face. As Sheriff Cotton walked past him to his horse he said, "Next time, when you know prairie dogs are about, keep an eye out for prairie dog *holes,* why don't you – this time it'll be one of Masterson's horses you'll be riding."

"You're lucky you ain't dead," Dwight said to Percy, and shoved the saddle at him.

Percy almost fell over from the weight of it, although Dwight *had* shoved it rather hard at him.

Towards evening they reached the bank of the North Canadian River without too much trouble, except from Kiefer, who kept mentioning the quicksand.

"There's quicksand in the *North* Canadian, too," he was saying.

"Suck a man right up."

"Good," Lebold said. "Finally it'll suck you up and shut you up."

The water was a muddy red colour and the river was bounded on either side by semi-submerged mud flats.

"How're we gonna cross?" Kit asked, taking in the distance to the other bank and the lengths of the smooth, muddy flats.

Dwight said, "We ought really to follow the river east and find a place where cattle've crossed."

"We ain't got time for that," Sheriff Cotton said as he rode up alongside them. "We'll cross here."

"Very well, Sheriff," Dwight said. "It's your show."

He rode his horse slowly onto the mud flat. Damp red mud slopped up out of the cups under his horse's hooves. As he got closer to the water's edge his horse's legs sank deeper into the mud. Then he walked it slowly down into the water.

This time, the horse had to swim, and swim it did. Once it was submerged it plastered its ears flat to its head and churned the water awkwardly with its hooves. Dwight held tightly to the reins and flattened himself along the length of its neck as best he could.

Soon he was across.

The boys on the other side of the bank hollered and cheered.

"All right," Kit said, and took a deep breath, letting it out slowly. He walked his horse out onto the mud flat as Dwight had, paused for a moment, and then spurred it gently down into the river. He felt his boots begin to flood as the horse's hindquarters dropped into the river.

The cold water rose around him and made him gasp. He felt the flow of the river trying to push him downstream.

"Good boy, Misty Blue," he said to his horse to calm it. "Atta boy. There you go, Misty."

They were halfway across the river; Kit had watched the way Dwight had crossed closely and attempted to imitate it. It was becoming more obvious with every mile that Dwight not only had a superior moustache, but was also a top hand. Back at the bank, Coe was walking his horse off the mud flat and into the river, Kiefer close at his heels, followed by

Percy on his new mount. Lebold had gone in right after Kit, noticing with concern that he had hesitated to be the next to cross and Kit had taken his spot.

While Lebold was crossing he thought he saw something moving under the surface of the water beside his leg, but when he double-checked nothing was there, and nothing happened so he shrugged it off.

Sheriff Cotton rode his horse in slowly once Percy's was swimming just ahead. Jeb Rawlins followed behind the sheriff solemnly. He seemed neither afraid nor concerned by either the depth or length of the crossing.

Finally Kit felt ground beneath him. Soon he felt the heavy pull and suck of the water as Misty Blue struggled to lunge up the mud bank.

He was out – and soaked to his boots.

He reined in next to Dwight and dripped. Even his hat was wet. Misty Blue shook his head and his ears made a pattering sound against his skull, like a wet mutt.

"Well, that weren't too bad," Kit remarked.

"They ain't all across yet," Dwight pointed out.

They watched as Lebold's big horse climbed the bank. Coe was right behind him on a smaller mare.

"Now you see that's just plumb stupid," Dwight said to Kit. "If Lebold's horse was to buck or fall backward, it'd knock Coe straight back into the river. He'd be lucky not to get crushed."

But fortunately nothing of the sort happened.

"Lucky," Dwight said. He spat in disapproval, but Kit noticed that a string of saliva had clung to one side of his walrus moustache, and that he had to wipe it away with the sleeve of his shirt.

Kit looked back out across the muddy river. All four of the riders' horses were swimming now, in single file: Kiefer was almost to the bank, Percy was about halfway in the river, Sheriff Cotton and Jeb behind him.

Then it happened. Percy shrieked in pain, and let go of one of his reins to reach a hand under the water. He seemed to be clutching his leg.

"What's he doing?" Dwight said in alarm.

At about the same time Percy was clutching his leg his horse touched the river bed, and as it did, spooked by his sudden shriek, it tried to rush to get out of the water, and Percy was pulled sideways out of the saddle.

"Whoa!" he cried, as his leg flopped over the pommel of the saddle – and then was suddenly submerged. Kit saw his open mouth fill with water.

Percy's mount lunged up the steep slope of the bank, riderless.

"I hope that tenderfoot can swim," Lebold said, a small smile tugging at the corners of his mouth.

Kit rode his horse to the edge of the bank, careful not to get too close to the edge in case the bank collapsed. He tried to look for Percy in the flowing, eddying water, but all he saw were swells and whirlpools where he had slid in – and a floating hat headed fast downstream.

Sheriff Cotton was still in the water and was also looking around for Percy.

"You see him?" Kit shouted across.

Then something unexpected happened. Jeb Rawlins turned his horse and started to swim it downstream, coming out from behind Cotton and cutting diagonally towards the other bank.

Kit watched as Jeb leaned sideways in his saddle, holding his hand out at the ready, as if timing a pick-up. Kit could see him spurring his horse underwater to get it to swim faster. Then Kit saw Percy's arm come up out of the swirling water briefly before disappearing again. Somehow Jeb saw where he was and swam his horse after him.

Jeb plunged his hand into the water and leaned right over into the river. He came back up clutching Percy Parker by the scruff of his shirt, and then held him there against the side of his horse while he swam it over to the opposite bank, some distance downstream.

He had to climb it up through a thick barrier of bushes.

"Come on!" Dwight said, and he spurred and rode after them, cutting through the trees and swerving around the trunks.

Sheriff Cotton was just coming out the river. Kit spurred his horse and followed.

When they reached the bank where Jeb had broken through the bushes they found Percy lying sprawled on the grass. He was coughing up mouthfuls of water.

"I reckon he drank half the Canadian," Coe observed. "'I God if he ain't drunk it shallow."

"What the hell happened?" Sheriff Cotton said. "I just saw him abandon his horse of a sudden."

"I guess the green bean felt like a little swim," Lebold said.

Kit was inspecting Percy's legs with a troubled brow. It had looked as if something had bit him; a water moccasin perhaps.

He jumped down from his horse. "I think he got bit," Kit said. "Something bit him on the leg."

"These rivers are full of snakes now," Dwight said. "Since all the beaver got trapped out."

Kit didn't doubt it. He crouched down next to Percy's leg and began to hitch up his legging. Soon he uncovered a large bite mark, about halfway up his calf. But it didn't look like the two distinct puncture marks a snake would have left. Instead, the bite mark looked as if it had been made by the beak of a bird, as if he had been bitten by an underwater eagle.

Lebold began to laugh heartily.

"He's got bit by a gosh dern snapping turtle," he laughed. "Now if that ain't a tenderfoot in the flesh, I don't know what is!"

Kit pulled Percy's legging back down over his boot and stood up. He looked at Jeb, who was standing next to his horse and holding onto its reins; this time Jeb was looking at him.

"I reckon this man owes you his life, Mister Rawlins," Kit said to him.

But Jeb looked shocked at this notion, or perhaps even just by being directly addressed – and by his second name at that. He looked down at his feet. Kit wondered why the man was so timid; he was evidently an able and reliable man and he was glad they had him with them.

Percy was sitting up now, coughing himself hoarse. He began to bash one side of his head with the palm of his hand, to get the water out of his ears.

"What happened?" he asked finally, looking around dumbfounded.

"You was bit by a snapping turtle," Kit said disappointedly, mounting his horse.

"A snapping turtle? I thought it was a snake."

Kit said, "I checked the bite. It's from a snapping turtle."

He pulled on his horse's reins and turned it away. The rest of them followed suit, even Jeb.

Lebold rode right up to where Percy was sitting, throwing mud all over him. "Now you're a *hat*less tenderfoot," he said. "Was me I'd leave you to drown." He spat and turned his horse, flicking more mud at him.

★ ★ ★

That night they camped several miles out from the South Canadian. Lebold, to his credit, had shot an elk; had come back with it draped over his horse's neck after riding out to the horizon where he said he had spotted something moving there. He had been whooping when he rode up.

"Looky what I got here, boys!" he shouted.

Everyone had been tired and looking forward to it. Kit offered to skin it but Lebold refused and decided to skin it himself, after sharpening his knife on a whetstone which he carried in his saddlebag. Kit reckoned he could easily have sharpened the knife quicker and have skinned the elk twice— no, three times – as fast.

They built a big fire even though it wasn't very cold and played cards while they waited for the strips of meat to cook. Coe had a deck in his saddlebags and they played poker. Kit played a hand or two, but decided to stop before he lost half his wages. Coe was either one heck of a card player or a cardsharp – he seemed to keep winning every time.

"It's not the hand you're dealt, it's how you play it," he said.

A sobering bit of advice, Kit thought – since it seemed to apply to more than just a game of poker.

Percy wasn't bad either, but then he played a lot back in Wagon Trail – usually as soon as he was paid out his wages he went off to play in the saloon.

Sheriff Cotton didn't play with the men; he sat to one side and cleaned his rifle, a roll-up cigarette dangling off his lip. Kiefer chewed on a plug of tobacco, occasionally spitting into the fire and making it hiss. Sheriff Cotton eyeballed him distastefully but didn't say anything.

Soon Kit got restless waiting for the meat to cook and took out the picture of the girls.

He looked at them for quite some time, wondering where they were now and if they were alright.

Supposing they *were* alright, and they could rescue them – what then? Kit took his hat off and scratched his head. What exactly did you do with a woman once you got one, anyway? He put his hat back on. Of course, you did the thing – the whatsit; what the buffalo hunters in Dodge paid the women behind the saloons to do, and what seemed to be the prime occupation and chief interest of almost every cowboy as soon as he collected his wages, whooping and hollering into town. Of course, *that*, but what else did you do with them? *Have* to do with them? Where did you put them? Kit wondered.

Kit tapped his finger on the girl in the photograph with the long, golden curly locks of hair. He certainly wouldn't be able to keep her in his small bedroom back at the rooming house in Wagon Trail. The more he thought about it, the more concerned he became.

This here girl wouldn't be content to waddle her feet and twiddle her thumbs in Wagon Trail the rest of her life. She'd want nice clothes and maybe a job in a general store – heck, she'd probably want her *own* general store. She wouldn't be content with a room like Kit's, either. She'd want a house of her own, to raise up a load of ankle-biters in – who'd in turn all need clothes and schooling and grub.

And what did you feed her? What did they eat, women?

Kit wished Old Morg was around so he could ask him, although Old Morg would probably just tell him he'd be better off spending the rest of his life collecting buffalo bones in a wheelbarrow and selling them at the railheads to be used as fertilizer – than take up with a woman, that is.

Perhaps some time he could ask Sheriff Cotton about it, although the sheriff didn't have a woman per se either; but apparently he had once been married, long ago, although he didn't talk about it. Kit wondered what had happened. Maybe she got carried off by Injuns.

Kit tucked the photograph back into his shirt pocket and buttoned it shut. He felt a bit confused – maybe Morg had been right when he said, "One day that imagination of yours is gonna get you into a world of trouble."

Kit remembered Old Morg's story about drinking water out of a hoofprint: hidden costs, that had been about, how nothing in this world is for free and comes with all kinds of concealed considerations and concerns.

Old Morg had even once said that whorein' is the oldest trade in the world and *all* women are whores basically, some just more subtle than others. "And those ones cost the most," he had told Kit. "Those ones a man can end up payin' for for the rest of his mother-lovin' life, until death does him a favour."

Kit put his hand to his pocket. Somehow, what was in there reassured him. He needed what was inside it, he wanted it, and he knew that now. He didn't exactly know what it was, but he needed it. The trade sort of made sense now, the fur pelt for...

For *it*.

He took the picture out again and looked at her, the girl with the golden locks.

I love her, he thought.

He wondered what she – they – must be going through right now, right this moment. Where was she, and what was she doing?

And was she alright?

"Kit, here's your meat," Sheriff Cotton said.

Kit tucked the picture away and stood up. Suddenly he didn't feel hungry any more. He wanted to saddle up and ride – they were wasting time, and every moment they remained here *she* was getting farther and farther away.

"Kit," Sheriff Cotton said. "You gonna eat this meat or'm I gonna?"

God Dog wound the horses through the narrow gullies at the bottom of the Palo Duro Canyon. He was excited. The cave where his Kiowa and Comanche brothers lived was near.

God Dog had heard that a ranch had been erected somewhere in the Palo Duro, and some months ago had ridden up out of the canyon to get an aerial view, scanning for a ranch. He hadn't seen one from where he had been sitting on his horse, so had spurred it on and followed the edge of the canyon around.

Soon he had spotted it, in an enormous grassy valley – in fact, where Lone Wolf, a brave Kiowa warrior who had helped the Kiowa become allies with the Comanches, had once made a stand against the US Cavalry. God Dog had once known Lone Wolf the Younger, the adopted Cheyenne son of Lone Wolf who had been killed by a party of raiding Texans.

As soon as he spotted the ranch buildings, God Dog became greatly angered. He could see that they had used an old Indian trail to drive the cattle down single file, and why they had chosen the location despite the difficulty in getting to it, for buffalo grass carpeted the valley of the canyon and no fencing was required due to the natural walls of the canyon.

Also, the whites had driven all the buffalo out of the valley and placed a guard at the mouth of the canyon to stop them from returning to eat the grass. Now the buffalo would die out in the waterless wastes of the Palo Duro, where even the white man would not dare to wander in search of food or water.

If only they had been there to spook the cattle while they were being trailed down; the whites could easily have been killed.

Nowhere could he now look in his land without being reminded of the whites encroaching upon them. Although they probably would not come further into the Palo Duro or onto the Llano, it was not a good sign. Where one white appeared, usually many whites followed. And if you attacked and slaughtered the few, soldiers came.

God Dog had decided the ranch was too big and well outfitted to attempt a raid, but had taken his Kiowa and Comanche brothers to see it. Big Bear had wanted to raid it by night, by climbing down the walls of the canyon or following the old Indian trail down. But the cunning Kiowa, Wanbli Cicala, Little Eagle, had pointed out that they could enter through the mouth of the canyon, since they knew how to get to it from within the Palo Duro, and the whites did not. Evidently the whites had entered the canyon from above and had lowered their lumber down, or they could not have gotten into it.

Iktomi, the trickster spirit, had been against the raid, fearful of the repercussions, of the soldiers who might come.

"But they will never find us in the Palo afterward," Maka Mani, Walks On Foot, had remarked.

Eventually they *had* decided to attempt a raid, but a guard had been posted at the canyon mouth, and two Kiowa had been killed and Little Eagle wounded in the leg. The whites had kept them away with a wall of fast flying steel, even faster than the guns that had fired at the Northern Forts long ago, for they had been armed with Winchesters, a rifle which loaded exceptionally fast via a quick back-and-forth flick of the wrist and hand within the wide trigger guard.

Now, God Dog looked back on his horse to check on the two girls. The one directly behind him was looking up and around at the high walls of the canyon. God Dog looked up himself, to see if she perhaps had seen someone on the lip high above, but there was no one. The only thing he spotted was an eagle nest on a ledge.

He looked at the girl on the last horse, and saw that she was asleep in the saddle. Not for long, though; for soon they would be at the Comanche and Kiowa hideout.

He entered a high, narrow gully, dark and cool, with a strip of light high above. The horses began to step and stumble over bones scattered upon the narrow path: the bones of birds and varmint. A human-like rib-cage.

Then the gully widened around them, but still remained just as narrow at the top where the strip of sky meandered along like a river, and they rounded a rocky corner.

There was a large enclave that went back into the rock and became a deep cave with a sooty ceiling, and here at its mouth a fire smoked and several Indians sat around talking, one coming out of the darkness of the cave.

"Dho!" the one coming out of the cave said. "Haho!" And the other Indians turned around and looked in surprise.

"Dho!"

"Ey-hee!"

They stood up from the smoky fire and smiles broke out on their gaunt, big-boned faces.

"Hao," God Dog said, and swung free from his horse.

Magdalena kept her eyes fixed on her horse's mane. She had risked a glimpse at the Indians and their bone-scattered camp, but had looked down as soon as she noticed a big Indian with no shirt on and only a small loincloth looking at her. She began to feel more eyes upon her, but resolved not to look up.

A big, dark hand touched her leg, and then another reached up and fondled her hair, twisting and twirling it around its fingers. She heard excited comments and exclamations, but could not for the life of her understand them. Indian-speak.

But a particular comment seemed to be levelled at her. "Nimitawa Ktelo," one said to her, and groped her breast painfully hard. She yelped, and there was a round of jolly laughter.

Fingers poked and prodded her. Her hair was pulled, at one point until a swath of it ripped out and she cried aloud, but still she kept her eyes fixed fast to the horse's mane. She felt that if she met any gaze, she would only provoke them further.

A hand reached up her leg, higher than any hand had reached up there before, sliding up her thigh, and she screamed and began to kick out in the stirrups. She felt her feet begin to bleed anew. Jenny was screaming behind her.

She felt hands tugging at the strings and trying to untie her feet–

Suddenly she was pulled from the horse. Hands began to rip and pull at her dress from every direction. She held her arms over her breasts protectively and squeezed her thighs together tight. When she opened her eyes to look up, she saw only heads crowded around her, blotting out the light; arms reaching down, hitting, pulling, groping and squeezing.

Then two big hands grabbed her upper arms, in a hold so hard she felt her bones ache, and he pushed himself on top of her. He wedged a knee in between her legs and opened them, pushing in another knee.

The top of her dress was suddenly ripped right down to her waist, and her bare breasts flowed out, unsupported, to her sides. A hand reached between the two holding her arms and took hold of one, squeezing and pulling it upwards.

She began to cry to herself, the deep and hopeless sobs of one effected to the very bottom of their being, tears squeezing out from the corners of her closed eyes; she had never been so violated, treated so terribly... thought that such a thing could or would ever happen to her.

She felt a mouth close over one of her nipples and suck painfully hard, and then suddenly the Indian was inside her, ramming her bony hips hard with his own, bruising them. Above, the Indians cheered and hollered. She heard echoed shouts from within the cave, and Jenny's own screams as they violated her. They must have dragged her into it.

Then the Indian on top of her tensed, and she felt something spurt several times into her. Her brow drew together in pained consternation, for she had no clue what it could be. Then he slid out of her, stood up and stepped away.

She felt something trickling out and running down her inner thigh.

What had just happened? Her head spun and the world whirled.

For a moment she thought the dreaded ordeal was over, but another Indian stepped up and then got down and lay on top of her, much heavier than the last. He smelled strongly of wood smoke.

She felt him enter her.

This time she didn't fight or struggle, for something inside her had just been broken, a part of her had died, given up – maybe forever. She wished she *could* just die, and hoped that they would kill her soon. But one Indian used her after the other, her hips aching immensely as each one bucked and rammed at her, some incredibly fast and hard.

One of the Indians was particularly nasty, and bit her breast, leaving a red bite mark that drew blood to the surface of each tooth imprint. He smothered her mouth and nose with one of his big hands while he ravaged her, blocking her air passages. When she managed to shake her head free from his hand and take a breath he bashed her in the nose, mashing her lips against her teeth. She felt her mouth flood with blood and a sharp metallic taste. Her nose, also, was bleeding.

But for some reason he could not finish inside of her like the others could, and soon he was pulled off...

Only to be replaced by another.

Then she felt something terrible – the worst, most abominable, confusing, confounding thing: a wave of inexplicable pleasure, greater than any she had ever felt in her life, swept through her body. It started between her legs and intensified, and then shot through her entire body. Her neck tensed, she arched her back and cried out in disgust. Then she fell back flat to the rocky floor. A feeling of great shame and nakedness came over her.

But the Indian on top of her did not stop, he continued on unaffected and the pain inside her became unbearable...

After some time her entire body felt numb and distant, and she felt there but not there. She thought of her ma, and wished also that she was dead; but even so, even with what she was going through, she did not wish to die the way her ma had: an unspeakable, unthinkable way. Even more unspeakable than what was happening to her now. But how else would she die at the hands of these Indians?

What if they in fact had no intention of killing her at all, but wanted to keep her alive – and do this to her for the rest of her life?

Magdalena fainted.

* * *

There was the sound of subdued voices, and the gentle pop and crackle of wood.

Magdalena swum up from the murky depths of a deep sleep, and surfaced with a gasp.

She had had a nightmare, *must have*. None of it had been real; she was back on the pallet in the crooked sod house on the Texan plains...

Only when she looked around she saw Jenny huddled up next to her in a horse blanket she had been given. Her arms were wrapped tight around her knees.

When she looked down at herself, Magdalena saw that she was also draped in a horse blanket. Then she felt the ache in her jaw, in her arms and legs, in her stomach and chest – everywhere.

Their backs were against cold rock and across from them she saw the silhouettes of backs hunched in front of a fire, vulture-like. The subdued voices came from there – more of that strange Indian-speak; a kind of broken-down monosyllabic language.

"Wi-ća-hća-la kiŋ he-ya pe lo ma-ka kiŋ le-će-la."

"Te-haŋ yuŋ-ke-lo e-ha pe-lo."

"E-haŋ-ke-ćoŋ wi-ća-ya-ka pe-lo..."

Magdalena looked at Jenny again. She was wide-eyed and frightened, but something in Jenny's eyes surprised her; it was a look that she felt was gone from her own, the look of life. Whilst Magdalena felt dead inside, as if she had in fact died and only remained here in the flesh, Jenny still looked intact. It wasn't that she didn't look like she had been through the same or a similar ordeal, it was that some part of her had somehow pulled through it intact, had somehow... en*dured*.

"It'll be okay," Jenny whispered, when she saw her sister searching her eyes. "It's going to be okay, Lena."

Magdalena began to sob quietly, but more deeply than she had ever sobbed. She felt her body heave and tremble and shake. Why was this happening to them?

Jenny put her arms around her and hugged her close.

"It's all going to be okay, Lena," she said again. "Someone will come and get us."

Magdalena looked up at her sister. "I don't want someone to come," she sobbed. "I want to die."

"You don't mean that, Lena. You know you don't. Be strong. Someone will come."

"I just want to die," she said.

"But I need you, Lena. Please don't."

Magdalena decided to stop talking, for it was a sobering thought: that if she died her sister would be all alone, with the Indians, and with her dead they would use her twice as hard.

Before sunrise, while night still lingered in the Canadian River Valley and the early morning dew drops clung to the prairie grass, they awoke sluggishly and restarted the fire, collecting nearby sticks and twigs, yawning and stretching themselves as they did so.

Last night's blazing fire was now a flat, fluffy puddle of ashes, but it soon blazed again as bigger branches and twigs were chucked on top of it. They were slightly damp from the dew and hissed and spat, but soon burned high.

They cooked the strips of leftovers from the elk Lebold had shot – the raw meat wrapped carefully into a bloody cutting of hide to keep it from turning overnight – and each man ate until he was full. Then they kicked sand over the fire to put it out and retied their bedrolls.

"Alright, boys," Sheriff Cotton said. "Let's saddle up'n ride. We're eatin' daylight. We got about five, six miles to go till we hit the river."

"Does he always say that?" Coe asked Kit as they climbed their mounts.

"I reckon so," Kit said.

They rode.

As the sun began to peek over the horizon, and a line of red light rimmed the earth, growing thicker and brighter, Lebold suddenly pulled hard on his reins while in a full lope.

His horse whinnied and lifted right up in the air, for a moment standing on its two hind legs, as steady as any bipedal beast ever stood, and then dropped back to earth.

Kit reined in his horse abruptly and saw that everyone else was reining in.

"What is it?" he asked, squinting ahead and trying to keep his horse under control. It was not easy to see, for the rising sun was now giving everything in sight a dull orange tinge.

"Over there," Lebold said. He pointed a hand directly out in front of him. But Kit couldn't see anything.

"What? I don't see. What is it?" he asked again.

"It's a campfire," Lebold answered, "and several men. Due southeast."

Then Kit saw it, the little flickering light and the small shadows bustling around it. It looked as if they were clearing camp and getting ready to set off, much as they had done themselves.

"Who do you think it is?" Kit asked quietly.

"Could be rustlers," Kiefer suggested.

"Or more horse thieves," Sheriff Cotton said.

"I don't see no cattle," Lebold said, scanning the plains ahead. "So they ain't with a cow outfit."

"Could be it's just overlanders," Dwight remarked.

"Let's ride up real slow," Lebold said.

Lebold led. It was by now well known that he had the best eyesight in the outfit – *that* Kit could not contest. He had spotted the elk yesterday when no one had seen anything at all, and even Kit had thought he was wasting his time riding out to it. And now he had spotted a campfire at dawn; a good thing, since riding up unannounced into someone's camp was a deadly thing to do. A good few had met their maker by stumbling accidently into someone's camp. Since Lebold had the best eyesight, he led this morning's little expedition and all followed him without question, relying on the strength of his sight to guide them.

They moved not much faster than a man could walk, but as they came closer to the camp Kit noticed that it was not being cleared, for the silhouetted men were still milling about, back and forth, and the fire continued to blaze.

In fact, Kit thought he saw a man *feed* a few pieces of wood onto it. "Huh?"

Then he spotted something highly irregular.

A short distance from the fire three men were holding down a longhorn steer. One was tying up the animal's front legs and had his knee pinned down on its head. Another was sitting on the ground behind it and bracing one of his feet against the animal's hind leg, stretching the other out to full length and pulling on it by leaning back – as if trying to rip it off with his bare hands.

"What are they doing?" Kit whispered.

"Looks like they're branding cattle," Dwight said.

Lebold had held his hand up and they had halted, trying to make out what was going on. The men in the busy camp had not yet noticed them.

Kit saw the man he had seen feeding wood onto the fire, and realized he was in fact poking it with a branding iron. Now he took it out of the fire and walked over to where the three men held the steer ready, but instead of pushing it down and burning a brand into the animal's hind, he began to use it like a pencil. Thick smoke sizzled up into the air, and the animal bellowed and tried to kick itself free. The men struggled to hold it there. For a moment the man sitting down on the ground lost the leg he was stretching out and had to grab hold of it again. Then the man with the poker went back to work.

Lebold said, "That's a running iron."

"They're illegal," Dwight remarked.

"Yeah, so's branding out on the open plains," Lebold said.

You were supposed to brand cattle in a corral, a measure taken to prevent hasty and illegal branding by rustlers on the open ranges. Even Kit knew that; you could get hung for this.

"It's a bunch of goddamn brand blotchers," Lebold said finally. "And we're too close to skirt 'em now."

"Let's ride up," Sheriff Cotton said. "I want everybody ready. Could be we have to shoot. Let's see."

They spurred their horses gently and trotted toward the rustler camp, riding abreast of each other – probably not good psychology, Kit thought, since they must have looked like a hanging party. The men blotching the brand on the steer suddenly noticed them coming and sprang up, dropping the running iron and letting go of the steer.

It jumped up and tried to bolt, but its front legs were still tied and it fell over onto its face.

The other men milling about stopped stock-still and faced them, frozen mid-task. Kit noticed hands hovering dangerously close to holstered weapons, and one man standing beside his horse at the ready, as if about to grab his rifle from his saddle scabbard – a Winchester, which in good hands could have quickly downed several of them. Kit marked him as his first target if he had to shoot.

"Howdy, boys," Sheriff Cotton said. "How we all doing this morning?"

No one said a word.

"That's a poor blotch job," Lebold said sternly. "If you want it to look old like the original brand you gotta do it against a wet cloth."

The man who had been leaning back against the steer's hind leg was still sitting, holding his hands out at his sides palm-down, as if not to provoke any sudden reactions.

"I reckon you boys've been caught red-handed," Lebold said.

"You are aware rustling's a hangin' offence?" Sheriff Cotton added.

"Looks like you boys've got plenty of rope," Lebold pointed out.

One of the rustlers spat insolently. Sheriff Cotton looked at him with distaste – finally he could justify shooting a man for chewing tobacco and spitting everywhere.

Still, nobody in the camp moved or said anything. There was a tension in the air. As much as they had caught them off guard, Kit realized if a gunfight suddenly broke out there was apt to be deaths on both sides and plenty of wounds, probably also a few dead horses.

Kit didn't fancy getting gutshot.

Suddenly one of the rustlers spoke up. It was the one who had been handling the running iron, a man with a thick scar on his cheek, as if he had once been shot in the face. He said, more to his boys than to them, "I reckon these're the ones got aholt of Tom and hung him up by the Cimarron."

Another one of them spat.

"That weren't us," Lebold said. "Though we seen him."

"You look like some kind of posse to me. Hey boys?"

"I hate posses," another one of them said, and spat – all over himself, it seemed.

"I want you boys to drop your guns nice 'n slow," Sheriff Cotton said, "and then lie down with your hands over your heads and cross your ankles."

Kit felt his horse relax beneath him. It could not have come at a worse time. He knew exactly what it meant when Misty Blue did that. It meant he was going to relieve himself.

He did.

A heavy stream of urine hit the earth and splattered loudly in the tense silence. That was all it took to tip the scales.

Kit saw the man by the horse reach into his rifle scabbard and pull out the Winchester. Kit drew his pistol and fired.

Suddenly gun shots erupted all around them, like a double broadside on the high seas. Misty Blue bucked beneath him and Kit was thrown. He flew backwards through the air and landed hard on his tailbone. A spike of pain shot up his spine and his pistol was jarred out of his hand.

He saw Sheriff Cotton trying to keep his horse under control while firing at the camp, but suddenly he was thrown back in his saddle and fell sideways out of it. He hit the ground with the side of his head and the horse began to bolt, his foot caught in one of the stirrups.

It ran straight for the branding fire and dragged Sheriff Cotton straight through it. A pall of embers burst and swirled up into the air, following in the horse's wake like a swarm of fire flies.

Kit saw Sheriff Cotton's body bumping lifelessly over the uneven earth, arms splayed out and pulled up on either side of his head.

A bullet whapped into the grass right next to Kit's hand and he snapped to. He clambered up and crawled along on his hands and knees, towards the pistol Sheriff Cotton had dropped as he fell from the saddle.

Lebold was firing his rifle from atop his horse, reloading rapidly. Brass shells flew out of the breech and rained down onto the grass. Kit saw a rustler knocked back off his feet and into the remains of the fire.

He caught alight quickly but didn't move.

Jeb had jumped down from his horse and, with his hand wrapped several times around the reins, had pulled the horse down onto the ground and was using it as cover, firing his long rifle over the top of it; a technique mastered by guerrilla fighters during the bloody Missouri-Kansas border raids in the aftermath of the Civil War.

Kit felt his fingers touch the pistol lying in the grass and he clutched it up. He stood and began to walk backwards, fanning the hammer with the palm of his hand. But the bullets flew wild and hit only a horse, Kit unused to fanning the stiffer hammer on Sheriff Cotton's big Colt.

But the sudden wild discharge of bullets caused two of the rustlers to hit the dirt, and another to risk mounting a horse without a saddle or bit. He leapt right onto the back of it and then simply slid along into its mane and slopped over the side again and landed back down on the earth.

Jeb stood quickly and fired, and Kit saw a patch of hair fly off the back of the man's skull as he tried to push himself up from the grass. He slumped back facedown and dead.

Kit had fanned the gun empty, and realized the danger he was in, for the men lying flat in the grass ahead of him were looking up now, their guns held out in front of them on the grass.

Kit slung the pistol aside and charged to close the distance. He was fired upon and felt a bullet zing past his ear, and then another tug at his hat and blow it from his head.

The two men clambered up off the grass and stood, the one on the left levelling his pistol and taking aim.

Dwight, who had also been thrown from his mount, shot him from where he crouched now next to Jeb. The bullet caught in the side of the man's cheek and tore his jaw out. Bones, teeth and blood splattered into the other man's face.

Kit dived him at the waist at full charge and went back over with him. He landed on top and there was a brief struggle for position, then Kit had him straddled and began to punch down into his face, hard.

The man squirmed beneath his legs and tried to turn over, giving Kit his back. Kit wrapped his elbow under the man's chin and cranked his head upwards, placing his other hand on the back of his neck and strangulating him, a trick Old Morg had taught him in case he ever ended up in a barroom brawl.

Kit squeezed hard and held on, and then he felt the life suddenly go out of him.

He let go and the man's head flopped into the grass.

He stood, beads of sweat prickling his brow.

There was no more gunfire. The camp was silent.

Kit looked around.

Christ Almighty, he thought.

Jeb and Dwight were peeking up over the horse to be safe. Lebold had dismounted at some point during the scrape, and now he was re-holstering his rifle.

Everyone else was down. Percy lay curled up in a ball, clutching his stomach and rocking. Kiefer lay silently in the grass, riddled with bullet holes – even his chaps were torn and bloodstained.

Coe had been thrown from his horse when the gunfire started and had hit his head on a sharp rock. He lay motionless.

"Christ Almighty," Kit said out loud this time.

They were all dead except Percy, who seemed mortally wounded, most probably by the look of him shot in the gut – one of the most painful wounds you could acquire in a gun battle, Old Morg had told him, almost certain to bring about a slow, agonising death.

Jeb let his horse back up and he and Dwight stood. Lebold came over after reloading his six-shooter with bullets from his belt. He still had it in his hand when he stepped up beside Kit, who was looking out across the plains... to where a body lay.

"Where'd the sheriff get to?" Lebold asked, but Kit heard it distantly.

He began to walk toward the body in the distance, a rut through the grass leading to it. He could see Misty Blue grazing a safe distance away, off to the east.

Stupid horse, he thought. *How can it eat grass at a time like this?* The sheriff's horse was nowhere to be seen.

Kit stopped, and looked down at the lifeless form before his feet.

Sheriff Rainbow Cotton was as dead as he was ever gonna get. There was a bullet hole on one side of his forehead. His jaw hung agape.

Dwight and Lebold came up alongside him.

"He's dead," Kit said, in disbelief.

"Well, he died fighting," Dwight said.

Lebold said, "He took two of 'em with him. I don't reckon I'd be standing here if it wasn't he'd taken out one of 'em was aiming right at me."

Kit felt tears welling up behind his eyes, but choked them back.

"Let's bury the dead," Dwight said. "Gather up guns and ammo – we'll divide them between us."

"And ropes," Lebold added.

When Kit turned he saw Jeb crouched next to Percy, tending to him. He walked up.

"How is he?" Kit asked.

"He daid," Jeb said.

Kit saw that Percy's fingers were curled up like claws, stiff and white, and that he was indeed dead.

"Daid like the rest of 'em," Jeb added.

At any other time Kit might have been surprised to hear Jeb Rawlins speak.

Kit sighed and said, "Let's find something to dig him a grave with."

Jeb joined him and they worked in silence. They gathered up rocks and stones, to place on top of the graves to prevent the coyotes from digging up the corpses – as fast. Eventually they would begin to decompose and the smell would attract bugs and varmints, dogs and wolves, and of course coyotes. Vultures would most likely come for the last of the pickings.

Kit felt a dark pall come over him, a grimness he had not expected to feel. Perhaps this was his fault; had he not suggested that they ride out to the herd and attempt to recruit volunteers, these men would not be dead. Even Percy would not be dead, would be back nodding off at the jailhouse.

For Kit, the death of Sheriff Rainbow Cotton was the hardest to come to terms with. He had liked the sheriff immensely, and somewhat like Old Morg had found a mentor in him.

Now he, too, was dead.

Kiefer and Coe's horses had both been shot dead in the crossfire, and Percy's extra mount was wounded in the belly.

Lebold made a point of shooting it, right between the eyes.

Together they dug several shallow graves, dragging the bodies into them and piling them up with rocks. Here and there a boot stuck out, a bit of shirt, the point of an elbow. They tried their best to cover up the spots with debris, prying lumps of soil and rock from the ground where they had to.

Kit and Jeb carried the sheriff's body back to the camp, Kit at his arms and Jeb at his feet, and they lowered him into the shallow grave waiting for him.

When the last rock was piled in place they stood back respectfully.

"I reckon someone ought to say a few words," Kit said.

There was an awkward silence. Kit looked around.

Lebold looked embarrassed. Dwight shuffled his feet nervously, and Jeb sure wasn't going to say anything.

Kit realised it was up to him to say something.

There was another awkward moment.

"I don't know nothing," Kit said finally, looking around again.

"Heck, we'll just say amen then," Lebold suggested.

Kit turned back to the row of rocky graves.

"Amen," he said hesitantly.

"Amen," they said behind him.

"Well, I reckon that's that," Lebold said.

"I reckon so," Dwight said.

"Yep, I reckon," Kit agreed.

"Well... should we go then?"

"I don't see there's any point in staying here," Dwight reflected.

"Let's go then."

"Yeh, let's go," Kit said.

The sight of so much death cast a gloom over him he had not expected, nor ever imagined during any of his many daydreams in which he indeed found himself in various gunfights, the last man standing at the end with a smoking gun.

The reality was far different. It had happened so fast and was over so soon, but the deaths on both sides had been numerous.

They rounded up the remaining horses, five in all. Dead horses lay scattered around them, and some had run off in different directions. They did not have time to go look for them or dig big enough graves for the dead ones. But they had plenty of extra rifles and pistols, ammo and even a saddlebag belonging to the rustlers full of tin cans. There was extra jerky they found on them: particularly dark, almost black twists of meat. Lebold found a block of chewing tobacco and a bowie knife and bandana.

As they rode off, Jeb trailing the one extra mount behind his own, Dwight said to Lebold, "What you gonna do with a dead man's bandana?"

"Why, lots of things," Lebold replied, several ropes belonging to the dead men hanging from his horse. He said, "I can use it as a dust mask. I can use it to protect the back of my neck from the sun. I can use it to sling a broken arm if I fall from my horse. Strain muddy water with it. Let's see... can use it for a towel, I guess. Uh... to tie a calf's legs together to brand it," he added. "Oh, as a blindfold for a skittish horse, I reckon. A hat tie maybe. And I reckon it'll make a nice face covering for a dead man. Heck, I reckon taking a dead man's bandana is well-nigh justified, wouldn't you say, Dwight?"

"I rescind the question," Dwight said.

"Yeah, well, you live and learn."

Kit had been listening solemnly as he watched the ground go by beneath his horse. In fact he was impressed; he hadn't known a bandana could be used for so many things and felt a little immature not to have had one on him.

After that they rode on in silence. Things were not looking up; it all seemed to amount to an unlucky start, is what it did. Whatever feeling of excitement Kit had had at the outset was gone.

They cut slightly to the east and the land became broken and rocky, and then lush and green as they neared the South Canadian River. Then the ground beneath their feet was heavily trampled by thousands and thousands of passing cattle, and they followed the wide, well-trampled cattle trail to the river.

It was steep banked with the land sheering off directly down into the water, but where the cattle had crossed the banks had been trampled right down into the gentlest of slopes. It was much farther to the other side of the bank than at the North Canadian.

But it was a well-navigated crossing and after seeing it Kit didn't feel his earlier fear was merited. Or perhaps he had changed, grown some, since the sudden gun battle with the rustlers. He wished now that they had ridden around them and not interfered.

On the other hand, rustlers often did not merely stop at rustling; they stole horses, robbed homesteaders and the overland stages. Often they could be hired as hitmen or agents to wipe out entire families who wouldn't budge from a claim, or to resolve a land boundary dispute. Most were ex-trappers and hunters, and when the furs had petered out on the plains they had simply taken the easy way and turned to a life of rustling.

They crossed the river without a hitch; Kit lost a stirrup for a moment under water and then found it again – a brief scare – but nothing more.

They climbed out at the other side and regrouped. This time they had not gone in single file but more or less alongside each other, getting to the opposite bank almost as if in a close race.

Kit had reached the other side in second place, Dwight getting there first – followed by Jeb and Lebold. But then Lebold had gone in last, fussing about his horse in an attempt to secure all his ropes.

They began to follow the river west and then started to cut inland as the plains grew more grassy and became tree-lined.

Then they entered a forest, about three miles southwest from the cross point. It was a matter now of riding abreast at some distance from each other and cutting through the forest in a line while searching for tracks, so as not to overlook or miss anything.

Again, it was Lebold who spotted something. He saw animals scattering every which way up ahead.

"I found it," he said, and spurred his horse to be the first one there.

They spurred their horses after him and came upon the overturned wagon.

"Urgh, what the hail's that smell?" Dwight said.

Lebold had dismounted and was trailing his horse as he searched around the wagon. He crouched out of sight, and when he came up he was holding the bandana over his nose.

"I found another use for my bandana," he said. "There's a dead kid here – and it ain't pretty."

Kit stepped down from his horse and had a look for himself.

The dead boy lay against the side of the wagon. His body had been ravaged beyond recognition. Kit couldn't believe that this had once been the boy crouched down by his mother's feet in the photograph. Another reality check.

He had been pecked and torn to tatters, his eyes eaten out of their sockets, the remains left like a half-eaten soft-boiled egg. His ears had been chewed down until flush with his face, the tip of his nose bitten and gnawed off, and even his lips eaten away, leaving behind a gnarled grin.

He had become the feast of the forest.

Kit checked in the wagon but could see it had been thoroughly rummaged through. A few yards from it he found a breaking plough and picked it up. He inspected the rusty end and then threw it aside.

"That would have been useful," he said to himself.

He spotted a broken arrow in the grass and inspected it, crouching to get a closer look but not attempting to lift it – he didn't want to risk cutting or splintering himself with an arrow that had been near any kind of snake venom. No other arrows were to be found; God Dog must have retrieved them.

Kit noticed that Jeb had picked up the breaking plough and was digging another grave with it. He drew a knife and cut a sheet of canvas free from the wagon cover, and then used it to roll the boy's body in, tight until only his bare feet poked out the bottom.

He dragged it over to the impression and then went to work at it some more with the plough, raising it high over his head and bringing it down with a clump.

"I found his track," Lebold called out.

He was deep in the forest on the other side of the wagon, where he had been inspecting the forest floor.

"Four horses headed west," Lebold said.

Dwight was inspecting the front of the wagon, where empty traces lay in the dirt. He said, "They were taken from the wagon team. All're shod and the lead horse poorly."

"I don't see why we're wasting time. We found it, let's go," Lebold said.

Kit helped Jeb cover the body of the boy and place a board of wood on top of him because they could find no stones. They mounted up and followed Dwight and Lebold. To Kit's surprise, both seemed as capable at tracking as each other, with Lebold's superior eyesight giving him a slight advantage.

"He's following the river west," Lebold said at one point.

Soon they were out of the forest and back in the burning sunlight. With all the morning's commotion, Kit had not in fact noticed it rise; but now it burned bright in the sky, and had not even yet reached its apex. It was going to be a hot day.

The trees began to become sparse on the plains, and were replaced by thickets and chaparral. The grass became brown and brittle.

"Whew, it's hot," Kit said, drawing from his canteen.

"Go easy on that water," Lebold told him. "Could be awhile till we find a creek."

The sun soon reached its apex in the sky and burned down upon them. Kit saw a rattler slither past in the grass, but it didn't stop to rattle so he continued on, glad that his horse had not spotted it. If it had he probably would have been thrown again.

They were riding now through a sea of brown grass, in some places as high as a horse's belly. The grassy landscape was no more broken by a landmark than as if they had been in the middle of an ocean.

Dwight had to backtrack several times to pick up God Dog's track again – he kept losing it. Even Lebold could not find it, and for a moment they were unsure if they were headed in the right direction, but when they came upon a trickling stream they saw the tracks again.

"Yep, four horses again," Dwight said. "He didn't stop to dismount. I reckon he just watered the horses and carried on at this one."

They refilled their canteens and let the horses water. Kit scooped up handfuls of water and poured them down the front and back of his shirt. He took his hat off and poked his finger through the bullet hole in the front of it, and then dampened it in the stream. When he put it back on his head the damp headband soothed his temples.

He drank several handfuls of water and then saddled back up.

They continued on.

The long brittle brown grass gave way to hard red earth full of broken rocks and bones. They constantly had to navigate thorny thickets and bushes, but here the track remained visible.

At one point they passed through what must once have been a large buffalo herd, for buffalo bones were scattered everywhere. But Dwight and Lebold couldn't find the tracks in it and had to retrace their steps.

"That's nigh strange," Dwight said. "He didn't pass through the buffalo bones but decided to skirt around them."

They followed around the slaughtered buffalo bone yard, and the track continued directly west – as if he had been respectful of the resting place of the dead and gone around it.

"You know if you round those bones up," Lebold said, "you can sell 'em at the Kansas railheads and they ship 'em back east to be made into fine china for rich old ladies' tea parties."

"I thought they turned it into fertilizer," Kit said.

"Yeah, that too," Lebold said. "I knew a guy used to go around with a wagon and a wheelbarrow collecting 'em up. He went insane and shot hisself in the eye."

Kit didn't know what to say to that.

His canteen was almost empty now; he titled his head back and shook the last drops into his mouth. He realized he had drank far too frequently, thinking that another creek would be coming sooner than it actually was.

He licked his lips. How had the girls faired on this trip? Had he watered them frequently enough, a man who rode horses to death? Dwight had said they hadn't stopped off at the creek – how thirsty had they been by now?

Kit realized it had been a horrendous ordeal for them – possibly they were not even alive, possibly not all of them had made it. An uncanny thought, for just as he was thinking it he saw vultures wheeling high overhead in the distance.

"Somethin' dead up ahead," Lebold remarked.

"It's just a creek," Dwight said. "Maybe they're just waiting their turn to water. Could be there's a cougar there watering himself."

Kit caught a pungent odour on the air, briefly, and then it was gone as suddenly. It was a putrid, sweet smell which reminded him of the emaciated body of the boy they had found lying near the wagon in the forest, but not quite as bad.

"You smell that?" Dwight asked.

"Yeah, I caught a whiff," Lebold said.

"I smelled it too," Kit said. He looked back to see if Jeb had smelt it.

"I cain't smell it," Jeb said to Kit.

Kit saw the creek ahead. There was a tree to one side of it, and another something hanging beneath it. Only the something was hung upside down, by the feet, which were strapped wide.

"'I God," Kit said under his breath.

The horses began to act skittish and nervous.

"Whoa boy," Kit said. "Whoa."

"Well... I'll be damned," Dwight said.

"That ain't somethin' I've seen before," Lebold remarked.

A woman hung upside down from a bare post oak branch – flies buzzed on and off her naked body. A fire had been built beneath her exposed head, which had been scalped. Her face was shrivelled and cooked, but the fire was stale and no longer alight below her. The flat sacks of her breasts hung groundwards; Kit had always wondered what a bare pair of breasts would look like, but had never expected they would look like this. There was nothing tantalizing about this at all.

Then he saw her dingus, between her legs; and for once even *he* had to look away. Flies buzzed and crawled about it; God Dog had sewn her shut there with coarse black thread, the ends of which stuck out untidily – a hasty but thorough job. Dried blood crusted the thread.

"It's the older woman in the photograph, the guy's wife," Kit said, but no one replied.

Reading the tracks, Dwight said, "He pulled them off their horses and let them water here. For some reason he butchered this one – the Lord alone knows." He held his elbow over his mouth.

Why a man would do such a ghastly thing Kit would never know; he doubted even if the Lord knew.

"Let's fill up our canteens and get out of here," Lebold said.

"I second that notion." Dwight began to fill his canteen.

God Dog did not resent not having a taste of the white girl with the golden locks, before handing her over to the Comanche and Kiowa; he had preferred rather the satisfaction of torturing the white elder before them, although most of the time they had not looked – but he was quite sure they had heard. He had not had time for both, for he knew he was not safe on the open plains, even as far west of the cattle trails as he had been.

After his Kiowa and Comanche brothers had ravaged her, he had no interest. He was not a scrap-eater; he would steal another woman and have his taste, would find one ripe for the picking.

Little Eagle, who still favoured one leg when he walked from the bullet he had taken in the thigh when they had attempted to raid the J.A. Ranch – as they later found out it was called – had had a taste of both the girls, and said the one with the freckles was in fact better. This had led to argument around the fire. Mila Hanska, Long Knives, did not comment, for although he had tried them both he had been unable to finish – suffering from some curse, he claimed, placed upon him by his wife who he had left on the reservation in Indian Territory.

He stared glumly into the fire.

But Big Bear was as jolly as always, and brought out some dusty bottles of red wine from inside the cave, which he had raided from a supply wagon headed to one of the Bent's forts. They passed the bottle around and drank. Every now and again they looked off into the shadows at the two frightened girls huddled up against the rock wall just outside the mouth of the cave, occasionally catching the white glare of their frightened eyes in the darkness.

Little Eagle soon went off and dragged the younger of the two girls back into the cave, but had to beat the other with a stick when she tried to stop him.

"You I will be back for," he said, in his best English, for Little Eagle had lived for a while on some of the reservations. The first had been the Fort Cobb Agency.

God Dog told his brothers of his recent exploits on the plains, and was met with similar stories and recent news from the reservations.

Quanah of the Comanches, apparently, had not only taken the white man's road, but had gone all the way east to the big cities – not to sign treaties, this time, or meet the Great White Father, but to live and trade.

"Hao," God Dog said, for he could not believe that the merciless killer that once had been Quanah and who had once been raiding and robbing and scalping during the wars like the rest of them, with whom he had fought at the battle of Adobe Walls and many others, had turned to the white way.

Quanah who had said at Medicine Lodge, "I am not going onto a reservation. Tell the white chiefs when they ask that the Kwahadis are warriors and that we are not afraid."

That had been not longer than a year before Sheridan and the great white warrior Custer had attacked the villages along the Washita River, and the Kiowa chiefs White Bear and Lone Wolf had led their broken people to Fort Cobb – and White Bear and Lone Wolf had been arrested.

Although they had surrendered in good faith and come forward to negotiate, the great white warrior Custer had threatened to hang them from the nearest tree at sundown if the rest of the Kiowa did not come in, and so the Kiowas had come in and taken the white road, and White Bear and Lone Wolf had been released to go free – at least, on the reservation.

But the small bands of Kicking Bird and Woman Heart had fled on to the Staked Plains to join the free Kwahadis, only to later return from them to set up a village near Fort Sill and work sincerely for peace.

But the call of the buffalo hunt had been too strong – as it was in almost all Indian blood – and White Bear and Lone Wolf and many other Kiowa had slipped away from the reservations.

Then White Bear had led a raid into Texas after hearing that the whites were planning to build a railroad across his old hunting grounds. He had taken with him a hundred braves and attacked a trespassing wagon train, killing seven people armed with little more than two rifles and a pistol between them. When he returned to the reservation he had been summoned before General Sherman and gone with Lone Wolf, Sitting Bear and Big Tree.

General Sherman had been sitting in a hand-woven chair on an open veranda, with two big shuttered windows behind him. The story had been told and retold around many fires.

General Sherman had said to them, "Why did you go down to Texas and murder those helpless overlanders who didn't know how to fight? If you want a fight, the soldiers here can always accommodate you."

White Bear said, "I heard the Texans were about to build a railroad down there, and I could not permit that. The road would frighten the buffalo away."

"You are all under arrest," General Sherman said. "You are to be sent back to Texas to be tried for murder."

Lone Wolf threw aside his blanket, revealing the carbine he had hidden beneath it. He raised and cocked it and stared defiantly at General Sherman. But General Sherman had stared back at him without any show of fear, which surprised the Indians.

White Bear and the other two chieftains also threw their blankets aside, following Lone Wolf's example.

But still General Sherman looked disaffected.

"Hao."

Then the shutters behind General Sherman had flown open and immediately the muzzles of two dozen rifles were trained on them. Lone Wolf had somehow managed to escape – which still had heads scratching today – but White Bear, Big Tree and Sitting Bear were held and arrested.

On the way back to Texas for the murder trial, Sitting Bear had been killed while trying to escape. He had slipped his handcuffs loose and grabbed a carbine off one of the guards, but in the resulting struggle he had been gunned down.

White Bear and Big Tree were tried and sentenced to death in Texas, but on advice of the Indian Agents, who feared an uprising if the Kiowa chiefs were killed, they were sentenced to life imprisonment instead.

God Dog had taken part in the retaliatory raids with the Kiowa all the same. Kicking Bird, now at Fort Sill, had warned officials that the trouble would increase if White Bear and Big Tree were not released, and that they would continue raiding until he was released.

They had persuaded the Cheyenne to join them, and so had started another big war against the whites.

Finally White Bear and Big Tree were released, and brought back to Fort Sill. It was a great day and there had been much celebration to do. But when another raid occurred in Texas shortly afterward, a raid that had nothing to do with White Bear or Big Tree, White Bear was arrested again and sent to a prison in Huntsville, Texas. The authorities had not been able to find Big Tree.

White Bear was put into a convict's striped uniform. He lived for two years sprawled morosely on the floor of his cell; he would stand for hours and stare out of the small barred window. But finally, at the time of the annual buffalo hunt, he slashed the arteries of his neck and legs, and when the guards tried to save him by taking him to the prison hospital, he suddenly broke free of their escort and leapt out of a two-story window, down to his death.

God Dog spat angrily into the fire, and his spit hissed and bubbled on a piece of blackened wood before it evaporated.

When news of this had come to them on the Llano, they had resolved even more strongly to stay clear of the white people. Quanah had been with them then, and he had repeated, "The Comanches will never go onto the reservations as the Kiowas have done."

But the settlers kept coming from the east – the buffalo hunters in the tens of thousands. It had seemed that all would be lost; they could not just sit there unmolested on the Staked Plains while their rich lands were free for the white man's taking, for this is what he wanted: to scare them off.

They would scare *them* off!

Once again they would have to fight, with all their concerted might, the settlers and the buffalo hunters. Quanah had called for a great council of the Comanches and their friends the Kiowas and those still free among the Cheyenne, to be held as soon as possible.

They had come together for a medicine dance near the mouth of Elk Creek on the North Fork of Red River. And this is how God Dog had become involved with Stone Calf and Lone Wolf and Quanah Parker, for shortly afterwards they had ridden for the Battle of Adobe Walls.

So Quanah had taken the white man's road; so be it, he would not. He was born an Indian, and he would die an Indian. He would be remembered as one of the few who held out to the very end. Perhaps it was the white blood coursing in Quanah's veins that had caused him to do so, since his father had been a Kwahadi chief and his mother a captured white girl, and he was a half-breed.

His Kiowa and Comanche brothers told him that when asked why he was deciding to take the white man's road, Quanah had said, "I am going to visit the white relatives of my mother, Cynthia Parker; if she could learn the ways of the Indians, I can learn the ways of the white man."

So be it.

When Little Eagle came back to the fire he was wet with sweat and they laughed at his appetite for the women, although he had not gone back for the other one.

Once he was re-seated, God Dog said, "So, my brothers, you have all had a taste. Now what will you give me for these white women?"

There was silence, just the pop and crackle of the wood. He was surprised; he had not expected such a reaction – or rather, non-reaction. They had all had a taste – some, more than once with both of the white women. They had all seemed eager enough, but now they sat silently, looking at one another.

God Dog was angry. "Dho! I come all the way from the Canadian River to bring you these women, and you all use them freely enough; but now when I ask for remuneration you look at me empty-eyed, like a child."

"We have only our horses," Iktomi protested, "and you have drunk with us the last of the wine Big Bear raided from the whites' fort."

"So you do not *want* the white women?"

"We have only our horses to trade." Long Knives repeated the sentiment.

"Then trade them," God Dog suggested, and drew a hand across the fire to suggest that be the end of it.

"But we need them, or we are stuck here," Long Knives replied.

"We have only a horse each," Little Eagle said.

"Hm," God Dog murmured.

"I have a stick of the dynamite," Big Bear spoke up. "Somewhere."

"A stick of dynamite?" God Dog said. "Why would I want to swap a white woman for a stick of dynamite?"

Big Bear shrugged, and then grunted.

"No, I will take two horses for the girl with the spotted cheeks, and three for the one with the golden hair, and I will throw in the scalp of the mother."

Big Bear grunted and shook his head – as if to say, no, the deal was not fair.

The others were shaking their heads in agreement when God Dog suddenly drew a pistol as fast as any white and put it to Big Bear's temple.

He pulled the trigger.

The shot was remarkably loud as it echoed up the walls of the gully. Big Bear fell sideways into Iktomi's lap and hot blood spilled out onto his stomach and groin. God Dog turned the gun on Long Knives, pointing it across the fire.

"Wait brother!" Long Knives cried, and held out a hand.

God Dog fired a bullet clean through the palm of his hand and it whacked into his chest, throwing him backwards into the red dust.

Then he moved it one man along and shot Walks On Foot through the face.

The Kiowas and Comanches who remained sitting sat still as statues, their ears ringing from the last flat bang in the gully. Their eyes were wide and spooked.

Finally God Dog put his pistol away, calmly.

"There," he said. "Now I will take three horses for the long-haired one."

Little Eagle was trembling with shock. He said, "But Walks On Foot did not have a horse. That's why he is Walks On Foot," he added.

God Dog considered this, and realized his mistake. "Hm, then I will take two horses for the ugly one. You do not need them now. Or is it the long-haired one you still want?" he added, and pointed the gun at Little Eagle, and then in turn at the others.

They each shook their heads vehemently.

"Mm," God Dog murmured. He drew his hand across the fire again, finished, deal done.

He stood up and went to look over their horses, selecting the two best ones, recently stolen. He put saddles on them and led them to the two girls.

"Get on the horse," he said to the one with the golden curls. "Or I'll kill you where you sit."

He hadn't planned on this, but now he would have to trade the girl elsewhere. He would go to a half-breed he knew, and see if he wouldn't take her. The half-breed could go among the whites as one of them, and he often traded with the forts or acted as messenger and interpreter, or bought women and sold them to the smaller towns that had not yet become subject to so much law and order, to the brothels and whorehouses. He had once done much business with God Dog selling stolen women to a two-storey saloon in Devil's Addition, a suburb of Abilene which had grown up to escape the laws and regulations of Abilene itself. They called it the Devil's Addition to

Abilene, and it was said that hell reigned there supreme. A place where unchecked money and gambling and whiskey met with youth and beauty and womanhood, and all were wrecked and damned.

And if he could not sell her he would do to her what he had done to her mother.

Magdalena was awoken by a startlingly loud gunshot, which echoed up the gully. When she opened her eyes her ears were ringing and she was clutching to her sister in instinctive fright.

At the fireside, she saw one of the Indians sitting next to God Dog staring ahead with his eyes open so wide it seemed they would pop out, and then he slowly fell sideways into another's lap. Someone had shot him.

She looked up and around, and hope suddenly soared in her breast – men had found them, white men, and were firing on the Indians' camp; but then another shot was fired, and she snapped her head around. At first she thought it was one of the Indians returning fire, but then she saw the big ugly Indian who had brought them here holding a pistol out across the fire. Another Indian fell.

She saw him move his pistol along and there was another big, flat bang and flash. He had killed another one. Did these people have no morals, now killing even their own? She found them even more unpredictable now, and although her initial soaring hope had been quashed, she still thought they might start shooting at each other and kill themselves.

But the remaining Indians merely sat stunned.

She watched as the big ugly one began to converse with them, seeming to be bartering over something, making some kind of deal. Finally, after pointing his pistol again, he drew his hand palm-down across the fire and then stood up. He went over to their horses, which were tied by their long ropes to a big thick jutting root that poked out between a crack in the rock.

He untethered two and then walked towards them.

She clutched her sister harder, who was also awake and watching the scene in amazement.

He stood before them with the two big horses. Magdalena didn't know what was going on. She looked to Jenny desperately.

"Get on the horse," he said to Magdalena. "Or I'll kill you where you sit."

They both began to stand, their stiff knees popping and clicking, but he lifted his foot and planted his boot on Jenny's shoulder, pushing her back down.

"Not you," he said. "You are for the Kiowa and Comanche."

Magdalena began to cry and hold on to Jenny, but the Indian pried her fingers loose with his strong hands and lifted her up by the waist, as if she were as light as a child, placing her in the saddle.

"It'll be alright," Jenny said. "I'll be fine, Lena."

"Jenny!" Magdalena cried, but she could say no more through her choking tears. Her heart felt like it was going to come up through her neck she was so terrified, terrified that she would never see her sister again, terrified of what was going to happen to her, of what they would do to her.

But the big ugly Indian merely mounted his horse and began to ride back down the gully-way through which they had come, trailing his horses.

Magdalena's crying echoed eerily in the gully. Where was he taking her now, in the dark of night? To another band of Indians in this labyrinthine canyon? Who would use her just as hard and eagerly as the last? She felt she would die if that happened to her again.

She wished, more so even than before, that she could just die.

As a little girl she had been raised to believe in God, but now she could not see how there could even *be* a God. How could he allow this? Why would he let this happen to them? If there was a God, then how could he create such people?

She had questioned the existence of God before, but never aloud, for her ma would have beaten her black and blue with a wooden spoon.

They had been raised Mormons, and although they had had to burn every page and even, in the end, the binding of their only Bible, her ma had justified it religiously.

"See," she had said that first winter in the sod house, "how the Lord provides."

But the Lord hadn't provided; he hadn't provided water – instead, by the sweat of their brow they had uncovered a load of black muck, boiling out of the earth, Pa said, as if he had struck hell itself.

He had been firmly convinced that his boots were in hell and the devil had tried to take him too.

What had the Lord provided then, and what good had He been?

The first time she had questioned the existence of God had been in Missouri, where they lived upon the river. There had been a small town nearby on the river, really just a few false-front settlements and a rickety dock where a flatboat would sometimes stop, headed up the river, taking people who could afford it west. They could not afford it; they had had to travel overland.

But before then, before the idea of coming west had ever entered their heads, each Sunday they had gone to church in the little town; only one Sunday the church had been closed. A hastily written message had been tacked to the door. It read: *Gone up the river on the flatboat, will be back within a week, God willing.*

No one had known why Father Zimerick had gone up the river, but the rumour was that he had gone to bless the first leg of the journey of a family headed westward. It didn't matter, because either way, he had never come back.

Evidently, God had *not* been willing.

The flatboat had been attacked by Indians on the river bank, and the entire family, Father Zimerick, and the boatmen were killed and the flatboat burned.

God had not been willing – if there was a God to will, that is.

It was an occurrence that Magdalena kept reflecting upon as she grew up. She never forgot the message on the church door: *Gone up the river on the flatboat, will be back within a week, God willing.*

Why would God not want a priest to return to the church where he preached?

What God? Magdalena thought now, as the gully began to widen again and the strip of starry night above became a wide gap.

She was angry with herself, angry that she had ever believed in a God – how could she have been so foolish? So... childish? *No* God, such as she had been taught in the church by Father Zimerick, could create a world in which what had happened to her... *happened.*

She felt angered at all the God-speak she had heard from the mouths of the church and the churchgoers, from her mother, mostly, who had justified everything with God.

She would like to see her mother have justified *this.*

Then she began to cry again; she had not meant to harbour such angst against her ma, her ma who was dead.

Where then, if there was no God, would she go?

Nowhere, she thought. *Not even into the ground. Into the bellies of beasts of the field, wolves and dogs, birds and worms.*

Perhaps when you died you just died, she thought to herself, and it was like a big sleep. Or perhaps you were just nothing.

But she found she could not comprehend what being 'nothing' would be like. But either way, she thought nothing would be preferable to this.

And to what was coming.

"You see that there? Those lights down there? That's Charlie Goodnight's J.A. Ranch," Lebold said.

The sky was a dark vault of stars and constellations overhead, cloudless and moonless but no less majestic with the earth falling away before them. They were looking down into the Palo Duro Canyon, according to Lebold and confirmed by Dwight, and in it they could see little dim squares of light here and there: the lanterns burning in the windows of the J.A. Ranch, apparently.

"Charlie's got a trail named after him," Lebold said. "It's called the Goodnight-Loving Trail."

"The Goodnight-Loving Trail?" Kit repeated. "Why Goodnight-*Loving*?"

"It was the name of his partner," Dwight added in.

Lebold said, "Loving was killed by Injuns on the trail. They had him holed down on one of the banks of the Pecos River, I think. And he got shot full of arrows. They had to amputate an arm but he died of infection. I think," he added. "Not so sure. Just what I heard on the trail."

"Where is the Goodnight-Loving Trail?" Kit asked.

"It follows the Pecos north to Fort Sumner," Lebold said. "Then it continues on out of New Mexico into Colorado, up to Denver."

"Any of you boys ever been on it?"

"Why, no, Kit," Dwight replied. "But there's a man in our outfit who has, and Mister Anderton's taken cattle up there before."

"Why?" Lebold smirked. "You gonna try your hand at herding?"

"I might," Kit said unsurely.

"It's the hardest thing to do on earth," Lebold said.

Dwight said, "Well, it ain't easy, I'll say that much."

"How do you be*come* a cowboy?" Kit asked. "And where?"

"Head down to Texas," Dwight said. "Ride down to San Antone; you're bound to find an outfit there or at least discover the location of an outfit. That or ride down to the Rio Grande and look along it. There a few big ranches there – they're always lookin' for hands."

"I thought you was a lawman?" Lebold said.

"I've had a change of heart," Kit said. "I think it's time to move on. After this," he added.

"There some big drives happenin' now," Dwight said. "Five thousand head of cattle."

"Five *thou*sand?"

"Yep, and they take 'em all the way up to Nebraska. To Ogallala. There's even a Texas trail goes all the way into Montana."

"I'd start with a small drive first," Lebold advised. "Oh, and they'll have you riding drag all the way."

"All the way?"

"Yep – you new to the crew you ride drag. Every cowpoke's first drive is on the drag. Then you move up, maybe get to keep the remuda. You still wanta be a cowboy, cowboy?"

"I don't see why not," Kit said. "I done everything else outside of trap furs."

Lebold snarled, but didn't say anything.

"If I live through this," Kit added, almost to himself. He was reflecting on how quickly they had lost half their posse, in one completely unforeseen and unplanned gun battle.

Probably they would all be dead at the end of this trip, if not before.

Kit looked around but couldn't see Jeb. Kit had noticed that at night you could often only see his teeth, and reflected that he could be a very useful man to head a night attack.

Lebold said, "This'd be a fine place to camp for the night."

"You must be kidding," Dwight said. "Put a fire on this ridge and every Indian holdout from here to Kansas'll see us."

"We could cold camp," Lebold suggested.

"No," Kit said.

"Whaddo you mean, no?"

"Tonight we're gonna ride."

"We oughta rest, be fresh in the morning," Lebold said.

"You got eyes like a hawk," Kit pointed out. "And the trail's old enough as it is. You said so yourself."

Just a short while before they had lost the trail and Dwight had begun to blame Lebold, and Lebold had begun to blame the wind and the number of days that had passed. Kit had a strong feeling they couldn't afford to stop or they might lose the trail entirely. They had picked it up again, but seeing the canyon ahead they had ridden to the edge to have a look into it.

Kit said, "We'll go back a ways and take up the scent. You said you reckon it'll lead down into Palo at some point."

"Yeah," Lebold said, "it's just a hunch, but from following so far I'd say he's gonna cut down into the canyon somewhere. Problem is he may have taken some narrow Indian trail down – we'd have to take the horses down single file, and without no moon I don't see how we'll see."

"We'll follow it as far as we can," Kit insisted.

Dwight said, "Well... I'm game."

"Alright then," Lebold said. "Suit yourself. But if you lose your horse down the canyon we only got one spare. Or if we lose the spare horse," he added.

"I'll worry about my horse," Kit said.

They turned and headed back along their own tracks, away from the canyon edge. They picked up God Dog's trail about a half a mile away, and continued to follow it, heading west. Again, to Lebold's credit, his eyesight was exemplary; the man was able to track even at night with no moon visible, on a three-day-old trail to boot. Kit found he had grown to respect the man, even if there seemed to be some grudge he held toward him. Kit figured maybe it was just his character and he couldn't help it.

Soon they found that God Dog had skirted the canyon a half-mile out and then cut in gradually toward the ragged rim of the escarpment.

Here rocky ledges, narrow paths and precarious steps and slopes led down into the shadows and the darkness.

"Jesus, I can't believe it," Lebold said. "It's like he just walked right off the edge, leading three horses."

Dwight dismounted carefully so as not to spook his horse and inspected the edge and the ledges below as best he could in the darkness.

Kit was as mystified; if he had thought Lebold impressive, what would he think of the abilities of the infamous Comanche Indian renegade? He had taken a path a goat wouldn't take, right down the canyon side – and he had done it leading not one or two but *three* horses.

Kit was stumped.

Part of him wanted to admit defeat; another would never admit defeat until defeated. If the Indian could have done it, and with two white girls on horses unaccustomed to this kind of country, they could do it. Maybe not by night, but they could do it.

Kit doubted God Dog had done it in darkness, or even *would* have done it. Perhaps it looked a lot more precarious in the darkness and was not in fact quite as bad during the day, or at least not as bad if the moon was out.

But still Kit felt awe for the Comanche. He had heard many stories of this sort of thing, the Indians using trails so precarious upon peaks and mountains and ravines that small rodents could fall to their death from them. How did a simple man become so adept at such arduous travel and intricate navigation of the wild?

"The only thing we can do is wait for daylight," Dwight said.

Kit couldn't see how it could be different; daylight it would have to be. They checked the rim several yards in either direction to make sure the tracks did not continue on, and that their disappearance into the canyon was not in fact a trick to throw them off, and then set up a cold camp for the night.

Jeb tied up the horses and stayed with them, lying against his saddle on the ground and wrapped up warm in his bedroll.

Kit, Lebold and Dwight set up their saddles and bedrolls in a circle, as if around a ghost fire.

Lebold sat up on his elbow and stared at the empty circle at their feet.

"Now that's a sad sight," he said. "Makes a man realise how comforting a simple good old fire can be. But when we got a fire goin' every night as a matter of course we sit there staring into it miserably and talking about how comfortable a town would be right now."

"A town'd do me just about fine right now," Dwight chuckled. "Warm bath and a good bottle of whiskey... a whore," he added.

They chuckled, and Kit joined in, although he didn't know what was funny, exactly, but he liked the mood of the talk, and it made him feel a part of these cowboys. It made him seriously consider that he one day might go down to the Texas border and become a cowboy.

"Stir me up a game of cards in a saloon," Dwight continued.

"Psh," Lebold said. "And there would go your next four months' wages."

"Naw, I figure I'd clean house. Head on down to the store and buy me a nice new hat. Pair of boots, some new duds – get my hair cut and my moustache trimmed. And then *paint the town red*."

"Whoohoo," Lebold whooped.

Kit felt the meagre growth of his own moustache; surprisingly he felt a good deal of stubble, if not a moustache exactly.

He marvelled at the way the two men spoke; they spoke as if there was nothing grander to look forward to on God's Creation.

Dwight said, "I remember the first time we reached Abilene, drove the herd right through the town, firin' our pistols and whooping and hollerin'."

"Rebel yells," Lebold said. "Yeah, I done that."

"Didn't that cause trouble none?" Kit asked.

"Hell no," Dwight said. "We were some of the first herds into Abilene back then. They welcomed us like we was royalty. The corrals and stalls were sittin' empty, just waiting for us. Folks lined the streets and watched us come like we was US Cavalry."

"The railroad'd just got there," Lebold added. "Why, Abilene was practically made for us."

"That's right," Dwight said. "There was brand new stores sellin' clothes and boots and hats. I 'member I had me on a nice white Stetson hat I paid ten dollars for, new pair of pants cost twelve dollars, good new shirt and fancy boots with Texas stars on 'em. The kind of clothes top hands wore. My Lord, I was proud of them clothes. I'd just collected my wages and we'd been three months on the trail."

"You remember old Josiah Jones?" Lebold asked. "Had them prairie dog pups he'd sell for five dollars? Did so well selling them he had no time to tend his saloon no more."

"Yeah," Dwight said. "I almost bought one myself. Reason he was doing so well is he'd get little kids to sell 'em to passengers on the Kansas Pacific. I guess the saps couldn't turn down those sorry lookin' pups."

Kit said, "So you boys didn't cowboy together?"

"No no," Dwight replied. "This the first time I've ridden with Lebold. We hired him on down in San Antone. Coe... Coe I'd ridden with before," he added hesitantly.

"Oh," Kit said, recalling vaguely that back in Duncan's saloon in Wagon Trail Dwight had mentioned that the men with him they had hired on in San Antonio, but that he and Coe had come up from the Rio Grande.

Lebold said, "You remember the Drover's Cottage? I stayed there a couple of times."

"Sure," Dwight said. "I used to like them iced drinks they use to serve."

"Yeah, with ice cut from the Republican River and stored from the past winter."

"That place had a hundred rooms," Dwight said. "And an adjoining barn that could house fifty horse and carriages."

"A hunnert," Lebold said. "But that ain't the cinch. I heard the whole thing's gone now."

"Gone?" Dwight frowned. "How does a hundred-room hotel with adjoining barn just *go*?"

"On the Kansas Pacific," Lebold said. "Lou and JW took the place apart and loaded it on a bunch of railroad cars and shipped it in sections to Ellsworth."

"So the Drover's Cottage is in Ellsworth now?"

"Correct."

"Well I'll be," Dwight said. "I never been to Ellsworth."

"I hear it's picking up now," Lebold said. "They only had a few herds come in there first season, but I hear they're diverting there every time some ill-informed foreman discovers Abilene is closed."

"Well, I'm sure you boys will like Dodge," Kit said, trying to join in the conversation.

"The herd ain't so far now," Lebold said. "I figure we get this son of a bitch in the next day or so, head back, we'll be in Dodge in about a week to collect our wages."

"What you gonna do when you get into Dodge?" Dwight asked him, and his face softened and his eyes stared dreamily, as if a fire really had been burning at their feet.

Kit got the feeling they were doing something they always did – or had done many a night on the trail.

"Heck," Lebold said. "First thing I'm gonna do I collect my wages, I'm gonna have me a hot bath and a haircut. Then I'm gonna fork out on some new duds, maybe a new hat. Then I'm gonna hit the saloon and drank whiskey – and I'm gonna take up with a whore for about a month, or until my money runs out."

"Yeah," Dwight said. "Me too. I'm gonna find me the best whore in town to bunk with."

"What do you do when your money runs out?" Kit asked.

Their expressions suddenly hardened, as if that consideration had no place in the conversation right now.

But Dwight said, "Well then I guess we'll head on back to Texas, take up with another herd."

Kit thought about that. What did they do it for then? He couldn't himself see. They risked life and limb and cattle stampede for three months across Texas and Kansas, in wind, rain, storm and hail, and then collected their wages and blew it all on nothing, only to then repeat the process.

Was that the point in life? Was it what you were meant to do? Maybe you just had to do it, to understand. Kit got that feeling again, that feeling that told him no any one pursuit in life was more virtuous than another; yet Old Morg had always inferred that hard work and the resultant reward was the utmost virtue to be found.

Kit realized then that men like these were perhaps just like his father had been; possibly they even gave an insight into his character.

"My mother was a whore," Kit pointed out.

"Well I got that one beat, Kit," Lebold said. "My mother was the best whore in Texas. Whoever my father was, she must have made him a *happy* man – for about ten, twenty minutes or however long it took him to squirt."

You see? Kit thought. *Why, half the men in Texas and Kansas must have had whores for mothers.* So it was no use looking for sympathy.

It was a notion as comforting as it was disquieting.

"My pa got kilt in the war," Dwight said. "And my ma had to become a sporting woman to feed us. Damn, but things was scarce back then."

That was true; it had taken years for the country to recover from the Civil War.

"What happened to her?" Kit asked.

"Some no good buffalo skinner strangled her to death."

"I'm sorry," Kit said.

"No need to be," Dwight said. "I avenged it."

"You a*ven*ged it?"

"Was the first time I kilt a man," he said. "I walked into the saloon he was at, where my ma used to work upstairs, and shot him in the crotch and then unloaded into him; then I lit out. Got work down in Texas rounding up and branding cattle. Then I ended up on the trails."

"Well I guess that makes you a *regular* outlaw," Lebold said, surprised at this admission. "How old were you when you shot this man in his pod?"

Dwight stared emptily into the ghost fire. "I was not fourteen," he said.

There was a moment's silence.

"You know, I think I'm gonna turn in," Dwight said.

Lebold nodded. "Well, g'night."

"G'night."

Kit wormed his head against his saddle to get more comfortable, failing miserably, and hugged his blanket around him.

Soon, he fell asleep.

★ ★ ★

The next morning before light they tied up their bedrolls and opened some of the tins they had found in the rustlers' camp; since the labels on them had been torn or worn off they had no way of knowing what was in them until they punctured them.

Kit used his skinning knife to cut around the lid of the tin he had taken from his saddlebag. It turned out to be a tin of beans. He ate them out of the tin cold. To Lebold's disappointment he opened a tin of peas, using his bowie knife.

"God damn tin of peas," he said. "What you got there, Dwight?"

"I got beans."

"Kit?"

"I got beans, too," he said.

"I got me beans," Jeb said.

"Why'm I the only one's got peas? Gimme those beans, you take these dern peas," Lebold said to Jeb.

Kit looked up. He'd emptied half of his tin. "You can have these," he said, holding them out, wanting to avoid a scene.

Kit gave him the half tin of beans and ate some of the peas, which were admittedly terrible.

"What kinda man tins peas?" Lebold said, using a small spoon he had taken from his saddlebag to scoop up the beans in the tin.

"What kinda man brings peas with him, that's what you gotta ask yourself," Dwight remarked.

"They're probably stole," Kit pointed out.

After their cold breakfast they put their saddles on their horses and led them afoot to the ragged rim of the escarpment. A strong easterly wind was blowing across the dry land, and a fine carpet of sand was being blown over the edge.

"This weather don't seem none too good," Lebold remarked. "Could be we get blown off the canyon if it gets up any stronger."

Kit looked down at the nauseating rock ledges and narrow steps and slopes that God Dog and the two girls had taken. He followed the precarious path down along the side of the canyon with his eyes. By day he could see that it was indeed feasible; the rock ledge was far wider than it had seemed the night before and the slopes more gradual than Kit had assumed. Still, one false step and you could wind up splattered on the distant hazy red bottom of the Palo Duro.

He looked around to the east and tried to see if he could spot the J.A. Ranch buildings, but they were hidden by high ragged peaks and narrow spires. Some of them looked as if they might topple or collapse they were so high and thin and crookedly stacked. He looked around at the multicoloured layers of canyon rock and the steep mesa walls. The Palo Duro Canyon was about a hundred and twenty miles long and twenty miles wide, with a depth of about a thousand feet.

How did such a great canyon come about? Kit wondered. What violent upheavals of nature could possibly have caused the land to fall away like this, to form these impossible... formations?

Kit became sorely aware of his lack of education and general knowledge as to such things, but he didn't have time to feel sore for long.

The wind was picking up, blowing their chaps against their legs and jingling the horses' bits.

"I guess we oughta go down on foot," Kit suggested. "And lead the horses. I wouldn't want my horse to try to throw me on a canyon ledge," he added.

They started down along the narrow rocky ledge, each man carefully leading his horse behind him. At first, the horses were reluctant to follow the ledge, attempting to turn and locking their legs so that their hooves scraped hollowly along the red rock, but with a few soothing goads and gentle words they managed to get them far enough along the ledge to prevent them from turning back.

Then they began to cut carefully down an uneven slope whose surface gave way under their feet, sending little stones trickling down like streams of water.

Once they were several feet below the rim of the canyon the wind cut out and they were unaffected. The air was still and hot. Around them, the canyon was a burning, seething cauldron of dramatic light and colour.

An eagle screeched in the vivid blue basin of the sky, and Kit saw it, a small shape hovering high above, riding a hot air current coming up out of the canyon. He could see its shadow rippling over the rocks and cliffs far below.

Leading his horse along by its lead rope, Lebold said, "They say Colonel Mackenzie couldn't find a path down for his troops when he came to get the Indians out. So he just plunged straight down the canyon cliffs and galloped down the scree slopes with the Fourth US Cavalry."

"He get the Indians out?" Dwight asked.

"Not all of 'em. There's still some holdouts, but sooner or later they're gonna hafta come in."

"Not the likes of God Dog," Kit remarked.

"Well, it's that or die, I figure. Mackenzie took all their winter supplies, destroyed all their villages and possessions. Took all their horses – more'n one thousand, I heard. And you know what? He slaughtered most of 'em."

Kit looked back briefly over his shoulder. "He slaughtered a thousand horses?"

"Well, Injun horses," Lebold said, as if that made it all right. "But he had to, on account of he couldn't risk them falling back into Indian hands. Most the Indians returned to the Fort Sill reservation, but some stayed hidden. They say Lone Wolf hid here after the battle, but then later gave up and came in, account of he had no provisions and was horseless. So I guess Mackenzie was right."

"Who's Lone Wolf?" Kit asked.

"He's a Kiowa chief," Lebold said. "He was one of them led that raid into Texas, where a group of teamsters was slaughtered – seven people

I think. Then the idiot just thought he could return to his reservation like he hadn't done more than hunt up some elk, and General Sherman got him. But just like what always happens they end up bein' pardoned and cutting some deal with the skunks."

"You know what really irks me about these Injuns," Lebold said, after a moment. "Their methods are cowardly. They're goddamn cowards. The only good one's a dead one. They come on the reservations and then sneak off and go on their little raids, robbing and scalping and whatnot, and then they return and act innocent, help themselves to the food and supplies. All they've ever been is a goddamn bunch of horse and cattle thieves, and raiding and murdering bastards."

"Well," Dwight said, "it don't much matter now, anyhow – they're close to bein' whupped all over."

"Yeah, but we still gotta go down a goddamn canyon after one 'cause he's bin murderin' and thieving."

Kit could detect the hate in Lebold's voice, but then he had heard much of the same talk from the buffalo hunters and mule skinners back in the day. He remembered a trapper who had complained that he had come down from the Rockies with a packhorse heaped with furs and a bunch of Navajo Indians had confiscated the lot as toll for passing through their territory. He, too, had called them a bunch of thieving bastards – but had added that they were also lazy and bone idle.

But Old Morg had once told Kit that the Indians never used to be that way. He had said that since the white man had started to steal all their land and violate the treaties and agreements they had merely begun to give him a taste of his own medicine, and the way they saw it, it was all theirs anyway, and what the white man took from their land without permission was their property – he was stealing it and no agreement had been made as to his right to it, and all they were doing was taking it back.

Kit was lost in thought when a sudden commotion broke out behind him. He swung around to see that one of the horses had lost its footing on the ledge and it was starting to go over, hind first.

Jesus!

"Get that horse!" Kit shouted.

One of its hind legs was hanging down into the canyon, and its unbalanced weight was pulling it over. He watched as Jeb grabbed hold of its lead rope and tried to pull it up. Dwight grabbed at its bit and tried to yank it back onto the ledge by its head.

Fear spread among the horses. Suddenly Jeb's horse bucked into the air behind him, whinnying as it lifted into the air, and as it crashed back down onto the ledge with its forequarters the rock cracked at the edge and fell away into the canyon.

Kit saw the inevitable but could do nothing to prevent it; the horse slipped and a moment later was plunging down the canyon side, turning over and over in the air, legs stiff. It hit a scree slope a hundred feet below and was carried away on a rock slide. Sharp rocks and boulders bounced and bounded down the slope alongside and ahead of it, and then spun off into empty space.

The sliding horse went over the edge of the scree slope and fell amidst a smoke-like red cloud of stone and sand. Kit watched its long freefall down to the canyon bottom; it fell silently, without making a sound, turning end over end with its hooves stuck stiffly out, and then finally it exploded on the rock bottom. Blood burst beneath it as if it had landed on a saddlebag full of red paint.

And then it was over.

"Jesus Christ," Lebold said, his eyes wide with surprise. He had not expected *that*; none of them had.

Dwight and Jeb were still holding on to the other horse's head; it had lost both its hind legs now and they were hanging over into empty space, kicking and scraping at the canyon side, trying to find a foothold. Its belly was against the ledge. Rocks, roots and little stones fell away beneath it, clicking and rattling down the cliff side.

"Whoa, girl. Whoa," Dwight said to it.

"Tch, tch, tch, tchtch," Jeb clicked with his teeth.

Lebold was holding his own horse by its lead rope and had his back flush to the canyon wall behind him, frozen.

Kit took in the situation before him, the horse hanging halfway between this world and damnation and the two men holding onto it, and felt himself become dizzy with vertigo. He could not cross Lebold's position behind him on the ledge and help them, for he would not only have to release his own horse but push past Lebold's, which could spook and knock him off.

"Walk back slow on three," Dwight said to Jeb out of the corner of his mouth.

Dwight was pretty much holding the horse by its teeth, clutching its bit. Kit saw its terrified black eyes staring at them and blinking, wild with the fear of its own impending doom. Its ears twitched and flapped and it whinnied in distress.

Dwight counted slowly to three and they began to back up slowly. Kit saw the horse struggling to get one of its legs up onto the ledge. It kept scraping the rock with its hoof and slipping, producing a hollow scraping sound.

Then, suddenly, it managed to plant its hoof firmly on the ledge while Jeb and Dwight pulled, pushing itself up as it straightened its leg. But as soon as its other hoof touched down it reared against the pull, and Dwight and Jeb were almost lifted off their feet.

They could do nothing but let go of the horse entirely, or else be lifted into the air with it – one of Jeb's feet was lifted right off the ground as it was.

Free, it reared up, lost balance and slipped as the brittle rock gave way beneath it, and then it was freefalling through the air.

It hit the scree slope below much as the other had done, and when at last it was tumbling down through the air Kit looked away so he didn't have to watch it burst at the bottom.

He heard a distant meaty thud.

Nobody moved for a moment. There was a light whistle from the wind.

Lebold slowly unplastered himself from the canyon wall, and walked stiffly to the edge. He looked over.

Buzzards were already on them, and more were taking off and gliding down from their hidden perches among the rocks.

Lebold looked back.

"There's nought we can do but move on," he said.

Without saying anything they began to move on along the ledge, their remaining horses acting skittish all over again, as they had when they had first started down the canyon.

But fortunately the ledges began to level off and the decent was far easier on the men and the horses. Finally, they found themselves descending a large scree slope which ran all the way down to the canyon bottom.

Streams of sand and small rocks trickled away around them and they set off little landslides with each downward step.

At last, they reached the bottom of the canyon.

"Well, I guess it could have been worse," Kit said, looking back up the slope. "*We* could have fallen."

"Hah!" Lebold exclaimed triumphantly. "Found his track already."

"Let's retrieve that saddle first," Kit said, for one of the two horses which had fallen had been saddled and had had a bedroll and rifle tied to it – Jeb's.

As they approached the grim scene, several buzzards cried out a warning and then burst into flight, fluttering.

Flies buzzed around the horses' bleeding eyes and nostrils. Ants, also, were milling around, large red ones. Blood was splattered in a wide radius around each of the horses, which were not several yards apart.

Jeb undid the saddle girth and pulled it off, but discovered that his rifle was broken, the stock shattered. He threw it aside and carried his blood-covered saddle in one hand as they walked away from the dead horses, to continue their pursuit of the Indian's tracks.

Slowly, one by one, the buzzards returned.

After some time following God Dog's tracks across the shrubby canyon floor, Kit turned in his saddle and saw that Jeb was sweating heavily and the veins were standing out on the arm he held his saddle with.

"Jeb can ride up with me," Kit said, and both Lebold and Dwight turned in their saddles, surprised.

Kit held out his hand. "Here, hand me your saddle."

Jeb hesitated at first, but then handed it up to Kit. Kit hung it over the horse's neck and then removed one of his boots from the stirrup.

"Here," he said, holding his hand out again. "Climb on."

Jeb put his foot in the free stirrup and with Kit's help climbed onto the back of the horse. Misty Blue gave a whinny in protest, and turned its head back along its flank.

Then it did something that, despite their situation, made them all laugh – even Jeb laughed when it happened.

Misty Blue took hold of Jeb's saddle in his teeth and flung it off his back onto the ground.

They stared at the sorry-looking flung-aside saddle and laughed.

"Horse must be a Texan," Lebold remarked. "Must've been a Reb during the Civil War; still bears a grudge."

After Kit climbed down to retrieve it and buckled the girth this time, Misty gave in and they finally trotted on toward the large entrance to a gully ahead, criss-crossed with light and shadow.

Kit thought the gully entrance loomed ominously.

God Dog looked back across the canyon from the north side and saw something that startled him, something he had not at all expected.

Riders were picking and working their way down the canyon, following the old Indian trail – the very trail he had used himself.

He had spent the entire night and following day working his way through the canyon to its northernmost rim, and then had climbed up and out. And now he sat on his horse looking back across the distance he had come, all the way to its southwest side, and there they were, riders.

They had to be following him. Probably they had a scout or a guide with them, someone who would know how to read tracks. Could be it was one of those traitorous Indian scouts who he despised even more than the worst of the whites, for during the wars they had led soldiers right into their most secret hiding places. They had sold out their people for whiskey and a few old carbines.

He spat. Anger boiled within him. He felt like grabbing the girl and throwing her off the canyon, or whipping and driving her horse right over the edge with her on it. The raid on the wagon had been so easy and the stealing of the women so effortless that he had not considered a posse might be sent after him at all. And now, there they were.

Then he saw something tumble down the canyon side in the distance. He squinted against the sun and followed it down until it struck bedrock. When he followed its fall back up the canyon he saw another one fall and hit a scree slope, spin about in a landslide and slide back-first, and then plummet into the canyon below.

They were horses.

The riders had lost two of their mounts trying to navigate the old Indian trail he had been up and down without difficulty half his life. That brought him some consolation; with any luck the riders would not even make it to the bottom – unless they *fell* to the bottom, that is.

But he watched as they descended without further loss of men or horses.

Perhaps the Kiowa and Comanche would kill them. There was still that possibility, if they did make it down, although he doubted it. These were able men, possibly soldiers or ex-soldiers, if they had tracked him this far.

It would take them about a day to get to where he was now, on the northern rim of the escarpment. The Kiowa and Comanche would slow them down, but he felt they would not stop them – they would come.

He now had a problem on his hands and would have to deal with it. God Dog was not one to underestimate white men.

He wished now that he had not shot Big Bear, or Long Knives and Walks On Foot – or at least if he had not shot Walks On Foot he could have slowed them down further and still made off with the two horses. Big Bear was probably the most resilient and fearless, a formidable warrior, and he had shot him dead. He wished they had traded with him fairly, instead of tasting eagerly enough and then behaving the way they had when it was time to compensate him for his days of hard hunting on the dangerous plains.

He grunted.

The riders were moving down the last of the slopes, sliding and stepping and going down diagonally so as not to trip and roll; they had made it down.

Ten miles or so west of where he was now, in a canyon-side cave where the elevation was comparatively mild, there was another small band of Kiowa. A young brave there still owed God Dog, for the time when he had equipped him with a rifle and ammo to defend against the whites when they had come to drive the Indians out of the canyon. The young brave had been with one of the bands who had held out, and was still here.

He put spurs to his horse, pulling the other mounts along with him and the two horses that had belonged to Big Bear and Long Knives.

He had a favour to ask.

★ ★ ★

When God Dog got to the little cave encampment he was greeted warmly by several braves and the squaws that were with them. But they were all very thin and gaunt-looking, especially the women, and he saw that they had slaughtered their last horse and were treating the hide and preserving the meats, which were hanging in the sun to dry.

Two young squaws swatted flies away from the meat. He saw that one was with child.

When they asked God Dog if he could spare a horse for them to eat, he told them vehemently that he could not; that the horses had come at a very high price. Since the men were with their squaws they did not express anything other than a curious interest in the white woman. The squaws themselves were more interested, pulling at her hair and inspecting her. Then they saw that she had been raped and left her.

God Dog spoke to an old Kiowa chief called Stands On His Horse and asked him where his son Wanabli Galeshka, Spotted Eagle, was. He was down in the canyon looking for varmints, according to the old chief. God Dog thanked him politely and asked if they could watch over the white woman while he went down to find Spotted Eagle, but not before tying her hands and feet with the same bloody string he used to fasten her to the stirrups.

He found Spotted Eagle amidst some boulders, pulling up rocks and uncovering centipedes.

"Dho!" God Dog said, and Spotted Eagle dropped the rock he had pulled up.

"Ey-hee," he replied. "Haho! I see you brother, and my heart soars like the hawk. What brings you?"

God Dog clasped him in a hug and then explained his situation; that he had raided one of the white's wagons and stolen two women, and now a posse was in pursuit of him. They were in the canyon right now.

"I need a favour of you," he said.

"What is it?" the young Kiowa brave asked him warily.

"First I need you to convince your people to move elsewhere, for the whites will be coming."

Spotted Eagle did not look impressed, and sighed. More trouble from whites; they would have to move again.

"What else?" he asked.

"During the Indian wars you were a great runner," God Dog told him. "You brought many good messages to your chiefs and to your people, you saved many lives."

That much was true. Spotted Eagle had once lived in the Washita Mountains, and he had alerted some of the Cheyenne tribes along the Washita River when he spotted the soldiers coming early that fateful morning when they had planned their surprise attack, but unfortunately he had not made it in time to the village of Black Kettle. He had also run across many a prairie, alerting the tribes to the fact that gold seekers and adventurers were driving new trails across their beloved old hunting grounds. In fact, he had even run out to some of the tribes to deliver the message of the big medicine dance instigated by Quanah near the mouth of Elk Creek on the North Fork of Red River, right before the three-day Battle of Adobe Walls.

God Dog said, "I need you to run to Tasunke the Half-breed and ask him if he will buy a white woman from me – the finest long-haired white woman he has ever seen. She will bring him great wealth."

"A white woman?"

"Mm, she is in your camp now. I will be following your trail; when you come back I will give you a taste, away from where your squaws can see."

Spotted Eagle brightened.

"Come, I will show you her."

They went back to the camp and he showed him the girl. Spotted Eagle licked his lips.

For a moment God Dog thought the girl looked guilty of something, but he could see nothing amiss.

"Okay, I will do this," Spotted Eagle said. "Let me first tell my brothers and sisters that the white men are coming, and that once again we must move our home."

God Dog did not think it was much of a home. The camp was messy and scattered with bones and chewed upon hides. The air smelt strongly of urine and defecation and sickness. He could see that such a band would be better off going onto the reservation, but a few young braves kept even the older ones from giving in with their youthful defiance and their sense of invulnerability. There were still, now, young braves who believed that the Indians' return to power was close at hand, and the day of the buffalo would reign once more.

God Dog did not only not believe it, he was convinced that one day there would only be whites in their lands – and the reservations would be death camps. Once they had rounded them all up, they would train their Hotchkiss guns on men, women and children and kill them all. He had seen it in a vision.

After Spotted Eagle told his band about the whites there was panic and they began to gather up their things, junk mostly, but they thanked God Dog for bringing them the warning, for they thought he had come to do only that.

God Dog gathered up his horses and the white woman and they set off, following a well-trodden footpath back out of the canyon. Once up on the plains Spotted Eagle bid him farewell and sprinted off across the plain. He would not stop until he delivered his message, and even then he would only pause briefly, just long enough to relay it, and then return, sprinting no slower or faster.

"Mm," God Dog murmured, satisfied, as he watched the young Indian brave become dwarfed by the immense distance.

Magdalena was confused; she had been brought out of the canyon and it had taken all night and the next day to get out again, and now they were returning. When she was brought to another Indian encampment she began to shake and tremble, fearing there was going to be another ordeal like the last, from which she already felt she would never recover, as long as she lived. But instead the men did not seem particularly interested in her, in that way at least, and it was the women who poked and pulled at her this time.

One grabbed her thighs and looked between her legs – a moment of extreme embarrassment for Magdalena. Then the starved-looking Indian woman said something to the others who were feeling and touching her hair and they all left her alone.

She was untied and taken down from her horse, and again expected to get set upon by the men, but instead she was tied again and left next to a rock. Then the big ugly Indian spoke to an old man, and left the camp.

She looked around; there was a fire smoking heavily nearby, and the women worked hard scraping flesh from the inner side of what looked like a horse's hide. Meat was slapped on top of a big boulder and two women stood over it, slapping away at the flies.

Bones littered the camp. When Magdalena looked at the men, she caught them glancing at her; but when one came near her for a closer look a woman started verbally berating him, it seemed, and he beat a hasty retreat.

That was fine with her.

She sat for some time, licking her lips. Her stomach grumbled and was aching. How long had it been since last she ate? She had watered several times out of streams and springs in the hot canyon as they crossed it, but even so she was now thirsty. It seemed the sun could suck the water from out of every pore.

But there was no water in sight, not a gourd or a canteen or anything. She wondered what they drank, and thought perhaps there was a creek or spring nearby.

She tugged on the bindings at her wrists, which were tied tightly together, and then reached down and fiddled with the bloody string at her ankles, but suddenly a young Indian who had been watching began to shout at her – and then he came over to her and slapped her hands away.

She gasped and shrank back against the rock, shuffling several paces backwards. She felt something pinch her backside, and she looked around beneath her. When she lifted one side of her buttocks, thinking it might be an ant or a beetle or some bug that had bitten her, she saw that she had shuffled back onto a broken arrowhead. It still had a small length of stick attached to it. The arrowhead appeared to be made from rock, a slate-like little piece containing many layers, the edges of which had been chipped very carefully along either side to a ragged point. It looked like a large tooth, the kind that might come from some sort of predatory fish, like a shark, although it was most certainly made from stone. Magdalena had seen a similar looking stone in one of the creeks she had watered from, though of course it had not been sharp like this one.

She looked around the camp cautiously, and then reached both of her tied hands over her side and scooped it up. Her heart flitted in her breast, and butterflies fluttered in the pit of her stomach. But to her surprise no one had seen her; the Indians in the camp continued to attend to their various chores, only glancing her way every once in a while.

She looked down at the arrowhead cupped between her tied palms, and then back up at the Indians. She could not exactly try to saw her way free here – there were too many of them, and anyway, even if she could, where would she go? Into the cracked and broken canyon, where she had no idea where any water might be? The big ugly Indian had an uncanny nose for water, in places where Magdalena could scarcely believe there could be any water at all. But then perhaps he knew the canyon well.

She realized she could not exactly take the arrowhead with her, clasped in her palms, because the big Indian would probably come back and untie them, and discover it.

She felt that if he did he would probably cut her with it, or worse.

She imagined driving it into his throat when he came up to untie her or move her again. But *how*? she thought.

What if she put it in her mouth? And held it there with her tongue? But what if it cut her?

She looked down at it; although sharp-looking, she reckoned it would not cut unless you sawed with it. Certainly it could saw at a piece of string and maybe eventually get through it.

But she would have to get the small piece of stick off it, and even then, when she put it into her mouth, in order not to look suspicious, she would have to place it point-forward against one side of her cheeks, flush against her teeth.

She checked that the coast was clear and no one was watching her and then quickly lifted her tied hands to her mouth. Holding the arrowhead there, she began to chew at the stick.

It tasted bitter and sour. She spat little shavings of wood and glanced up. Several times she lowered her hands quickly and tried to act nonchalant, usually when an Indian woman passed close by.

Finally she managed to gnaw the stick down far enough to make fitting it into her mouth a possibility.

She quickly raised her hands to her lips and popped it into her mouth, using her tongue to position it against one cheek. At first she felt the point against the back of her gums, and struggled to turn it around to face the other way.

The arrowhead was surprisingly bitter, and saliva began to fill her mouth. She could do nothing but swallow it.

Soon she had it turned the way she wanted it; once she felt it scraping against the side of her teeth she was satisfied that it looked inconspicuous. Her jaw closed perfectly with the arrowhead in it, and it was not that much of a discomfort.

The only real discomfort was the saliva that kept forming in her mouth because of the bitter taste of the arrowhead, or perhaps the dried and crusted remnants of the last animal it had been shot into.

She swallowed.

Knowing the arrowhead was there brought her some hope, though the idea of actually attempting to use it to cut free of her bindings brought with it great fear. She turned, rather, to the idea of stabbing the Indian in his neck with it.

Soon he returned with a young Indian who looked thin but wiry with ropy muscles. She looked up at them guiltily, and for a moment thought they had noticed something.

But instead she was lifted to her feet and her hands untied. The young Indian helped the other load her back onto the horse and tie her, but when the young one tried to tie one of her ankles, the big ugly Indian pushed his hands away and grunted. He untied what little he had done and retied it tight so that it cut into the scabs and dried lacerations there.

She gasped around the arrowhead, but was careful not to open her mouth, breathing through her nose.

The young Indian went off briefly and spoke to the women and older men, and soon they were hustling and bustling to clear the camp. Magdalena detected worry among the women.

Then they set off. She noticed that the young Indian was afoot and did not have a horse. Nor did the big ugly Indian offer to let him ride one of the four extra horses he was trailing.

Once they were up on the plains and moving north they stopped, and the ugly one spoke to the young one. Then, to Magdalena's surprise he turned and sprinted away, running fast.

She had absolutely no idea what was going on, but she felt it could not have been something good. Probably he was running ahead to another hidden encampment to tell men she was coming, and once they got there they would all set upon her.

Well, if they did, they could do with her as they pleased, but one unlucky one would get it. If that happened she intended to take the arrow out of her mouth and slash at the neck, or if her hands were bound she would move it out from the side of her cheek and clench it in her teeth and then jab it at both the eyes above her, peck at them wildly like an angry hen.

For the first time she felt fight in her – what had she to lose? Mostly she feared for her sister, poor Jenny.

She wondered what she was doing right now...

The gully walls began to narrow around them, and Kit felt claustrophobic. He did not like small confined places, having spent most of his life skinning hides on the open prairies, and the deep gully looked only like it was going to become narrower.

Lebold said, "I have a feeling we're close. The track shows horses coming and going, and one guy goes on foot. There's bare footprints among these."

Kit thought that strange, that someone would go unmounted, let alone barefoot, upon this sharp bone-and-rock-scattered path between the gully walls. Bones crunched like dry leaves under hoof.

"A *woman's* feet?" Kit asked.

"No, I don't think so," Lebold replied. "They're too big and flat. They're the feet of a lifelong outdoorsman."

Kit saw one of the prints in the dust amidst the mess of horse tracks going back and forth. It was indeed a large-looking foot.

"I say we be ready," Dwight suggested. "Could be he's anywhere."

Kit checked his pistol, and made sure it was loaded and the cylinder clicked freely. Again, needless – for if anything Kit's gun was always ready. He drew it to make sure it wasn't sticking in the holster, which could sometimes happen after hard riding and sweating. He replaced it and asked Jeb to hand him his rifle from its scabbard on the side of the horse.

He checked it and handed it back to Jeb. "You use that," he said, for Jeb did not have a pistol. Kit assumed it was because he was not good with one, or had preference for a rifle. Many men did, though Kit preferred a pistol in a close scrape, for it allowed for more range of motion.

"Maybe one of us should dismount and go ahead," Lebold suggested.

"Shhh," Dwight said. "You hear that?"

They stopped and listened.

"What?" Lebold asked.

"Shhh. Listen," Dwight said.

"I don't hear it," Kit whispered.

"I cain't hear it neither," said Jeb.

Then they heard it, distant voices, vaguely echoing down the gully from somewhere up ahead.

"That sounds like a goddamn passel of 'em," Lebold remarked.

Kit felt butterflies in his stomach. He figured if they got into another scrape like the last they'd be whipped, wiped off the face of God's Creation. They could no longer afford to experience a sizeable loss, for they were so few. Nor could they afford another dead horse.

"I thought it was only one Indian, Kit," Dwight said.

"I guess he's got a band," Lebold commented.

"I heard me a good idea a moment ago," Kit said. "Let's dismount."

They got down from the horses, Kit giving Jeb the stirrup and Jeb climbing down from Misty Blue first.

Once they were dismounted they drew their rifles and pistols quietly and held them ready.

"I got an idea," Lebold said. "But it's chancy."

"What is it?" Kit whispered.

"We'll have to chance a horse."

Kit didn't like the sound of chancing another horse. "Whaddo you have in mind?" he asked him warily.

Lebold said, "I've got a lariat in one of my saddlebags; if there's a passel up ahead, I say we take one horse with us and then whip it and charge it ahead into their camp, that'll give us the element of surprise – and that's half the battle."

Kit did like the sound of it as opposed to just pitching up and shooting. If anything, the recent past had taught him that a battle plan was well-nigh necessary, and indeed may give one the upper hand in conflict.

"Alright, I'm game," Kit said.

"Sounds like a good idea," Dwight said.

It was dim and shadowy in the gully, and Kit remembered something. He looked back at Jeb.

"We'll send Jeb in front with the horse," he said. "On account of he's dark."

"Alright," Lebold said. "Which horse?"

Although he didn't want to admit it, Kit knew Misty Blue was the least skittish of the horses. He had only thrown Kit when fired upon directly and unexpectedly, and after relieving himself to boot.

Lebold's horse was too large and Dwight's had bright white markings on it.

"We'll take Misty," Kit said reluctantly.

"Alright, let's move," Lebold said.

They let Jeb lead the horse ahead of them and followed close behind, half-hunkered and stepping quietly, careful to avoid standing on a bone fragment or, worse yet, crunching a dry set of ribs underfoot.

Dwight and Lebold both carried Winchester rifles, but had pistols at their waists. Dwight had a big Colt like Sheriff Cotton had carried, a weapon Kit reckoned required only a set of wheels to qualify as a cannon.

The voices echoed louder as they moved up the gully. They seemed to be coming from around a rock corner ahead.

Lebold looked at Kit and whispered very quietly. "Once I whip the horse, if we hesitate for a second they'll look back to see which way it came. We can't afford that. As soon as I send it, we move and fire. Got it?"

Kit nodded and squeezed his pistol tightly. He resented the fact that Jeb did not carry a pistol as well, since he realized he only had six shots before he would have to reload. At such times a man wished he carried a two-gun rig, but Kit knew that was asking for trouble – the reason he never kept one. A two-gun rig could earn you the reputation of a gunfighter, and was perceived as a challenge by most men.

Now they were so close they could see firelight reflecting off the rock sides of the gully-passage and the overhangs above.

Lebold held out his hand to halt them, and looked to everyone to make sure they were ready. Kit and Dwight nodded that they were.

Lebold stood to his full height slowly, lifting an arm overhead, moving in slow motion. Kit saw that clutched in his hand was the lariat he had taken from his saddlebags.

He let go at one end and let it coil out to his feet. It was almost as long as he was tall, and that with his hand held over his head.

Lebold nodded.

Suddenly he flicked his hand back, like a man about to cast out a fishing line, and whipped.

The lariat whipped up into the air overhead and lashed downwards onto Misty Blue's rump.

There was a flat crack in the gully-way, almost as loud as a gunshot. It was followed by another *whap* from the end of the lariat as Lebold managed to flick the end again with a quick movement of his wrist, whipping the horse a second time.

Misty Blue burst into undignified flight, charging down the gully and whinnying madly.

They charged after it as it disappeared around the rock corner.

They heard startled voices and several "Dho"s and "Hao"s.

Kit came around the corner with his pistol held out in front of him, looking for a target to shoot at. He fired at the head of the first Indian he saw, and a moment later the bullet ricocheted off the rock overhang behind the Indian's head.

Kit realized the blunder too late; he had missed the Indian by a good foot and a half and had spoiled the element of surprise caused by the horse diversion, for the four Indians had been looking in disbelief in the other direction before he fired, after the horse that had sprinted past, but now they whipped their heads around.

They scattered.

Lebold fired his rifle and caught one in the shoulder, but the Indian was knocked to the ground where he had been racing for a carbine. He spun over onto his back after he had grabbed it up and fired back at Lebold.

Kit heard a bullet thud into Lebold next to him and Lebold was thrown. Meanwhile, Jeb and Dwight were firing every which way. One of the Indians had fled in the direction the horse had gone.

Kit fired back at the Indian with the carbine, who had shot Lebold, and struck him; but he managed to scamper up and dart into the darkness of the cave, where another one of the scattering Indians had disappeared.

Kit crouched down over Lebold as loud shots and ricochets whined off the walls. Dwight and Jeb were firing into the cave, where several carbine shots were now fired in return.

"Cease fire!" Kit shouted above the gunfire, for he could see it was going wild. "Stop shooting!"

There was a ledge of rock leading up to the campfire and the cave, and crouched they were relatively safe. Lebold had been hit in the thigh, and was clutching the wound with both hands and squeezing. His face was a twisted white mask of pain. It looked to Kit like the bullet had thudded right into bone.

The rate of fire slowed, to a few pops and cracks, but the Indians still fired their carbines from inside the cave, and when they did Dwight and Jeb tried to fire back at the muzzle flashes.

"Cease fire!" Kit shouted again.

Suddenly they heard the growing pound of hooves.

"Huh?"

Kit spun around where he was crouched, and saw Misty Blue come galloping back along the gully – only on top of him was an Indian!

The son of a bitch had not fled like some coward, but gone after the horse and come back mounted on it.

He bore down on them at a full gallop, hooves pounding loud in the gully, driving his bare heels hard into the horse's flanks.

Kit saw that he was riding with one hand on the reins, and his other hand was held up above his shoulder and had a long, thin, spear-like object in it.

He launched it at Dwight and Jeb, who had turned their rifles and started firing upon him.

"Don't hit the horse," Kit shouted, but didn't think they heard him.

The thin spear wobbled through the air and came down like a javelin. Kit heard Dwight begin to shriek with pain.

Now the galloping Indian was almost on top of Kit. He was going to run him down!

Kit fired twice at the mounted Indian and missed both times, and now knew he had only one bullet left and one option.

In what little time he had he aimed for Misty Blue's head, and fired.

The bullet caught the horse in the neck and blew out the back of its mane. Blood splattered up the Indian's front and the horse reared and toppled over to one side, landing on top of the Indian.

Kit felt Jeb waddle up next to him on his hindquarters and take aim. The Indian was struggling to free himself from under the horse.

Kit watched his futile struggle to get free. The Indian looked at Kit, still struggling, pushing against the horse's body with his hands.

Kit had never seen such hate in a pair of eyes as in the pair that looked back at him now; but they could not hide the fear he must have felt: it was the eyes of an animal that knew it was trapped and was about to be preyed upon.

"Shoot him, Jebediah," Lebold said in a strained voice.

A shot rang out, and suddenly the Indian stopped his struggle and lay back.

Just then a slug ricocheted off the rock across from them and bounced back to land next to Kit's leg, with a plunk. It had come from the cave.

"Jesus, they're still firing on us," Kit said.

Jeb waddled along and pushed himself up against the rock which led up to the campfire and cave mouth.

Kit looked across at Dwight. The thin spear had pierced his boot and gone right through his foot; he lay on his side with the length of the spear alongside him and Kit could see the spike sticking out of his sole. Blood oozed from the bottom of his boot.

"You all right, Dwight?" Kit called across.

"Yeah, I'm aright," he said. "Damned Indian tried to stick me."

Kit looked back at Lebold. His face was white and feverish. Kit could see he was in agony. His pupils were dilated, his eyes watering and bloodshot.

"What we goan do now, Mister Kit?" Jeb said, clutching his rife across his chest, back to the rock. Beads of sweat covered his face and brow.

"We're gonna hafta charge that cave," Kit said. He appeared thoughtful for a moment. Then he said, "Jeb, that a belt you're wearin'?"

"Yeahsir, Mister Kit."

"Can I have it? I need it to stop the bleeding. He's losin' blood!"

Jeb looked reluctant, but put his rifle up against the rock and began to unbuckle his belt. He threaded it out of his belt loops and flung it across to Kit.

"This is gonna hurt," Kit said matter-of-factly.

He lifted Lebold's leg and the man groaned.

"I told ya."

Kit began to wrap the belt a few turns around his thigh, just above the leaking bullet wound. Since the belt was too big to buckle around, he pulled it tight as he could against the buckle and Lebold gasped.

"Okay, hold that end, partner," Kit said to him. "And keep it held tight."

He looked across at Dwight, who didn't look like he could be of much use himself.

Kit duck-walked back to Jeb and shoved himself up against the rock cover next to him.

"We gotta move to the mouth of the cave," Kit said, holding his pistol ready. "How 'bout some covering fire? Once I get to the mouth, you follow and I'll fire in, all right?"

Jeb was just about to say yes when they heard a peculiar sizzling sound; it passed overhead and then hit the opposite wall of the gully with a soundless explosion of sparks. It rolled into the middle of the gully-floor and continued to sizzle on the sand.

"That's a goddamn stick of *dynamite*!" Lebold said.

"*Dyn*amite?!" Dwight said in alarm.

For a moment Kit was frozen, staring at it and blinking his eyes hard; he couldn't believe it and thought he must be seeing things.

When a rattlesnake rattles I git, he remembered Sheriff Rainbow

Cotton saying, *I don't stand round waitin' to be bit.*

Kit jumped up and made a run for the sparkling stick of dynamite. Shots immediately rang out from inside the cave and there were more whining ricochets around him.

He dived at it with his hand out; not a moment to lose. As he skidded across the ground and came to a sliding stop, he felt the ends of his fingers touch the stick. He grabbed it up.

The Indians in the cave began to fire at him frantically, and good old Jeb turned and meted out some heavy covering fire from behind the cover of rock.

It gave Kit the chance he needed.

He whipped his hand back, much as Lebold had done with the lariat, braced his legs wide apart, one forward, one behind, and winged it at the cave.

Its trajectory was high in the air, and for a moment Kit thought it might explode above them, for the fuse had looked awful short, but it tumbled down toward the cave, turning end over end, and then disappeared into the darkness of the cave mouth.

"Hao!"

Kit hit the ground and held onto his hat.

Dwight buried his head into his armpit and turned away.

Lebold rolled over hurriedly, despite his leg.

And Jeb hesitated.

There was a deafening *BOOM*, a heart-rending blast that drove a thick pall of dust out from the mouth of the cave. Rocks and stones rattled down from above, shaken lose by the blast, and showered down on top of them. Rubble came pouring down like a waterfall and palled in the bottom of the gully like broiling water.

Kit was blinded by dust and had to breathe it right in, coughing and choking. He could taste it on his tongue and feel it on his teeth.

The dynamite blast had been so loud Kit felt shaken to the bone, winded even. All he could hear was a din. Rocks still rattled down from all the way up at the top of the gully, where the rock narrowed almost until it closed out the sky.

Slowly the dust and debris settled.

Kit stood unsteadily in the silence. He was white with dust. He took off his hat and knocked the dust off it.

"Jesus Christ Almighty," Lebold was saying.

"I reckon," Dwight said, "I reckon you didn't miss this time, Kit."

"I cain't see," another voice said.

Kit could feel little particles of sand grinding in the back of his eye sockets, an extremely unpleasant affliction, but when he walked over to check on Jeb, he saw that the man's eyes were full of sand, muddy tears coursing down his dark cheeks. He had been peeping over the rock at the cave mouth and firing when the dynamite had exploded, and hadn't been able to lower his head in time – that is, hadn't been able to lower his head at the speed dynamite exploded, which to Kit's knowledge was about five to twenty-five thousand feet per second.

"Use a canteen to wash that out," Kit told him.

The mouth of the cave was still smoking, sending a roiling pall skyward.

There was a long period of silence.

The din in Kit's ears suddenly cleared and he clicked his jaw, opening and closing his mouth several times.

"I hate to be the one to point this out to you, young Kit," Lebold said slowly, propping himself up on one elbow, "but is it just me, or could maybe them girls have been in that cave?"

Kit's mouth hung open, and stayed open.

"I reckon," Dwight said, "I reckon I second that notion."

It had proved a satisfying turn of events.

As they rode across the open range, in the rough direction Spotted Eagle had run, God Dog noticed the woman's face becoming whiter – soon it developed a sickly tinge to it, and beads of sweat sprang out on her forehead.

He rode on unperturbed, but stopped when she started throwing up over the side of her horse. She retched hard, but they were dry retches, with small strings of spit coming out at best. The retches were no less violent for it, however.

God Dog dismounted to check what little she had thrown up, in the hope to determine what had caused her to become sick. Perhaps she had somehow plucked up a poisonous mushroom back in the Kiowa camp, or eaten a piece of putrid meat – or swallowed a mesquite thorn.

He had once captured a white woman who, after a month of captivity, had swallowed a handful of thorns in an attempt to kill herself. He had watched her die slowly, agonisingly, and had forced her to eat more.

He examined the vomit in the grass and frowned at what he saw there. He looked up at the girl. She was running the back of her wrist along her lips, which had turned purple. There were dark circles under her eyes, and she looked racoonish.

He crouched and picked up the arrowhead. Confused as he was, at first he thought it might have been there in the grass by chance, but then saw that it was wet with saliva.

He stood up and looked at the girl, and once again felt anger boil within him. He wanted to cut her mammaries off, cut off and make her eat each of her fingers. Just when he wanted to sell her she looked awful.

He began to untie her ankles and then dragged her off her horse. He continued to drag her by her hair along the grass, and she reached up and grabbed hold of his forearms to try to take some of the pull off her hair.

Then he let go of her and straddled her. He held the arrowhead close under her nose.

"You *stupid* bitch dog," he said as he shook her violently with his other hand. "What were you planning to do with this? Hah! All you have done is poison yourself and now you will die. And die slow. This is a poison arrow. That is why it was discarded. *Fool.*"

If there had been a creek he would have dunked her head several times and half-drowned her; in fact he had a good mind to do so when next he came upon one. The white bitch dog!

He slapped her in the face several times and then clasped her jaws in his hands and squeezed until she was pouting like a fish and crying like a child. He almost could not contain his rage; he wanted to spend a long time torturing and killing her, worse even than he had done to the elder. He would cut her toes off as well and cook them and force her to chew and swallow each one. He would find an ant mound and bury her next to it, stir them with a stick and sit and watch as the ants swarmed into her nostrils and ears.

He let out a wild roar of rage, and then unstraddled her.

He doubted she would really die, but he knew she could, depending on how strong- or weak-willed she was. He knew he must take her to water, for she was dry retching and blood was coming up in small clumps.

"Stupid bitch dog," he said again, and slumped her over her horse, not bothering to tie her this time, for in this state she could not even stand, let alone run.

He rode northeast over the high grassy range and found a creek in about seven miles. All the while he rode the girl burped and retched on the back of the horse.

When he reached the creek he walked the horses right into it and dismounted. He threw her off into the water.

"Drink!"

He dunked her head under and held it. She began to squirm and reached out of the water in attempt to scratch and claw at his hands. Soon the fight went out of her and she stopped, and just as she did he pulled her head up.

She gasped and spat water.

He pushed her head away and again told her to drink.

She drank, lapping up the water like the dog he had called her. God Dog filled his canteens and let the horses drink.

While he was tying his last canteen on his horse she was vomiting again, but now her retches we no longer dry, and a pale, milky liquid poured out of her mouth and nose.

He waited impatiently for her to stop vomiting. Finally she did. She crawled weakly on her hands and knees through the creek, and collapsed on the bank, lying there exhausted, as if she had been shipwrecked and at last was washed ashore.

God Dog picked her up and draped her back over the horse. He saddled up and rode, cutting back northwest to return to the path Spotted Eagle had taken.

He rode for another several miles, now over hills and gentle rises and falls in the land. From the top of one of them he could see the Canadian River vaguely, snaking across the horizon, like a long brown spillage across the land. He could see a small speck crossing it, possibly an animal, possibly not.

He galloped down the hill.

The girl was quiet now, and when he rode back to check on her he noted that she was asleep – though not dead. Her back lifted gently and lowered as she struggled to breathe.

When he noticed the speck coming towards him and closing the distance quickly, he realised it was the young Indian runner. An elk or deer could have moved as fast, but no elk or deer would run toward a man, let alone one with a pack of horses.

Finally Spotted Eagle came running over a rise and stopped before him. He was slick with sweat, and was breathing heavily, but not as heavily as most men would have been breathing, having run the distance he had, and swimming a river to boot. The sun was now low in the sky, turning orange-red with dusk. Soon the prairie would swallow it up, and God Dog would feel much safer travelling with a white woman over the back of one of his horses. When white men apprehended you you could at least tell them you were headed towards one of the reservations – if their numbers were too great – but with a white woman draped over a horse...

"I see you, brother," God Dog said.

"And I you also," Spotted Eagle said, panting. "And my heart sours like the hawk."

"And?"

"Tasunke says to come and bring the woman."

"Is he in his lodges?"

Tasunke the Half-breed had many, but the one God Dog referred to was his log house on the other side of the Canadian River, some ten or twelve miles northwest from it, alongside a little creek. It had once been an abandoned cabin, half-built by some settler and then deserted as Indians drove him off, but the Half-breed had built it back up and lived in it for many years unmolested.

"He is, brother," Spotted Eagle said. "But he was leaving for the town when I got there or I could not have delivered your message. He says you are to come to his lodge and change, and bring the woman into the town tonight."

God Dog did not like the sound of that, and was annoyed. He knew of the town, a lawless whoreman's paradise that was the Half-breed's preference; a way station for travellers on their way to Fort Lyon, which was a good two hundred miles from it, situated between the South and North Canadian Rivers and well west of the cattle trails, erected solely for the damned, full of the white man's evil...

A town called Farlow.

"How can I enter a town?" he said angrily and spat.

"He said you should dress in some of his clothes in his lodges and bring the woman. He has a proposition for you."

That perked his interest. "A proposition?"

Magdalena was aware of being interfered with, but too weak even to open her eyes. When the big ugly Indian had pulled her down from her horse and dragged her kicking and screaming across the land by her hair, and then sat astraddle of her and told her she was now going to die while holding the arrowhead under her nose, she in fact felt relief.

It was a relief to know she was going to die, only she didn't die – or else his words were going to ring very true: that she was going to die and die slow. Certainly the symptoms leading to death – if that is indeed what they were leading to – were unbearable. The retching tore her throat out, and the nausea came in waves and troughs. But she retched and retched, and nothing came out. Her stomach was dry as a desert bone, and the back of her throat burned.

She felt weak and stiff, particularly in the elbows and knees. She could not believe that her plan had turned out so badly; that the arrowhead had been poisoned. But it stood to reason, since it was Indians she was dealing with here, and she had heard they poisoned their arrows, with strange poisonous frogs, snakes, mushrooms and roots.

When they got to the creek and he had held her head under, she thought he was finishing her, for now she could be no use to him. Dying itself may well have been a relief to her, but for some reason she fought it. The *idea* of dying may have been a relief, that is, but the actual process of being killed was not one she could readily go along with. The feeling of being drowned was so unpleasant she protested in every way she could, pulling and scratching and trying to tear his hands out of her hair above the water.

When it finally felt as if her lungs would implode, and her vision began to tunnel and she felt a long way down it, receding into herself, he let go of her and she jerked her head out of the water and gasped in a breath of air. She shot back down the tunnel and her normal vision soon reasserted itself.

Her hearing was off, as if water had got into her ears and filled her head – but that, too, quickly cleared.

Once she recovered and realized he was not going to do anything else to her – he was crouched at the creek's edge and filling a canteen – she drank slowly but without stopping, for the crisp, clear water seemed to reinvigorate her and drive away the nausea.

But once her belly was full she felt the waves of nausea crashing through her again, and this time when she retched white water jetted powerfully out of her mouth and back into the creek. This happened several times, uncontrollably, and when at last it seemed over she crawled weakly along on her hands and knees and collapsed upon the bank.

At one point she raised her head and was briefly aware she was hung sideways over a walking horse, but it was only a moment of consciousness.

But now she was aware of being interfered with. Still, her eyes were too heavy – which was probably just as well – for she felt a weight on top of her and a sharp dry stabbing pain between her legs. It continued for a while but then became numb and was no longer as sharp, and soon it was over.

And then she fell into a deep, dark, dreamless sleep.

★ ★ ★

When she awoke she was on a pallet, made soft by thick furs and buffalo hides. She looked around the cabin – it looked like a cabin. It was lit by dim lantern light, and she could see that the walls had been constructed from unpeeled logs. It felt surprisingly cosy and comfortable, after the hard canyons and unremitting plains; a mix of soft shadows, rich browns and reds. Indian blankets and animal heads decorated the walls. Various books and jars and other oddities lay around on various rough-hewn bits of furniture, shelves and small tables and stools. There was even a glass window, although one of the panes was broken. Starry night showed above. She listened intently; she thought she heard running water in the distance – a small stream or creek or spring.

Then she saw a sight that sprung hope in her. Had she been rescued? She knew she could only have been rescued, no longer that any of it could have been a dream. Reality had hit her too hard for that.

A man was standing in the dim light and buttoning a waistcoat – a waistcoat that looked somewhat too small for him. He appeared to be struggling with the buttons on the front, and then decided to just leave them open. He was wearing a chequered red and black fabric shirt, a white bandana around his neck, held in place by a silver clasp, and a pair of worn cowboy chaps.

She tried to speak up but produced a weak, whiny sound instead. Her throat stung and felt swollen. She could not form a single word with her lips.

He did not hear her. He was busy grabbing a hat from a hook on the log wall and trying it on. It seemed an ill fit and he took it off and crumpled the top, and then tried it on again.

Was she rescued? What had happened to the big ugly Indian?

She tried to make another sound again, even if just to attract his attention, and she noticed something that stopped her in her tracks.

Animal skin clothes lay on the wood floor around him, and his boots! They were of soft animal hide!

The man turned to face her, for he had heard her little squeal, and she saw that it was him – the big ugly Indian. He was now wearing clothes that a white man or Mexican would wear, but his face was too big and square and Indian for it ever to be mistaken – too mean and cruel.

He stepped over to her and grabbed her up by the arm.

"Come," he grunted.

His thumb was digging hard into her arm, and weak as she was she could do nought but follow him. She looked around hurriedly for anything in the cabin within hands-reach, that she might be able to grab.

She saw a letter opener on a rough-hewn desk, but it was too far to grab at. When she stepped over his discarded clothes, she noticed his big, sharp-looking eagle claw, but there was no way she could have at it.

He pushed open the big cabin door and they stepped out into the cold, brisk night. A creek glinted nearby in the starlight.

She heard the horses nicker nervously.

She thought he was going to lift her onto the saddle again but instead he grabbed up the lead ropes of the horses and led them through the night, to the trickling creek.

Here he took the bandana from his neck and dipped it in the water, then he began to wipe and clean her face with it. He did it hard and rough, not as a mother might. When he took his porcupine quill out of a pocket she flinched back, but he held onto her hard and began to brush it through her hair.

The sharp ends of the quills scratched her scalp, and when he ran it down the length of her hair and encountered stiff knots, and there were many, he simply jerked it hard through them, pulling it downwards and ripping out swaths of her hair and yanking her neck back.

It was a painful ordeal, but she had been through worse.

Then he drew his knife and took hold of one of her hands, straightening out her thumb. For a moment she thought he meant to cut it off, but instead he drew it sharply across the soft pad of her thumb and blood sprang to the surface of the cut in big beads.

He dipped the end of a finger in it as if on a pallet and began to smear her cheeks with it, rubbing it in and around.

She was going to be given to men, surely – more men. But why had he changed, and into white man's clothes?

Finally he lifted her by the waist and put her in the saddle. Her entire backside and hip girdle ached from riding, and from constantly swinging back and forth against the saddle pommel from the motion of the horse. But again, she would have to ride.

He did not tie her ankles, but then, when he rode, he constantly checked back on her. She could break free from him and try to hide in the darkness, but she felt he would find her – for he seemed to know the wild as well as any animal.

He *was* an animal – worse than one. She could not think of a worse animal than he.

After hours of painful riding she noticed something in the distance on the dark plains; low lights and distant noises. The cheery pings, pangs and bongs of a honky-tonk piano, and the bawling laughter and cheer of rowdy men.

Men. She had never felt more terrified of men than now – probably forever she would feel terrified. Just the idea of men, leering and gawking at her, or even just the sight of them, horrified her. Her entire perception of men had changed: Indian men, white men – the male gender itself. For she reinterpreted every look she had ever received from a man. The men who had come to the sod house to see if they could buy buttermilk and eggs, sometimes coffee or a rind of bacon, which they had readily sold them – she had always felt their looks and not quite understood them. Now she knew what they had all wanted to do with her. Their eyes would always wonder from her face to her chest, more so as she had grown up. One man had even stood over her and watched as she sat on a stool and milked a cow, leaning over – she felt – and peering down her dress.

The noise grew louder and the lights in the night grew larger and brighter. Then she saw the dark shapes of the buildings in the night, a large two-storey lane of clapboard buildings with stairs going up and down the sides of them. Cowboys clunked up and down the steps and opened and closed the doors, as if coming and going. Briefly she would see a hatted silhouette against the light shining through the glass panes in the doors at the tops of those flights of stairs. There was the laughter of women, maniacal, false laughter; the pound of hooves, the mad laughter of men; shouts and jolly yells, glasses chinking and some breaking, the honks and pinks of the pianos.

It sounded as if they were riding towards some sort of man-made hell.

They came in off the plain, onto the trampled grass and mud which led into the first buildings of the town, every single one of which seemed to be a saloon – and more.

They trotted slowly into the town, and as they entered the main street, light shining down onto the street in shafts from the building windows, Magdalena saw a man vomiting into the street while holding on to a crooked sign staked deeper at one end than the other.

It read: FARLOW.

Kit managed to fashion a crutch for Lebold, from one of the long carbines he found in the camp. It had a strap to it which fitted nicely over his shoulder and helped hold it in place.

They had managed to stop the bleeding by undoing the belt and stuffing the hole in his chaps with his bandana – yet another use they found for it. Then they closed the belt over it again and strapped it tight, which caused Lebold some deal of pain.

Kit had examined the wound as best he could, with what little knowledge of wounds he had. He had never considered himself much of a student of wounds, and neither had his old mentor Old Morgan. Old Morgan often maintained that a bullet wound in any limb would cost you that limb; and that he knew an old sawbones who recommended removing a limb even if it got slashed or cut, to be on the safe side.

But Lebold was lucky, as far as Kit could see. The bullet had gone through his thigh but had not entered his thigh bone. It had passed right beside it, probably so close it had nicked the bone, and when they got him up on his feet a slug had fallen out from his legging.

"You oughta keep that," Kit had said, trying to cheer him up. "That's your lucky slug."

"I don't see what's lucky about bein' shot."

"You're alive, ain't you?" Kit said.

Now Lebold was standing, with the makeshift crutch under one arm and Jeb standing nearby in case he fell – Jeb who had helped Kit bring him to his feet. But he still looked pale and feverish, out of sorts.

The cave was still smoking at its mouth, though now a lot less than before – they were waiting for it to clear before going in, an event Kit was dreading. He hoped it would smoke forever; better yet, that there had been a cave-in just within the mouth, and an impenetrable barrier of piled rocks had sealed the entrance.

Kit braced Dwight and then yanked the Indian's lance out of his boot, which caused him to yell out in pain.

"I could swear one of my toes is cut off," he gasped, holding onto his boot.

"Well don't take off that boot," Kit said. "Find something to bind it up with tight and don't touch it."

Once again Lebold's looted possessions of the dead proved useful; Kit used one of his ropes to tie around Dwight's bleeding boot. It may not have been even, and one foot may have had to stand higher than the other, but the boot was sealed and tied tight.

Dwight was able to stand, and even place pressure on the wounded foot, although he had to place it lightly and hop along.

"Jeb and I're gonna go check out the cave," Kit said nervously.

"I'm comin'," Lebold said. "I gotta see *this*."

Kit swallowed.

"I'm comin' too," Dwight said.

Kit helped Lebold up onto the rock buttress before the cave; helping him sit on the edge of the buttress and straighten his leg out, sliding his rifle-crutch next to him. Then he climbed up himself and picked him up under the armpits and lifted him to his feet.

Jeb handed Kit the carbine, and he passed it to Lebold, helping him position it under his armpit and looping the strap over his shoulder.

Jeb had given Dwight a hand up and Dwight had taken it.

They turned and faced the cave. Kit felt a stone in the pit of his stomach.

"Now where the hell'd you think they got that goddamn stick of dynamite?" Lebold wondered. "I ain't heard of Injuns lobbin' dynamite before."

"Probably out of a supply wagon up to one of the forts," Dwight said.

"Well, one way or another, Indians with dynamite don't get *my* vote," Lebold remarked.

They stepped slowly into the dusty darkness of the cave. Lebold managed to take several steps with his crutch but had to stop to catch his breath just under the sooty ceiling of the cave. He seemed to turn even whiter.

"I found one," Dwight said from deeper in the cave. "I think. He's got no skin left on him. And one of his arms is gone," he added. "Urgh!"

Kit found another, down on the floor, blown against the rock. He was frozen stiff and had his hands held up protectively before his face, but his fingers had been blown off in the blast. Only his thumbs remained. Patches of skin were missing all over him and the orbs of his eyes had burst in their sockets, leaking out onto his rock-blasted face and running down his dusty cheeks in two long, jelly-like tears.

Kit turned away. Deeper in the darkness he stumbled over another, a tangled pile of blackened limbs he could neither make head nor tail of. The head seemed to be between the legs, and the spine where the stomach should have been. A glistening pile of guts were coiled in the dead Indian's stiff fingers, as if he had held them up to his face in disbelief after they had been blown out.

Then Kit came across something strange. Three Indian bodies were piled in a row behind a boulder in the cave. They all appeared to have been shot, execution-style.

That's strange, Kit thought. *I never saw these Injuns.*

The one which had shot Lebold was still outside, dead by the fire. He doubted these would have been placed here so neatly during the shootout; they appeared cold and blue, one even purplish, as if dead at least twenty-four hours or more.

"I found something," Dwight suddenly said.

Kit looked up, his heart pounding.

"Now that's a damn shame," Dwight said quietly.

Kit stepped up next to him and looked down.

There was a dead girl there. She was covered in dust, and rocks had showered down on her. Kit looked up and saw that a part of the ceiling had collapsed and come right down on top of her in many pieces. Her neck lay at an odd angle, and there were big gashes and cuts on her skinny shins and arms, which she had held up protectively.

"There's one of 'em dead here!" Dwight called back to Lebold.

"Figures," he said back. "Nice throw, Kit," he added.

Kit felt his spirits sink. He had killed the girls he had been trying so hard to save; probably she still would have been alive if it wasn't for him. How could he have been so stupid? How could he have thrown a stick of dynamite back into this cave, knowing that the girls could be in it?

But the truth was, not only had he not known, he hadn't even been thinking of the two girls. His mind had been solely on the fight with the Indians and making it through alive.

Dwight noticed Kit's low spirits. "Don't worry, Kit. If you hadn't got rid of that stick of dynamite we'd all be dead."

Lebold overhead that remark and called back, "He could have throwed it elsewhere, you ask me."

"Nobody asked you," Dwight said irritably.

"Well I figured they might have wanted my opinion anyhow."

"Well they didn't."

"Jebediah? Help me back down. I wanta look at something," they heard Lebold say.

"Where's the *other* one?" Kit said suddenly. "The other girl?"

He could tell this was the girl with the freckles on her cheeks, and the bucked teeth, although in truth she didn't look half as bad as she had in the photograph, even dead. Perhaps she had been younger then, a young teenager going through those dramatic changes that come during those confusing years.

Kit had certainly found them confusing – still did.

He looked around, and then began to search vigorously, even lifting rocks and stones and kicking aside fallen piles of rubble.

"Help me look," he said to Dwight, who was still staring down at the dead girl.

They scoured the entire cave, right to the back and out again. Even Jeb helped in the search.

There was no second girl. Not a trace of her.

They came out into the light.

Lebold was crouched over his crutch and staring intently at the ground.

He looked up. "Gentlemen, I think I know what's happened here."

"What?" Kit asked. "Where's the other girl?"

"She's bin taken."

"Taken?"

"It's the same Indian. The same hooves go back the way he came. I only didn't notice it 'cause he's trailing different horses now. He must have traded one of the girls and taken the other."

"Yeah, but... *where*?" Kit asked eagerly. At least there was still hope, for the most beautiful of the two girls was still alive, through no plan of Kit's own, mind. That was just the way it went.

Lebold said, "Well, that's what we're gonna find out. I would have noticed the track if it hadn't been amidst other horses. I thought it was a different track. I can tell his horse. He still ain't changed it; its horseshoes have been nailed in badly, and the ends haven't been clipped and filled off."

"Maybe we should bury the girl before we go," Kit suggested, feeling guilty.

"We've buried enough people on this trip," Lebold said impatiently. "And now I even got a slug in my leg, and Dwight a hole in his foot. I say there's no more time to lose. This is it. If we don't catch him soon, I don't give that girl much of a chance."

"What about that leg of yours?" Dwight asked.

"I'll get it checked out in a town."

"You're apt to get it sawed off."

"Any man tries to saw my leg off I'll fill him with lead."

"Well pray it don't go infected then," Dwight said.

"You mind that foot of yours don't get infected, or you'll be the one seein' a sawbones."

"Okay," Kit said. "We'll share horses and ride. We still got plenty of daylight left. I'll ride with Jeb. Lebold can ride shotgun with you, Dwight."

"I need to be sitting in the saddle to read the tracks," Lebold reminded him.

"I can do that," Dwight said.

"Alright. Let's ride," Kit said.

He thought of adding "we're eating daylight", but decided it best not to.

* * *

It took them most of that day to work their way out of the canyon, but they managed it without incident.

What Kit feared most was that one of the horses would slip or break a foreleg somehow, what with bearing double loads and all.

But none such happened. The elevation out of the canyon at the northernmost side was nowhere near as sheer or high, and even riding shotgun both horses made it out. Kit looked forward to hitting the plains after spending all day in the seething cauldron of the canyon, but instead as soon as they were out they discovered the track returning to the canyon, but all it led to was an abandoned Indian camp that looked like a junkyard amidst the rocks.

Dwight found a dropped piece of meat several yards from the camp, covered in ants.

"They beat a retreat," he said.

Lebold discovered that the tracks backed over themselves again and returned, leaving the canyon once more; finally they were back up on the plains and moving north again.

Kit enjoyed the wind in his face, at such times as he could block the memory of the young dead girl. She kept cropping up in his mind.

Dwight had said to him earlier as they picked through the canyon, "Maybe it wasn't you killed her," but Kit had a strong feeling it was. He felt terrible. How could he have caused so much death in such a short period of time?

Now Lebold said, "You won't believe this. This Indian follows him right here, and I mean on foot, and then takes off ahead like a rabbit with a fox on it."

Later, as the sun was climbing down the sky and just beginning to go orange, a gunshot rang out and clattered across the plains. It clattered again as its echo came back from the horizon.

Kit looked up. He had been staring at the mane of Dwight's horse, on which he rode because Lebold refused to ride it, and daydreaming – although not one of his usually fantastical daydreams: he dreamed miserably now, of rescuing the young girl and then telling her that he blew her sister up with dynamite.

That was when the shot had rung out.

When he looked up, he merely saw Lebold pointing his pistol out over his horse's head, Dwight leaning to one side behind him and looking ahead.

"What'd you shoot at?" Kit asked.

"A Injun," Lebold said. "The idiot just come running over the hill and I put one in him."

They crowded around the young dead Indian lying in the grass. Lebold had plugged him right in the chest.

He spat down from his horse into the Indian's dead face – which Kit thought uncalled for.

"Whoever he was he was with the other one," Lebold said. "And I got a feeling we're gettin' real close."

Close to our graves, probably, Kit thought.

Lebold holstered his pistol and told Dwight to spur the horse's flanks for him. He was looking his whitest, which worried Kit, but he didn't say anything. Lebold was a hard man, he realized, and now he felt honoured that he had ever felt challenged by Kit. He did not know if he would have fared as well in the same situation, a big wound in his thigh and still riding and tracking.

They set off across the grassy plains. Miles and miles of unvarying emptiness lay before them, and somewhere on it, the girl and God Dog: the Indian renegade who had cost so many of them their lives, before they had even come face to face. The man was killing them off one by one merely by way of what he left in his wake.

Some hours later Lebold stopped them.

"Look at this!" he said. "Here someone's been throwing up, and then been drug and sat on. The girl."

They circled the area looking for signs of anything else, and even though the light was going, Kit spotted something in the grass.

He dismounted and picked it up, handing it up to Jeb after inspecting it.

"It's another arrowhead," Kit said.

"His?" Lebold asked, riding his horse up alongside Jeb.

Jeb passed it to him.

"It looks different," Kit remarked.

"Yeah," Lebold said. "The other was fashioned out of some base metal."

He handed it to Dwight, who had a look himself before handing it back to Kit. Kit put it in his top pocket, together with the photograph.

"What do you think happened here?" he asked.

"I dunno," Lebold said. "But we're wasting time. Let's go."

Jeb helped Kit back into the saddle. They set off once more.

"We're gonna hafta cross the Canadian again, only I reckon by the time we get to it it'll be in darkness."

The river Kit had once feared crossing by day, they would now have to cross by night, and this time with two men to a horse. He found he didn't care. He just wanted to get the girl back and end this manhunt; it had not been the adventure he had thought it would be when he started out, and he just wanted to end.

One day that 'magination of yours is gonna get you in a heap of trouble.

What had Old Morg always meant by that? Was it this? That it would get him into this? Perhaps so *willingly* into this? He didn't know.

The river crossing was cold in darkness, and Jeb clung on tight behind him. The horse sunk deeper in the water than before, and took so long to scoop itself across Kit thought they would never get there and would have to abandon horse. Several times it dropped its snout into the water and had to snort its nostrils clear.

But finally ground jarred beneath them and they were across.

Lebold wasted no time to stop, as was the usual custom after crossing a river. "Let's ride!" he said, and Dwight spurred the horse's flanks on cue, a strange sight – two men operating a horse.

They galloped away.

Finally it was too dark to see God Dog's tracks and they stopped.

But Lebold squinted cunningly into the darkness. "I have a hunch where this son of a bitch is headed," he said.

Kit could hardly credit that. "Where?" he asked.

"There's an old cabin not far from here, beside a creek. Owners got run off by Injuns," he added. "And if my sources're correct, there's a town not far from it now. Farlow, 'bout fifty miles hard ride. Hell of a place. They say it won't last, like the Devil's Addition."

"Well he wouldn't rightly be headed to a town," Dwight said.

"I know, but he might try to sell her there."

"Whoa, whoa, whoa. Wait a minute," Kit said. "What do you mean 'sell her there'?"

"I mean, *sell her there*. They drug 'em up with opium powders and laudanum, get 'em hooked, keep 'em in the rooms."

"What kind of town *is* this?" Kit said in disgust.

"A hell of a town," Lebold repeated. "There's two forts between it, Fort Union to the west and Fort Lyon on the north bank of the Arkansas, in Colorado Territory. They say that's why it cropped up – for the soldiers to drink theirselves silly and dip their wicks. There ain't no law there worth a damn. It's a hell of a town."

"There a doctor there?" Kit asked. He was looking at Lebold's pale face. He didn't like the look of it; it was the face of a man suffering a high fever. In fact, Kit had once seen Mister Masterson's brother in town, before his tuberculosis had bed-ridden him, and this is how he had looked; this same gaunt paleness.

"I doubt it," Lebold replied. "Let's head to that cabin, if we have to bed down we can bed down there, roof over our head."

"I say we head to that town," Kit said. "After we check the cabin, of course," he added. He didn't think he could sleep. Something was chasing him inside. He felt if they were going to get the girl back it would have to be now.

They spurred the horses and set out.

Kit was considering the ramifications, were the Indian to sell the girl to someone in the town.

Well, they would just have to take her back. Which should, in effect, be easier than getting her from the Indian. Perhaps he would be long gone by the time they got there.

Kit wondered what Lebold had meant by a hell of a town.

He didn't know what the future held, had no idea – perhaps it would soon hold no future at all for young Kit, and Old Morg's immortal words would come true.

Well, they would just have to see what they would see – and live through it. With any luck the next confrontation – hopefully the last – would not involve any dynamite. And anyhow, if it did, he would no more pick it up and lob it than he would a live rattlesnake.

As Kit rode toward his and all of their uncertain fates, he had never felt less eager in his life.

Now the only thing he couldn't wait for, was for all of this to be over.

PART
III

"What I can't stand for is all this range fencing," the old man said. "They fence off any more of these dern ranges and soon they're gonna kill off the entire cattle trade. Not that I'm a cattle herder. But if I was I wouldn't stand for it, I wouldn't."

"So what are you then?" Bandito asked, and turned over his cards. He didn't really care, but since he was cleaning the old man out he might as well try to be polite.

"Me? I'm a buffalo hunter," the old man replied proudly. He turned over his own cards. "Shoot," he said.

"Well, you ain't no slick-haired gambler, that's for sure," said Bandito, scooping up the winnings from the centre of the table, which happened to be several bits and a pair of old gauntlet riding gloves, which the old man had staked once he was broke, in a final attempt to claim back his winnings.

Bandito said, "Anyway, there ain't no more buffalo. You missed your calling."

"I know there's no more buffalo, young man – I was there huntin' the last ones out. Now I collect the bones. Yeah, you heard me right. I collect 'em. I know, I know," he said, "but I can't shake the life. I done it ever since I come down out of the mountains."

"You collect the *bones*? Buffalo bones?"

"They take 'em off you at the railheads," the old man claimed.

"What the hell for?"

Bandito had never heard of anyone making money out of buffalo bones.

The old man hesitated. "Well... I never thought to ask. Must do somethin' with 'em, I guess. I just heard they took 'em, so I started rounding them up. Most of 'em were mine anyway, I figirt."

Bandito reckoned the old man was mad, but thought he'd humour him.

"So how do you do that, then?" he asked, shuffling a deck of cards quickly in one hand, over and over. "You go about with a 'barrow or somethin'?"

"Oh no," the old man said. "I do it with a covered wagon, pick an' toss 'em in. There's more buffalo bones out there than you could pick up in a lifetime. It's all waiting out there like white gold, only you don't even have to dig it, it's all right there layin' on the surface. Whenever I run out of cash, I just head on out."

Bandito said, "Yeah, well, why don't you head on out and come back when you got some?"

"How 'bout we play another game for bones?" the old man suggested.

"I ain't gamblin' for bones," Bandito said indignantly. "Besides, I don't think they allow bones up on the tables in this saloon."

"Dern it. Hoot! It's a full wagon of bones, piled right up. It's right next door in the livery stable. How 'bout we play another hand, put the stakes back on the table? You win, I'll give you all the buffalo bones and throw in the wagon. Sturdiest wagon you ever saw, three-inch wheels held on by bolts, not nails."

Crazy old man, Bandito thought.

"*Nails?*" he said incredulously. "Why, I ain't heard of nails bein' used to hold wagon wheels on since the days of the pathbreakers."

"I know – I changed 'em to bolts. But it's no less sturdy than your modern contraption. Why, it's hauled about a dozen tons of bones in its time, never lost a wheel – and once rode over an Injun."

Bandito wondered whether he should humour the old man further. But what would he do if he won a wagon full of bones? Life threw some strange questions at you. There was no railhead in Farlow, that was for sure. No rail line would come this far west of the cow towns, or even any law. Farlow was strictly for those who preferred towns the way they used to be. That's what Bandito liked about it. In Farlow you could get away with things. Once Devil's Addition had run dry, he had ridden the plains in search of such a town for years, and finally found it, riding into Farlow some several months ago. The women were willing, the whiskey flowed free and the gambling was good. The funny thing is that he had had to come to a town like Farlow to make an honest living for a change – well, almost honest. But it was a living.

He had come to gamble, at first – the archetypal slick-haired gambler, half-Mexican on his late mother's side. But he was also an opportunist, as the good gambler must be – and he knew an opportunity when he saw one.

So he became a carpenter, buying a barn and a false-front store with his brother, Manito, and he fashioned coffins out of pine during the day and gambled by night.

It was a living, though his true calling in life was gambling. His brother Manito didn't like to gamble, but only because he was no good at it. Anyway, he had taken a whore for a wife and worked her in a saloon owned by the Half-breed, the Hog's Head, though it was more a whorehouse than anything else, largest in town. Then his brother had gotten more involved in the sporting trade, and had deals going with the overland stages, importing his powders and drugs and doing more and more business with the Half-breed.

Perhaps he would humour the old man then; he thought now he could simply sell the wagon itself easily enough. Offload the bones somewhere and sell it.

"Okay, my friend," he said, with a glint in his eye. "We play another hand."

The old man perked up.

Bandito began to shuffle the cards, despite having skilfully shuffled them continuously throughout.

"What's your name, sonny?" the old man said. "I like to know the name of the man I'm about to whup."

Bandito looked up from the cards with a sly smile and began to deal them out. "My name is Bandito José Heurta, señor."

"Bandito?"

"I am half-Mexican."

"Don't that mean bandit?"

"My mother called me it when I was born, in Mexico, by the Rio Grande. My father was a sheep herder, until a Comanche got him."

He pronounced Mexico "Meh-hee-co", which the old man seemed to find amusing.

Bandito put the deck down and fanned his hand of cards in front of his face, immediately putting on his poker face.

The old man watched him closely, and then looked down and scanned his own.

"I never used to believe in games of chance," the old man said casually, picking through his cards and rearranging them.

"Mm-hmm, and what changed your mind?"

"I realized the whole of life is a game of chance."

"Indeed, but there is some skill required in both."

Bandito laid out his play of cards confidently, as if to prove this.

The old man took one look at them and then dropped his own cards in resignation.

"Shoot," he said. He looked around the saloon hopelessly as Bandito cleared up the winnings again.

The saloon was bustling, the round tables full of rustlers and miners whose claims had either petered out or had nothing in them to begin with. Here and there a whore occupied a knee, usually the knee of a good gambler – or at least the best card player at the table.

The bar – which was a long pine plank set atop several sawhorses – was packed with mule skinners, freighters and fortune hunters – big, wild-looking men, rosy-cheeked and bright-nosed from drinking beer and whiskey.

Soldiers from the forts went up and down the stairs, visiting the sporting ladies who went from knee upstairs to room and back down again.

Earlier the old man had gone up and spent some time with one, Bandito had noticed, and then had come down and set at a table after acquiring an entire bottle of whiskey from the barkeeper, and a single shot glass.

Bandito had noticed him, turning back from the bar. Mostly he had noticed the bottle of whiskey. He had made his move, and successfully stirred up a game – and cleaned the man out of everything he owned, now even his wagon.

It beat hammering coffins together, although admittedly, opportunist that he was, it was an opportunity he could not pass up. Bandito would even eye customers coming into the saloon, from head to heel, measuring them for a coffin.

The old man had looked out of place, ancient; he was dressed as if he had come out of the Rocky Mountains, in thick furs and hides. And he smelt strongly of cured leather.

Now, Bandito decided there was nothing more to be had from the man, other than a huge old rifle leant against the table, which didn't even look as if it worked, more an ornament from the past, and decided to excuse himself. As well as an opportunity when he saw one, he could notice a lack of it.

"Well, it has been fun, panjero," he said. "But now, if you'll excuse me…"

He stood, and when he did, a queen of hearts fell out of his sleeve.

The last moments of Bandito José Heurta's life played out before him in a strangely disassociated way.

As he felt the card flutter out of his sleeve and saw it land face-up on the round table top in the corner of his eye, he immediately went for his gun. He carried a two-gun rig, and had never been beaten to the draw. He had been caught cheating at cards before, a simple matter of odds, and his response was always to shoot – a response he was more than willing to go through with.

He went for his gun, in the usual confident and assured way he always had, and it all should have played out the way it usually did – with the man taking a bullet before he could even stand up, toppling over in the chair and spilling out onto the floor. The old man did not even have a gun belt about him – he had checked for it earlier in the evening. He was easy prey.

But all Bandito José Heurta heard was a dry squawk, as of chair legs shooting back, and then he could scarcely credit what he was seeing.

The old man was already up and had the butt of the huge, long buffalo gun shouldered before Bandito even had his hand on the handle of his pistol. He had drawn an old, heavy Henry rifle faster than a man could draw a light and carefully balanced pistol.

He did not see it fire, only flash silently – like lightning in a low-lying cloud – and he registered the impact of the shot almost in slow motion, for he could not believe it.

Then he took two unsteady steps back, hand still on the handle of his pistol. He stared across at the old man in disbelief, and tried to raise the gun at his hip, but it felt as heavy as an iron anvil, and once out it simply swung to and fro by its trigger guard on the end his finger.

He toppled over and fell.

Every man in the saloon was silent.

Bandito José Heurta touched the tips of his fingers to the gaping hole in his stomach, held them up in front of his face, and stared in even greater disbelief at his life's blood.

Then he looked up at the old man, still unable to believe how he could have been beaten to the draw by this ancient relic of the past.

"Huh-huh-How? How did you beat me?" were the last strangled words he uttered in this world. But not the last words he heard.

"From a lifetime of not dyin', sonny," said Old Morgan.

★ ★ ★

"Cheatin' at cards," Old Morg explained to the silenced saloon.

Slowly, the stunned inhabitants of the saloon went back to their beers and cards and conversations, the current topic of conversation heard all over being about the range fencing. Old Morg had heard it all over, about the rolls of barbed wire being shipped over on the Kansas Pacific. A cattleman had complained to him just the other day, claiming he had set up camp one night and awoke the next day in a quarter-mile enclosure. He had attempted to get his horse to jump the fencing and then had to shoot it.

Another cattleman complained that his brother had been killed after they had clipped a fence to pass their herd of horses, only to be ambushed by the owner. But range fencing was apparently legal, and Old Morg reckoned it was going to spell the end of everything, shut down the entire cattle trade in Kansas, shut down all the ranches in Texas, once it caught on.

It was just starting, but Old Morgan had lived long enough to know that things changed quickly in the west.

He bent over the dead bandito and retrieved his winnings, plus whatever the slick-haired gambler happened to have on him – almost a good seven hundred dollars. Playing the slick-haired bandito had turned out to be quite prosperous.

Old Morg reckoned he wouldn't mind another bottle of whiskey and a whore. You could never have enough whiskey and enough of a whore, in his book. He had once been a Christian man – relatively Christian, anyway – but after the buffalo got hunted out life just wasn't the same. His one vocation in life had suddenly vanished, and he had taken up with a one-eyed Pawnee woman on a reservation, and had become heathen. He had learned how to chant all day and talk to the Great Spirit, united in the Pawnee cause, which was to chant for the return of the buffalo – which he neglected to mention he had had a hand in wiping out. Then one day her brother had come to the reservation, and convinced her that he was a government spy working for the Indian Office, and she had tried to scalp him in the middle of the night.

He still had the scar on the front of his forehead, for he had only just managed to prevent her. Any longer and she would have had his hair, such as it was: his head had grown through most of it. But still, a man's hair was his hair and no one was gonna take it.

He had fled the reservation and had continued to be heathen. There was just no turning back to the Christian God after mescal whiskey. It had been a miserable time for Old Morg, for none of the cow outfits had been willing to hire on such an old man, not even as a cook, and he had found sustenance in the only way he knew how: rounding up the buffalo bones. In a way, he was cleaning up the mess he had made nearly two decades earlier, and getting paid for it.

There had, however, been a great – if short-lived – time to prosper. The Year of the Grasshopper.

It may have been a very unprosperous time for most, but for Old Morg it was as fine a time as ever he had had. Farmers virtually everywhere had begun to see the strange silvery spots circling in the sunny skies; finally they discovered what they were: millions of grasshoppers in flight.

Old Morg remembered thinking: *Uh-oh, someone must have added something to The Bible, again. Or subtracted it.*

The grasshoppers had descended upon the plains, in columns over a hundred and fifty miles wide and a hundred miles long. Old Morg had seen 'em. With his own two eyes. They had carpeted the plains three inches deep, covered farmhouses and ranch buildings, sod houses and wagons and even entire herds, causing frenzied stampedes. They had lined tree limbs, their weight so great the branches had cracked and fallen to the earth, leaving trees entirely branchless.

Old Morg had been picking up bones and tossing them over his shoulder into his wagon on the plains when they hit. He had had to tie string around his trouser bottoms to keep them out, and climb in his wagon with his bones, the canvas completely covered in hoppers in a matter of seconds, so's you couldn't see any white anywhere.

When finally they left, they had eaten the canvas right off his wagon, leaving only tatters and tethers and its skeletal wooden framework behind.

And all that day he had seen what they had done to the land, the damage they had left in their wake...

Hundred-acre cornfields had been obliterated from end to end, the corn eaten and annihilated right down to the stalks. One man who he came across was stumbling blindly across the plains, his throat and wrists bleeding from the bites of the starving grasshoppers. They had even taken bites out of his eyelids and eaten half his hat.

They ate entire saddles off of horses' backs, harnesses, reins, window curtains, the ears off cattle, even each other.

Old Morg had comforted one old woman in a sod house he checked in on, who had just hung out the laundry to dry across a washing line running from the side of the house to a mesquite tree before the grasshoppers hit. Her wet shirts and trousers and undergarments vanished. Only the wooden pegs and little pieces of cloth remained, clipped between them.

'I God!

The grasshoppers had even stopped a *train*, covering the tracks and crossties so heavily that the crushed grease inside the insects set the wheels free-spinning – a sight Old Morg had marvelled at.

"I never seen a train set there and do that," he had said to himself, passengers lining the windows of the train and hanging out and peering down at the free-spinning wheels in disbelief. "You better believe it."

Many farmers just up and plumb gave up. Wagon after wagon full of household goods set out, headed back east. When news of this hit the reservations, word was the Indians started celebrating with their ghost dances and thought the day of the Indian was close at hand, again.

Following the hoppers, the settlers who did decide to stay had a hard run of it. They had no food, no fuel, nothing for the coming winter, no money, no clothes, no means to either. Some even took to picking up buffalo bones.

The government even passed a Grasshopper Act, declaring the insect Public Enemy Number One, a declaration that upset many an unruly outlaw, who filled signs and posters stating as much with bullet holes and throwing knives.

Some Christians thought it was even the end of days – and Old Morg might himself have believed it, if he hadn't turned heathen on account of his one-eyed Pawnee wife who had tried to scalp him.

But Old Morg was a firm believer that the west was a grand land of opportunity, and you only had to be in the right place at the right time with the right frame of mind. In fact, that pretty much summed up the entire wayward western march of civilization. It had worked for him in the past, with the beaver pelts and then the buffalo hides, and it worked again...

Old Morg became what was briefly known on the ranges as a Grasshopper Vigilante. A job description too good to be true, which didn't last, but was good while it did.

The government in many states established a bounty of fifty cents per insect, dead or alive. Old Morg let the buffalo bones to rest! He tipped the bones out of his wagon and constructed boxes out of chicken wire. And he went around the plains and the farms and fields filling them. Made a killing when he turned 'em in at the nearest towns accepting.

It wasn't all easy sailing, though. One farmer ran Old Morg off his land with a pitchfork, accusing him of "poaching his grasshoppers".

Fun while it lasted; soon so many people were dealing in the lucrative round-up and sale of grasshoppers the government, offering fifty cents a bushel, went bankrupt. And Old Morg returned to his buffalo bones – most of them he had made anyway. Maybe he would run people off with a pitchfork for picking them up.

But Old Morg's gloom was to return. He had liked his Pawnee wife, who introduced him to Mescal whiskey as a holy sacrament, even if she *had* tried to scalp him and had only one eye. Kin was known to be persuasive of that kind of thing.

One of the main reasons for his gloom had been his inability to get a holt of enough of the mescal whiskey, since he was no longer welcome on the reservation. He took to drinking the white man whiskey, in the cowtowns, and soon he was lapped up by some whore woman. That had been in Devil's Addition.

She caught him at a hard time, still struggling with the loss of his one-eyed Pawnee wife.

But after that there had been no turning back.

The deadly web he had once so outspokenly warned against had him, and he didn't feel he would ever get out. His life became buffalo bones, whores and whiskey. He was a lost man – old man, anyway.

He no longer even knew how old he was. The buffalo skinners he had hired on himself in the good old days, when he bumped into them, would stare in disbelief.

"Old Morg?" they would say. "Why, I thought you was dead."

"No," he would say, "the truth is I spread that Injun story myself, after I met my Pawnee wife, though I did almost get scalped."

The ones who hadn't heard that story would say, "Old Morg? Why, I thought you'd have died by now. Why, you was nearing the grave twenty yeer ago."

Not even Old Morg knew how old he was. He suspected, in fact, that he had somehow cheated the grave. Even *he* had expected to be well under it by now. Old Morg had always maintained that man's relationship to the earth was being buried in it. And as for staking and claiming the plains, that the only land a man was really entitled to was a small allotment beneath the earth roughly measuring the same length from his head to his heels with an inch all round give or take to account for the pineboard box.

But here he was, now in Farlow, where you could sometimes buy Mescal Whiskey, and even Peyote cactus buttons, from a half-breed Indian up a ways who ran a sporting saloon, if that's what you wanted to call it.

Old Morg mostly kept out of that saloon on account of there was too much killing in it. He had nothing against killing, just against wasting ammo. And in this one, at least the coffin builders could keep up.

Now, stepping over the dead bandito – slick-haired but not slick-haired enough – Old Morg nudged in at the bar with his big gun and held a hand up to summon the barkeep.

"Barkeep! Another whiskey over here! Bring me the bottle."

The barkeep was a fat, jolly-faced fellow by the name of Pierce. He came over with his stubbled jowls and the bottle of whiskey and Old Morg paid him with his loot.

When he came back with his change, Pierce said to Morg, "I wouldn't want to be in your shoes right now."

"And why's that?" Old Morg said smugly. "Son, I 'spect you'd have never wanted to be in my shoes – you ever outrun a avalanche?"

"Are you gonna listen why or not?"

"Okay, sonny, why wouldn't you want to be in my shoes right now? Though I can think of plenty reasons myself. You know what a bunch of grapes looks like? Ever heard of piles?"

"No I ain't," Pierce the barkeep said. "But I have heard of Manito Heurta, and he fills half of the coffins he builds in this town."

"Who's he?" Old Morg said, uncorking the bottle with his teeth.

He spat the cork out into a spittoon, and missed. "Shoot."

Pierce said, "He's a coffin builder – but not only that. He's got a hand in a lot of the goings on in this town. Brings in laudanum and other things, if you know what I mean. Not a man to be taken lightly."

"So? What's he to me?" Old Morg asked, taking a swig from the bottle.

"Well," Pierce said, "I believe you just shot his younger brother with your buffalo gun. Do you have to resort to a rifle that's so loud?" he added.

"I like something with a bit of kick," Old Morg said. "I don't see the problem. He was cheatin' at cards. It's a game of chance – he himself admitted it."

"Well I'd say *you've* just taken a chance – a big one."

"Look on the bright side, he can build his brother a coffin and it won't cost him a cent."

"He's gonna build *you* a coffin."

"That'll be nice of him."

"I were you, I'd leave town."

"Leave town? Son, you don't get it. I've lived to a grand old age, and my hootsit still works. I intend to dip it in as many of these here fine young ladies until my time comes. I ain't goin' anywhere. I've spent my whole life not dying, and I'm not about to start now."

With that he took his whiskey bottle and latched onto the nearest whore, and after saying a few words to her convinced her to take him upstairs.

Old Morg had never run from a fight in his life, and wasn't about to. If some man had a beef with him for shooting his brother while cheatin' at cards, then so be it. Certain things came down to principle, and Old Morg had always been a man of principle – always *would* be.

The whore closed the bedroom door and Old Morg put his whiskey bottle down on a dresser, where half-full perfume bottles and a bunch of beauty powders stood.

There was a window beside the bed, and he hopped to it, pulling off a boot. He pulled off the other and stared out.

The back of the two-storey saloon faced onto the open prairie, and he looked out at the dark miles of grassy plains. Tents could be seen pitched in the darkness: cowboys and mule skinners and young soldiers and suchlike who couldn't afford to stay in the rooming houses or hotels, or bed down with a whore for the night, which cost ten dollars – and you got the whore with the room.

Here and there he could see lone riders and little posses coming in off the plains, and an overland stage – probably containing at least one new slick-haired gambler on the make, come to try his hand in Farlow.

He thought he saw lightning flash, distantly at the far horizon, illuminating a low-lying purple bank of cloud.

"Looks like a storm's a comin'," he said, turning around.

The young girl was taking a big swig from a bottle, one of the ones he had seen on the little dresser.

For a moment Morg was confused.

"Now, there's no need to drink all that perfume, missy," he said to her. "I ain't particularly picky, and anyhow my own mouth turned foul about three decade ago."

The young whore smiled at him nervously and put the little bottle down.

Then she came to the bed and sat down timidly on the end. He shrugged out of his big hides and skins and hung them on the back of a chair, and then stood there in his faded pink full underwear, old and tattered and covered in holes. White hair poked from the holes.

"Are you going to take those off, mister?" she asked him, impatient now as he stood there in them. "Or are you going to put your pod through one of those holes?"

But curiosity was keeping him.

"You know anything about a man called Manito?" he asked her.

"Oh yes," she said. "That's his brother you shot downstairs."

"He was cheatin' at cards."

Old Morg hesitated.

"That door locked?"

"Yes, mister, but if it's Manito you fear he'll likely just have his men kick it down and shoot the both of us."

"Hmm, that don't sit pretty."

"Are you going to take those johns off or should I?"

"Would you mind if I bring my buffalo gun into bed?"

The girl sighed. "Mister, it's your money," she said.

"I'll bring the gun."

It was a long ride to the little log cabin on the creek.

Kit fell asleep in the saddle several times and almost fell out of it. Fortunately Jeb caught him by the collar and saved him a nasty fall into a prickly pear.

Lebold had switched places with Dwight, so that he could catch some rest, pointing them due northwest before nodding off. When he later awoke and they stopped briefly to let the horses rest – for they were riding hard to close the distance of fifty miles – he did not look well.

Kit noticed he had been getting steadily worse.

It was fortunate that they had his hunch to go on, for he was in no state to track, least of all by starlight, and after waking, complained of blurred vision and vertigo.

They pushed the horses hard, and Kit felt a saddle sore coming on under his left thigh. The hard shoulders of the horse pistoned up and down beneath him and turned his legs numb, for they rode at a full lope and drove their spurs deep, the horses slick with sweat and foaming at the mouth.

When finally they reached the little unpeeled log cabin, they let the horses to graze by the creek and washed and watered. A coyote yipped nearby and a night owl screeched from a post oak branch, and behind all the night noises there was the constant but somehow comforting *ee-ee-ee* of tree frogs and crickets.

Kit slapped at a mosquito, which added to the night cacophony its not so welcome whine.

Lebold was limping heavily, his leg lame. When he walked it was with a determined grimace on his whitened face.

They entered the cabin and Dwight and Jeb lit the lanterns. It smelt of old cooking fat and wood smoke.

"Geronimo," Lebold said, standing amidst a pile of discarded clothes – Indian clothes. "Our little friend's headed to town. He's gonna sell that girl. He stopped here for a change of clothes – though I don't know who's."

"Well, what are we waiting for?" Kit said. "Let's leave."

"I'd say there's no hurry now," Lebold said. "She's gonna be in that town come tomorrow."

"But... how're we gonna get her back?"

Dwight interrupted the question with another of his own. "What about the Indian?" he said tiredly. "We come all this way to hang him and I reckon we oughta hang him. Kiefer and Coe're dead 'cause of that son of a bitch."

"Getting the girl back is more important," Lebold said. "There's no more time, and I ain't wasting any more time chasing that Indian. If the Texas Rangers couldn't even catch him, how we suppose to? The herd'll be halfway to Chicago in a bunch of boxcars and the boys'll be back in Texas rounding up the next ones at this rate. I don't know 'bout you, but I'd like to spend my wages in Dodge City," he added. "And I'd like to collect 'em, too."

Kit felt an argument about to break out between the two.

"We'll bunk here for the night," he said. "We can head in to town tomorrow. Anyway we could use the rest. But I aim to go after that Indian, with you boys or not. And by God, he's gonna hang."

Lebold looked at him angrily, but didn't say anything. For a moment the old Lebold who Kit had first met back in the saloon in Wagon Trail flashed in his pale face. The one who felt extremely challenged.

"I reckon you'll get scalped and he'll sew your pecker shut," he told Kit.

"Well, then that's a chance I'm willing to take," Kit maintained.

Jeb had already slid down one of the log walls and was sitting with Kit's rifle between his legs and his head against one knee, exhausted.

Lebold looked around the cabin.

"I'm havin' that pallet," he said, and walked his crutch across the weathered-wood floor.

Kit slid down the wall next to Jeb and sighed heavily as he sat. It was a relief to sit on a surface that wasn't galloping up and down beneath him. He rubbed at his saddle sore.

Lebold dropped his crutch and with his leg stuck out stiffly managed to drop onto the horse blankets and furs draped over the pallet.

Dwight was tearing pages out of a book and stuffing them here and there amidst fresh logs of wood left in the fireplace. There were also a few buffalo chips amidst them.

"There's shit in this fireplace," he said.

"Throw it out," Lebold said testily. "I didn't ride fifty miles to no cabin to breathe in a load of buffalo shit. I do that out on the cold prairie but I ain't about to do it under no roof."

"Alright, alright," Dwight said. He plucked out the big pieces of buffalo dung and chucked them into a thick wooden bucket.

Then he struck a match along the rough wooden mantelpiece and put fire to the paper.

Soon they had a nice warm fire going, popping and crackling. The yellow-orange flickers in the room were comforting after the long night's ride – fifty miles without stopping over hard terrain, across rivers and high creeks, through hills and over and down rocky ridges, and most of the time in cracking blackness.

Dwight took an Indian blanket off one of the walls and lay it down on one side of the fireplace. He got his saddle from where they had dropped them by the door and made a headrest out of it. Soon, he was lying back, his boots in front of the fire, the one coiled up in rope. During the ride, when he had switched places to let Lebold rest, only the end of the boot had been able to fit in the stirrup.

"Ain't nothin' quite like a good roof over your head," Dwight remarked, staring into the fire. "That's all I need in life, I figure. A good roof over my head and a fine lookin' lady."

"Amen," Lebold said tiredly. He winced, at a spike of pain that must have suddenly shot up his leg.

They had finished all their food, the tins from the rustler camp and all but a few dry sticks of jerky and hard tack, which they tugged on miserably. There was nothing in the cabin, not that they had expected there to be. At least, not in the way of food, anyway.

Kit took the photograph out of his pocket again, and looked at it miserably. Mostly he looked at the girl he had blown up now. The photograph itself had become even more battered and faded than it had been to begin with; it smelt of Kit's sweat and was damp with it.

"Why're you always lookin' at that picture?" Lebold suddenly asked.

Kit looked up guiltily and tucked it away quickly.

Lebold didn't say anything else, surprised at Kit's reaction.

Why *did* he always look at it?

Kit looked at Jeb, whose head was now up off his knee. He was looking around the cabin curiously with his big, wide, white eyes, which had an innocent quality to them Kit had noticed from the beginning, ever since they let out. He wondered about the black man, this strange, black, silent companion, who seldom spoke or said anything. He wondered where he had come from and how he had got here. He liked the man's long silences, strangely peaceable. He felt they were friends, after all the riding they had done together on the horse, Jeb reaching around Kit and holding onto the reins – but it was a peculiar detached kind of friendship, if it was one.

He had shot and fought alongside them without hesitation, trailed horses and crossed rivers unflinchingly, without needing to be told what to do. He had saved Percy in the North Canadian, even if he had merely lived to die near the South Canadian. Kit recalled him tending to the gut-shot Percy, there with him in his last moments.

Kit wanted to ask him so many questions, but when he caught Jeb's eyes as he was looking curiously around the cabin, Jeb quickly looked away – as if he was not meant to meet him in the eye for too long, as if he might be in trouble for doing so.

Kit wondered, with the entire cabin available, why he had sat next to Jeb, who everyone more or less avoided or hardly even acknowledged, nor *had* nearly this entire trip. Kit wondered, especially, since he should have wanted to be free of the man, after having been on the horse with him ever since his own horse had fallen to its death in the Palo Duro.

Kit supposed Jeb was the way he was on account of having been a slave before the Civil War. He always looked as if he might flinch, if you looked his way or addressed him or stood too close. As if you might suddenly strike him.

Kit felt appalled that such an able and good man would think he would ever strike him.

Kit had been too young to fight in the Civil War, but Old Morg, who had served as a trail guide during it, had told him stories about it. When Kit had asked him what side he was on he had said, "I was on the side that paid most. Best side there is."

Although Kit's father had probably been a Texan, trailing the herds north and visiting the cow towns when he could, Kit decided he would have been with the Union if he had had to fight. It galled Kit to think that any man should be a slave, even a black man.

Kit realised he hadn't blinked for almost five minutes and that his eyeballs had gone dry. He blinked them wet again and looked around.

The fire was burning low and Lebold was snoring loudly, snorting and gargling every now and again. Dwight was snoring at a more even and gentle keel.

Jeb's head was back down on his knee and he was breathing gently.

For a moment Kit thought he saw a flash through the cabin window, but when he looked all he saw was darkness. He wondered if it was going to thunder.

Kit sat back and pulled his hat down over his eyes, as was his habit.

He listened to the fire crackling and popping.

Soon he drifted off.

He dreamed that he was below the deck of a slave ship caught in rough seas, being thrown back and forth in a small cabin – and when water came in under the door he ran down a rocking hallway and up a flight of wooden steps.

When he came out onto the deck it was pitching back and forth and from side to side, and dozens of big, black cannon balls were rolling up and down and back and forth along the decks, rumbling terrifically and crashing into the sides with big hollow booms, and into the wooden masts, one of which came crashing down.

Then a huge wave came over the side and Kit was swept from the deck.

★ ★ ★

When he awoke the first thing Kit noticed was the heavy pattering of the rain on the roof.

It was cold in the cabin and still dark, but the darkness was weak with the promise of dawn. The fire was cold and pale and down to ashes, with a few dying embers glowing here and there.

Rain beat against the cabin's one window, and Kit watched beads of water snaking quickly down the glass in the pre-dawn darkness.

He got up stiffly and set to waking the men up, shaking Jeb awake before he stood.

He rocked Dwight with his boot and Dwight came awake.

"Dern it," he said as he stirred. "I was havin' a fine dream till you woke me up. I'm liable to hold a grudge against you, Kit. I was about to dip my rod and it wasn't going to cost me a dime."

Kit didn't know what to say to that, so didn't say anything. He crouched next to Lebold and inspected him. His face seemed less pale.

When he awoke him, Lebold looked around the cabin as if unaware of how he got there. Then he seemed to come around to his senses. He face did indeed look less pale, and there was no more sweat upon his brow; his skin looked relatively dry.

There was a sudden flash which filled the cabin with white light, and then as it faded thunder rumbled across the sky like big, rocky boulders rattling against each other over them.

"Dern," Lebold said. "Would you hear that? I ain't lookin' forward to riding in it. Help me up, Kit."

Kit held out his hand and helped Lebold to his feet, once again helping him position the rifle crutch under his armpit.

As they tied their bedrolls and gathered up their saddles, Kit drew his pistol and checked it, weighed it expertly in his hand, and then replaced it.

Dwight saw him doing so and did the same.

"Well, this is it, I guess," Kit said.

Lebold said, "We may not even have to use those."

"Yeah, well, we'll see," Dwight said.

They came out of the cabin.

Water immediately began to stream over Kit's hat and patter in big hard drops on his shoulders. Soon his shirt was soaked through.

The rain was cold and icy, and it made Kit feel even more miserable. He felt well rested, but obviously the sleep had done nothing to shake his feeling of dread; not for what he was about to do, but for what he had already done.

The horses were huddled together and whinnying, almost as annoyed with the weather as they were. They pulled up the stakes and placed the horse blankets quickly so as not to get them too wet, then they buckled the girths of the saddles and climbed on.

"We're gonna look mighty funny ridin' into that town two to a horse," Lebold remarked.

Kit ignored the comment.

Thunder crashed in the sky and rolled across the prairie distances like big black cannon balls rolling along a galley deck.

Kit spurred the horse and felt the tug of Jeb's arms around his waist as the horse jerked into a trot.

The darkness was beginning to recede and the oncoming morning light looked pale and grey, the prairie muddy.

It was going to be an unpleasant ride, though Lebold assured them that the town of Farlow was not further than twenty miles.

W hen God Dog entered the town of Farlow he felt something he seldom had ever: fear.

This was the white man's world, and he didn't belong. How Quanah had decided to take it, he did not know – though perhaps where Quanah had gone was not like this.

Then he saw a sight that made him feel less nervous. Three Crow Indians were sitting on a set of steps that climbed the boardwalk. They were passing a whiskey bottle among each other and raising it to the night sky. Their eyes rolled in their sockets and they laughed like fools and jabbered at each other. They were probably from the forts, scouts or guides for the white soldiers.

The sight calmed him – for his presence here in the town would not attract the kind of attention he had thought it might – but it also enraged him.

Still, he decided it better to skirt the back of the buildings by taking the first alley he found, between a saloon and an opera house. Passing the batwings of the opera house, he saw an isle leading up to a stage; chairs were lined in rows before it and were filled by a noisy and crude audience, some of whom were drawing pistols and firing them into the air.

The air in the opera house was thick with cigar smoke, and on the stage a small balding man who was introducing the next act held a hand to his mouth and coughed.

God Dog passed it and turned down the alley. He looked up. The saloon next to it was a high clapboard building. He went around the back of it trailing the horses and the white woman, whom he had warned he would shoot stone dead if she attempted to scream or dismount. Her feet were untied and she could jump down and run if she wanted to, but if that eventuality arose he was prepared to draw his pistol and blow the back of her head out.

He travelled several buildings down and came to the back of The Hog's Head saloon, another big two-storey clapboard building. He turned down the muddy alleyway and saw another drunken Crow Indian sitting next to a pile of refuse, old crates and bottles and rotting food stuffs, empty tin cans and broken glasses. Probably, as with the others, he had wandered over from one of the forts to get drunk and lose himself and sit destitute in the white man's alley.

Look what he has sold out his people for, God Dog thought to himself.

He stopped by the Crow and waited for him to look up, then he dipped his hand into his saddlebag and dug for a dollar. He flicked it down into the mud.

"Go into the saloon and tell the Half-breed I am waiting in the alley," God Dog said.

The Crow, a member of one of the more peaceable of the Indian tribes – though God Dog preferred to think of them as one of the more cowardly and traitorous – stood unsteadily and bent down and picked up the silver dollar piece from out of the mud.

He looked at the white woman.

"Mind your business," God Dog told him. "Go."

The Crow Indian went down the alley obediently and turned and disappeared around the front of the building, stepping up onto the boardwalk.

God Dog waited, watching people passing in the street, mostly white men: soldiers and skinners and gamblers, though women passed among them too. They wore too much make-up and had powdered their faces heavily, and their busts were almost bursting from their bodices.

The white women were disgusting things; they were pale enough as it was yet made themselves even paler with their even whiter powders. God Dog had never understood those chiefs who had taken white women for wives. They would keep the captive children and then take them once they were of age.

He realized that in retrospect they should have killed the whites' women and children too, during the raids – especially the female children. In order to prevent the half-breeds. God Dog had never had anything against the half-breeds. None of them had, for they had Indian hearts pumping in their breasts and Indian blood was stronger than white blood – for when a half-breed was born he always appeared more Indian than white. A fact that in fact made many Indians proud. Quanah himself he had never treated any different, or ever considered him to be. And yet the fact remained that had it not been for his half-blood he probably would not have taken the white man's road as he had with such conviction that he would succeed upon it.

A wooden doorway in the alley suddenly opened inwards, and a large rough-looking cowboy looked out. He was wearing a black, wide-brimmed hat with a low crown, and had a waxed moustache twirled at the tips. His dirty chin and cheeks were covered in a dark stubble.

"Bring the girl," he said. "Tie your horses to the rail out front and then come up; Michael's upstairs waiting to see you."

Michael? Was that what the Half-breed was calling himself? God Dog had always known him as Tasunke Hinzi, Yellow Horse.

God Dog spat, for he did not like the officious tone of the white cowboy, and then dismounted slowly. He lifted the girl down from the saddle and pushed her in front of him as he walked to the doorway.

The cowboy took one look at her and his dirty, bony face lit up. When he smiled, God Dog saw that his teeth had rotted in his face; they were stained a dark yellow and one was even completely blackened and dead.

"Well ain't she a beaut," he said. "Why, the boys are gonna be all over you, missy. They been waiting for a new filly. I reckon you're gonna fetch top dollar, you are. And I reckon I'm gonna pay to ride you myself, before the mule skinners rip into you."

"Tell the Half-breed I want two hundred dollars," God Dog said.

"Two hunnert dollars! Why, no girl's worth that much. Michael ain't gonna pay you *half* that."

"He's gonna pay it."

The cowboy looked uncertain.

"Well, you'll have to talk to him." He had pulled the girl into the doorway behind him now. Beyond, a narrow flight of steps led up to a lantern-lit hallway.

God Dog spat again, onto the clapboard wall of the building, and then turned and took his horses out into the street.

Horses lined the hitching rails on both sides of the big saloon, and there was no space for his horses. So he turned six hitched horses loose and slapped their rumps, driving them riderless into the street, where they swerved wildly and dodged the startled pedestrians.

A drunk sitting on a bench under one of the windows watched him incredulously, but God Dog gave him one look so full of hatred and anger that the man looked quickly back down at his lap, and started picking straw off himself.

God Dog hitched his sixth and last horse, and then walked back into the alley. The door had been left open and a shaft of weak yellow light shone onto the boards of the building opposite.

He entered and closed the wooden door behind him, ascending the creaky wooden steps that led up into the narrow hallway with several closed doors running down it on either side.

He knew that the whites were coming and that if he was going to make a stand he would have to make it here. He could expect help from the Half-breed, who at least owed him that much for all the business he had brought him over the years: the young white women, some merely teenagers and even then only just that, the stolen whiskey and horses and carbines.

As he walked down the hallway he wondered if all along he had himself taken the white man's road – and not realized it.

Magdalena was pushed down the hallway by the disgusting man who had opened the door in the alley. The look he had given her in the doorway under his wide-brimmed hat had terrified her all over again. She had imagined that rotted mouth clamping over her own, and felt she would die on the spot if ever it did.

He pushed her along to the third door down and then stepped in front of her and opened it. Beyond it was a small plank-walled room with a bare cornshuck mattress dumped on the floor. It smelt strongly of body odour and she saw that the window was misted over, even though no one was in the room. Coming through the floor, she could hear the half-muted sounds of a bustling and busy saloon, and the clump and jingle of boots and spurs on floorboards and wooden steps.

A hard hand pushed her from behind and she tripped and fell onto the hard mattress. When she rolled over and turned around, the disgusting man was holding onto the brass door handle, about to close the door.

He said, "You just set tight, missy – company's comin'. I might just come back myself," he chuckled, smiling at her delightedly.

It was the most disgusting smile she had ever seen in her life. He seemed worse even than the Indians.

He closed the door and she heard a key rattling in the lock.

After a moment she got up and tried the door. It was locked. There was nothing else in the room and all she could do in the end was sit back down on the mattress and wait. She considered jumping through the high window, or breaking the glass and cutting her wrists, and then jumping out of it.

She had the growing feeling inside her that she would never see her sister again; she couldn't bear the thought of her sister going through the same as she was or worse, and she found herself wishing that she, too, might be dead. At least then no one could do anything to her any more. She wished her*self* dead; why wouldn't she her sister?

Jenny. She regretted that she had not been able to say more to her before they had parted; to her mother too. She regretted the bickering fights she and Jenny had had, which had then seemed perfectly justified but now seemed to have been over absolutely nothing.

She wished she could have just said sorry, for those fights. They were usually fighting over chores like whose turn it was to milk the cow or clean the skillet. Before George had grown wise to the fact that he was one day going to be a man, they had managed for a while to get him to do chores too, and that had prevented some of the bickering, until George had started bickering too. He was a man and it wasn't right that he was doing woman's work, according to him, and Ma had surprisingly supported that notion, accusing the girls of bulling him into doing their chores. George had expressly stated that if he was to do any chores it was helping Pa to shoe the horses and tend to the livestock, which were several oxen, two mules and some cows. Most of which they had had to eat.

And George had. He liked mostly to play with his rope, and catch the milk cow. Once she had told George off when he had roped it around the neck while she was sitting on a stool beneath it, pumping the teats. She had been particularly mad at him, because it seemed he got away without having to do any chores that were exactly that, a chore.

Men had all the fun and adventure; none of the responsibility. But she regretted ever having exploded at her younger brother, and wished, also, that she could have said sorry. They had not particularly gotten along well back then.

She felt now that the world was a most unfair place, and woman's place in it was worse even than horses or mules, or almost as bad. And men just wanted what women had, and if they could would take it. She had seen that, and she recognized the intention in the eyes of the disgusting man clear enough.

If she lived through this, somehow made it, she never wanted anything to do with a man ever again. No sir.

Suddenly there was another rattle in the lock, and the round brass doorknob began to turn this way and that. Then the door opened and the disgusting man was back.

He opened the door only enough to admit himself, and snuck in. He closed it quietly and locked it again, and then turned around and rubbed his hands together as if he had come in out of the cold, only with excitement in his eyes. Looking at him, she thought of a fly rubbing its little feet together hungrily before sucking on a piece of meat.

"Tolt you I'd be back," he said, pulling off his gun belt and casting it aside. It fell with a heavy clump, and she glanced at the gun in it.

He climbed down on top of her and her worst fears came true. He began to smother her mouth with his, and stick his tongue down it! She gagged and turned her head away in disgust, but he simply began to kiss and lick at her neck. The stubble on his cheeks rasped and stung her soft skin.

What had she done to deserve being so violated in life? Why was life this way?

She struggled against him as he tried to pull apart her legs, and managed to turn over onto her front, her back to him.

"You want it like a bitch dog, I'll give it to you that way."

He was rough and hard with her, hitching up her dresses.

"The Half-breed just bought you for a hunnert dollars," he said. "He'll probably come for a taste hisself. Tell him I was here first and I'll come back and gut you like a fish."

The threat did not hold up after all the things the Indian had said he would do to her.

"And look at this," he said behind her, pulling something out of his pocket. He held out two fifty dollar notes in his hand. "He cut a deal with your Indian friend; I got me a hunnert dollars just to get my boys to kill those men comin' after you. That's more'n two months' wages. You and that makes for a fine evenin', I'd say."

Magdalena was stunned with what she had just heard. Men, coming after her? Who? What men?

Suddenly she felt hope; not much more than she had felt when she had found the arrowhead, for there were men who were going to try to kill them according to this disgusting man, but hope just the same.

Hope.

She wondered how many men there were, and what kind of men. Perhaps they were Texas Rangers. Her pa had once told her of the Texas Rangers, how they would chase horse thieves and stage robbers to the ends of the earth to hang them, only ever stopping once they got their man. They had even chased after the formidable Comanche when they had terrorised the trails, most notably the Santa Fe and Old Spanish Trails, along which had passed much trade.

She gritted her teeth and strengthened her resolve, ready for what this disgusting man was about to do and the mind frame she would need to get through it.

All this time men had been coming after her – if only she had known, she would not have felt so hopeless.

Texas Rangers, she decided. Texas Rangers were coming to rescue her.

And they had to be close.

When they came to the muddy outskirts of the town Kit was shocked by something he saw.

The rain had let up some and there was a light drizzle needling out of the grey sky, but it didn't make much of a difference: they were as wet as if they had crossed a river – wetter. Not only Kit's hat was soaked, but his hair under his hat too. And he was chilled to the bone; his toes at the ends of his boots were aching with cold. His boots squelched when he pushed down against the stirrups, and water squeezed from the seams and stitches.

What Kit saw when they entered the pounded mud outskirts of the dripping town of Farlow was a load of erected tents and encampments. All of the darkness had gone from the sky and it was light now, the sun nowhere to be seen, the sky a pale dirty-washtub grey. The men were stirring in their camps. Some were attempting vainly to get their fires going again and quietly cursing and complaining. Others looked to be sleeping off a heavy hangover, still huddled in their wet bedrolls, oblivious.

Then they rode past a tent with its flaps open and Kit saw a man performing the sex act, his legs half out the tent and his chaps down at his ankles, connecting them like shackles. His pale, hairy, bare backside pumped up and down in the grey light. Dress skirts were hitched up underneath him and Kit caught sight of a pair of milky white legs – woman's legs – open on either side of him.

It was the first time Kit had ever seen the sex act – or heard it, for that matter. The woman beneath the man – whose face he had not seen – was mewing like a hungry kitten, while the man on top of her huffed and panted.

Kit looked away – although not quickly.

"It's barely daylight," Lebold remarked. "And it's wet as the Republican River, to boot. You'd think they'd do it indoors."

Kit noticed another tent pitched in the wet mud in which something unsavoury sounded to be happening. The flaps were closed, however, and he couldn't see anything. After passing several tents he realized that women were servicing the men who couldn't afford to stay the night in the town; perhaps the women themselves could not afford to do their business in a bedroom and had to do it in a tent instead.

Kit did not feel his dingus twitch. The sight, rather, was on the whole off-putting.

Kit saw a man squatting over a hole in the mud and defecating, who appeared to take a lively interest in them as he strained. He had a newspaper tucked under one arm.

Probably the worst thing he saw was a woman holding her skirts up out of the mud, squatting with her legs planted wide apart in plain sight. There was a hissing noise and a thin steaming yellow stream squirted down between her legs and pooled in the mud.

Muddy dogs and pups ran excitedly alongside their horses, barking and yipping up at them, their shabby coats splattered with mud.

"Git out of it!" Lebold shouted at one, which was aggravating his horse, trying to nip at one of its forelegs. "Go on, git! Little bastard! Goddamn dogs are alerting the whole town we're comin'."

Some of the people who were awake in the camps and fixing coffee and breakfast stopped to look at them as they passed. Kit thought the looks were hostile, although some of the men looked highly amused at the sight of them riding two to a horse, and chuckled among each other, tapping one another and pointing.

Then Kit took in the town itself.

It was a long single lane on the open prairie, but by no means a 'one-horse' town. Hitching rails all the way up and down and on either side of the street were tied with horses. There were carts and wagons being loaded outside general stores and gunsmiths; men loading big barrels onto wagons and sacks of seed and grain. Some appeared to be carrying farming tools.

Even at this time of morning the town was busy and bustling.

Hungover drunks staggered across the streets, dodging horses and stages, some litting out of town and back onto the prairie already. The main street itself was one long, wide, muddy rut. The rain had pooled in wagon ruts, in hoofprints and footprints. In areas where the muddy brown water had pooled particularly bad, long planks had been laid down. Two or three had been laid down one after the other so that people could cross along them to the other side of the street and keep clear of the mud.

A stagecoach driver had to stop his coach and move one aside and was cursing and blaspheming.

They entered the town proper.

Grubby men were plonking up and down the muddy planks of the boardwalks, entering and exiting various utility stores and saloons and coffee shops. Kit could smell frying eggs and bacon wafting out across the street from one of them, a narrow-looking ground-floor establishment with windows on either side of the door, that appeared to be an eating house of sorts, with a long bar down one end and wooden booths on the other.

"Dern, I could use me some breakfast," Kit said. "Those eggs smell right tasty."

His stomach had begun grumbling as soon as the smell had hit his nostrils; after a day or two of beef jerky, bacon and eggs would have gone down a treat.

Dwight said, "I could use me some bacon."

"All the goddamn hitch rails are full," Lebold pointed out. "Unless you boys have it in mind to take the horses in for breakfast too."

"There must be a livery somewhere," Kit suggested.

They set up the street looking for a livery stable. Kit caught more unfriendly looks from some of the men he passed, and made sure to look down and not hold the stare, as appeared to be the challenge. The men looked to be an unfriendly mix of cowboys, miners and mule skinners – and soldiers.

Then Kit saw an Indian lying in the street, right in the mud, holding onto a whiskey bottle with a little of the brown liquid left at the bottom. At first he thought the Indian might be dead, but when he passed saw that he was snoring up a storm.

"They must be the pride of their people," Lebold remarked.

Every next establishment seemed to be a saloon, though Kit did see a gun store and a blacksmiths and a saddle-maker's.

Finally, halfway through the town, they found a big livery stable. They entered the high doors and dismounted onto the damp hay. A few flies buzzed gently in the air and there was a strong smell of horse manure.

Kit saw that Lebold had dismounted without help, and wasn't using his rifle crutch, though he limped along awkwardly.

The owner came over wiping grease off his hands with a rag. He had been shoeing a horse at the back of the barn when they entered, holding a hoof up between his legs and scraping it out and filing it, a nail between his teeth.

"How can I help you boys?" he asked, throwing the rag aside.

Lebold said, "We'd like to stable these horses."

"That'll be four bits each."

Lebold pulled his rifle from his saddle scabbard and dug in one of his saddlebags. He handed the man eight bits and stuffed the rest of his money into his duds.

Kit drew the rifle from his own saddle scabbard and handed it to Jeb.

As the owner took hold of the lead ropes and walked the horses away he said, "I'd watch out, if I were you boys. Folks don't like niggers none too much in Farlow. In fact, some of 'em hate 'em even more than Injuns."

Jeb looked at Kit with his big white eyes.

But to their surprise it was Lebold who spoke up; even Dwight was taken aback.

"I guess he'll go where we go," Lebold said.

"Just don't say I didn't warn ya," the man said, and disappeared with both horses into one of the stalls.

"Let's go get that breakfast," Lebold said impatiently.

When they made it back to the eating house they had passed on their way in, and had stepped up out of the muddy street onto the boardwalk, Jeb did not follow them. He sat, instead, on a water barrel.

"It's probably for the best," Dwight pointed out.

"I'll take him out a plate," Kit said.

They entered the eating house; the smell of bacon and eggs and coffee wafted into their faces as soon as they pushed the door open. They found an unoccupied booth and slid in. Lebold went to the bar and ordered four plates of bacon and eggs and some coffee.

He came back and sat down, shouldering through the crowd. The other booths were full and the establishment was busy.

"How're we gonna find her in such a place?" Kit asked. "She could be in any one of those saloons."

"I think better on a full stomach," Lebold said. "We'll ask someone once we've et."

After looking around for a while and waiting, the barman slapped four plates down on the bar and called across the room. Kit and Lebold got up and carried the plates back to the table. Before sitting down Kit took a plate out to Jeb and gave it to him at the water barrel.

When he got back to the table the boys were busy devouring the bacon and eggs. Kit sat before his plate and attacked his eggs with a ferocious appetite. Once he polished them off he held the plate up and licked it clean, and then washed it down with scalding hot coffee.

When he finally put his plate down he said, "I coulda et two of those."

Dwight was licking his own plate – as Kit had done. Soon, even Lebold was doing it.

"I second that notion," Dwight said.

"So far I ain't heard a notion you don't second," Lebold remarked.

"I guess I don't second *that* notion."

When they came out of the eating house, bellies full, several grubby cowboys were crowded around Jeb.

"I swear he had a hand in one of my saddlebags," one of them was saying.

"Is that right, nigger boy? You try rob my pardner's saddlebag?"

Suddenly there was a *whap* and Jeb flew back against the water barrel, jostling it. A wave of water splashed over the side and onto the boardwalk and ran under their boots.

The cowboy who had struck Jeb a blow across the face grabbed him up off the water barrel by the collar of his torn shirt and began to dunk him. His little posse of cowboys cheered him on.

"Drownt that son of a bitch," one of them cheered.

"He had his black hand in my saddlebag," the one maintained.

Suddenly a round went off right by Kit's ear, and a slug whacked into the wooden overhang overhead. Damp woodchips floated down.

The startled cowboys who were crowded around the water barrel jumped back. Jeb pulled his head out of the water barrel and spat water, gasping.

The man who had held him under walked slowly back, holding up his hands.

Kit saw that Lebold was holding his rifle out in front of him, pointing it at the man. Then he walked forward toward the edge of the boardwalk.

"Let him be," he said sternly.

"He had a hand in my pardner's saddlebag," the man holding up his hands said, lowering them slowly.

"Jeb don't put his hands in other people's saddlebags," Lebold said. "Jeb, take up your rifle and step up here."

Jeb's rifle was lying in the mud; it had been propped up against the water barrel and fallen over as he flew into it.

Jeb picked it up and wiped away the mud, then slowly stepped backwards, training it on the group of cowboys. He walked backwards up the steps until he was next to Lebold.

Kit had his hand ready to draw and fire; so did Dwight. Kit couldn't believe it; already, they were almost in a gunfight – and it hadn't any thing to do with why they were here.

"You boys run along now," Lebold told them.

Mostly they looked mad at having a negro hold a gun on them. Several of them spat and turned away sulkily, but three stood their ground – the biggest and meanest of the bunch, Kit noticed.

"You draw a gun on me," the one who had hit Jeb said, "and you had best use it."

"I tend to shoot low right after breakfast," Lebold remarked, and lowered his rifle so that it was aimed for the man's groin.

He spat and turned away, slapping his remaining boys on their shoulders and telling them to get moving, there'd be another time.

Lebold heard the remark and said, "I shoot low after lunch and dinner too."

But the cowboys were trudging off across the street.

They lowered their rifles.

Kit was relieved.

"I reckon we keep Jeb with us from now on," Dwight suggested.

"I reckon so," Lebold said. "Let's go pop into one of the saloons and see what we can see."

They went up the busy boardwalk, stepped briefly down into a muddy alley, and then back up onto the one opposite.

They pushed through a pair of batwing doors that had several broken slats, one of which looked like it had been shot out, and entered the saloon.

She had waited all her life for a man like him to come walking in through those saloon doors – fearing that by then she would be too old and used up to be of any interest to him – and then today, just like that, he had.

He was the most ruggedly handsome cowboy she had ever seen; the three men he came in with were of no consequence and she hardly even saw them – although she noted one was black.

He was everything she had imagined he would be; strong and wide-shouldered from handling broncs and cows, tall and lean.

There was only one thing she had not imagined, and it was the thing she thought made him look more handsomely rugged than any man she had ever seen.

It was his big horseshoe-shaped moustache.

He seemed to be travelling with a man who had a lame leg with a belt tied high around one thigh, a young man who looked not much older than twenty, and a negro. She supposed the young man was handsome, too, but he lacked what she wanted in a man; an air of maturity, that promise that he could take care of a lady, financially and physically of course.

Glorietta got up from the table and straightened her dresses, deciding that she would have to make a move now or one of the other younger sporting women would. The saloon was busy, at least, and the other women were presently occupied with the usual crowd of miners and soldiers and the foul mule skinners.

As she was straightening her dresses she saw them walk over to the bar, and decided to sidle up.

"Howdy boys," she said in a seductive purr. "Where you from? I ain't seen you around here before."

They were looking around with wide eyes, surprised to have been addressed. Bill Hutchinson, who owned the saloon, was presently not behind the bar. He had gone upstairs to resolve an issue with some cowpoke who had throttled a girl for making fun of his pod.

To her disappointment it was the one with the lame leg who spoke up.

"I'm from San Antonio, name's Lebold; this young man's from Dodge City and Dwight over here comes from down by the Rio Grande. Jeb's from a Kansas trail town – same one Kit's from."

He indicated the negro and then the young man. Close up he looked like a boy who was large for his age, with a light growth of stubble and the first showing of a moustache on his upper lip.

"I've always wanted to see the Rio Grande," she said, smiling.

To her further disappointment the cowboy called Dwight was acting embarrassed and nervous that she was addressing them.

"I dunno why," the one called Lebold said. "It's a shallow brown river with a load of ugly Mexican bandits on the other side."

She didn't know what to say to that; it wasn't this man with the lame leg she was interested in.

She decided to address Dwight directly. "Care to buy a woman a drink?" she asked him, purring her voice as best she could.

But it was the lame one who spoke again, to her annoyance.

"He ain't got time for that – we're lookin' for a young lady."

"Why there's a young lady right stood in front of youse."

"No no," he said. "She was brought here last night about."

"So what?" she said. "Dozens of girls come here."

She had herself been brought here – and been left. By a crooked gambler she had met in Ogallala. He had run into debt in this very saloon, and left her to Bill Hutchinson to pay it back.

Anyway, Bill Hutchinson was a far better man. He didn't beat her like the gambler had, and at least Bill gave her a quarter of what she earned pleasing the boys, unlike the seedy, spineless son of a bitch, who had taken every cent she ever owned and gambled it.

Still it was the lame one who addressed her.

"Who owns this saloon?"

"Bill Hutchinson," she said, and batted her long eyelashes at Dwight, who looked down at his boots, embarrassed.

That was a turn-off; by the way he had walked in she had expected him to be the confident type, not like the young cowboys who wanted a prod but were too embarrassed to come up and ask, and you had to wait for them to get totally drunk so that they could work up the nerve. And even then you still had to ask them.

Suddenly she was put off. The young man was even worse; she had barely even looked in his direction and he was acting so embarrassed he looked about to jump out of his skin.

Only the one called Lebold had the confidence; but he wasn't the one she was interested in.

He was saying, "If a young girl was to be brought here – let's say for argument she was brought against her will – where would she likely end up? Which one of these saloons?"

"I was brought here against my will," she said. "And didn't no men come looking for me."

"She's a young girl," he said testily. "She's had her family kilt and we've come to bring her home."

"Oh, that's cute. My whole family was burnt in a wagon train by Injins when I was nought but a five-yeer-old girl. Didn't no men come rescuing me."

She could see she was galling him, but she was galled herself. The man of her dreams had just walked in and not only was too embarrassed to look at her, but here to rescue some lucky little whore from the life she had always wanted to be rescued from herself. It was her dream: to meet some man who would take her away from all this – before it was too late.

"Let me rephrase that," the one called Lebold said to her. "Did any new girl come here, yesterday or last night?"

"Not that I know of," she said reluctantly.

"Come on, boys, let's get out of here. We're wastin' our time."

As they began to move away an impulse came over her, one she could not control. She reached out and grabbed onto Dwight's arm, startling him.

"Wait. Maybe I can help. I could ask around."

Lebold said, "You do that. We'll be along in one of the saloons."

She had to let go of the man's arm and then stand there and watch him walk out of her life. Probably the embarrassment could be brought out of him, with whiskey, and then he would be perfect.

Perhaps if she helped them find the lucky brat they were looking for they would take her too; she could plead to them to take her. Ply every one of her feminine wiles...

"I reckon that whore had eyes for you, Dwight. Wanted to lap you up and make you take her to San Francisco."

Dwight stuck a finger in the neck of his shirt and tried to loosen it some.

"I don't see why you'd think that," he said to Lebold awkwardly.

"That moustache of yours is why I think that; you never should of drank that tonic."

Kit had noticed the way the woman had been transfixed by Dwight, and now, walking along the boardwalk to the next saloon, he felt his own pitiful moustache with his fingers; to him, it felt thoroughly inadequate.

They went into the next saloon, where a honky-tonk piano was being played loudly, binging and bonging, but after speaking to the owner – a fat unhelpful Mexican with an eye-patch that gave him even more of a piratical air – they left again. There had only been three sporting ladies in there in any case, all big and Spanish-looking, and it hadn't looked as if the girl might be there.

Finally, after coming up short in another saloon, they entered one called The Hog's Head, which looked more promising.

It was bigger and busier than the others, the tables full of card players and gamblers and loud drunks. Provocatively dressed women went from table to table, plying their wiles. Two rough-looking customers served drinks from behind the bar. Kit stared, dazzled, at some of the sporting ladies in the place.

He felt his dingus twitch.

This is what Old Morg had always warned him of; this den of depravity and its dangerous lure. Even then Kit thought that, if alone, he might have tried to go with one of the women – find out what it was all about, whoring, just do it. He had been born of it. Surely it wouldn't be wrong to see how? To see the conditions under which his own mother had once lived and worked...

Then it struck Kit that he, too, could produce a son just like himself: the son of a thousand fathers...

Never. Never would he do that. Old Morg had been right; this was a place to avoid with all your inner resolve. This was...

"Old Morg?" he said.

Dwight and Lebold turned to look at Kit, confused as to whom he had addressed, and then followed Kit's stunned gaze to a table not less than a yard away. An old granddad sat there with a big-busted woman on his knee and a bottle of whiskey and two glasses in front of him. He was cackling.

Kit appeared to be stunned by the sight of him.

"Old Morg?" he said again, even more incredulously than the first time.

"Who the hell's Old Morg?" Lebold asked.

But Kit didn't answer. He walked slowly up to the table and stopped before the old man with the whore.

"Now what do you suppose's got into him?" Dwight asked.

Kit couldn't believe it. Unless his eyes were deceiving him, it was Old Morg – and not only was it Old Morg, but Old Morg with a sporting lady sat on his knee and a whiskey glass in his hand. That was impossible. All of it was impossible.

"Old Morg?" he said again, standing over the table.

The old man heard his name and stopped cackling and looked up, frowning.

"What is it?" he asked. "Do I know you? If you're here about your brother, he was cheatin' at cards."

"No, it's... it's *me*. Kit."

The old man frowned and scratched his head. The sporting lady was looking up curiously from where she sat on his bony knee. Kit was surprised that such a knee could even hold the weight of the woman.

She had the largest pair of whatsits Kit had ever seen; if her bodice had been any tighter it looked like they would explode.

"Kit? You're too young to be Kit Carson," the old man said. "I knewed him. He was a mountain man and a guide. And a fine one at that."

"No, I'm Kit Cope."

Suddenly the Old Man seemed to remember.

"'I *God*," he said. "Why, it *is* you. Well look at this. Young Kit all growed up and doin' the town. How are ya, son?"

"I... I thought you was dead." Kit slowly pulled a chair out and sat down.

Lebold and Dwight exchanged confused glances and then walked up behind him with Jeb, their weapons held casually in their hands, barrels pointed to the floorboards.

"No, son, I ain't dead," Old Morg said. "I oughta be, but I ain't."

"But... but I heard you got scalped by Injuns."

Old Morg checked his head hurriedly, patting what was left of his hair as if to make sure it was still all there.

Relieved, he said, "'I God, no. I spread that rumour myself. Though my Pawnee wife almost did scalp me on the reservation. See? Take a look at that scar, son. Caught her just in time."

"Pawnee *wife*?" Kit said.

"When I left after the last buffalo, I bumped into a load of Injuns lookin' for it too. Then I took me a Injun wife; it was a good life while it lasted. We never did find the buffalo, though. But I did discover a lucrative business in the bones. Who're your friends, Kit?"

Old Morg could no longer ignore the men standing there. Kit looked around.

"Oh. That's Jeb Rawlins, Dwight and Lebold."

"I see. You're ridin' in a posse now; thought I tolt you not to do that," Old Morg said. "Whyn't you all sit down?" he suggested. "I'll buy youse a drink. We got some catching up to do, Kit. It's been a coon's age."

At the invitation Lebold grabbed a chair from another table – to the annoyance of the man sitting there – and squawked it over. Jeb and

Dwight took a seat on the sides.

"Who is this old man?" Lebold asked Kit.

"The name's Morgan."

Kit said, "We used to skin buffalos together in Dodge."

"That's right," Old Morg said. "Young Kit here was one of the best skinners on the plains, and a fine shot too – I taught him, of course," he added.

Kit still looked confused.

"Why didn't you come back, Morg?" he asked. "All this time I thought you was dead."

"Well, it was time to move on, son," Old Morg explained. "I'm a man's got itchy feet; you know that. Always got to move on, master the next thing."

He turned to the woman on his knee.

"How 'bout you go get us some glasses, honey – my knee's startin' to ache. My dern arthritis is playin' up again."

She smiled and then got up and went for the glasses.

"When did you start... drinking?" Kit asked, looking down at his glass.

"After my Pawnee wife tried to scalp me and I left the reservation."

Kit shook his head in disbelief. He felt truly lost: the one man who had instilled every principle within him and held dear to heart was sitting here and breaking them all.

He was lost.

"Now now, son," Old Morg said. "Don't get teary-eyed on me; I always warned ya of what a woman could do to a man. I warned ya. Stay away from them, the whores, I said. Now I guess I'm a livin' example of it."

There was a moment's contemplative silence. The sporting lady who had been sitting on Old Morg's knee returned with a couple of glasses clutched on the ends of her fingers like big see-through thimbles and put them down on the table.

Morg lined them in a row and then picked up his whiskey bottle and began to pour them full, skilfully moving the bottle across them without stopping. Once they were brimming full he shoved them across the table, spilling them everywhere despite his prior effort to pour them full perfectly.

He pushed one toward Kit, but Kit didn't take it.

"I drink to your health, gentlemen, and to those who have it comin'," Old Morg said, and knocked back an entire glass.

"I kilt a man yesterday," he said matter-of-factly, when he put the glass down. "Cheatin' at cards."

"Oh," Kit said, still distant.

"Now I have to keep lookin' over my shoulder, account of he had a brother, apparently. What're you boys doin' in Farlow, anyhow? None of youse look like slick-haired gamblers to me, more like cowpokes. You're all dustier than drag riders."

Kit slowly came around to his senses and snapped to. He said, "We're here lookin' for a young girl's been kidnapped, Morg. She got stolt by an Indian."

Old Morg whistled. "Is that so?" he said. "Well, there's a good few Indians in Farlow, mostly Crows from the forts. Though I doubt they'd steal a woman – they're liable to get lynched they do that."

Lebold spoke up. "Nah, this one was stole by an Indian renegade by the name of God Dog."

"God Dog?" Old Morg said. "Why, I encountered that son of a bitch once. He stole one of my pack mules when I was goin' through Nebraska. I trailed that snake for fourteen days and then lost him in a river. The son of a bitch outsmarted me, 'I God!"

Kit said, "He was likely here last night, with the girl we're tryin' to get back. We think he may have sold her."

"God Dog? Here?"

"He may be gone now," Lebold said. "But we reckon the girl's here in town."

"Well," Old Morg said. "Well, what do you plan to do?"

"Get her back, of course," Lebold replied.

"I was you I'd check the back rooms in each of these saloons. There's some nefarious goings on in Farlow, I'd say that much."

Kit looked up at the railing above the barroom floor. There was a narrow corridor there that disappeared around a corner. A cowboy was going up there right now, hopping up the flight of steps merrily.

"What's this girl's name?" Old Morg asked.

"Magdalena," Kit said. The name sounded strange on his tongue. With the unexpected meeting of Old Morg, Kit had forgotten about accidentally killing her sister – briefly, anyway.

He remembered his pocket.

"Here," he said. "I got this, a photograph of her."

He handed it across the table to Old Morg, who took it and then held it so close to his eyes he almost touched them with it.

"Which one is she?" he asked.

"The one with the long hair. Think it's blond," Kit said.

"That's a damn shame," Old Morg said, lowering the photograph. "Fine young woman like that nabbed by that rotten scoundrel. I'd like to skin his hide, turn him into a blanket."

Kit looked to the railing again, and then back at Morg. Morg handed him back the photograph and Kit tucked it away.

"Well, whyn't you go up and take a look?" Old Morg suggested.

Kit said, "Well... *me*? Why, I wouldn't know where to begin."

"Nonsense, son. Ain't nothin' to it. Just go on up there and knock. The ones're occupied have got great big alarm clocks outside 'em. When they go off, the cowboys've gotta come out. Or else the Half-breed's goons'll throw 'em out, though I just saw them leave before you boys came in."

"The Half-breed?" Lebold said.

"He runs this place." Old Morg began to top his glass again, and then lowered the bottle. "Well, what're you waitin' for, Kit? You look like a young cowboy, go on up there. Go on, git."

"Why, I–"

"Son, there ain't nothin' to it. Just go on up there and git."

"Well... alright. I guess."

"Don't guess, just git."

Kit slowly stood up, the chair legs squawking on the floorboards behind him.

"I guess I'll be back in a while then."

"I said don't do that."

Kit gave Dwight and Lebold an uncertain look, and then nodded to Jeb. He tipped his hat to Morg and started across the barroom for the stairs.

★ ★ ★

Kit climbed the stairs. It felt surreal. Old Morg was back in his life again, all of a sudden, just like that. He supposed once he got over the shock of it, it might actually be something to be happy about. But right now he was too nervous; things were happening far too quickly, life taking unexpected turns at every corner. Now he was going around another, in fact, and found himself standing in a hallway lined with doors on either side. At the other end there appeared to be a narrow flight of steps, descending into darkness.

Several white alarm clocks sat on the floors outside the doors, ticking and tocking. He could hear bedsprings creaking and groaning.

Kit decided to knock on the doors without alarm clocks out in front of them. Figured it might be prudent, and something in the way of a preventative to getting shot at.

He felt his heart blip. Despite his noble reasons for being here, he couldn't quite shake the feeling that it wasn't a place he was supposed to be.

Kit tried the handle of the first door on his right, and then realized his mistake – he had meant to knock first. He let go of the handle in a hurry but before he could knock the door was pulled inwards, and he ended up knocking on thin air.

A ghastly looking woman stood in front of him. She was overweight by a dern sight more than most and Kit could see the particles of white powder and thick, over-applied make-up on her face. Her hair was tied up in a neatly-netted bun that looked like something a dog might leave on a boardwalk while its owner pretended not to notice.

"'I God!" he said, couldn't help but say.

But the overweight woman looked delighted at the sight of him.

"Well ain't you the young cowboy," she said. "I'm Gretaline, honey – and you came to the right door today."

"I... I'm looking for a young girl," Kit blurted.

The delight on her face disappeared.

"A young girl?" She peeked her head out the doorway and quickly looked this way and that, as if checking to see if the coast was clear. Then she grabbed Kit by the collar and pulled him into the room.

"Why, you don't want no young girl," she said. "You want a lady experienced in these things to show you the way."

She pushed the door closed with one plump hand and then turned a key in a lock. Kit was regressing on the spot.

"You see?" the woman was saying. "Look how affright you are. You need a mature lady to show you how it's done. Come here, cowboy."

She grabbed hold of Kit's gun belt and pulled him towards a spring bed. Before he knew it his gun belt landed on the floor with a loud clunk, along with his duds.

He tried to reach down and pull them up but she slapped his hands away. Then she turned to a basin of soapy water and dipped her hands in it.

"You're lucky," she said, lathering up her hands. "You're only the third one today, this water's even still warm. Lukewarm," she added.

Suddenly she turned and took hold of his john thomas, in a pair of soapy and slippery, if all the same freezing cold, hands.

Kit gasped, at both the shock of the cold soapy wetness and the shock of... well, it.

Kit was paralysed.

She began tugging on his johnson. Kit felt his midsection being tugged helplessly back and forth. To his absolute terror, not only did he feel his dingus twitch, but he felt it growing.

And then she was tugging on him like a maid under a milk cow, only there weren't no pail of milk that he could see. He felt his face become red and his cheeks flush burning hot. As she worked her big callused hand back and forth she used her other to roll her sleeve up over her bicep, which was as big as a blacksmith's, only it swung back and forth like an udder.

Then suddenly she pulled him right against her and pushed him down on top of the bed.

She lifted her skirts, not just hitching them up but lifting them right over her head and throwing them into a corner of the room.

Kit stared on in horror. Her naked torso was a fold of fatty flaps, her breasts hung down to where her belly button ought to have been but wasn't, hidden somewhere beneath another flap, and there was nothing between her thick tree-trunk thighs but another big fold of fat, and a rusty growth of red hair that ought to have been under an armpit.

Suddenly she was atop of him, straddling him like a horse. She began to wiggle her behind on his thighs until, satisfied, she started to ride back and forth at his midsection.

He shot up and down beneath her. The weight of the big woman bearing down on his legs was suddenly replaced by an acute, if momentary, weightlessness. He saw only folds of flesh piled around his waist, as if the woman somehow grew out of his own belly.

He felt his dingus beginning to pulse, as strange a sensation as ever he knew. She seemed to be delighted at the strained look on his face.

Then Kit felt an even stranger sensation, probably the most unexpected and inexplicably pleasurable experience in all his life.

And the next thing he knew it was over.

The feeling was immediately replaced by a feeling of acute dread, deep embarrassment and guilt.

He shot out from under her and rolled off the side of the bed, landing on his dingus and almost snapping it.

Kit shot up to his feet and began pulling up his trousers; before they were even up he was headed for the door, hopping and tripping, clutching his gun belt in his one hand and his duds in the other.

"Why, that'll be four dollars!" she was calling after him. "Just you wait a minute now, young man!"

Out of sheer survival instinct, Kit pulled the key out of the lock as he opened the door, and when he turned and slammed it shut he found himself jamming it in the lock frantically and rattling it this way and that, until he felt the tumbler fall.

He let go and stepped back, heart pounding. His back stopped against the opposite wall.

The door began to boom, jumping and bouncing in the frame.

"Open this door, you little scoundrel!" he heard her shouting behind it as she banged her fist. "I don't give it away for free, you know!"

Kit looked this way and that, desperately seeking an avenue of escape.

Within an instant he decided there was no point in trying to enter one of the other rooms to escape this beast, and to run to the landing with the rail over it and try to hightail it down the stairs.

No sooner had he decided this than the door before him shuddered with a terrific wooden *bang*, the frame creaking and breaking out into the hallway and the door collapsing top first against Kit.

He ducked under it as it clapped against the wall and shot out the side, glancing back over his shoulder as he headed for the railing over the barroom.

The overweight woman was stepping one of her big thighs over the broken door, jowls abounce and big and red with anger.

She levelled a shotgun.

Kit hit the railing with his waist and went over.

When Glorietta passed Jackson's Gunsmith she saw an alarming sight.

Several of Mister Manito's men were looking at rifles and testing pistols in their hands, one sighting down the long barrel of a Sharps rifle and another practicing his draw.

Jackson was behind the glass counter trying to sidestep out of the way, but they kept training the guns on him.

She saw Bill Pearl, a particularly grubby man who for some reason had always had a thing for her and usually spent a good deal of his wages visiting her in the saloon. He was weighing a pistol in his hand. Thomas Felton was with them too, an ex-boxer who now was a ref for the fights sometimes held on the outskirts of Farlow. He was looking into the breach of a Winchester. Greg Jackson was swiping the air with a big brand new bowie knife. And Calgary, a miner and mule skinner, was pointing a pistol at his own eyeball and inspecting the barrel.

She'd serviced almost every one of Manito's men at least once, and didn't like a one. They were bad news. And they looked like they were getting ready to fight a war.

She had been into a few saloons across the street and asked around, but nobody seemed to know anything about any new girl coming into town.

She knew most of these men on a first-hand basis, if all the same grudgingly, but thought she might as well see what they were up to.

She stepped in the doorway and leaned against one side of the frame.

"Howdy, Bill," she said.

Bill Pearl looked up from the breach of the Winchester he was looking at now. There was a cigar clenched in his teeth.

"Why, howdy, Glory."

"Boys," she said.

"Miss Glorietta."

They lowered their guns for a moment and Mister Jackson looked mighty relieved not to have the Sharps rifle and all the pistols trained at him.

"What you boys up to?" she asked curiously, giving them the once-over. "You plannin' another Civil War?"

"Why, no, Glory," Bill said. "Fact is, some gambler kilt Mister Manito's brother and stoled his winnings. An ace fell out of his sleeve and he shot him."

That wasn't so surprising. Mister Manito's brother was bound to get shot sooner or later, and Glorietta had always thought it would be the former rather than the latter. She supposed it was theoretically possible that someone could have cheated in a card game against *him*, but knew it wasn't likely. He was a well-known cardsharp, and usually he only played new faces in town because of it – hanging around the saloons and preying on them, scanning for new faces and looking for the chance to make his move. No one local dared bother him – because of his brother Manito – nor spread any warning to others.

In a way she was glad he was dead, for he had once promised he would take her on a buggy ride, and she had thought – if all the same briefly – that he might have been genuine about her, but soon she had discovered otherwise. He had done it only to get as many free prods as he could until she cottoned on, and cottoned on she had. He had even stayed with her for a while, in her room over the saloon – and hadn't had to pay the usual ten dollars.

That had been when he had first come to town; she had been impressed by his skill with cards and, of course, the amount of money he seemed to always be winning, playing unusually high stakes poker games. He'd killed two men since he'd been in Farlow, too, both times over a card dispute.

Bill Hutchinson had been the one to warn her, although she had ignored his warnings at first. Then, one evening, Bandito had come up to the table she was sitting at – waiting and watching the batwing doors as she always did for a better prospect to come waltzing through – and had asked her if she had any money for him to carry on playing and win back his stake.

She had almost given it to him, too, but her better senses had kicked in. And that, for the most part, had been because of Bill's previous, though admittedly ignored, warnings.

Men, on the whole, Glorietta found, were useless things – with the odd exception. And then the exceptions happened to be uninterested or the types who were too shy and had to be coaxed into the whole thing. But the fact remained you couldn't do anything without one – or get anywhere, for that matter.

Even as far back as five years old, she could remember her mother telling her in the wagon train pushing west from Missouri, "You ain't no kinda woman if you ain't got a man."

Glorietta's mother had been extremely proud of her husband, not for succeeding but for finally providing a solution when their family was on the brink of financial destitution, as were so many during Missouri's period of financial panic that led to the great depression. A bill had been passed by a senator in the government and there was free land in the west, rich and fertile, and all you had to do was go to it and stake your claim. Three hundred and twenty acres to single men and six hundred and forty to married men.

And so they had.

Her father had promptly sold their house and wheat farm at a time when wheat was selling for twenty-five cents a bushel when the profit margin only began at fifty cents, and he used the money to buy a wagon and a milk cow and other provisions they would need for the trip.

Only their entire wagon train, a train of eight families headed west for similar reasons, had been burned to the ground on the banks of the Platte River by Comanche Indians. Both her mother and father had been killed, but Glorietta had managed to hide in a prairie dog hole and was later found by members of the wagon train who had fled when the

Indians had attacked, returning to salvage what was left of the blackened and burnt wagons. Indians back then were always burning up perfectly good wagons.

She had made it a priority for the rest of her life to search for a man, the right man, the man of her dreams. But she was starting to believe such a man did not exist, or if he did she had better hurry up and find him – because her looks were failing her. She was always sitting in the saloon and watching the doors these days because her popularity with the men had waned, and the younger girls tended to get what would have once been her eager clients. But it consoled her that their time would come too, when they had to sit and watch the door hopefully.

If she was ever going to have a chance in life, at a man who would take her away from this life, it would have to be now. There was no more waiting.

She realized, then, that she could not be too picky – she had always had a preference for good looks, finding herself particularly attracted to rugged handsomeness; usually that of the more experienced and mature cowboys.

But the fact was, not many men came to Farlow with good intentions. She realized, also, that she could not be so picky as to be put off by such a perfect specimen as the man she had briefly met, Dwight. By his embarrassment and shyness, that is.

Mister Manito's men – men like Bill Pearl and Thomas Felton and Carl Calgary – were the kind of men she had decided to give up on in life; she needed no more experience to warn her away from such men.

She had to have that man, *had* to. His embarrassment aside he looked like an able and reliable man, the kind who could take care of her and pull her through a hard scrape. He–

"Excuse me, missy," a voice said behind her.

She spun around in the doorway, slightly taken by surprise as she had been watching Mister Manito's men testing and trying their weapons.

It was another posse of men; she recognized them at once. They were the men who hung about the Hog's Head saloon, and worked for the Half-breed, another one of the major players in Farlow – only his men were even meaner than Manito's.

She stepped slowly backwards, away from the smile of the man who had addressed her. It was Frank Gunson, a man with an infamous reputation even for Farlow. He had killed a Texas Ranger; shot and hung him. You could tell him over a crowd anywhere in Farlow, for he was the only man who wore a low-crowned black hat with a broad brim, and if he caught another man wearing a similar style of hat he would knock it from their head. He had shot a man once, after he had picked it up and placed it back on his head.

"Why, it's Glory, ain't it?" Frank said. His lips peeled apart in a sly grin, revealing a row of furry yellow teeth, one completely blackened.

She stepped further back into Jackson's Gunsmith, until she bumped into Bill Pearl.

"Billy," Frank said. "What you boys doin' here?"

"We're after a man shot Mister Manito's brother, in Pierce's saloon. Over a card game," he said.

Frank looked around at his boys, that sly smile still on his face.

He said, "Yeah, I heard about that. All of youse to take out one man?"

Bill said, "He's a gun hand. Has gotta be to have beaten Bandito to the draw. They say he didn't even manage to get his gun out of its holster."

"We're after four sons of bitches ourselves," Frank said. "Ain't that right, boys?"

There were obedient nods from several of his men.

"What they do?" Bill asked. He handed the Winchester across the glass counter, to Jackson. "I'll take it," he said to him. "And gimme two boxes of ammo with it. Boys?"

His men started handing the pistols and rifles they had been looking at across the counter for purchase too.

Glorietta had backed against a cabinet containing old ball and cap muskets and pistols, forgotten.

Frank was saying, "They're harassing one of Michael's girls, and one of 'em's tryin' to make off with her. They're travellin' with a nigger."

Glorietta felt a frightful beat in her breast. *They* had been travelling with a nigger, those men who had come into the saloon, with the cowboy Dwight.

"I've already had words with that nigger," Frank was saying. He raised his fist and she noticed that his knuckles were red and raw. "Though I didn't know it was them at the time; they'd just come in. But I'm gonna look forward to killin' 'em, especially that nigger."

"He put his hands in my saddlebag," one of his men remarked.

"Shut up, Dan." Frank said, "What's this man you're after look like?"

"He's an old fart dressed in furs," Bill said. "Looks like he come out of the Rockies."

"Well, there's safety in numbers, boys," Frank said, looking around. "Whyn't we cut a deal? Me and my boys'll help you get your man, and you help us get ours."

"But we only gotta get one, you gotta get four," Bill protested.

"But the one you gotta get's a gun hand. These boys of ours are just reg'lar cowpokes. Some of 'em don't even got guns."

Bill Pearl appeared to consider the proposition.

Glorietta wasn't about to wait – this was her opportunity if ever there was going to be one. It was even better than trying to find the girl they were looking for, which so far she hadn't been able to anyway, and which wouldn't guarantee that they would do anything but thank her.

She could see now how it would all play out. She would find them quickly and warn them that two large posses were coming after them, right now, and that they had to get out of town. These were dangerous men, desperate men, all dead shots – would tell them that whether they were or not. It was true of some of them, at least.

And here was the clincher. She would tell them they had to take her with them, *had* to, or she would be killed for warning them.

It was a perfect plan. All she had to do was execute it.

Frank Gunson had asked Jackson to see a rifle in one of the racks behind the counter and Jackson had handed it to him; the rest of his men had crowded in behind him. It was about twelve or fourteen men altogether, a formidable force.

She saw her opportunity as the men were distracted and dinked out of the door, hoping none of them had noticed.

She rushed down the boardwalk, passing each busy saloon and glancing quickly in, scanning the barroom floors and then continuing on. She dropped into an alley and then jumped back up onto the next boardwalk, and when she passed the next saloon's batwing doors – the slats shot apart several weeks ago during a gambling dispute – she saw them, sitting at a table!

This was it. She took a deep breath, steadied herself, and prepared to push through the broken batwings. She thought about the men in Jackson's Gunsmith, buying guns and ammo and loading up.

One thing was for certain, there wasn't going to be much time.

Lebold said, "Now what do you suppose is taking him so long?"

"Kit was always a little slow," Old Morg admitted. "I hired him on in the first place 'cause I felt sorry for him. He'd take twice as long to skin a hide as anyone else on the plains, even One-armed Sam, but I always tried to keep his spirits up, give him a helpin' hand."

"Didn't nobody give me no helpin' hand," Lebold said.

"Well, I don't suspect you needed it."

"Maybe," Lebold said. "But I coulda used one, just the same."

"Kit on the other hand needed one," Old Morg said. "When I found him he was pitching hay in a livery, and that pitchfork stood taller than he did. I stabled my horse and hired him on."

"First work I did was rounding up steers," Dwight remarked.

"I did chute branding," Lebold said. "It was much easier than regular branding. A lot of young hands were doing it, before they learned how to bulldog tie a steer and brand it out in the open."

"I done chute branding, too" Dwight added.

"What about you, Jeb?" Old Morg asked.

Jeb looked surprised to be asked a question.

"I done fought for my freedom in the Civil War."

"Is that so?" Old Morg said. "Where'd you come from?"

"I was solt on a block in New Orleans."

Jeb Rawlins pronounced it "New Orlins".

"Yeah, but where'd you come from before that?" Lebold said. "You sure didn't come from here."

Jeb's eyes clouded over with pain. After a moment he said, "When I was jes a boy 'nother tribe come to our village, kilt our chillun an' olders, stole us and we was solt in chains to the A-rabs. Stacked us in under them decks like we was spoons in a rack, layers and layers of us on top each other. When they offloaded us in 'Merica, quarter of us had drownded in the… in the mess and urine that done run down from the decks above while we was at sea."

"I'm mighty sorry to hear that, Jeb," Lebold said, guiltily, for he had always been against the abolitionists after they had won the war, taking up the cry in Texas and carrying the dispute right into the Kansas cowtowns, where there were always plenty of Yanks to get in a scrape with over it.

But Old Morg said, "There ain't no easy roads to America, and you got here on one of 'em. Although I'll allow it was against your will. But there's many who don't make it, either way. Ain't no easy roads to America. In fact, when I come down from the mountains—"

Just then a flustered female voice behind them said, "Oh, am I glad I found you boys!"

Old Morg looked up, caught in mid-sentence. Lebold turned in his seat, at first not realizing who it was. Dwight half-turned on his chair, and then slowly turned red in the face.

The woman they had met in the first saloon they had walked into was standing behind them, looking panicky and out of breath. The batwing doors were swinging back and forth behind her.

"Did you find the girl?" Lebold asked, frowning.

"No, but you boys've got to get out of town, right now – there's men coming."

Lebold exchanged confused glances with Dwight and Jeb.

"What men?" he asked, when he looked back.

"They're in Jackson's Gunsmith right now, about twenty of them, loading up and getting ready to shoot all of you boys dead. Two posses of them combined."

"That just don't make no sense," Dwight said.

"They're comin', right now – I seen 'em," she insisted.

"How'd you know it's us they're comin' for?" Lebold asked her.

"They said they was after four men travelling with a negro."

That convinced Lebold enough to clutch a hold of his rifle, which was leaning up against the empty chair Kit had sat in.

Glorietta looked at Old Morg. "And they mentioned an old man too. Did you shoot Mister Manito's brother by any chance?"

"He was cheatin' at cards," Old Morg maintained.

Glorrietta dashed to the saloon doors and peeped out, returning quickly. Mostly she addressed Dwight, "You've gotta go, they're comin' right now down the walk."

Old Morg grabbed up his big Henry rifle, also leaning next to him against the table. "Why I ain't had a good gunfight since my Dodge City days," he said, "I ain't gonna miss this for the world."

"They're going to kill me too," the woman added breathlessly.

"Why're they gonna kill you?" Lebold said.

"Why, for tellin' youse, of course. These are desperate men, boys; every one of them's a sure shot."

"We'd best go get Kit," Lebold suggested. "Maybe we can all dink out back."

"Well I'm stayin'," Old Morg said stubbornly.

"You're just gonna get yourself kilt, old man," Lebold said.

"Why, I ain't been killed in several decades. I don't see why I'd get kilt now."

"Suit yourself," Lebold said. "Jeb, Dwight, let's g–"

Suddenly there were a dozen hollow thuds on the boardwalk outside, accompanied by the jingle of spurs.

The batwing doors creaked open.

They flapped back and forth as more than a dozen men flooded right in through them, holding rifles and pistols at the ready, even knives.

Glorietta had not counted on that – for she had not really seen anyone coming along the boardwalk when she had peeked out of the saloon – and she was caught at the table red-handed with the rest of them. She looked at Frank fearfully, who had come through the batwing doors first. He spat from the side of his mouth, and a long streak of brown spit splattered across the floor.

Lebold found that he was up and standing, but didn't remember doing so. His hands were held out at his sides, frozen.

The saloon had gone silent.

Slowly, Dwight raised his hands. Lebold and Jeb began to raise them too. Old Morg merely remained seated, hand frozen on his Henry.

"Well, well, well," Frank said, to Glorietta it seemed. "What do we have here?"

"I was just comin' to find 'em for you, Frank. Honest I was. I had a hunch where they were, so I came to check. Bill?" she said, in a pleading voice. "Didn't I, Bill?"

She thought Bill might lie for her, since he had always been fond of her, for even now he still visited her whenever he collected his pay.

Bill Pearl stood off to one side, next to Carl Calgary and Thomas Felton, clutching the Winchester whose breach he had been inspecting earlier in Jackson's Gunsmith.

"What you doing here, Glory?" he asked instead, frowning.

"Why, Bill, I was just–"

"She was just warnin' 'em we was comin', that's what she was just doin'," Frank said, smiling that sly, sadistic smile of his again. "I reckon we'll just treat her like she's with 'em."

He thumbed back the hammer of his big pistol, which clicked into place loudly in the silence. Several pistol hammers followed its lead and clicked into place in his men's hands.

They were caught off-guard, Lebold realized, and there was nothing they could do. Their rifles and pistols were within hands' reach, but they had the jump on them. One move and they were leaving God's Creation in a hurry.

He stared at the dark hole of the barrel of a pistol pointed right at his stomach, sitting smugly in the hand of the man who had punched Jeb against the water barrel. Lebold wished he had shot him now, although a gunfight would likely have ensued even then – but at least they would have had the jump on *them*, and not the other way around.

"I'm gonna shoot the cripple first," Frank said to his men out the corner of his mouth. He raised the pistol up from Lebold's stomach to his chest.

Lebold saw his finger tighten on the trigger, beginning to squeeze it home. He flinched and waited for the bullet to come. Kit had said you felt the bullet before you heard the blast. He squinted his eyes shut, and waited for–

Suddenly there was a shotgun blast; a big, loud, deafening noise which filled the saloon and rattled the glasses and bottles on the bar shelves in its wake.

The blast stunned all of them; attention was suddenly shifted to the railing above the bar, from which the blast had come.

Kit was falling through the air. The entire railing was hanging in splintered and grapeshot-shattered tatters.

Kit fell through the air, headed head first for a fully occupied card table of frozen players below.

The entire saloon, as one man – outlaws included – stared and watched incredulously.

Kit hit the card table head first, crumpling the crown of his hat in; then his shoulders struck as his neck folded beneath him, followed by his back and behind. He landed in a kind of half-somersault, stopped midway by the obstruction. The table legs snapped and blew out beneath him, the table top itself clapping flat to the floor as it collapsed with the weight of Kit suddenly coming down on top of it. Poker chips, playing cards and change flew into the air and spun and rattled on the floorboards around them; beer sloshed up out of the mugs resting on the table top and then the mugs themselves were launched into the air, landing on the floor and bursting in frothy explosions of glass.

The card players found themselves sitting on their chairs around the broken wreckage, still holding up their hands of cards, frozen.

Lebold looked up from the crumpled form of Kit and examined the shattered wooden railing over which he had suddenly come, now torn away by what must have been nothing less than a double-barrelled blast of grapeshot.

Wood chips and splinters and pieces of railing still rained down onto Kit and the collapsed card table below.

The saloon still stood frozen.

Then a big woman came bounding out of the hallway – a *big* woman; bigger than any mule skinner or buffalo hunter that ever lived. She cracked the breach of a smoking shotgun in half and fed two fat blue shotgun shells back into the barrels, after plucking out and casting aside a spent pair of smoking shells.

Now she flicked the shotgun upwards with her wrist, like an expert gunman, and clicked the barrel shut, still bounding towards what was left of the railing.

Lebold could hardly credit his own eyes – neither could anyone else, for that matter.

The big woman was thumbing back the heavy double hammers with one thumb, and then she held and aimed the shotgun down at the card players, who were now all looking up, terrified.

When they saw the big black mouths of the shotgun barrels pointing down at them they dropped their cards into their laps and scattered. One grabbed the seat of his chair and quickly rocked it to one side, tipping it over. He fell shoulder-first to the floor and spilled out of the chair, army-crawling away and huddling under the nearest table.

She was going to shoot Kit!

Lebold wasn't sure what to do, just that he had to do *some*thing. The situation could be turned to their advantage or wasted; it would otherwise have been a perfect diversion to capitalize on, if Kit hadn't been about to get peppered with two barrels of grapeshot.

Lebold quickly glanced at Jeb, Dwight, and the old man – who recognized his intentions.

Lebold nodded once, with his eyes, and then raised his rifle to his shoulder and took aim quickly, bringing the foresight and rear sight into alignment, and then adjusting the focus of his one open eye to the large figure of the woman training the shotgun down at Kit from the upper landing.

He curled his finger around the trigger and squeezed.

There was a flat crack and a flash from his rifle.

And then the saloon broke into chaos.

Jeb launched himself at the nearest man, swinging his rifle up by the barrel. The thick wooden stock connected with the man's teeth and knocked several of them into the air. Blood spurted from the man's mouth like water out of a whale spout.

At the same time Dwight picked one of the chairs up at the table by its back and swung it through the air, knocking the pistol out of Frank's hand, which went off with a loud bang before it clunked onto the floor.

He threw the chair at the disarmed man and dived for the gun on the floor. Frank drew a blade and set to beat him to it, but Jeb kicked it from his hand and it went sliding across the floor.

Bullets zipped and whined through the air around them.

Old Morg pulled a big heavy pistol from his belt and fanned it, hammering the back of the gun with the hard bony palm of his hand.

A bullet caught Bill Pearl in the leg and kicked it out from under him.

Thomas Felton caught one of Old Morg's wild slugs in his shoulder, and it spun him around into the batwings. He grabbed onto the top of one of them and hung there, until the top hinge blew out under his weight and he dropped onto the floor, the battered batwing door hanging askew, before tearing away and falling on top of him.

Men dived for cover in several different directions simultaneously, overturning tables and chairs and quickly taking cover. One dived straight back out of the saloon via the nearest window, which crashed around him and sprinkled out onto the boardwalk.

The air was suddenly filled with a new volley of gunfire, pops and cracks and echoing bangs from various high-calibre pistols and rifles.

Lebold had dived under a table himself after taking a shot up at the woman, and when he crawled out the other side to see and he looked up, he saw that the slug had hit her square in the chest.

She teetered on the edge. Her eyes had widened in disbelief, and her mouth was opened in an amazed O and was pouting at the sides. She let go of the shotgun and clutched at her chest.

It fell end over end through the air and then landed butt first against Kit's unconscious head with a *clonk*, which surprisingly woke him and made him come to his senses. He was shaking his head from side to side and struggling to push himself up onto his hands and knees.

"Kit!" Lebold yelled. "Kit, look out! Above you!"

Kit looked up, rubbing his head.

For a moment Lebold thought the woman was going to fall backwards, safely onto the landing, but then she teetered dangerously on the spot, like a ladder kicked away from a wall with a workman balancing at the top rung, and fell forward.

She fell through the air with the weight of an anvil, still clutching her chest.

"Holy shi–"

Kit grabbed the shotgun up and rolled out of the way, coming to a dizzy stop against the bar.

There was a rending *bang* as the fat woman landed on the broken table top, and then a splintering *crash* as the floorboards gave way beneath her and she disappeared through the floor, landing on the bare earth under the raised saloon.

Kit watched from where he lay against the bar, stunned at how close he had come to being killed. A falling fat woman had for a moment been all there was between him and eternity.

Suddenly the table was yanked away above Lebold, and crashed over onto its side. Frank was standing there, enraged. He reached down for Lebold but Lebold dropped to his belly and turned over onto his back. He tried to raise his rifle and fire, but Frank stomped a boot down onto the barrel and it slammed into his chest, pinning it to his body.

He kicked it away from Lebold, and then pulled another knife and tried to bury it in his heart, the blade already bloody. Lebold clutched hold of Frank's wrists as he pressed down on top of him, the point of the knife straining an inch from his pumping heart.

"I tolt you I was gonna kill you first, cripple!"

Kit wanted to fire, but all he had in his hands was the loaded and cocked double barrel shotgun. He had been clutching his gun belt in his hands as he had gone over the railing, and unfortunately it had disappeared under the saloon along with the section of floor and the broken table top.

He was still winded terrifically and catching his breath, not to mention knocked a little senseless.

A bullet *thunked* into the wood at the base of the bar, right by Kit's head, and he realized he had to get behind it, and in a hurry. He jumped up to his feet and rolled over the bartop, taking the shotgun with him.

Before he even landed on the other side bottles began to kick and explode on the shelves above, raining him down with glass. A broken bottle neck landed by his hand and exploded. He felt the sharp sting of glass cuts.

Liquor was glugging all about him, running in rivulets down from the shelves and spattering on the floorboards.

More bullets whacked into the shelving and shattered glass. Packages of cigars and tobacco exploded and showered down.

Then there was a loud *whoomph*, and suddenly the shelves were on fire.

A Henry rifle roared from behind a table in the saloon, catching one of Frank's men who had sprung up from behind another toppled table and had fanned his pistol at Kit as he leapt and rolled over the bar.

The slug caught him in the eyeball and blew the back of his head out against the window behind him, and then with another roar from the rifle he was thrown back against the bloody glass itself, crashing through it backwards and spilling out onto the boardwalk, where innocent bystanders were desperately running for cover.

Across the street, men, women and children hid behind barrels, carts and carriages; some had even dropped to the mud and crawled for cover under boardwalks.

A man lay dead in the street, after catching a stray bullet in the stomach. A horse lay on the mud under one of the hitch rails, whinnying and kicking painfully at the mud: it had been shot in the neck and was bleeding into the street.

People were fleeing the town itself, racing out onto the open prairie; some afoot, others on horses. There were whips and cracks as mule teams were sent galloping, pulling their wagons through the thick mud.

Pistol cracks and rifle shots still rang out from the saloon.

Lebold had managed to kick Frank in the groin, a move which caused them both considerable pain, as Lebold had used his wounded leg to groin him.

Frank's eyes rolled into his head as he gasped at the pain; he dropped the knife and clutched at his groin. Lebold rolled over and picked up his rifle.

Bullets zipped and ripped through the air over his head. He decided to make a dash for the burning bar and dive over it.

He got up and ran, keeping low, slugs whistling past his head.

Meanwhile Jeb was busy wrestling Thomas Felton for possession of a rifle, over in one corner; Jeb clutched the rifle long ways against his own chest as Tom Felton pushed it against him and drove him back, and then yanked it back toward himself, trying to tear it from Jeb's grasp.

Instead Jeb turned the grip of his hand clutching the barrel so that it was palm upwards, and push-turned the rifle until it was vertical between the two of them. And then he pulled the top of the rifle toward him like a leaver.

The butt swung up beneath Tom Felton and cracked him hard under the chin; his teeth flew into the air in a scarlet spray of blood, knocking him back and sending his arms pinwheeling.

Jeb swung the rifle back the right way round and fired, stepping forward and yanking the big trigger guard open and shut.

Spent bullet casings rattled hollowly across the floorboards, and Thomas Felton was riddled with bullets. Several ragged holes ripped into his flannel shirt, and one caught him high in the cheek, exiting the back of his head in a brief mist of red.

He dropped to the floor lack a sack of sand, dead.

Some of the gunmen were now scattering for the street. A bullet zipped past Jeb and buried itself into a wall plank with a *thud*. He ducked and dropped behind an overturned table. Several bullets instantly thudded into the table top. He stared at a hissing slug protruding from beneath the table. It had almost made it through. Blackened splinters flowered around it.

The fire had grown now; at first it had sooted and blackened the landing above, but now it was burning it. The railing had caught alight and was blazing right along its entire length to where it turned and followed down one side of the stairs. The fire rippled and flapped like an Indian blanket.

Lebold had flown over the bar top and landed on top of Kit in a tangle of limbs. The situation was getting well-nigh hot behind the bar, and deciding to take cover behind it any longer was chancy. Lebold regretted ever diving over it.

He said, "Kit, use that shotgun and fire at the tables they're hiding behind!"

Kit nodded and got to his knees. He half-stood and peeped carefully over the bar top.

"I'll give you some covering fire," Lebold added.

He raised and began to fire his rifle into the room, loading and cocking, firing and reloading.

From where he was crouched, peeping over the bar, Kit saw a hand raised over the round top of an overturned table over by one of the broken windows. A pistol protruded from it and was firing blindly at the bar. Beer mugs and glasses exploded behind them.

"Fire one barrel at a time," Lebold yelled from the corner of his mouth.

Kit pointed the shotgun at the overturned table and pulled the first trigger.

The left barrel exploded, driving the wooden stock hard into his shoulder.

The table across the room was torn into a thousand pieces, peppered so heavily by the shotgun blast it split in two. Kit saw the man who had been hiding behind it clutching at himself on the floor; his shirt was shredded and blood was pooling out around him. One of his boots kicked and jerked.

Kit trained the other barrel on another table, behind which two men were ducking and firing. He squeezed the trigger.

The table top was obliterated, so devastating was the blast. Grapeshot tore through the thin wood and the men behind it, slashing and lacerating them. They fell and clutched at themselves, gargling mouthfuls of blood, and then lay still.

Then they saw Old Morg crouch over Frank, who was still clutching at his aching balls from Lebold's well-placed kick. Old Morg had picked his knife off the floor.

He scalped him.

"My Lord," Lebold said, and looked sidelong at Kit.

Frank tried to clutch at his hair and hold it onto his head as Morg drew the knife across his forehead and began to rip it free from his skull, opening a large red sinuous flap, but he failed miserably.

Morg tore the hairy flap free and tucked it, bleeding, into a fold in his furs.

The man was screaming, a shrill shriek that scared the remaining men straight out of the saloon. They crashed through the batwings and broken windows and jumped off the boardwalk and landed in the muddy street, bounding across it and diving through the windows and doors of the saloon opposite.

Kit heard alarmed footfalls on the floorboards above, and he and Lebold saw several half-dressed women and cowboys, clutching their duds in an attempt to keep them up without their belts, come bounding down the stairs: whores and their customers.

They stepped over the dead and fled the saloon, running out into the street.

Lebold and Kit slowly straightened up.

The saloon was a wreck.

"Anybody hurt?" Lebold called.

"I'm fine as paint," Old Morg said, and slit Frank Gunson's throat as methodically as if skinning a deer. He gargled briefly and died. "That'll teach you, sonny," Morg said. "Normally I ain't gratuitous, but I saw you try to carve up one of these bright boys and it sticks in my craw."

Kit saw that Jeb was standing up from where he had been crouched behind a table turned on its side.

He glanced at Lebold.

"Where's Dwight?" he said.

Old Morg looked up. "I saw him get hisself knifed and shot."

"Jesus," Lebold said.

Old Morg grabbed the only table in the room still standing and crashed it onto its side.

Dwight lay wounded beneath it. There was a long diagonal slash in his shirt, and several knife holes. Strangely, he also appeared to have been peppered by grapeshot.

He wasn't the only one beneath the table. Glorietta was crouched over him, grabbing at his slashed shirt and shaking him, blubbing for some reason, teardrops falling into Dwight's strained face.

Morg crouched next to him. "I reckon he'll live if he's a mind to," he said. "I've seen a man survive a bear attack on the Platte looked a sight worse than this."

Then they heard the screams for help, half muffled by the crackle of the fire that engulfed the upper landing. They heard the banging, as of a fist being hammered against a wooden door.

"Sounds like there's a woman stuck up there," Lebold said.

Kit dropped the shotgun and leapt over the bar, rushing to the end of it and bounding up the stairs.

"I'll get her," he called back.

When he came to the top of the steps the landing was awash with fire. Thick smoke pooled and flowed across the ceiling. Fire rippled over the wooden walls and had blackened two frames hung there. One fell and clapped to the floor in two pieces.

He prepared to charge the fire, and took a deep breath...

Magdalena had no idea what was going on, just that something huge was happening. At first there had been a huge blast, like a cannon being fired. It had been shortly followed by a single rifle crack, and then a barrage of gunfire had ensued. She could hear tables crashing onto their sides and glass popping and breaking, yells and screams and dying shrieks.

Once again, she had awoken to the madness. After the disgusting man had had his way with her and left, locking the door, she had fallen into a deep and exasperated sleep, so tired had she been from all the tension and hard travelling.

Now she felt a new tension. It was a point of regret to be awake. She felt if she could just somehow sleep for the rest of her life, it might be okay. Sleep seemed to be the only thing that could afford her any comfort now.

There were muffled, if all the same alarmed, yells from the neighbouring rooms, and she could hear doors flying open and boots and bare feet hammering along the floorboards and down the stairs: people leaving the upper hallway in a hurry.

What was happening?

Soon the rate of gunfire slowed, and then she heard rapid rifle shots, followed by two big blasts, somewhat like the first one she had heard. A shotgun, maybe.

Then she smelt smoke. She stepped away from the door and looked down at her feet. Thick, dark smoke was filtering in.

Oh my God, she thought.

Then it clicked in her head. It was the Texas Rangers! They were fighting a battle downstairs with her captors!

She began to bang a fist hard against the door and cry for help.

"Help! Somebody help me! I'm stuck!"

She tried to kick the bottom of the door, which produced a somewhat louder bang, but hurt her toes.

"Hello?" said a muffled voice.

"Hello?" Magdalena said. "Help me! I'm stuck in here! *Help*!"

"Okay, step back from the door!" the voice called.

Magdalena walked back until she felt the cornshuck mattress under her feet.

The door shuddered against the frame, several times, though didn't budge.

Then the muffled voice said, "I can't get it open."

Magdalena sighed. What kind of incompetent moron was this? It sounded like a man. Surely he should have been strong enough to kick open a door?

The door began to shudder in the frame again. Then the handle began to rattle, as if he was trying to see if he could just open it. The idiot.

She heard him coughing and choking.

"I can't get it open!" the voice cried again.

This was unbelievable. She hoped this wasn't one of the famed Texas Rangers.

"Is there a window in there?" the voice was saying now.

"Yes," she replied, flustered.

"Do you have a mattress?"

"Yes!"

"Break the window and throw it out. I'm gonna go around and... and... and make sure it's in the right spot."

Terrific, Magdalena thought. She was going to have to jump out of a two-storey window, down onto a cornshuck mattress.

Thick black smoke wafted under the door, and some of it caught in her throat, causing her to cough.

Magdalena strained to pick the mattress off the floor, and then used it to ram against the glass of the window.

It broke from the frame and fell, tinkling two storeys below. She moved the end of the mattress around to clear the edges of the frame and then dropped it onto the floor in the room, stepped over it and looked out.

It was the back of the building, and the ground two storeys below was mostly composed of mud with a few hopeless tufts of dying grass here and there.

She saw a boy in a hat with a bullet hole in it looking up at her – at least he looked like a boy, if all the same a big one. He was waving a hand at her.

"Throw the mattress down," he called up.

She disappeared back into the window and picked the mattress up at one end, ramming it out and letting go. Down it went.

When she looked out the window again she saw that it had landed on him and he was pulling his hat out from underneath it, now flat and covered in mud. She saw him slap it against the side of his riding trousers and then poke a fist into it. Then he placed it back on his head. He kicked the mattress into a better position for her to fall on and looked up.

"Jump!" he called. "It's okay, you can do it!"

"Move it more to the left!" she cried. It didn't look positioned properly.

"No, it's in the right place. Jump!"

"It's too far over to the right," she called down.

"Trust me, it's right – jump! You can do it!"

Yes, she found she could. However incompetent he was, or at least so far had appeared, he was here to rescue her. This was her one way out. She was going home, away from this filth, and there was no time to hesitate.

She looked back into the room briefly – she saw that the smoke coming under the door was incredibly thick now; it even leaked through the keyhole – and then she half-climbed out of the window.

Balancing on the frame, she suddenly lost her resolve, but when she tried to turn around and climb back in she slipped, and the next thing she knew her feet were dangling in the air and she was hanging down the side of the building.

She looked down past her shoulder desperately, and saw that the boy was kicking the mattress closer to the side of the building for her to land on.

"Just drop!" he said. "Just let go and drop!"

She didn't have to; one by one her fingers gave way, and then suddenly she was falling.

She landed in the mud.

God Dog turned in the saddle, and looked back.

A gigantic ball of smoke was palling into the sky over the town, a sight that surprised him. He had heard the distant pops and cracks of gunfire, knowing what it meant.

The deal he had made with the Half-breed was underway. He was to have his men kill the riders in pursuit of him.

An hour later he looked back again, and saw that the pall of smoke had grown into a huge mushroom-like formation that now towered on the horizon. The entire town must have been burning down, the buildings catching successively alight, for it to have been that big.

He rode only one horse now; he had sold his horses to a livery stable, and now – together with the takings from the girl – he had a substantial sum. It was tucked into his saddlebags, and it brought him great satisfaction. He had traded the first girl for the horses, and those for cash money, and he had sold the second girl for a high sum. He was able to convert both the girls into cash money, and have his followers taken care of for a fee.

He was satisfied with the outcome. Now he would return to the Palo Duro; he thought he would at least stay for a while with Spotted Eagle's clan, if they had not left for the reservations already. He would lay low for a while, and then leave to spend his money; he would buy food and whiskey, new weapons for capturing and killing, invest in new items for trade.

Things were looking up.

God Dog had not been impressed by the Half-breed, *or* his men, most of whom had been in his office when he had entered to collect his payment. He had told the Half-breed he had no intention of staying, but the Half-breed had insisted. Since it had been late and he was tired from travelling and having to deal with the white woman, after collecting his money and securing the deal that would deliver death to his pursuers he had taken a room in the back of the saloon.

He had not slept well in the enclosed room, preferring the open sky, and he had left early, before light, taking his horses down to the livery to sell and keeping one to leave on. It was the best horse of the bunch, one of the stolen ones he had gotten from his Comanche and Kiowa brothers in the Palo Duro – the one Big Bear had ridden.

Suddenly his horse threw him – just as he was thinking what a fine mare it was.

He landed hard on his back, and spent several minutes catching his breath. In the meantime the mare was hopping along skittishly, one of its front legs wounded.

It confused him, for he had not felt the horse step into a hole.

Finally he got up onto his hands and knees and then managed to stand. He took a few steps forward and then spotted it in the grass.

A rattlesnake.

He drew his pistol fast and fired it, and then fired it again.

The first shot broke its rattler off, severing it instantly from the tail of the snake. The second bullet ripped into its scaled skin, and blew blood and thin brittle-looking bones into the ground. They looked like the kind of small bones found inside a fish.

Surprisingly, the rattlesnake was still alive, although it could no longer slither along and was coiling back in on itself.

He stomped the heel of his boot onto its flat head, and ground it into the dirt like a cigar until the snake was finally dead.

Anger boiled inside him, for now he was in a spot. He managed to get hold of the mare's reins and pull it to a stop. When he checked its foreleg he saw the bleeding bite mark in its hairy flesh.

He looked back at the town, still burning far in the distance. He could just make out little figures fleeing out onto the plains, some riders not stopping to turn back and watch but continuing to ride, leaving the town completely.

He knew the horse would not live, but also that he would have to ride it as far as he could until it did die.

He jumped up into the saddle and spurred it hard, pushing it as hard as he had ever pushed any horse – even to get to water on the Llano.

He managed to get about an hour more out of it, but by that time, despite spurring it so hard it caused him to become out of breath, it merely walked along slowly, not even able to trot. Finally it came to a stop, about twenty miles from the Canadian River, and hung its head in defeat.

When God Dog dismounted it fell to its knees, and then pitched over onto its side. He began to kick it violently in the belly with the sharp tips of his boots, a final measure he had used on many over-ridden horses in the past; sometimes if you kicked them hard enough, you could get a few more miles out of them.

But as he became breathless again from the kicking, he realized this one was done.

He pulled his saddle from it and unbuckled his saddlebags and scabbard. Then he slit its jugular and continued on, walking.

Hopefully he would come across a lone rider or find a herd and could sneak one of their horses out.

But he saw nothing in every direction he looked but the empty, unvarying plains.

Mostly he hoped the men in pursuit of him had been killed.

Kit had to help get the horses and other livestock out from the livery.

The slope of its roof had caught alight along with the roofs of several other buildings on the same side as the saloon, which had now, for the most part, collapsed in on itself. When they had rushed to get their horses from the livery where they had left them, the owner was the only worker who hadn't left for the prairie, and they helped him to get his frightened livestock out of the stables and stalls. He also had several pigs and some goats in a partitioned enclosure.

The only thing they could do was turn the horses loose and slap their rumps to get them to run out of the town.

When Kit had picked the girl out of the mud, he had done so only to discover that she had badly sprained her ankle and couldn't put any weight on it. He had draped one of her arms over his shoulders and helped her to hop-walk around the building.

When they came out of the alley, Old Morg, Lebold and Jeb were standing at a safe distance in the middle of the muddy street, and watching the saloon burn. Licks of fire had blown out the front windows two storeys up, and were flapping and fluttering like curtains in the wind.

Kit saw the woman from the other saloon tending to Dwight, tying his arm in a sling with, Kit noticed, Lebold's bandana.

It was only once Kit reached them and turned, himself, to watch, that anyone spoke.

"Looks like she's gonna burn right to the ground," Old Morg said matter-of-factly, watching the flames, mesmerised by them.

"We thought you was in there for a moment, Kit," Lebold said.

"I was," Kit said. "But I couldn't get her door open; she had to jump out the window."

At that Lebold turned around to have a look at her.

The girl seemed terrified, on edge, nervous to be out in the open. She blinked constantly and looked away from him as he looked her over.

"Is she..."

"It's her," Kit said.

Kit had known it was her the moment she looked out of the window; that hair of hers was unmistakable, long and blond and curled. And after having looked at the photograph of her every night and at every opportunity he had, there was no mistaking her, even though she was older than in the photograph. Older, although not much older.

Her cheeks were gaunt and she looked as if she had not eaten at all since she had been taken. Her hair was greasy and had particles of sand and other muck in it. And her dress was ripped and torn and muddy and stained.

Kit had noticed the crusts of dried blood on her ankles, and the big grazes on both her elbows and knees.

She hadn't said anything since crying out for help and dangling over the side of the saloon.

Soon they saw that both the buildings on either side of the saloon had caught alight.

"Looks like this whole side of the street's gonna go up," Old Morg remarked, holding his Henry rifle in one hand.

Dwight was on his feet, his arm now in the sling, and he was looking the worse for wear. One of his eyebrows had split open and was bleeding into his eye and onto his cheek.

"How you doin', Dwight?" Kit asked him.

"He's doin' just fine," the woman tending to him replied in his place. "He's just a bit beat up, is all."

Dwight looked too weak to comment or protest, and she dabbed a white handkerchief on her tongue and began to wipe at his split eyebrow. He winced and jerked his head away, and she apologized for hurting him, but continued anyway.

Lebold said, "Uh-oh! We better go get our horses, before they're all burnt alive!"

Kit glanced in the direction of the livery and saw that the fire had spread along the rooftops and then onto the thatched roof of the building next to the livery barn, which had fired up so fast it had sent burning swaths of hay into the air and onto the roof of the livery, now burning up.

"Let's go!" Lebold said urgently.

And now Kit was clearing the livery of horses, pulling open the stalls and leading the horses out, then slapping their rumps. Lebold assisted him, first releasing the goats and then the pigs.

"Go on, git!" he shouted, kicking at a shoat. "Git on outta here or you're gonna be wasted bacon. Git!"

The pigs grunted and whined as he kicked at them, and left the barn in a little comical-looking line, single file.

They ran off down the main street squealing and out onto the open prairie.

The owner of the livery was looking for a key to a chain wrapped around the handle of a stall door. A horse bucked and kicked within it.

He tried an ill-fitting key in the padlock and then shouted from the corner of his mouth.

"You boys get out of here! When I let this horse loose it's gonna buck and kick like a devil – it ain't broke."

They led their own horses out into the bright sunlight.

On their way out, the owner muttered under his breath. "I *told* you boys not to take that nigger to town."

Old Morg was standing next to the girl who had been taken by God Dog, watching her closely to make sure she didn't fall – she looked about to topple over at any moment.

When Kit walked up leading the horses, Old Morg said, "She can ride in my wagon. It's in a livery next to a saloon at the other end of town."

"You've got a wagon?" Kit said.

"Well of course I do. It's my home on wheels. Take these lot out onto the prairie and I'll take her and put her in the wagon. She ain't in no shape to ride. Be with you in a moment."

Kit looked at the tired and weary girl, who looked away as soon as his eyes met hers, as though scared he might see something she didn't want him to.

"Well, alright," Kit said reluctantly.

Lebold put a foot to a stirrup and mounted. Jeb helped Kit get Dwight into the saddle of the horse they themselves had ridden into Farlow. Jeb handed the rein into his untied hand.

"We'll catch you boys up," Kit said. "We'll walk."

Glorietta went with them as they followed the two men trotting ahead on the horses.

Behind them, the town of Farlow – on one side anyway – was busy collapsing plank by burning plank and falling to the ground.

"Pardon the bones," the old man said.

Magdalena stood behind the canvas-covered wagon, staring in at the piles of powdery white bones.

"Well go on now, missy, they won't bite ya – not any more, anyway. My name's Morgan, by the way. You can call me Morg or Old Morg – everyone else seems to."

He made a stirrup by interlacing his fingers and she stepped a foot into the hard, leathery palms of his hands.

Bones rattled away under her feet and she almost lost balance and fell.

"Best set down, missy. My mules're apt to throw you out the wagon if you try to stand while I whip 'em."

She sat down on the bones obediently. She immediately took a liking to the old man, though didn't dare talk to him. She felt she couldn't. She could happily have remained mute all the rest of her days if it meant she would never have to tell anyone what had happened to her.

The other men frightened her, on the other hand, even though they didn't seem particularly bad – compared to the ones she had encountered, anyway, in the recent past. She liked the youngest one least, the one who had draped her over his shoulders – after causing her to sprain her ankle, so that now it was puffed and swollen. But that wasn't why; already he seemed to look at her expectantly, as if he expected something of her.

The other two men and the black man had just looked at her with relief. The one with the wounded leg somehow seemed to know her, or at least of her. He had asked the one who had misplaced the mattress in the mud, "Is it her?" or something.

She realized, of course, that these men were no Texas Rangers

– certainly the youngest one was not. He was as big as a man, yet had the face of a boy, a boy just beginning to show signs of stubble and hair growth.

She hadn't liked one look he had given her; each one had seemed charged with nervousness and shyness, coupled with expectation. Although he had supported her weight as she hopped on her one good foot through the mud of the alleyway and the main street, he had acted awkward to have her body touching his; she could tell that. It made her feel that he was yet another man who wanted something from her, or had some sort of underlying issue with himself he hoped she might resolve.

At least that's what she felt from his looks so far.

She watched the old man who had said his name was Morgan pull open a stall in the livery barn they were in and then lead out a mule team after buckling harnesses and bits onto them.

He disappeared around the wagon, and after a moment she heard a creak and the wagon tilted slightly to one side as he climbed it. Then there was the crack of a whip and soon they were in the sunlight.

The bones jumped and jostled around her, and she looked out the back of the wagon as the mules pulled it through the mud.

One side of the town seemed fine, although deserted save for a few store owners afraid of having their shops looted – for she saw mule skinners and miners pillaging some of the abandoned stores, even the ones on fire on the other side. They carried out sacks of feed and farming tools, and one had a big glass jar of candy in either hand and a ghoulish grin on his face.

Soon the town began to fall back, and they rode further out onto the open plains, the wagon wheels moving more firmly now, over hard ground and lush grass.

After a while the wagon stopped, and she heard voices.

It was the old man's she heard clearest.

"You boys who don't got mounts can ride up with me on the wagon."

Then she heard, "No, I don't think you should ride up in back, Kit."

"Why not?" She recognised the voice of the young man who had tried to rescue her – Kit.

"If she's been with Injuns she's been through a hellish ordeal. She ain't gonna want much to do with men for a while, if you get my meaning. I seen girls after they been captured by Indians throw 'emselves in front of a galloping horse."

"Keep your pecker in your duds, is what he means," a voice said bitterly. She recognized the voice as belonging to the man with the lame leg, who had asked if it was her.

"What about *me*?" a shrill female voice said.

Magdalena didn't pay much mind to it; she was relieved not to have to have company, especially not his. She just wanted to be left alone right now, and she was grateful to the old man for being so understanding.

"What *about* you?" she heard the old man say. "Who the hell are you, anyway?"

"My name's Glorietta."

"Since when were you part of our outfit?" the one with the lame leg said. "What do you want with us?"

"I'm scared of Frank's men. Some of them are still alive."

"I reckon they won't bother you none now."

"Quit the yappin'," the old man said. "Get on up on the wagon. I wanta go shoot me a deer or somethin' to eat before the sun cools off."

"I say we turn south and head for a river, and then follow it along to the herds."

"Whatever gets us movin'," the old man said impatiently.

She felt the wagon tilting on both sides as people boarded it.

"Kit, what you doin'?"

"I'm swappin' places with Dwight, Morg; he don't want to ride hard with only he has one hand to use."

"Well, come on up then, Dwight, before there's no space and you have to sit on one of these mules. And don't walk too close to 'em – they bite."

She heard the whip crack and then the wagon was moving again, rattling, bouncing and creaking along. It turned to the south, and soon was rocking steadily back and forth over the open plains.

Magdalena cried; all the emotion she had been holding back burst forth in a flood. It was the relief of being rescued, coupled with the ordeal she had been through, the underserved things that had been done to her. The deaths of her family.

When she looked up from the piles of bones later, water still flooding from her eyes, she saw something that annoyed her.

The one called Kit kept dropping his horse back behind the wagon, and looking in at her. When she caught him at it, he pretended to be inspecting one of the wheels at the back of the wagon.

That is, until the old man admonished him.

"What you doin' back there, Kit? Get on over here up front. You're ridin' slower than these mules, I want you scouting up ahead. Go on now!"

She watched him spur his horse with relief and disappear from sight. She lay back against the bones and closed her eyes, trying to get some sleep. She felt safe in the enclosure of the wagon. Covered but not locked in. The sunlight on the canvas blocked the harshness of the sun but let its warmth filter in.

It felt good, and soon she drifted off to the gentle sway and rock of the wagon.

L ebold had been riding ahead, scouting the plain for something to shoot, but he came galloping back after having been gone for no more than ten minutes.

The wagon was moving slow across the plains, moving even slower than a wagon normally would due not only to the load of bones but all the passengers. Neither Kit nor Lebold had had the patience to keep up with it, but kept it in sight.

When Kit saw Lebold come galloping back he stood in his stirrups; from the look on his face he thought Lebold might be being pursued.

But there was no one in pursuit of him and when he rode up Kit sat back in the saddle.

"I found a dead horse," Lebold said, the horse under him panting and lathered with sweat. "Looks like it's been snakebit."

Kit touched his spurs to his horse's flanks and Lebold turned about and followed, loping alongside him.

Soon Kit saw the buzzards turning in the sky, a sure sign of death on the plains. He saw the dead horse directly under them in the distance, a big, brown blot in the grass.

When they rode up Kit dismounted before his horse even stopped and jumped free of the stirrups.

A buzzard cried a shrill warning overhead.

Lebold got down off his horse and pointed out the bite mark on its foreleg.

"Probably a rattlesnake," he said. "They plague these plains."

"Whose horse do you think this is?" Kit asked.

"You see here? It's been stripped of its saddle, and not long ago – the buzzards ain't yet et much of it."

That was a point; there were only a couple of pecked wounds in its hide and neither one bled, the holes merely red-rimmed. Nor did the animal carcass smell of anything other than horse. In this kind of heat meat turned quick; they all knew that.

Lebold said, "Kit, this horse was headed south right back along the Indian's original tracks, like he's headed back to the cabin on the creek. Or the Duro."

"You think this is God Dog's?"

"I don't think anything. But if it *is* his he's not much farther ahead, and he's on foot with nowhere to hide but a prairie dog hole. It's open plains all the way to the Canadian."

"We may get this bastard yet," he added.

They rode back to the wagon to inform Morg and the boys of their finding. Kit resisted the urge to ride around back and take a look at the girl, but kept looking past the wagon seat to the canvas of the wagon cover, as if he might catch a glimpse of her clean through it.

Which of course he didn't.

"We're gonna ride ahead," Lebold told them. "Kit and I."

Old Morg said, "Well, make sure you got enough ammo, and if you catch him wait for my wagon. I wanta see this Injun hang as much as you do, and I'm sure the girl does too."

It was typical Old Morg, Kit thought, already taking over and telling everybody what to do.

They turned their horses' heads and put spurs to their flanks. They rode so fast across the plains Kit felt cold tears streaming out of his eyes and running back behind his ears into his hair.

They scared the buzzards back into the air as they rode past the dead horse, but soon they returned and settled, only to have to rise again as the wagon pulled up and stopped.

Lebold's horse was racing just ahead of Kit's. He could see now why Lebold favoured it over any other animal, refusing to ride any but his own. It was a fast and durable horse, seldom tiring, and could sprint and maintain a high speed for long distances. It seemed slightly wilder than

Dwight's, too, though Kit knew that slightly wild horses were favoured all over the ranges. If a horse maintained an element of its original nature, it remained defiant and that kept its instincts sharp and its pride up.

The only thing with slightly wild horses was that they were often skittish, and might throw their rider or kick while being mounted. Misty Blue had been the best of both worlds, Kit thought solemnly now. Misty Blue had been the least skittish of all the horses they had trailed with. It was unfortunate that Kit had had to shoot him.

He realized he, too, would like to see the Indian hang – hang for what he had done and all the lives he had cost them; of horses and of men.

Lebold began to slow and Kit eased up on his horse, until they were going at a trot. Lebold was squinting into the distance.

"I see a figure up ahead," he said. "Looks like a man on foot, alright."

If it was, they had him. Kit knew a man on foot against riders was done for. That's why the US Cavalry had been so infamous, for every soldier had been mounted and a fierce force to the Indians. Kit remembered being told by a young buffalo skinner outside of Dodge that the famed US Cavalry had originally been formed because sending troops out against mounted Indians was considered to be suicidal: thus began an entire mounted infantry.

Lebold drew his rifle from its scabbard, and then whacked the barrel hard against his horse again and again to get it to burst into an explosive gallop.

A moment later Kit drew his own and did the same.

The prairie began to blur by beneath them and the figure grew in the distance as they closed the gap. Soon Kit could see, even from his galloping mount, that the figure was heavily laden. He carried a big saddle in one hand and a heavy rifle and scabbard in the other. Saddlebags were hung over one shoulder.

As they closed the last twenty yards Kit saw the Indian spin around and drop his saddle and bags. But Lebold saw this early and fired his rifle twice into the air, and then reined in his horse, training his rifle on the Indian.

"Hold it!" he shouted. "Don't you move, Injun! Or I'll blow you a hole in your stomach."

Kit galloped up and reined in, and then shouldered his rifle and aimed for the Indian's chest.

"I got you covered," he said to Lebold. "You can get down."

Lebold slipped off his horse and grabbed a coil of rope that was hanging from the pommel of his saddle.

He walked slowly towards the Indian with it. The Indian – God Dog – was wearing standard cowboying clothes, but there was no mistaking that face. He still held the rifle scabbard in one hand.

"Drop that rifle and kick it away," Kit shouted from his mount.

God Dog dropped it and did as he said.

Lebold had stopped and was waiting, not wanting to step into Kit's field of fire.

"Now slowly take the pistol out of that holster and drop it," Kit continued. "And drop that scalping knife too."

God Dog slowly reached down and lifted the pistol from his holster with two fingers. He dropped it to the grass. Then he drew a knife from a leather sheath on his belt.

Kit tensed his finger on the trigger, thinking for a moment that the Indian might try to throw it, but he simply let go of it and it stuck, quivering, in the dirt.

Lebold stepped up cautiously and kicked it away. With the side of one boot he sent the pistol skidding off along the grass. Then he drove a fist hard into the Indian's stomach, and dropped him.

Kit swung one leg over his horse and slid off, keeping the rifle trained. He sidestepped to where the pistol lay in the grass and kicked it even further away just to be on the safe side.

Then he stood over God Dog and prodded the muzzle of the rifle into his side.

"One move and you're in a world of pain," Kit told him.

"What other world is there?" the Indian said, to Kit's surprise, and then spat.

Lebold had pulled the Indian's hands behind his back and now tied them tight. With the remaining length he pulled the Indian's feet up and wrapped them several turns, tying and securing them to his hands.

"Okay, Kit, let's get him up."

They yanked God Dog to his feet, each with a hand gripping him under the armpit, where two large sweat stains had formed. Then they looked around the plains.

Kit was looking for the wagon; Lebold, for a tree to hang him from.

"I see them," Kit said.

"Where?"

"Northwest."

Lebold spotted the wagon, the sunlight on the white of the canvas.

"We'll wait," he said. Still, he was looking around.

Then the Indian spoke. "Which reservation am I to be taken to?"

Lebold laughed. "What makes you think you're going to a reservation? You see those ropes hanging from my horse? One of those is for you."

The Indian's mouth set reptile-tight, and he stared grimly at the rope-laden horse – accepting his fate, it seemed to Kit.

Kit had seen a man hung, now he was going to see a man hang.

Well, he thought, *if ever there was a man who deserved to hang, it's this one.*

As the wagon came over a little rise in the grassy plain they heard whoops and hollers from Old Morg and Dwight. Even Jeb seemed to be overjoyed; he was raising his rifle in the air, clutched in a triumphantly curled first.

Kit smiled; it *was* a good feeling to finally have him.

Morg pulled on the riding reins and the mules' necks were yanked back. The wagon rolled to a stop.

"Lookit what we found," Lebold said sternly. "We found us a Injun. Now all we need's a tree. I reckon we'll find one on the banks of the Canadian."

But they didn't even have to go that far; they found one standing in the middle of the plains, a mesquite tree, with a long, thick branch jutting out on one side that looked like it had grown to hang a man from.

On their way south towards the Canadian looking for the tree, Kit had risked riding behind the wagon briefly, to inform the girl of the good news. First he offered her a pull on his canteen after having a sip himself, and she shook her head – impatiently, it seemed to Kit. Perhaps he should have remembered his manners, and offered her a pull first.

He clipped it back onto his horse and then told her they had caught the Indian who had captured her. It took a while for her to take that on board, it seemed to Kit, for at first she stared blankly, and then her eyes began to fill with tears.

Kit went red in the face, embarrassed to see her cry. He stuttered for words.

He decided to say, "Well, I 'spect you'll want to see him hang." And then wished he hadn't.

She let out a loud moan and then the tears really came, dripping and pattering onto Morgan's sun-bleached buffalo bones.

Kit decided it best to hightail it out of there. He nodded politely to her, even though she wasn't looking, and said, "Ma'am."

As he rode ahead alongside the wagon it seemed an inadequate thing to have said: "Ma'am". He wanted to ride back there and comfort her, but he hadn't a clue how. At the sight of her he seemed to freeze inside every time.

He spurred the horse gently until he was alongside the mules. Lebold had the Indian draped over the side of his horse and rode ahead.

"She's cryin' up a storm back there," Kit said.

"Let her be, Kit," Old Morg said. "I 'spect she's got a lot of cryin' to do yet."

"What did he *do* to her?" he asked, looking ahead at the Indian slung over the horse in the distance.

"Only she knows that, but I wouldn't ask her if I were you. She's liable not to want to recall, least of all to a stranger."

Kit had a hard time accepting that; that he was a stranger. He didn't feel like *she* was a stranger, not after all they had been through to get her back, not after all the times he had stared at her in the photograph, worrying about her, thinking about her, thinking about what he would *say* to her.

Most of all, thinking about how grateful she would be toward him, for rescuing her from the ghastly Indian who had captured her.

Instead, she didn't seem grateful at all. If anything, she acted the opposite. He just couldn't make sense of it.

Perhaps Old Morg was right, and it was too soon to be talking to her – she'd come around.

The thought seemed to comfort Kit, and he decided it was so.

Just then they had seen the tree in the distance, and Dwight had said, "Is that what I think it is?"

Old Morg said, "The Good Lord's Gallows."

Lebold had ridden his horse in under the tree, and now Kit dismounted. Old Morg and Jeb climbed down from the wagon seat, and Glorietta helped Dwight down as he had difficulty getting off with his one arm in the sling, and his right one at that.

Kit said to Morg, "Has she had anything to drink yet? Ain't she thirsty?"

"Maybe it's best *I* tend to her, Kit."

Kit didn't understand that, why it would be better for Morg to tend to her and not him.

He said, "Naw, it's alright – I'll do it."

As Lebold was pulling the tied Indian off the horse and dropping him to the leafy circle of grassless dirt under the tree, Kit walked around to the back of the wagon.

The girl was sitting on a pile of bones apprehensively.

Kit had his canteen in his hand and handed it to her first, this time. But she shook her head sullenly.

"You got to drink," he said. "You sure you don't want none?"

She shook her head once, solemnly.

Kit cleared his throat. "We're about to hang him. I thought as you might like to watch."

Kit half-expected her to shake her head again, but instead she got up off the pile of bones she was sitting on and tried to climb out of the wagon. Kit hastily made a hand-stirrup for her to stand into and stared at his intertwined palms, waiting for her foot.

Instead, she sat on the end of the wagon and slipped off the back. He saw her wince and hop as her sprained ankle touched the ground, but when he went to give her support – as he had done the first time – she held a hand out sternly, stopping him.

Then she turned and hobbled around the wagon, bracing herself against the side, and then along and past the grazing mules.

Kit couldn't see any reason why she shouldn't have wanted help. Her ankle was clearly paining her. She was a strange girl.

He shrugged it off and went over to the tree.

God Dog was sitting against the bole of the mesquite, while Lebold draped one of his ropes over the big jutting branch grown to hang a man from. He pulled it tight and tested it, and then adjusted the noose open and shut to make sure it was knotted right.

"Here, Kit," he said, holding his skinning knife out by the blade. "Cut his legs loose but leave his hands tied behind his back."

Kit took the knife and approached the bitter-looking Indian warily. He expected to be spat on, the man looked so embittered, but he wasn't, and Kit pulled him away from the bole of the tree and then pushed him over onto his front. He crouched and with one upward tug of the skinning knife cut the rope connecting his feet.

Lebold came over leading his own horse.

"It's time for your last ride, Injun," he said.

They picked him up by his armpits and made him stand on his own feet, Lebold checking that his hands were properly secured and there was no way he could break loose – never underestimate a Plains Indian, he knew. Kit noticed that the two large patches of sweat under the Indian's armpits had grown to the size of dinner plates.

God Dog looked up at the noose hanging from the branch, and then at the group waiting to watch him hang. He scowled at them with such a look of hatred as to transcend words that could ever suffice to give it description.

Magdalena stood next to Old Morg, stood close to him in fact. Her eyes were glazed over with tears, though she looked straight at the Indian, with firm resolve. Her lower lip trembled and she shook.

"Now now," Old Morg said to her gently. "It's okay, missy. We're just gonna hang this man so he can't ever do what he did to you and yours again."

She sniffled and whimpered, but her eyes remained firm in their resolve to watch him hang.

"Put your foot in the stirrup!" Lebold was saying sternly, pointing at it. "Do it!"

The Indian was not complying, just watching the little crowd, so Lebold bent, picked up and raised the Indian's boot and placed it into the stirrup. Then Kit grabbed his waist while Lebold pushed him upward under the armpits.

Soon they had him in the saddle.

Jeb had mounted Dwight's horse so as to be at the right height to put the noose over the Indian's head.

But when he tried to put the noose over, God Dog yanked his head out of the way.

"Don't touch me, you dark nigger devil," he said.

"Take your hangin' like a man," Lebold said. "Old Jeb ain't the dark devil. The dark devil is who you're goin' to meet in a moment."

Still, the Indian struggled, but Jeb grabbed hold of his long, greasy hair and held his head steady long enough to get the noose over it.

But the fight had not gone out of him yet. The Indian cleverly tucked his chin into his neck, so that when Jeb tried to tighten the noose, it closed over the front of his mouth instead. God Dog bared his teeth in a snarl against the tightening rope, for Jeb could not see what the man was doing from behind him; he yanked the noose tighter against the Indian's teeth, until it forced his mouth to open. The thick rope pulled tight into his mouth, biting against the back of his cheeks, like a gag.

Lebold said, "Hang him like that, if that's how he wants to hang!"

Kit was horrified; he could only imagine what it would be like to be hanged from your jaw – would the Indian even die if he was hung like that? Certainly he doubted he would die instantly.

The idea of watching him hang had filled Kit with both awe and repulsion, for it excited a part of him, and disgusted another. But he would go through with it, for this man deserved to hang. He did not think, however, that he deserved to hang from his jaw.

"Maybe you should redo that, Jeb," Kit suggested.

The Indian's eyes were wide above the rope, and he tried to say something, though all that came out were muffled garbles.

"No, no," Lebold said. "He's gonna hang like that for what he done."

Kit decided to leave it at that; Lebold had made a lot of sacrifices because of this God Dog, and had watched a lot of his friends die – had almost died himself, even.

Jeb rode out under the tree, ducking the branches, and then tied the horse to the side of the wagon, then dismounted and returned to join the little crowd.

Kit stepped back until he fell into line, deliberately coming to a stop next to the girl. Lebold stepped behind the horse the Indian was sitting on with a coil of rope in his hand.

Kit glanced sidelong at the girl, but looked quickly away when he saw her give him an admonishing look. She didn't want to be looked at. Her face, he saw, was a mess of tears, her eyes intent.

Kit looked up instead at the Indian about to hang, with the rope in his mouth.

The horse on which he sat with his hands tied behind him wasn't quite standing still, and he seemed to be trying to will it to stop stepping forward and backward with his mind alone.

The noose that Jeb had pulled tight into his mouth and around his jaws had cut into his cheeks. Already Kit could see blood running out the side of his mouth. Not much, but blood all the same.

His big nostrils flared and pulsed and his chest heaved up and down under his shirt as he struggled to breathe from only his nose. Big blue veins stood out on his forehead, pulsing due to the constriction below his nose and around the back of his head.

The little group realized they would be in the way of the horse when it was whipped and bolted, and slowly parted like the Red Sea for Moses.

Lebold lifted the coil of rope into the air behind the horse.

Kit saw the Indian's nostrils pulsing rapidly. He saw *fear* in those bulging eyes – something he had not expected to see. Though he saw no remorse.

Magdalena stared without blinking, right at the terrified eyes of the Indian, willing her pain into him. He deserved this ten times over for what he had done – such was too good for him. He had ruined her life and taken the lives of her ma, pa, and brother – and maybe also her sister. This was right, what was happening. It was what was called frontier justice on the plains.

Dwight watched with wide eyes, shocked by the way the Indian was about to hang – had he not have frustrated Jeb as Jeb had attempted to put the noose over his head, his neck probably would have broken instantly and that, more or less, would have been it.

He had brought it on himself, he figured. But that didn't make it right.

Dwight had seen a man hang before, a rustler who had made off with a remuda of horses belonging to the owner of an outfit he had once worked for, but had never seen a man hang by his jaw until dead – a grisly thought.

Even Old Morg thought the noose should have been retied – but what was, was what was.

The Indian began to let out a barrage of muffled pleas, his temples pulsing.

"Tell it to your friends in hell!" Lebold said.

He whipped the coil of rope hard onto the horse's rump.

It launched out from underneath the Indian with a startled squeal, and as it did his eyes bulged even wider and he let out a muffled scream.

He was drawn forward as the horse lunged out from beneath him, the hang rope swinging forward overhead until it pulled taut against the branch, and then he was pulled backwards out of the saddle and off the horse's rump.

He dropped.

The noose pulled tight *with a whap* and the top half of his head was yanked upwards with a sound like a piece of cracking wood. His jaw dislocated instantly, tore loose and hung slack.

As he started to swing to and fro his back arched into the air like a bow, and his feet began to kick together in pulses. The hang rope creaked like an unoiled hinge above and he slowly twisted around on the end of it.

Strangulated gargles and dry chokes came from his stretching neck.

The noose had pulled tight around the flaps of his ears and the drums began to bleed, sending rivulets down either side of his neck, the rope squeezing the sides of his skull with the weight of his entire body.

Then two streams of bright life-blood began to gush from his nose, as he continued to kick in uniform pulses and arch his back, his hands bound behind him.

Magdalena cried out, unable to watch any longer, and turned to bury her head into the chest of the nearest person behind her – which happened to be Morg.

He put his hand on her head gently and stroked her hair.

Still, the Indian kicked and jerked at the end of the rope.

Kit had never seen a pair of eyes bulge like that. He almost expected them to explode and splatter. Within seconds of hanging and twisting there they had shot through with red and become the colour of uncooked meat.

The Indian began to spasm in the air, shaking and juddering.

Kit saw a wet spot form at his groin and then he watched as a stream of urine began to run out over one of his black boots and spatter into the dust. As the stream slowed and came to a stop, droplets flicked into the air from the tip of his jerking boot.

"Jesus!" Dwight said. "Somebody stop this!"

The Indian wasn't dying, and didn't even look about to any time soon. Blood was still gushing freshly from his nose and ears.

Then his whole body began to pulse, jerking and pulsing as if lightning was striking him in the head and leaving his body via his boots. His popping eyes rolled up into his head, blood began to foam and bubble around the rope in his gritted teeth, and then finally the tiny vessels in his eyes burst, and a single crimson tear formed in the corner of each eye and coursed quickly down his cheeks and onto and over the stained rope, dripping and pattering rapidly to earth like the last contents of a tipped paint tin–

A pistol shot rang out, and then another and another.

Slugs smashed into the Indian's jerking body, into his chest, his stomach, his neck.

And then suddenly he was hanging still.

Dwight, who had been the one to fire, slowly holstered his pistol.

Magdalena was crying uncontrollably against Old Morg's chest.

Lebold had slowly walked backwards as the sight had grown more gruesome, and he came to a stop next to Kit. His face was white.

Kit felt sick to the stomach; he finally knew what it was like to hang a man, and he wished he didn't.

"I think I'll let him keep that rope," Lebold said. "He earned it."

"Should we put a sign on him?" Kit asked.

"I think he is a sign, Kit."

No one said any more. Slowly, one by one, they went back to the wagon and climbed it. Even Magdalena went around the back and got in.

Kit untied the horse Jeb had hitched to the side of the wagon and led it away and then mounted it.

Lebold caught his horse ten yards away, grazing on some grass. He swung up into the saddle, to its annoyance.

Old Morg cracked the whips and the mule team began to pull the wagon away. Lebold spurred his horse. As the wagon wheeled past, Kit couldn't help but look into the back: the girl was crying steadily. She did not look up.

Kit found himself the last one before the tree.

He stared at the dead Indian whose horrendous death had produced such pain he had cried tears of blood to release it, before his body had been riddled with the merciful death bullets. His bottom jawbone hung askew, and blood oozed out along his hanging tongue in long elastic strings and pooled in the dust below.

It was what it was:

Frontier Justice.

PART
IV

They camped that night on the north bank of the Canadian. Despite having left the wagon to watch the Indian hang, Magdalena would no longer leave it and she stayed inside the entire night. It was Morg's idea to have the other lady, Glorietta, take her food and water. Lebold spotted an antelope and he and Old Morg took the horses and rode off to hunt it. After an hour or so they returned with its dead carcass, the antelope's neck hanging limply as they carried it into camp between them.

It was Morg who skinned it, and even Lebold was impressed with the speed in which he did so, to say nothing of the aptitude. He skinned the animal so well the hide peeled back in one piece and came off after they cut all the useful strips of meat from it. Old Morg dug in the back of his wagon, disturbing Magdalena for a moment, and came back with six wooden stakes and a hammer with a large iron head, like a miniature sledge.

"What you doin' with that?" Lebold asked curiously.

"Curing it," Old Morg answered.

He walked a few yards from the camp and staked it into the grass.

"Come the morrow it ought to be dry, if'n the clouds don't let loose."

The light was leaving the prairie rapidly, and the sky overhead was banked with thick wisps of cloud. Kit hoped it wouldn't rain.

It didn't while they cooked and ate, anyway.

The cuts of meat sizzled on the embers over which they were draped and bubbling juices steamed into the air. It set Kit's buds to jetting saliva in anticipation, and he found he had to swallow several times.

They pulled their tin plates and cutlery from their saddlebags and passed them out. Kit offered to eat his meat by hand so that Magdalena could use his plate. He allowed his tin cup to be used as well.

Morg filled it with water from his canteen – Kit had taken upon himself the task to fill them in the river earlier – and then selected a large cut of steak from the fire with his fork.

He handed it to Glorietta, who got up from where she was sitting next to Dwight cross-legged and took it to Magdalena.

They sat and waited for her to return, half-suspecting that Magdalena would not eat it – at least Old Morg had said she probably would not. But when Glorietta returned it was without the plate or cup.

It relieved Kit, at least. He had been worried she wasn't even going to drink the water from his cup, let alone eat. It satisfied him somewhat that Magdalena was eating from his own plate, with his own cutlery, drinking from his dented tin cup. He only wished he could somehow let her know it was he who had given up his cutlery for her to eat with. He wished somehow she could see him eating his own piece of meat by hand, which caused him some considerable discomfort. It was burning hot and he had to keep shifting it from hand to hand and take quick bites. Even then the meat itself was too hot in his mouth, and he had to blow around it as it sat painfully on his tongue. It burned the back of his throat as he swallowed it.

Jeb was sitting with them for a change, the horses tied to the side of the wagon and grazing on the grass beneath. It pleased Kit to see the black man sit among them. This time it had been Jeb who had sat down next to Kit, after helping collect the wood for the fire. Old Morg also had a sack in the back of his wagon, full of cow chips, but when he had mentioned going to fetch it to help the fire get started Lebold had protested, seeming not to want to have to breathe in shit out on the open prairie either, if he could help it.

Kit felt that Jeb, in his silent way, felt a safety emanating from Kit; a safety he did not feel from the other men, even Morg.

But mostly Kit just stared into the fire, on which they had placed new logs of wood after removing the meat. He felt a sad confusion inside, and kept looking to the wagon. After he had eaten he wanted to get up and go talk to her, telling himself that he would do it any minute now, get up and walk over – but he found he couldn't do it.

Glorietta was a strange woman. She seemed almost to stick to the side of Dwight, as if she were actually physically attached by flesh, but Dwight seemed too tired and pained to give it much more notice than he did. He seemed slightly bothered by it, however, and kept looking at Lebold as if for help.

Lebold noticed his pleading looks, but didn't say anything.

He and Morg were talking about range fencing, a subject Old Morg himself had brought up.

Lebold said, "They must just be starting it, then, 'cause I ain't seen any fenced ranges."

"It's on account of the new invention. They call it barbed wire."

"Barbed wire?" Kit said.

"Livestock can get caught and cut up in it," Old Morg explained, "and a man can't even climb over it without he gets his duds torn or his shirt stuck. And I hear if you try to cut it you can get shot at."

"It sounds like a ploy to prevent the herds from free grazing," Lebold remarked.

"I 'spect that's just what it is," Old Morg said. "Well, and to stop herds trampling all the grass."

"Well ain't no barbed wire gonna stop me," Lebold said. "The open range is everybody's. Who do they think they are closin' it off?"

"Landowners," Old Morg said. "Well, I 'spect it's just one more obstacle on the trail when it comes to herdin', I suppose."

Dwight said, "Barbed wire ain't gonna stop a man like Mister Anderton."

"Who's he?" Old Morg asked.

"Our trail boss," Lebold said. "Speaking of which, tomorrow we're gonna follow the river east until we come to the cattle trails, then we're gonna push north and try to catch up with the herd, if it ain't already in Dodge."

"I have a mind to try the cattle trade myself," Old Morg said.

"Though I'm a might worried about this range fencing putting an end to it."

"My livelihood depends on cows; always has," Lebold said. "No self-respecting hand is gonna allow some land-greedy sons of bitches to close off the range."

"Well then I guess there'll be blood," Old Morg said.

"Then blood there'll be." Lebold stood up and went off to relieve himself.

"Young Kit over here mentioned tryin' his hand at cowboying himself," Dwight remarked. "Seeing's you two know each other, whyn't you head down to Texas and join an outfit? Summer's nearing its end, but there's always work to be done on a ranch. The round-up ain't till spring."

"I don't intend to join no outfit," Old Morg said. "I'd like to gather together my own herd and trail it north. One last adventure before my old age puts a stop to me."

"I guess we'll be leaving east tomorrow," Dwight said to Kit. "But I hope to see you again on the plains. Heck, maybe I'll come down to Texas and hire on, if you boys have got you a ranch by spring next year. I could come for the round-up."

Kit didn't know what to think of it, but it sounded great. If Old Morg really did intend on starting up a ranch of his own he would need a lot of help. But the question remained what would happen to the girl.

Lebold stepped back into the circle of firelight and sat.

"What you girls talkin' about now?" he asked.

"Old Morg's thinkin' of rounding up some cattle and trailing them north," Dwight told him.

"It's a bit late to start a drive, ain't it?" Lebold said.

"I still got it in me, sonny," Old Morg remarked.

"I don't doubt you do, old man. I mean the summer's nearin' its end."

"Why, that's perfect," Dwight said. "You can head down to Texas and build your ranch. Put up your corrals and stock buildings, dig a well and whatnot, then wait for spring next year and head over the Grande into Mexico and round up some steers, start the drive by next summer."

"It's a thought," Old Morg said. "I been thinkin' mostly about cattle these days. The fur trade's over and I'm tired of picking up old bones."

"I knew a guy shot himself in the eye doin' that," Lebold said. "Suicided hisself."

"I know the way he felt – I near did myself," Old Morg said.

"Are you really thinkin' of starting your own ranch and herd?" Kit asked Old Morg.

"I been thinkin' it a long time, son. I got some money put away and that there wagon load of bones – once I sell 'em off to the railhead I might have enough for a plot in Texas and some lumber, maybe a few saddles and some traces."

Dwight said to Lebold, "While you was off I said if they have a ranch ready by next spring I may hire on."

Lebold smirked. "If these fellas have got a ranch up and runnin' by next spring I'll hire on myself," he said sceptically.

"When I say somethin', sonny, I do it," Old Morg said. "There ain't nothin' I said I'd do I ain't done yet – ain't that so, Kit?"

Kit smiled and said, "Never truer words were spoke, Morg."

"Thank ye."

It was a happy thought, and it got Kit's mind to thinking. He imagined being a top-hand, working the ranch with Old Morg and taking part in the spring round-up, branding the animals to get them ready for the drive. He realized the prospect was the *real* adventure, the one he had dreamed about all his life – not this one. Not the rescuing of the girl from the Indian renegade.

To boot, if Kit worked with Morg on the ranch he would be one of the main hands about the place, and the way Old Morg looked at him now, with that familiar glint in his eye and slight smile on his face, told him a good future awaited and Old Morg's intention was to include Kit without a second thought. It was that same look he had given him all those years ago, on the outskirts of Dodge, as Kit had struggled to skin a carcass and Old Morg had shown him how and helped him.

The only thing bothering Kit was the girl in the wagon, Magdalena

– where did she fit in the future?

"Well," Lebold said, "I think I'm gonna turn in. It's been a hell of a day. Tomorrow we'll push east. Dunno 'bout you boys."

"Where are you goin'?" Glorietta asked.

"Didn't you hear?" Lebold said testily. "We're going back to the herd. They're near Dodge by now, if not in it."

She turned to Dwight hopefully. "Oh won't you take me with you, Dwight?" she said.

"What do you mean, take you with him?" Lebold asked angrily. "We're going back to a herd of cows. Ain't no place for a woman. Ain't no place at all."

Dwight looked at her nervously, but didn't say anything – he seemed too afraid to tell her what he had to.

"Dwight?" she said.

"He's right," Dwight said regretfully. "A herd ain't no place for a woman to be. It's too dangerous. Plus the trail boss would never allow it."

A pained expression came into her face. "Well then take me as far as Dodge," she pleaded desperately. "Please! I ain't got no place to go."

"You women," Lebold said distastefully. "You think a man is a kind of mule you can hitch onto your wagon, then you find your cunning ways to whip him along to where you want to get to."

She shot him an angered glance, and then looked hangdog at Dwight.

Even Kit didn't like her – who was she anyway? Some woman who latched onto them because they bumped into her in a saloon? Now she expected Dwight to, what? What obligation did he have to her? Kit couldn't see a one. Yet the woman seemed to behave as if he owed it to her. Perhaps for tying his arm in a sling, Kit thought; a high price for an amateur doctoring at best, it seemed to him.

So far, women were strange.

But Dwight, to Kit's surprise, looked somehow as if he didn't want to disappoint her.

He said, "Well I suppose I could take you as far as Dodge, but then you'll have to find your way from there."

She seemed to be content with that, and sat back with a look of poorly concealed satisfaction. But Kit saw it, and noted it; it was as if she had won some sort of age-old battle.

"Well I'm against it," Lebold said. "She certainly ain't ridin' shotgun with me. I'm turnin' in, I'd appreciate it if you boys would quieten it down a bit."

He pushed back his saddle, against which he had been sitting, and then unrolled his blanket.

"What are *we* gonna do, Morg?" Kit asked.

"That depends," the old man said. "I gotta sell these bones, so we could push north to the nearest railhead. After that I guess we can get some provisions and trek down to Texas."

Kit realized he would need a new horse, since the only remaining horses belonged to both Lebold and Dwight.

"What about you, Jeb?" Kit asked. "I suppose if we push north we'll pass Wagon Trail."

Jeb seemed to consider that unhappily. Then he said, "If youse could use a hand with that ranch of yours down in Texas, it'd be my honour to help out."

Kit looked at Old Morg, like a kid looking at his father for permission he eagerly wanted.

"It's fine with me, Kit," Old Morg said. "Any able and willing man is welcome, but there's a lot of work to be done and I'll have no slackers."

Kit was overjoyed, and suppressed a big celebratory *Yesss!*

He looked at Jeb happily. "It will be a pleasure working with you," Kit said.

"Why, you too, Mister Kit," Jeb said. His face lit with the brightness of his white teeth as he smiled.

It seemed to Kit that everything was coming to a fine resolution, despite all that had happened. He, Jeb and Morg would sell the wagonload of bones at the railhead and then push south to Texas, to start a ranch there with the intention of trailing a herd north next spring. Kit could not have dreamed up a brighter future for himself, overjoyed that he had crossed paths once more with Old Morg.

Even Dwight would come down and hire on next year, and maybe Lebold. He looked forward to driving a herd with them, experienced men from whom he could learn to cowboy.

He felt the sense of adventure and was sure of it this time. This time an adventure was sure to follow.

There was only one thing that irked him: the girl. Well, two things: letting the girl know how her sister had died, and the girl herself. Where was she to go, with her entire family dead, unless she had some other family somewhere? He found there was no way around it. He would have to ask her some questions and get her talking.

He thought about doing it now, and then thought against it. Perhaps after a good night of sleep she would feel better and her attitude would change. Often a night of sleep was all Kit himself needed to have a change of mood; going to sleep with a bad notion and waking to find that it wasn't so bad, after all, in light of a new day.

He decided he would talk to her tomorrow, or at least try to. He thought of ways to start a conversation. Definitely not with a canteen of water or a plate of food, he figured.

I know! he thought. He would give her back the photograph, say to her, "I have something I kept for you." No, "I have something of yours." Maybe. He would say something like that, and then hand it to her. That was bound to please her.

He thought of giving her the arrowhead in his pocket, the one he had found on the plains next to the vomit they had discovered; for her, as a memento of her travels.

That was bound to work as an opener, get her to see that he was a good guy, on her side – gentle and nice.

He tried to think how he might approach her with his questions. He needed to ask her where she wanted to go. What she wanted to do. How she intended to do it.

He found himself feeling anxious about tomorrow, and when finally he decided to turn in, pushing his own saddle back along the grass and getting into his blanket, he found he could not sleep.

He had no idea at which point he drifted off, just that he had been sure he wasn't going to be able to sleep at all, so much was going on in his head, but finally he did.

★ ★ ★

He awoke in the middle of the night, wet and cold, shivering in his blankets. Big pregnant drops of rain were falling out of the night sky, starless and low with dark swaths of cloud.

Then the intensity of the rain increased, until it was so hard a drop stung Kit's eyeball as it splashed into his eye. He sat up and climbed out of his blanket in the rain, rolling it up hurriedly and tying it. Already water squeezed out of the coarse fabric as he pulled tight on the strings.

The ground was rapidly becoming mud at his feet, pooling with water, and the fire was out, washing away in a growing puddle.

The horses and mules were nickering and neighing. When he looked at the figures around the fire he saw that Lebold had sat up and was holding his blanket over his head in an attempt to keep the rain out.

"Just dandy, huh, Kit?" he said.

Kit looked around and saw that Dwight was doing the same, and Glorietta, who had nothing in the way of a single provision, was huddled under the blanket with him. It was amazing how quickly a woman could take up with a man, Kit thought.

Jeb was lying flat but had pulled his blanket up over his head.

Old Morg, to Kit's amazement, lay sleeping oblivious – even oblivious to the rain pooling in his closed eye sockets.

"Is that old man even alive?" Lebold asked from under his blanket.

Kit saw that his chest was rising and falling gently.

"He's breathin'," Kit said.

He decided to go sleep under the wagon to get out of the rain, an idea that Lebold begrudged him for having first. He watched Kit walking towards the wagon and cursed under his breath. He cursed the girl, too, for if she hadn't been so skittish some of them could have slept in the wagon. It was a deep annoyance to have women with you, he thought to himself, and he was not looking forward to this Glorietta latching onto them until Dodge. Women belonged in towns and in houses, but moreover in sporting saloons, and the way he saw it it was their job – their duty, rather – to bring comfort to the boys coming in off the trails. Things worked out better all round for everyone if you just paid a woman for her company and time, and then left her. Everybody was happy, no one inconvenienced. That's how it ought to be, far as he was concerned.

Kit huddled under the wagon on the small patch of dry earth, and lay with his head on the roll of his wet blanket. He had left his saddle in the rain and regretted not bringing it now, but was too wet and tired to do anything about it.

He lay under the wooden boards and looked up at them. Magdalena was up there, but he couldn't hear her. All he could hear was the steady patter of rain on the canvas of the wagon, and the nickering and whinnying of the mules and horses. The two horses were hitched on one side of the wagon, and they stomped their hooves into the mud agitatedly and jingled their bits.

He wondered what Magdalena was doing in the wagon. Had the rain awoken her? Was she awake and unable to sleep? What was she thinking about? Was she perhaps afraid?

He indeed loved her. He felt it now, what must indeed have been love – as strong as it had ever been felt.

On the other hand, what did he know about love? He had never felt it before, or even really seen it. Sure, he had heard the buffalo hunters bragging about being in love; in fact, distinctly recalled one having said, "I'm in love with that Marcy. She only charges me two dollars when I take a bath."

On the other hand, another had once said, "I love that whore, but she's taken up with some young cowboy. I have a mind to shoot him."

The more and more Kit thought about it, the less certain he felt about love at all. Did he even have any idea what it was? Was the woman who had latched onto Dwight in love?

He stared at the wood miserably, despite his good feeling earlier – but then rain often brought him to a gloom.

Magdalena was in there. Actually in there. Kit felt that his future and life would be like a dream if he could only convince her to love him – especially if she would accompany him to Texas.

Imagine that, he thought.

The idea alone brought him a warm feeling, even in the cold. He would build her a home in Texas, right on the ranch they were going to erect, and not out of sod; he would build it from lumber and fell trees if need be. He would dig her a well, build her tables and chairs and get a smithy to make her a Dutch oven, so that she could cook sourdough biscuits. He would make sure it had a chimney, and windows, and a nice board floor instead of pounded mud.

Surely when she heard that she would fall head over heels for him?

Surely...

Wouldn't she?

Magdalena awoke to a new day. The sky was a clear blue basin above, the air crisp and fresh. She could hear the river not far from the wagon, swishing and swirling against the muddy banks and around the mudflats. Somewhere birds were tweeting, a sound that put life in her breast.

She felt well rested. Although the bones had been hard and uneven to sleep on, and had continuously shifted under her weight, she had managed to sleep well on them all the same. She had felt exhausted, both physically and emotionally; in fact, in every possible way one could feel exhausted – especially after watching the Indian hang.

Watching him hang had brought her a mix of emotions, some she had not expected. She had felt anger and righteousness, had felt satisfaction, mostly before the horse had been whipped out from beneath him. Then she had felt sadness and even pity – but most of all she had felt disappointment. Especially after he was shot and had hung still.

It was not enough. That is to say, not enough in so far as it amounted to nothing, seemed in the end pointless. The hanging itself had been horrific, so horrific she had not been able to watch all of it. But in the end it didn't change anything, what had been done had still been done, and she was the one left to live with it.

She felt she would never be able to live with what happened, refused to in fact. How many girls her age had gone through the same thing? Not many, she thought. Why, then, had she had to?

Thinking over the course of events, and listening to the river running past nearby, she felt there was one thing that would make her feel in keeping with this fine morning: a wash. She had been dying for a wash ever since the first Indian had done the thing to her. Sitting with Jenny against the cave wall, she had even taken up a handful of sand and wiped it over her legs and arms, which is one of the reasons they looked so dirty now.

When she looked out of the wagon she could see the rut its wheels had made running off behind it into the distance, but she noticed that the prairie grass was soaking wet, and not just with dew. There were pools of water in the mud. When she looked up she saw that there were puddles of water on the canvas above, and now that she noticed it she could in fact hear the wagon itself dripping.

She had been so exhausted she had slept through the rain, and by the looks of things it had been heavy enough.

She had decided to stay in the wagon when they stopped to camp to avoid the looks of the men – the looks of the youngest one, mostly. Kit. She wished he would stop looking at her the way he did.

She listened carefully for other sounds, and found that she could hear gentle snoring somewhere. She frowned.

Someone was snoring under the wagon. Someone must have crept under it last night when it rained. She listened, and also found she could hear someone else snoring, further away. Everyone was still asleep, it seemed.

It annoyed her that someone was underneath the wagon, for she would have liked to climb down quietly without waking anyone and creep off to the river to have a wash. She felt a wash would be better than anything right now. She wanted to get right in there and clean every pore, as well; wash the memory of those filthy Indians away for good.

Perhaps she could still climb down without waking them. She put the empty plate and tin cup aside carefully, and moved quietly over the bones, trying not to upset them. She had eaten the entire steak hungrily, leaving nothing . She had even eaten the fat, which normally she would not have. It had tasted fantastic, and she wondered what it was. Certainly it was no mule or ox – she had tasted them before.

She sat on the end of the wagon and pushed herself slowly from the edge, until the tips of her feet touched the ground. Her ankle was able to take more weight, she noticed, though was still sprained and sore.

Once she was on the ground and out of the wagon, she listened carefully to hear if she had awoken anyone.

The snoring continued blissfully under the wagon. She wondered who it was under there, and decided to bend over and have a look.

That was annoying. It was Kit. All night he had been sleeping beneath her. Probably it was just to get out of the rain, a part of her tried to console her; but another was more cynical and reminded her of the way he had been looking at her the day before, the way he had kept riding back behind the wagon to look in at her.

She crept around the side of the wagon, and the horses looked up at her in surprise, blinking their long lashes. They were beautiful horses, she thought, though, of course, she loved all horses, always had.

Even the mules looked at her in surprise, turning their heads and following with their eyes as she snuck past.

The camp was wet and the fire was a mash of damp ash. Bedrolls lay around it in the wet, and snorts and snores came from them.

She continued past until she was well out of earshot, and then sped for the river, eager to get into it and bathe before anyone awoke and saw her. They had all seemed sound asleep enough to allow for a quick wash. Of course, she wouldn't go right in, but at least would wade in to her knees and pick the water up to wash herself.

Fortunately she found a thick wall of green bushes along the bank, offering cover from the wagon camp. She went behind it and looked around one more time to make sure that nobody was watching. Then she lifted her dress over her head.

The gentle morning breeze felt reviving on her skin.

She looked down at herself, inspecting her arms. They were a dark brown colour, like her lower legs and feet, but the rest of her was fish-belly white. There were streaks of dirt on her stomach and thighs, and scrapes and scratches all over her knees and forearms. The bite mark around her nipple had turned blue.

That brought tears to her eyes, though just enough to wet the balls and not enough to run out onto her cheeks.

She made water behind the bush, which stung, but she had gotten used to the sting by now. She had made water in the little room she had been placed in in the town, in a chamber pot with a lid, and it had stung far worse. She used a leaf to dry herself, and then stood and went to the edge of the bank. It was a small drop to the water, and she didn't want to hurt her ankle again, so sat down on her bare bottom instead and pushed herself off into the water.

It was icy cold, enough to make her want to climb back out again, but she strengthened her resolve and waded out until the water was running by above her knees. Then she quickly bent and scooped up handfuls of water, wetting herself. Goosebumps broke out over her flesh. Once she was wet and shivering, her lips blue, she reached deeper into the river and brought up a handful of brown mud. She lathered it under her armpits and smoothed it out over her belly. She scraped her scratched legs clean with another handful of mud, and then her shoulders and breasts.

Finally she braced herself and dropped neck-deep into the river, the water incredibly cold but refreshing. She could feel little fish nibbling at her toes, which brought a small smile to her face.

She looked back at the bank once or twice, feeling for a moment that someone was watching – but no one was there. She dunked her head and wet her hair. She washed herself thoroughly below, in the place where the Indians had fouled her.

When finally she walked out of the water and climbed the bank, she felt refreshed and relieved. It was great to feel clean for a change, though it was strange; a part of her still felt dirty, a part of her felt it would never be clean – no matter how many times she washed, no matter what she washed with. A part of her would be dirty forever.

She stood behind the bushes in the sunlight, drip-drying and squeezing the water out of her hair. She still did it the way her mother had showed her to do it, twisting the braids of her hair tight, as if weaving a rope, and then squeezing them in her fists so that the water pumped out between her fingers.

When she felt dry enough not to wet what was left of her dress, she pulled it back on over her head, and then came out from behind the bush.

That's when she saw Kit quickly ducking back under the wagon, a sight that infuriated her. Had he seen her naked? Had he been watching her wash herself from behind the bush all this time? Had he – an awful, repelling thought – watched her make water?

She felt her blood boil, and her lips tremble. Were men all the same, just wanting to put themselves inside her? To do it by force, if they could? She felt they all would, if they could. And this one was no different.

As he quickly ducked out of sight she noticed him bang his head under the wagon, a sight which brought her some satisfaction. It knocked his hat from his head and it landed in the mud.

A hand shot out quickly and collected it, disappearing back under the wagon.

She started walking again and when she went past the wagon she purposely made sure her footfalls were heavy and flustered, despite the pain it caused her ankle. Then she climbed back up into the wagon, and decided she would not step a foot out of it again. Mostly, it was just extremely embarrassing to think he had seen her – worse, *spied* on her.

K it had been watering the green leaves of the wall of bushes absent-mindedly when he heard the splash.

He had awoken under the wagon with a distinct pain in his bladder, and had needed to go urgently. Kit had never been one to go in plain sight, like some. He fancied his own space to do his business in, and all he asked for was the privacy to do it in. Sometimes he couldn't even go if he thought someone else was watching, even if it was only a horse. Often he had had to tell Misty Blue to stop looking when he had dismounted during the trip to relieve himself.

His box of thearaputic papers was empty now; had emptied, in fact, long ago. A new lesson he had learned about travelling with T.P. was not to let anyone else know you had it. As soon as Dwight had seen it he had told Lebold, and Lebold had asked to borrow the box, which Kit kept tucked in a saddlebag. He had leant it, of course, not wanting Lebold to take a further dislike to him at that point. And soon Dwight had asked to borrow it too. Then one morning he had gone to do his business with it and when he opened the box there was a single sheet left in it and he had had to finish off with prickly leaves.

So that was one to tell Old Morg, who had originally schooled him in the use of such paper and the provisioning of it before setting off on a journey across the plains.

He wished he had still had it – wished he had just used the leaves all along, in fact – for it would have been a nice gift for Magdalena, and she would certainly remember him fondly each time she used it, for the difference between a leaf and a piece of T.P. was considerable, in Kit's opinion. As always, Old Morg had been right: nature just wasn't cut out for the task.

When Lebold urinated, he would dismount and do it behind his horse, looking over the top of it. Dwight was more modest, like Kit, and did it out of sight, usually some distance out on the plains, peeing into the wind. Once he had come back to camp cursing because the wind had blown some back onto him. "That's what happens when you piss into the wind," Lebold had remarked.

Jeb, Kit never saw. He went off mostly at night and did his business, so dark he simply disappeared. Kit envied his ability to go off and do his business at roughly the same time every day, at night. And he must have had a huge bladder, for he seldom stopped and dismounted even to relieve himself.

Kit was peeing onto the leaves when he heard the splash, and the stream of yellow water instantly stopped as he tensed, then slowly resumed as he frowned and looked around. At first he dismissed it for a snapping turtle, probably launching itself off a mudflat into the river, but then he heard it again.

By this time he was shaking himself dry, and slowly he tucked his jolly rodger away, buckling his pants. Then he sidestepped along, away from his urine, and crouched, peering through a dead patch of growth in the bush.

Oh my God, Kit thought. He didn't know whether he should look away from what he saw or on the other hand even blink in case he missed even one split moment of it.

It was Magdalena. She was as naked as a new born baby; white as a fish belly, Kit thought. He felt his dingus growing and growing fast. The more he looked the more it grew, until it was a hard rod down one legging of his duds, like a third, if somewhat stunted, leg.

His eyes inspected every inch of her. He felt guilty for doing so but the impulse to look while he could seized him far more powerfully than his sense of guilt.

She had her back to him and she was wading out into the water, her lower legs getting deeper and deeper. He hoped she didn't go out too far and get carried away, for it would have been mighty suspicious if he suddenly had to pounce out from behind the bush and come to her rescue.

He looked at her plump milky bottom, and felt his dingus throbbing.

Then his eyes almost popped out of his head. She bent over to scoop up a handful of water, and for a moment he saw a flash of... a flash of *hair* under her bottom? Right in the middle where her legs met, as if a little rodent was hiding there.

Kit's heart began to beat harder, and the naughty excitement he felt was undeniable – this was wrong and he should have looked away in shame, but he couldn't – he wasn't about to miss this for all the horses in the world.

She began to wash her belly and then lifted an armpit and rubbed her hand beneath it. The side of her plump white breast was showing, like a big milk-white dewdrop hanging off the side of her.

Then she turned as she searched the riverbed with her hand, coming up with a handful of mud.

Kit saw her shivering from the cold, and her skin tight with goose bumps, though that wasn't what really called his attention.

Her bare breasts were facing him, and her nipples were hard and erect, a deep purple-blue colour. There were lighter circles of purple around each one, prickled with goose bumps.

Then he saw what was between her legs, a dark V of wispy hair. The single most fascinating sight of his life, second only to the breasts. This was nothing at all like the big fat whore in the saloon, who had done the thing to him and then tried to blow him away with a shotgun. This was young, firm womanhood at its height, ripe for the picking, Kit thought. There were no flaps of fat around her waist, or *any*where on her for that matter. Her belly was flat as a washboard, her breasts round, firm and plump.

She began covering herself in mud, a sight so tantalizing Kit found that he was rubbing at himself.

Then she dropped neck-deep into the water and he stopped disappointedly. He tried to crane his neck, but could see nothing.

But then she walked out of the water and he saw everything, her breasts swinging and bouncing gently as she tiptoed out of the water, the large V of hair between her legs beaded with water drops.

When she stepped a leg up onto the bank his breath caught in his throat, for as she stepped up he caught a glance of something pink hidden within the thatch of curly black hair between her legs.

Then he realized how dangerously close she was getting, and he turned and hightailed it out of there, running on tiptoes. He hoped no one awoke as he raced awkwardly back to the wagon, for if they did they would see the large lump down the front of his legging and he would be disgraced.

Once he got alongside the wagon he risked a quick glance back, and saw her coming, now back in her dirty tattered dress. He hurriedly ducked under the wagon, and hit his head. The edge of the wagon scraped his hat from his head, too.

He quickly reached for it and snatched it back under the wagon, in case she saw it as she walked past.

Then he waited under the wagon, holding his hat in one hand the growing lump on his forehead with the other.

Soon he heard the horses and mules nicker and saw her bare feet sloshing by in the mud. The back of the wagon creaked as she climbed up into it, and he heard bones rattling.

He let out a sigh of relief.

That was close, Kit thought. *Thank God Almighty she didn't see me.*

Kit remained under the wagon as long as he possibly could without bringing disgrace upon himself; even as it was when finally he ducked out and stretched theatrically, Lebold said, "I didn't know you were so early to rise, Kit," – sarcastically, of course.

Sleeping late was a point of shame among these men, used to starting the day on the drive well before light, so that by the time their coffee and breakfast was in them and their bedrolls tied and hitched, they were ready to put in a full day's work from sunup until sundown and often even well into the night.

Eager to get an early start for the herd, Lebold and Dwight had already saddled their horses. They were no longer tied to the side of the wagon, but grazing a few yards away, ready to go.

No fire had been possible, due to all the wet wood and puddles. Kit saw Dwight chewing on a piece of jerky. Glorietta stuck to him as if she was as much a part of him as his own arms or legs. She was also chewing, Kit noticed, on a small piece of jerky.

Old Morg was pulling up the stakes he had hammered into the ground to cure the antelope's hide. He rolled it up now, even though it was nowhere near cured, thanks to the rain.

Kit felt embarrassed. He had woken earlier than anyone – well, except Magdalena – and usually always did, and now he looked like a lazybones. Certainly Lebold was looking at him with distaste for being the last one up. And, perhaps, for not only being the last to wake but for getting to spend most of the night out of the wet, for most of Lebold's clothes were damp, and everyone else's too.

Kit saw his saddle by the fire, most of which had washed away. It was the last item to be cleared around the camp, another point of embarrassment for Kit. He picked it up and then realized he had no horse to put it on.

"Hey, Morg," he said, walking over to Morg with his dripping saddle, who was tying the roll of hide with a length of string. "Would you mind much if I store this in your wagon?"

"No, I wouldn't, son," Old Morg said. "I 'spect my mules'll mind, though – they're the one's gonna hafta pull the extra load. Just go on back and plop it in there. And watch them mules don't kick ya."

Although Old Morg always warned everyone about the temperament of his mules, they seemed fine, intelligent animals to Kit – for mules, anyway. Whenever you walked past them they looked up, usually from grazing, and followed you with their eyes. Though perhaps that was a sign of their ill-intentions, the mules watching for an opportunity to successfully bite or kick.

Kit went along the wagon with his saddle and around the back, his heart suddenly beating again. He had seen Magdalena stark naked, and he didn't think he would ever be able to look at her the same way again.

He felt even more embarrassed than he had before, now.

When he came squelching around the back of the wagon, the mud sucking at his boots, Magdalena looked up – angrily, Kit thought.

He stuttered several times before he could get his tongue to work together with his teeth. He said, "Why, howdy – I mean, good... good morning. Ma'am."

He felt like slapping himself over the head for sounding so stupid and uncertain of his greeting.

"Good morning," she said sullenly. She didn't look any too happy to Kit.

Perhaps she had seen him, a thought that was unbearable to Kit. Blood flushed to his face. If she had seen him, it meant he had cause to be deeply embarrassed. Though at least she had spoken to him, which had to be a good sign – of sorts.

"Why, I... I just come to put my saddle in the wagon," Kit said. "Morg... Morg said I could."

She reached out a hand to take it from him and put it in the wagon for him.

He said, "Why, no, that's all right, ma'am. I'll – I'll, I'll, I'll... I'll put it in there. It's a might heavy. Heavier than usual, on account of it got wet."

"I'll, I'll, I'll," she said, mimicking him slightly.

That made his face even redder.

"Give it to me," she said impatiently. "I think I can manage."

"Yes – yes, ma'am."

"Call me Magda or Lena, or Magdalena – but don't call me ma'am. It makes me feel older than I am."

"Why, certainly. Yes... yes, ma– Magda. Lena."

He felt like hitting himself upside the head again. *Jesus.* His heart beat hard in his chest. It hadn't even beat this hard during the gunfight in Farlow, in the Hog's Head saloon.

He handed her up his saddle, which she took in two hands and placed in a corner, where Old Morg kept a small barrel and a few other provisions necessary for the Wagoneer. Kit wondered what was in the small wooden barrel – water, perhaps? Though it didn't look like a water barrel.

There was an awkward moment. Magdalena was looking at him expectantly, as if she deeply wanted to know why he was still standing there and hadn't beat it.

Kit braced himself. A part of him wanted to walk away, but that part of him that insisted on going through even the most arduous of things kept him from leaving.

He cleared his throat. "I... I have something for you."

That seemed to surprise her, that he could possibly have had anything for her. For a moment Kit was so pleased with himself for pulling off the line he had practised over and over in his head the night before, he forgot to move. Then he hurriedly unbuttoned his top pocket and dipped the ends of his fingers into it.

He smiled at her nervously as he dug for the photograph. Finally he found it, and handed it to her.

"I got it from your pa."

She took it from his outheld hand and stared at it in disbelief.

"You saw my pa?" she said softly. "Is he... where is he? Is he still alive?"

"I'm afraid not, ma'am– Magdalena, I mean," Kit added hurriedly.

"I thought that Indian killed him."

Kit thought of telling her that her pa had very unwisely faked death and lost his scalp for having done so, but thought it best not to make bad news any worse.

He said, "He did kill him, in the end. If it wasn't for your pa's... bravery we never would have found you. He rode into Wagon Trail, near dead in the saddle, and we took him to Doc Benton."

"It was a poison arrow killed him," he added.

She glanced up at Kit, and then went back to the photograph.

"I'm sorry about your brother," Kit said. "If it brings you any peace of mind, we give him a decent Christian burial."

"We're Mormons," she said, frustrated.

Kit didn't know what Mormons were – sounded like some kind of Indians to him – but he figured a hole in the ground was a hole in the ground, to most anyone.

"What about my sister?" she asked, finally confronting Kit with the dreaded question he knew would have to be answered eventually.

Kit hesitated, but something fortunate happened. Lebold was bringing his horse back into camp, walking ahead of it and leading it by its long rope, and overheard.

He tied the horse back to the side of the wagon and came around back.

"Howdy, ma'am," he said, taking off his hat and holding it – something Kit himself had neglected to do. He said, "Pardon me, but I just happened to overhear. I'm sorry about your sister. I'm afraid she passed. If it's any consolation to you, she passed quickly, and we killed the Indians who kept her captive. She passed during the battle." Then he put his hat back on and nodded at her, "Ma'am."

He gave Kit a knowing look, as if Kit now owed him one, and

walked away, back around front of the wagon.

"I'm sorry," Kit said.

In truth, he was relieved. He could quite happily have gone the rest of his days without having to let Magdalena know that he had bombed her sister with dynamite. He was very grateful to Lebold, for putting it the way he had.

What stuck in his craw, though, was that Lebold had called her ma'am, and twice, and she hadn't admonished him even once.

"Miss Magdalena?" Kit said. "I was just wonderin' if you have any other family elsewhere, that you could go to?"

When she looked up from the little, worn photograph Kit saw tears in her eyes again; they were coursing down her cheeks. A sight that made him feel for her, though also a sight that embarrassed him.

"I don't got nobody," she sobbed. "He killed my whole family, everyone."

"You ain't got nowhere to go?"

"No," she snorted.

"Well, reason I ask is, we're gonna start headin' north, to sell those bones you're sittin' on. Then we're gonna head down to Texas and build us a ranch."

She tried to compose herself, flicking her head to get her hair out of the way.

"Our sod house was in Texas," she said matter-of-factly. "This one, in the photo."

"It's a mighty fine home."

"No it wasn't. It was practically caving in on our heads and Ma hated it."

"Oh," Kit said. He was silent for a moment. "Uh, Miss Magdalena?"

"Just call me Lena, okay? Not miss or my full name – it sounds strange, okay?"

Kit found it hard to have to call her Lena; a further embarrassment, since he thought it sounded too informal. But he decided not to disobey her.

"Uh, okay. Lena. Can you go back there? Mean to say, did your pa still own the claim?"

"No, he sold it. It's not ours any more. Anyway, it was useless. Had no water beneath it."

Kit thought he ought to tell her that it had sounded like it was oil actually, one of the most useful and profitable resources in all the west, but again did not want to be the harbinger of bad news.

"Well, I guess we could drop you off in Dodge, or Abilene or Ellsworth. The doc said that's where you was all headed, according to your pa."

"No. No, I don't want to go to a town. All this happened in the first place because my pa got it into his mad head that we should go live in one."

"Well then I guess we could take you to Texas," he said. "Provided Old Morg don't mind."

Kit thought Old Morg might, though it would likely save him having to hire on a cook. Kit didn't know what else they might do with her; if she didn't want to go to a town, they couldn't just leave her out on the cold prairie.

"Well, it was nice talking to you, Lena," Kit said. "Oh, I got one other thing for you."

He dipped into his pocket again and held his fist out to her, closed around the arrowhead.

When she held her hand open beneath his, he released his fingers and dropped the arrowhead into her palm.

"I found it on the prairie while we was following you. Thought you might like it. It's an Indian..."

Magdalena was staring at the arrowhead on her open palm as if Kit had just given her a black widow spider.

She gasped in disgust and then cocked her hand back behind her ear and threw it into the grass, as far away from her she could get it to go.

"Wha–" Kit said, but was cut off.

"Just leave," Magdalena said. "Just... just leave me alone. I want to be alone."

"Why... why certainly, ma– ma'am."

She let out a frustrated little groan, and he decided to hightail it out of there.

On the whole, actually, he felt it went rather well.

“Even if you’re gonna head north,” Lebold said, “along the same cattle trails as we are, we ain’t gonna be able to ride with you.”

“Why not?” Kit asked.

“We can’t keep up with that wagon, or we’ll never get to the herd in time. It moves at a goddamn snail’s pace; the herd’s busy doin’ ten, fifteen mile a day.”

“Oh,” Kit said. He had not considered that, but supposed it was as good a reason as any. He himself had not been fond of keeping up with it as they had hunted ahead for the renegade Indian.

“Well, I guess this is goodbye then,” Kit said, looking from Dwight to Lebold, and briefly glancing at the Glorietta woman.

The camp was all packed up and ready to let out on the trail. Old Morg was sitting on his wagon seat next to Jeb, holding onto the mules’ reins and waiting to whip at them.

“It was a hell of a trip, Kit,” Lebold said. He held out his hand, and Kit took it in his own.

This time Lebold did not add his challenging squeeze, as he had the first time he had met Kit; it seemed he finally had a sort of respect for Kit.

“Maybe I’ll see you on down the trail,” he added, and walked to his horse.

Dwight stepped up and held out his left hand, which Kit at first tried to shake with his right, and then had to shake awkwardly with his left.

“See you on down the line, Kit,” he said. “Maybe next spring I’ll see you down in Texas, huh?”

"I'd look forward to that," Kit said.

There was something unpleasant about goodbyes. Kit realized he didn't like them, and looked forward to nothing more than next spring, when these fine men might come to join them for their drive.

Glorietta helped Dwight up into the saddle and then climbed on behind him. In the meantime Lebold had ridden over to the wagon seat and was shaking Old Morg's hand.

"Take it easy, old man," he said to Morg.

"You take it easy yourself," Old Morg replied. "And if you and your young friend there are thinkin' of joining my outfit next spring, you best know now that I don't put up with slackers and I pay forty dollars a month and not a cent more."

"That's about what we get now," Lebold said. "Fine with me, though I never said nothin' about joinin' no cow outfit of yours. That was Dwight."

He rode around the mules and pulled his horse to a stop on the other side of the wagon seat.

"Jeb," he said, and held out his hand.

Jeb hesitated, and then held out his own and shook it.

"It was an honour riding with you," Lebold said. "You're a good man."

Jeb was mighty taken aback by that comment, since at first Lebold had been wary of him, and had been for most of the trip, for that matter, too.

He rode around the back of the wagon and tipped his hat to Magdalena.

"Ma'am," he said to her. "Wishin' you luck now."

"Why, thank you," Kit heard her reply from the back.

Then Lebold reined in next to Dwight and Glorietta, her hands around Dwight's waist.

Boy, that woman sure got holt of him, Kit thought from where he stood in front of the mules.

"Goodbye, boys," Dwight said.

"G'bye," Lebold said.

They turned their horses' heads and without saying any more touched spurs to their flanks and loped away, following the slithering line of the river east to the cow trails.

Soon they were specks in the shimmering distance.

Kit felt gloomy.

"Come on up on the wagon, Kit," Old Morg said. "Unless you tend on walkin' to the railhead."

Jeb shuffled along as Kit climbed up onto the wagon seat. He sat and sighed.

"I hate goodbyes," he said.

"Why, I do too, Kit, I do too," said Old Morg, and whipped the mules.

Travelling with a wagon over the plains proved to be a pain.

By the end of the first day Kit's backside was sore from all the juddering the wagon did as it wheeled over various bumps and rocks while he sat on the seat. Furthermore, he reckoned he could have walked faster – the wagon could do no more than two miles an hour with the load it was bearing.

They pushed east most of that morning, making sure to keep the Canadian River in sight on the southern horizon.

Finally, they came upon the wide, trampled road used by the cattle herds, though they saw no cattle. Things went more smoothly from here on out, as they swung north and took the well-trodden trail.

In the late afternoon, however, they found themselves at the top of a steep rise in the plains, and they all had to climb down off the wagon, and Magdalena out of the back, to go through the downward process.

Kit was glad to see Magdalena, though she did not seem glad to see him. She waited at the top of the rise with her forearms folded impatiently as Old Morg got a thick coil of rope out of the back of the wagon and attached it to the wagon's tongue.

Old Morg got Magdalena to sit up on the wagon seat and rile up the mules, whipping their traces. As they began to pull the wagon down the decline, Kit and Jeb, aided by Morg, prevented it from descending too fast in a sort of one-way tug of war.

Afterwards, Kit was covered in sweat and had rope burns on his palms, which stung terrifically when he opened and closed his hands.

That night they camped at a creek and found plenty of firewood. Magdalena still remained in the back of the wagon, and took her supper there, though Kit made a point to rise to the task of bringing her her plate of food. Well, *his* plate, though still, she did not know that. She didn't seem to want much to do with him, and mostly he sat with Old Morg and Jeb, listening to the old man's reminiscences.

The North Canadian and Cimarron River crossings were not a pleasant thought to Kit, but the next afternoon when they reached the North Canadian, it wasn't as bad as he had thought it was going to be. Firstly, the cows had trampled the banks on both sides into gentle slopes, and the crossing was not too deep or fast moving, though the rain had charged the river up some. None of the mules had to swim, though. Secondly, they had the rope and the team of mules.

Kit swam across arm-over-arm with the thick end of the rope gritted between his teeth, and helped to pull the wagon along from the other bank. Old Morg and Jeb stood waist-deep in the river, their backs to the wagon-end, planting their feet on the riverbed and pushing the wagon along. Magdalena, who claimed she could not swim, sat on the wagon seat and whipped the mules, who seemed to be taking an intense dislike to her. Already one had tried to nip her after they had taken the wagon downhill and re-boarded it, and one had tried to kick Kit.

He saw now why Old Morg warned them. His mules were tricky; they even tried to bite Jeb. The only one they didn't seem to mind was Morg, who could walk right up and scratch them behind their ears without being bitten or kicked.

Once the mules were up the bank and straining in their traces, Kit let go of the rope and jumped down into the river, to help Jeb and Morg push the rest of the wagon out of the water and up the muddy bank.

It had bogged slightly and took a lot of grit. All three of the men were covered in mud from their boots to their armpits by the time they got it up onto the bank, and had to go back into the river to wash off.

Indeed, it had been tiring, but Kit had thought the wagon wouldn't make it across the river at all, full of bones as it was, and thought it might sink like a stone or turn over onto its side. He had also expected the river to be much more up than it was, after the rain.

They crossed the Cimarron in much the same manner, though this time the wagon didn't even bog and Jeb could help Kit pull it across, a point at which Kit learned how strong Jeb actually was. He took more than half of the load when he pulled, and the muscles of his arms stood out and popped and pulsed, veins as big as snakes running along his biceps and forearms.

The days and nights blurred together and things went slow. They ate what they could catch, which happened to be a skinny prairie chicken and some rabbit. Old Morg shot a prairie dog but even Jeb refused to eat it, and Magdalena refused to take part in preparing it. Magdalena had finally come out of the wagon and taken to helping around camp, particularly with cooking and watching the meat and making coffee.

Old Morg was more than content to eat the prairie dog, explaining to them that he practically considered it a delicacy after his Pawnee wife had introduced it to him on the reservation.

He even skinned it and cured its hide, from force of habit, he said. The only animal he didn't skin was the chicken and even then probably only because he couldn't. He even made little fluffy balls of the rabbit pelts. "Reminds me of my beaverin' days," he had remarked.

Old Morg had decided they would sell the bones in Dodge City, and Kit was looking forward to it. It would be interesting to see Dodge again, he felt, and see how much – or indeed how little – it might have changed over the years he had been away, busy patrolling the streets of Wagon Trail.

Dodge City was right on the other side of the Arkansas river, and though they had no more rivers to cross, which was a relief to Kit, he realized they would have to cross the river on the flatboat ferry. Mules on a flatboat, he knew, were no joke. Old Morg told him that an entire wagon was once pulled into the Arkansas by a team of mules spooked by the motion of the flatboat as it pushed away from the south bank, and a kid was drowned.

On the last leg of the journey, just when everything was going good, a squall hit. It caught them right out on the flat, open plains of the Arkansas River Valley, and blew so hard it almost tipped the wagon over. The mules were spooked and had to be blindfolded with hats tied on by their hatstrings, and neckerchiefs and shirts.

The canvas cover on the wagon rippled against the skeletal wooden bows within it, causing such resistance that the wheels on one side began to lift off the ground as the blinded mules were whipped along.

But Old Morg's experience soon put an end to their problems.

"We're gonna hafta ride bareheaded," he shouted over the squall on the wagon seat.

Kit was amiss. He put his hand on his bare head to see if he hadn't lost track of things. No, he hadn't. His hat was indeed presently covering the eyes of one of Old Morg's ungrateful mules.

"No, not your head, Kit," Old Morg shouted. "The *wagon's* gonna hafta go bareheaded."

Magdalena was cowering in the back and was none too pleased to have them undo and fold back the canvas cover, so that she had to sit there and deal with the full brunt of the wind. Her hair blew to one side, revealing a small white ear, and the squall wailed and screamed its banshee cry into it.

But with the wagon cover off, and the wagon itself bare to the bows which arched over its wooden bed full of bones, it moved much smoother along the wind-ravaged plains. With most of the resistance gone, the mules also managed to recover their strength and after a while they collected their hats and clothing from them.

The squall lasted well into the night, letting up no less – only a hard driving rain added itself to the mix. It was a miserable night, and they saw no reason to stop and make camp, so decided to push on instead.

Soon the rain turned into icy cold, stinging sleet, which kept driving into Kit's eyes and blinding him. The mules didn't like it none too much either. Eventually the wagon and the bones in back were covered with a fine carpet of melting sleet, which began to settle as the wind turned down a notch or two.

Then suddenly it stopped, so quickly and completely that they halted the mule team and looked around into the dark night suspiciously.

"I seen this happen in the Rocky Mountains," Old Morg said. "And usually it meant a storm like no other was gonna hit."

Kit swallowed and checked back in the wagon bed to see if Magdalena was alright. She was hiding under a corner of canvas sheeting, which she held over her head like a blanket.

Just as soon as the squall had stopped, little balls of white ice began to fall out of the sky. They dropped and bounced off the wooden sides of the wagon, and hit the arched bows above with loud *thonks* and *dinks*.

Kit was glad he had his hat back and a mule wasn't wearing it, because they were getting bigger every second. Old Morg whipped the mules and they pushed through the hail.

It stung their arms and legs and the little stones fell down their shirt necks, an extremely unpleasant feeling.

All around, the dark plains were covered, from end to end, in brilliant white balls of ice.

Then a ball of ice the size of a pullet's egg hit the wagon seat at one end and put a big dent into it. Old Morg stopped the mules quickly and they stared at it.

"'I God, Mary, Mother of Jesus!" Old Morg said. "Everybody who don't want a hole in their head get under the wagon!"

They jumped down immediately and crowded in under the wagon, Kit offering Magdalena help before he did, but she refused it and got down on her own.

Huddled under the wagon and shivering, they lay and listened to the occasional loud *plonk* amidst the smaller noises of the landing hailstones. By the sounds of things, every now and again there were some real big ones, and one must have hit one of the mules, for it let out a loud squeal.

"I just hope them mules don't take it into their heads to leave without us," Old Morg said.

If they did get it into their heads to do so, they most likely would all have been run over.

One thing pleased Kit: he was shoulder to shoulder with Magdalena. But still, when he looked at her and smiled she merely looked away. He was beginning to feel there was no chance she was ever going to like him, even just as a friend.

Finally the hail petered out and stopped, and they decided to cold camp right there, all under the wagon where they lay with exception of Magdalena, who climbed out and slept under the canvas in the wagon bed. That depressed Kit, because for a moment he thought he was going to have the extreme good fortune of spending the night next to her.

In the morning when they awoke the weather was just dandy, and by midday they found themselves boarding the flatboat on the Arkansas River and waiting to be ferried across. There were only a few other passengers: a man on horseback and a thin lady with two curious-looking if poorly fed children. Kit gave one a piece of jerky, and then had to give the other kid one when they started fighting over it.

But when he looked at Magdalena she smiled at him, for the first time, which filled his breast with joy – but then he noticed that she was smiling at the two kids eating his jerky, and wished he hadn't given it to them.

Morg paid the toll and they were ferried across the Arkansas without incident, even the mules behaving themselves and looking down at the water curiously, glad not to have to be pulling the wagon through it and seeming to marvel at how this was possible...

And shortly after midday they rode the wagon into the city of Dodge.

When they rode down the wide main street of Dodge City, Magdalena was stunned.

She had never seen such fancy-looking stores and saloons, even if they did have false fronts. There were fancy new carriages and stages parked outside various establishments, and men and women dressed in the fanciest new clothes she had ever seen. She saw men wearing suits, with new-looking stovepipe hats, and one carrying a cane, walking along with a regal air. She saw a woman in a big green dress, and another – a stunning sight if ever there was one – wearing trousers and walking along with her partner, hand in hand.

She could hear a steam train hissing and sputtering somewhere behind the row of false-fronted buildings on the left, and railcar doors sliding aside nosily on their runners and big gangplanks being lowered into place with loud claps.

Groups of hardy-looking men on horseback passed them by, looking at her and undressing her, she felt, with their eyes – for the wagon cover had not yet been put back into place. Their hungry looks unnerved her. *All* the eyes that fell upon her unnerved her.

When she looked down at her own filthy dress it filled her with shame. She had always been interested in fashion and dressing well, though had never had the money to practise doing so. Now, the town just made her more conscious of how poorly dressed she was; how poorly dressed, come to think of it, she had always been, and how poor she was and what little she actually had to her name, not even having family any more.

She feared the well-dressed women crossing the streets and walking along the boardwalks might look at her with condescension and distaste, but most walked along with an arrogant cock to their chins and didn't look at her at all.

Then the buildings dropped away on her left and she saw the railcars being loaded with cattle. Cowboys on horseback herded the steers up the wide gangplanks, and she saw one of them lasso a steer expertly after it turned away and refused to enter the rail car.

She enjoyed getting to see the cowboys work, especially since they were too busy to see her seeing. She liked the clothes they wore, and the looks of their determined faces. It seemed to her that every one was a strong-willed, well-fed and able man who took pride in what he was doing.

There were cattle pens nearby, chocked full of cattle waiting to be loaded onto the freight train. She had always wanted to travel on a train, though didn't know where she would go once she got on one – or indeed where it even was they went. She had heard that some went even as far as Chicago, to the slaughterhouses where they offloaded the cattle.

It was a frightful thought that all those cattle were going off to be slaughtered, after travelling all the way up from Texas, most likely. She wondered if they would have put up more of a struggle if they could somehow have been informed of where it was exactly they were being taken.

Suddenly the wagon pulled to a stop at the side of a wooden train building or depot, it seemed, and the men descended.

"I'm gonna go make a deal with a man I know," she heard Old Morg say. "You boys are free to roam round but don't you go into no saloons or get into fisticuffs."

Old Morg handed Kit a ten dollar note. "That's an advancement on your first month's wages," he said. "Don't waste it. That's five each."

She saw Kit looking at Jeb happily.

Old Morg said, "Take care of that girl and don't let her out of your sight. And leave your guns in the back of the wagon."

"Yes, sir," Kit said.

She watched the old man enter an open doorway and disappear into the big clapboard building.

She wondered what was going to happen now, looking around at the busy town. She decided to get down from the wagon and stretch her legs.

Then wished she had stayed in it, for Kit was coming over.

"Hiya, Lena," he said shyly. "Would you maybe like to go for a walk with us? Or not," he added, as if to make the decision easier on her.

What annoyed her is it seemed she had no choice. If she said she would stay with the wagon, she would be on her own and didn't doubt some man would soon step up and bother her. But at the same time she didn't want to walk around in a town – *city* – where people were so well dressed, not in the old torn dress she was wearing, anyway.

She decided to say to them, "I ain't going into town wearing a dress like *this*."

She saw Kit look reluctantly down at the note in his hand, and then apologetically at Jeb.

"Why, I guess we could go buy you a new one, but I don't know what size you are. I reckon it best you come with us."

That was good but also bad news. She doubted you could get much of a nice dress for five dollars, which, if she had heard Old Morg correctly, was what they each had to their names. Even if they would both club in to buy her a dress, she doubted it would be as good as the ones she had seen some of the women wearing as they had entered Dodge. Almost all those women had been with men, although not every one; but there seemed to be a clear correlation between well-dressed and with a man.

But what was mostly depressing was that she had no other choice than to go with them, to allow them to buy her the dress. How else would she get a new one? It was depressing; depressing that a woman was forever dependent on a man to have anything, to go... anywhere. To live.

She had not wanted anything to do with a man ever again, and yet in order to survive – or even have a single dress – she would have to. And sooner or later he would want the thing that the Indians had wanted, and she would have to give it to him.

She told herself she would never give it, to anyone, ever. They could help her and clothe and feed her and do everything they wanted, but it would never get them the one thing she knew they really wanted.

It was what *he* wanted – Kit. Why else would he act so nervous and insecure around her all the time? He wanted it, and not only that but he wanted her to make it easy for him to have it – to *help* him have it, to ease his shyness and nervousness.

Not a chance in this world, she thought.

"Okay, I'll come," she said irritably.

They found a clothing store after searching one side of the main street for several minutes, passing a few general stores and a saddle-maker's, a dry goods store that was closed, a big saloon – the biggest Magdalena had ever seen – and then found it next to a utility store.

A little old man with a monocle stood behind a glass counter, in which were set earrings and jewellery. Jeb waited outside and Magdalena felt acutely embarrassed with her appearance, for she saw the old man adjust his monocle and give her a surprised once-over, but after scanning the dresses hanging in the racks along the walls she found a durable-looking green one she liked. It looked a little like one she had seen a woman wearing earlier.

To her surprise, it was only six dollars, and Kit went outside to have a talk with Jeb while she tried it on in a little curtained changing room. She was glad Kit was outside while she tried it on, for she suspected he might try to spy her through the curtain, in which case she was prepared to have punched him in the snout.

It was heavy but fit nicely, and when she came out Kit was waiting with the eager little old man who owned the store.

"Why, you look smashing in that, young lady," the owner said.

"Do you like it?" Kit asked nervously, not knowing, it seemed to Magdalena, where to look.

"Yes, but it's six dollars," she said.

"That's fuh– fine," Kit said. "I spoke to Jeb outside. He's going to contribute."

That was nice of Jeb, she thought, who didn't look like a man to whom money came very easily. She felt a connection to Jeb, for he was the one man who didn't seem to look at her with the same expectation as Kit or the other men had, and he often wore a pained if contained expression, as if he had come a great distance and through a great ordeal, which is exactly how she felt.

Kit paid the man and Magdalena left her old dress with him, which he said he would gladly incinerate, and when they got outside Kit gave Jeb the change.

"Why, that was mighty kind of you, Jeb," she said to the black man, and gave him a friendly and appreciative smile.

He nodded and a small, forced smile tugged at the corners of his mouth.

Two men came out of a saloon as they headed back to the wagon. They stepped off into the dusty street and started circling each other and swiping at each other with knives.

No sooner were they doing so than a rider galloped over from the other side of the street on a big gelding. He had a big, bushy, black moustache and combed-back black hair, and an air of authority about him.

He pulled a pistol from a leather holster on his hip and fired into the air.

Magdalena noticed that there was a sickly-looking man riding up as well, also from the other side of the street, with a pale, thin face.

The two men swiping at each other with the knives stopped as soon as the gun fired into the air, and lowered them slowly, uncertainly.

When the sickly man rode up he stopped next to the man who had ridden up and fired his gun, and pulled out a handkerchief and coughed into it.

"I'd let them carve each other up, Wyatt. At least they're obeying the firearms ordinance," he said.

"That's Wyatt Earp!" Kit said in amazement.

Magdalena thought he was a magnificent-looking man, who carried himself proudly and fiercely, yet had an air of danger about him. He held himself with the regality of an eagle.

She heard him say, "I don't know, Doc. There ought to be a law against the carrying of knives too. We enforce the firearms ordinance, and all that happens is the whole town starts carvin' itself up."

"You boys chuck those knives in the dirt," Wyatt Earp, if that's who he was, said.

They immediately obeyed, even more fearful of him than they were of each other, which impressed Magdalena to no end. How could a man so easily command such obedience?

She watched him dismount gracefully and pick up the knives from the dust, handing them up to the sickly man on his horse.

"I dunno who *that* guy is," Kit said. "He looks like an outlaw."

Wyatt had passed the two knives handle-first to the man he had called Doc, and then remounted again.

"Clear away, folks," he said to the sidewalk. "And if you boys want your knives back you come one at a time to collect 'em from the jailhouse."

For a moment, as he turned his horse away, his eyes met Magdalena's. It was only a moment, but they were the brightest blue eyes she'd ever seen.

If ever she did have to have a man, she thought, it would have to be a man like that – a fine man.

"I can't believe I just saw Wyatt Earp," Kit said.

"I never heard of 'im," Jeb said.

They crossed the street and returned to the wagon.

Two men were offloading the buffalo bones into boxes and carrying them off into the building. They stood and watched the men work, which appeared to annoy them, one saying, "I wisht I could just stand around and watch other people workin'."

Old Morg was nowhere to be seen.

They waited for him for a good hour, leaning up against the side of the opposite building in what little shade it afforded, until finally Old Morg came around the corner of the boardwalk, carrying a big wooden box full of provisions, a new saddlebag slung over his shoulder with the pouches apparently stuffed full.

From what Magdalena could see, the wooden box contained jerky sticks and ammo, boxes of Therapeutic Papers, coffee and sugar, some rope and... and other things beneath them she couldn't quite make out without actually going through the box itself.

She had a curious nature and wanted to know, and realized that later, in the wagon, she could sneak a look. Old Morg had said on the flatboat that they were not going to stay in town for long, certainly not the night – which would have cost too much, particularly to stable the mules – and would be going across the Arkansas again before afternoon.

As he slumped the box into the back of the wagon, which was now empty of bones save for the white powder, which could not be collected, Old Morg said, "Right, that about does her. Got everything we need to take us to Texas. Got money if we need anything else along the way, though I don't intend to stop until Doan's Store on the Red River."

"We saw Wyatt Earp," Kit said.

"Is that so?" Old Morg said, turning from the box he had placed in the wagon bed.

"Yeah," Kit said excitedly. "Two guys tried to carve each other up in the street and he stopped them. He and another man," he added. "Sickly-looking."

"Did he call him Doc?" Old Morg asked.

"Why, I believe he did," Kit said, surprised that Morg had mentioned it.

"Then I 'spect it was Doc Holliday," Old Morg said.

"Who's he?"

"A dentist."

"A *den*tist? He didn't look like no dentist."

Old Morg said, "That's 'cause he became a gambler. I don't get that. Man has a perfectly good trade but prefers to gamble. He carved up some card player in Abilene, if I recall correctly. And a saloon got burnt down. Did you see Big Nose Kate?"

"Who's Big Nose Kate?"

"The whore who burnt down the saloon in Abilene to help him escape after he carved the card player up. They say he cut him open from his belly-whatsit to the nape of his neck. Not a man to take lightly. I could never quite work out why Wyatt's even friends with him – he's supposed to be a lawman."

"What's wrong with him?" Kit asked.

"Who?"

"The dentist? He looks sick."

"He's got tuberculosis."

"Oh," Kit said. "Like Mister Masterson's brother."

"Who?"

Magdalena decided to interrupt them. "Could you boys put the canvas cover back on the wagon before we go, please?"

"Why, sure, missy," Old Morg said. "Nice dress. Who bought that for you? Young Kit? Here. Gimme a hand, Kit."

Kit helped Old Morg to cover the wagon again, standing awkwardly on the sideboards, balancing on the tips of his boots and throwing one end of the canvas cover over the tops of the bows.

Then he climbed down and Old Morg told them all to climb on or get in; there was one other thing they needed to pick up before they set out.

They stopped at a big livery stable near the entrance to the main street and Old Morg went in and came out soon after leading two horses. Not the finest horses Magdalena had ever seen, but certainly durable-looking creatures.

He tied them to the back of the wagon and they looked in at Magdalena curiously as they walked along behind it.

In fact, she found she enjoyed their company, and to boot they blocked the wagon entrance and made her feel more secure in it. There was much more space now, and without the bones it was a lot more comfortable – and not so many people could look in at her now that the canvas cover was back on and the entrance obscured.

When they stopped on the north bank to wait for the ferry to come, Old Morg got down from the wagon seat and came around back to speak to her, standing between the two horses.

"Well, this is it, young missy," he said. "Which is it gonna be? You can either get on off here or come with us to Texas, though it ain't gonna be an easy trip. The next civilized place I intend to stop is Doan's Store, on the Red River in Texas. That's about three hundred miles or more from here."

But she had already made up her mind to go. Going back to Texas was what she had wanted all along, ever since they left it, and certainly after being taken captive. She didn't know what she would do once she got there, just that she would find her way.

"I'll come," she said, and smiled lightly.

"Well, I'm glad to hear it," Old Morg said. "We sure could use the help of a woman at the ranch – you are aware that's what we're goin' to Texas to do? You've got no obligation to take part in it, of course."

"No, I want to," she said agreeably.

"I don't put up with slackers."

"I ain't a slacker."

"I didn't think you were."

They crossed the Arkansas on the flatboat ferry again, without incident either way, which seemed to be a good start. Magdalena wondered what life on a ranch in Texas would be like; surely it couldn't be any worse than life in a sod house on the treeless plains?

Once they offloaded on the other side and rolled on for the endless prairie plains, Magdalena watched the city of Dodge beyond the river slowly shrink down beneath the horizon.

And soon even the Arkansas River was gone, and they were headed south for Texas.

PART
V

Kit had been disappointed that they had not spent longer in Dodge; he had wanted to explore and visit the old haunts he used to know, like the spot where all the buffalo hides used to be piled up, in a big fly-infested mound higher than a house. He was also disappointed that they had not seen Lebold or Dwight; for all Kit knew they could have been in any one of the saloons, and they had not looked in a single one. He would have liked to see them one more time before they headed off.

It seemed to him it was all the girl's fault. Not only had he had to spend the money Old Morg had given him on her, but a part of Jeb's, too, which he had promised to pay back. And what stuck in his craw night and day on the trail was that she had thanked Jeb for it and not him.

Had it not been for her he could have spent that money on himself, gone into one of the saloons and bought himself a shot of whiskey or two. Or gone looking in some of the general stores – he would have liked to buy himself some candy, and another box of Therapeutic Papers. He was tired of wiping with leaves, and on the plains there was sometimes nothing but sharp blades of grass, the nearest tree as far as a day's ride east.

He was beginning to see that Magdalena was not much different than Glorrietta had seemed to be, with one exception: whereas she had wanted to have everything to do with Dwight, and Dwight nothing to do with her (at least, to begin with), Magdalena wanted nothing to do with him and he everything to do with her.

He loved her, but she didn't seem to see it or if she did, *care*. It was completely not the way he had imagined it was going to turn out. She seemed to have no appreciation of what he had done for her, or that he had even done it. The only one she really talked to was Morg, sometimes sitting up on the wagon seat with him when Kit and Jeb used the two horses to scout ahead and look for something to shoot and cook.

The problem with following the cow trails south was that the animals had cottoned on to the herds and cattlemen that could be coming, and you had to ride further west – and quite a ways, at that – in order even to see a rabbit.

The new horses were a pain, too. Especially the one Kit mostly rode, which he had decided to call Apache, and not as a compliment. Apparently it had belonged to reservation Indians before being traded and sold, and it seemed to have as much a dislike for the white man as any Indian. His luck to choose it, when he had had the choice of the two, since it didn't seem to mind Jeb much.

Often it tried to kick Kit when he walked around it to mount, and he had developed a method of never stepping around the back of it, always around front. But even then it tried to bite him.

One day after they had crossed the Cimarron it tried to throw him, but Kit was expecting it and managed to stay on, only for it to start bucking like an unbroken bronc, until Kit indeed was thrown. He hurt his collarbone and elbow and had to spend three days up on the wagon seat.

When they came to the North Canadian and finally crossed it, using of course the well-trodden highway of the cattlemen, Kit decided to approach Jeb and ask if he wanted to swap.

At first Jeb seemed unwilling, afraid the horse might do the same to him, but Kit persuaded him it was the horse's shared temperament with the Indians and its distinct dislike for whites.

Jeb didn't want Kit to get injured any worse, so gave in. With Kit injured it had been a lot harder to get the wagon across the rivers, though it was a lot lighter without the load of bones, which counted for something at least.

The new horse was just dandy – at least, after having done at least a hundred miles or more on the ill-disposed Apache. It was so dandy Kit decided to call it Dandy, for Jeb had not named it and found the practice of naming an animal alien to him.

For a while it gave Jeb some trouble too, reaching back and trying to bite his knee, though the second time it tried to do it, Jeb booted it in the face before it could. From then on it tried to bite his other knee, and Jeb socked it under the chin with his boot tip on two separate occasions. Eventually it learned to be wary of Jeb. Kit didn't like to see animals get hurt or hit, but he agreed with Jeb's method, since the animal was almost unmanageable and it was that or let it go – and of course they weren't going to do that.

Old Morg said to Kit one afternoon on the wagon seat, as Jeb scouted ahead on Apache, "All that horse's done with all its fussin' is set itself up to be the first one to get eaten if it ends up we can't catch anything."

Kit chuckled at that. "Have you ever et horse?" he asked.

"I et a packhorse."

"Really?"

"That's what I said, didn't I? I was stranded up in the Rockies in winter, trappin' furs, and I et him."

"Jeez."

"His name was Kansas, and I was hungry enough to eat the whole of him. He didn't do a thing to deserve it either," he added, "except stand there and look right tasty."

When they came to the South Canadian, it seemed to Kit he had been back and forth across it a thousand times, though he had only in fact been across it twice, that he recalled. Of course this would make it a third time.

Getting the wagon across turned out to be half a day's work, mainly because a torrential shower decided to add itself to their misery. It turned the river's banks into mud slush and this time Kit got covered in mud up to his hatband. He even got mud in one of his eyes and couldn't see out of it.

On the opposite bank the wagon bogged, and Kit had to grab a hold of one rear wheel and Jeb the other, while Old Morg and Magdalena waited on the bank in the rain with the two horses.

The main problem was that Jeb was strong enough to get his wheel turning, while Kit's didn't budge an inch. He kept slipping as well, and sliding front first into the mud, as the river flowed by behind him, raindrops bouncing up and down all over its torrent-agitated surface like fleas on a mattress.

The wagon ended up turning sideways, and landing above the bank at a canter. For a moment Kit thought it was going to tip and fall on him, in which case he would have been crushed into the mud, but soon Jeb's big hands were on the spokes of the wheel with him and together they were able to get it firmly on land.

After that, other than the rainy weather, it was plain sailing – comparatively plain sailing, at least. The horse Kit swapped with Jeb certainly made things easier, though he felt guilty every time Apache gave Jeb any trouble. Especially when Apache took a big bite out of Jeb's old saddle. Kit promised him a new one, or at least to have it mended once they got set up down at the Rio Grande. That was another debt to his already growing costs, although Kit made light of the incident, telling Jeb his saddle had sure been through the wars, what with having fallen down the Palo Duro Canyon on the back of a horse that got kilt.

The days blurred into each other, as often was the case on the rolling plains. Intermittent rains spoiled many days and left them all feeling wet and gloomy and chilled to the bones – even Old Morg. There were no trees on the plains, either, or even bushes, just miles and miles of grassy prairies, as far as the eye could see and far further, Kit knew. At times it seemed they would never ever end.

Kit often had to ride a good half-mile to do his business; normally he wouldn't have, but with Magdalena around he became more modest – excessively so, Old Morg told him. To make things worse, the boxes of T.P. were for Magdalena's use only, and even Old Morg didn't use them. Where or when Magdalena went, Kit didn't know. She must have gone every time he scouted ahead, waiting for him to leave before she went, because he sure never saw her go.

When the sun was uninterrupted the days were stifling, so hot even Magdalena jumped out of the back of the wagon to walk alongside it. If her ankle had been injured before it certainly wasn't any more, though still it seemed to Kit she spent more of her time inside the wagon than outside it.

She hardly ever said a word to Kit, or even looked at him much, he felt. Often he would ride out and skirt the wagon wide, riding so that she could have seen him if she had looked out the back; he stood in the stirrups and spurred the horse, pretending he could see something in the distance and trying to impress her with his riding skill. Though usually once he reached his fake target in the distance, he merely stopped and looked back, to see if she was looking. It seemed to him she never was.

It was depressing. Life seemed pointless if she wasn't going to like him. Whereas life would have been heavenly if she just would even talk to him. His attempts to get her into conversation at the fireplace usually caused her to get up and take her plate to the wagon, until she started to take her food in it each night again, and Kit decided to do the same – in a way.

He would come into camp and collect his plate, and then walk off into the distance and find some place to eat it – though Morg warned him not to go too far.

Soon he stopped, however, for away from the fire it was cold and lonely and he kept thinking an Indian might pop out of the long grass and scalp him, for they were presently passing through Indian Territory, and he would have to go around like Magdalena's pa had, without no hair.

Snakes became a problem as they worked their way deeper into the Territory, covering their path and spooking the mules. Mostly they were rattlesnakes. Kit and Jeb rode ahead each day shooting the snakes from their horses whenever they spotted them. Kit was shocked at how often his slugs merely kicked up the dust around them and they continued slithering on, while Jeb managed to hit them with his rifle every time. Kit suspected his pistol, though when he asked Jeb to borrow his rifle and gave Jeb his pistol, the same occurred. Spurts of dust shot up around the slithering bodies even though Kit had them firmly in his sights, while Jeb merely pointed the pistol over the side of his horse, took aim carefully at an arm's length, and fired. And then the snake was whipping and lashing in the final throws of death, except when Jeb hit them in the head, in which case they lay there still, headless, messy red tatters at one end.

When Kit mentioned this to Old Morg, Old Morg made a show of inspecting his pistol and told him it was poorly weighted, and when Kit pointed out that the very same had happened with the rifle, Old Morg simply dismissed it and said, "Some weapons work better in one man's hands than another. I suspect all you need is the right kind of hand-banger. Tell you what, we'll have a look see if we can't get you a new one at Doan's Store."

The next big river they would cross would be the Red, though Kit's dread of taking the wagon across this wide, brown, muddy river was offset by the fact they would be visiting Doan's Store, a small trading outpost on the north banks of the river. He looked forward to getting a new gun and maybe Morg would give him some money again and he could buy some things.

Kit had always considered himself a fine shot. Certainly he was a fast draw – which wasn't much use if you weren't one – and even Old Morg had always told him the same, teaching him how to shoot at tins back in Dodge in the grand old days. Although Kit recalled Morg had almost invariably been firing at the same time as he.

When he reflected back on past events, however, the only thing he seemed to be able to recall hitting was his horse, Misty Blue. And the two tables in the saloon with the shotgun, but even then he had somehow wounded Dwight with grapeshot, unless someone else had fired a shotgun. But the only one he could remember firing a shotgun was the big, fat whore who had choked his member.

One night he choked his own member, doing it in his bedroll and thinking of Magdalena. He came to realise that you didn't need no whore to soap up her hands and do the thing; you could do it all by yourself and didn't have to pay no four dollars or get shot at and have to jump over a barroom railing, but before he could finish, Old Morg suddenly awoke and there was the loud click of a pistol hammer.

"What's that noise?" Old Morg asked, in a startled voice. His pistol was pointed in Kit's direction – more worryingly, towards Kit's midsection.

"It's, uh... it's nothin'," Kit replied.

"That weren't nothin', I heard it. I near shot at it."

"I didn't hear anythin'."

"It sounded like a fox with its snout in an empty bean tin."

Kit was extremely embarrassed, but at least it was dark and Old Morg wouldn't be able to see his face flushing.

"Why's your face red?" Old Morg asked him. He unclicked the hammer of his pistol and slowly lowered it. "You look like you've been runnin' butt-neckid in the moonlight."

"Why, I ain't, I been right here in my blanket," Kit insisted.

"Well... I hear that fox goin' at it again I'm apt to shoot it, you unnerstand?"

Kit was just settling back down to sleep when Morg added, "It'll come off in your hand and then you'll have to pee like a lady, I tell ya."

Kit froze in the darkness, but Old Morg said no more. He tried to console himself all night that Morg had not known what he had been doing under his blanket, and failed miserably. He didn't dare finish, either.

★ ★ ★

One day as they neared the Red, Kit got down from his horse to inspect a rabbit hole, and found a black widow in it instead. He stared at the small red hourglass shape under its fat belly as it went about mending its web. It seemed to have some huge catch in there, a big, silky, round ball in the middle. For some reason it was fascinating to think that one bite from that tiny little insect could kill a man.

He found an old piece of planking, which must have come from a corral fence or something, and used the end to dig it out, breaking its web. Suddenly hundreds of little black widows were swarming everywhere; he had hit a nest of them – the black widow must have been a female. Females were trouble, he knew!

He used the end of the plank to whack them with, squishing the mother, but when he hefted the plank up to whap at them again, hundreds of little spiders had adhered, and flew through the air like ants.

Suddenly they were all over him, dropping down the neck of his shirt and abseiling down from the brim of his hat like little corks on a string.

The sight that followed was enough to make Old Morg stop the wagon and laugh so loud from the seat that even Magdalena climbed out of the back and up onto the wagon to see from its vantage point. In fact, Old Morg almost laughed himself off the seat.

Kit didn't know this until afterwards, by which time he was in his underwear. He jumped up and down on one foot at a time while he pulled off his boots and even socks, and then without unbuttoning it pulled his shirt clean over his head, taking his hat off with it. Finally he frantically jumped out of his trousers, and began to beat at them with the plank.

Then he dropped it and whacked at himself with his hands as if being attacked by a swarm of bees.

Old Morg shouted from the wagon seat. "What's the matter, Kit, you got ants in your pants?"

Kit looked up, and to his deep embarrassment saw Magdalena looking at him, standing on the wagon seat next to Morg.

He held his hands over the lump his dingus made in his long johns, and his face near turned as red as the hourglass marking *on* a black widow.

"They was black widows," he said. "Hunnerts of 'em! Little baby ones!"

"I don't think they can do you much harm," Old Morg called. "Did any bite you?"

"No, I don't think so."

"Well get on back in your duds, afore one bites your ting-ting and it off 'n falls off – if it ain't already."

Kit had been extremely embarrassed, mostly to have Magdalena see him in his underwear, and hear what Old Morg said.

That night they ate bacon and beans from some tins Old Morg had bought in a food store in Dodge, since Jeb had been unable to find any game out on the plains. He had spent most of the day looking, and hadn't been around to witness the spider incident, an event that Old Morg poked fun at all night and seemed highly amused by.

"You should have seen young Kit," he said. "I didn't know he could dance like that. He ought to take up a job doin' it in a saloon."

Even Magdalena laughed at the jokes, and it drove Kit from the camp for the first time in three weeks. She didn't laugh much, but it was enough to upset him severely.

As he stormed off with his beans Old Morg added insult to injury.

"You oughtn't to have fooled with that nest of widows and you know it," he called after him. "What were you thinkin'? I knowed a man who got kilt by one of those."

But all was forgotten the next morning – everything that had happened on the entire trip so far – for when Magdalena awoke, she complained of dizziness and nausea...

And then began to throw up.

Kit had no idea what could be wrong with her; he thought at first she might have food poisoning – which caused him a conside able deal of alarm, since he knew that out here on the plains she could die from it – but it appeared to pass fairly quickly, and after taking a pull on one of Old Morg's canteens she said she felt herself again.

Kit watched her closely all that day, whenever he could find the opportunity. He kept annoying her, to boot, by continuously inquiring after her, asking if she felt okay – and despite her insistence that she was fine, he continued to ask.

That afternoon Kit discovered what was in the small barrel Old Morg kept in his wagon. It was thick, white animal fat. Old Morg took it down and plucked up the round lid, placing the barrel down before one of the wheels.

"What's that for, Morg?" Kit asked.

"It's wolf fat."

"Wolf fat?"

"That's right. I learned to do this when we ran out of store-bought grease when I was leading a party along the Oregon Trail."

There was a flat piece of metal in it and Old Morg scooped up a load on the end and began to work it around the wheel's axle and bearings.

Kit knew that Old Morg had served as a guide. Many a mountain man had, for they were some of the first people to explore the Rocky Mountains and find paths through their barrier and into the west before there were even maps, but he did not know that he had taken people along the entire Oregon Trail.

Working, Old Morg said, "When we run out of grease for the wagon wheels and the axles, we shot buffalo and wolves and scooped and stored all the fat. Of course, there ain't no buffalos any more, but wolves'll do."

Kit helped Morg grease the axles and soon they were underway again.

Just after midday, Kit saw Magdalena sitting up on the wagon next to Old Morg and decided to ride back and tether his horse. He tied it to the back of the wagon and climbed up, sitting on the other side of Morg, which he noticed seemed to annoy her some. But he was tired of riding in the saddle and wanted to have his tailbone whacked by the wagon seat some, for a change of hurt. He had another saddle sore, too, which Morg had noticed and advised him to go open the barrel in the back of the wagon and smear some of the animal fat over.

"How's it goin'?" he asked Morg now.

"Oh, I was just enjoyin' some fine female company," Morg replied. "Till you rode up, that is."

"I thought you might wanta go hunting," Kit said. "With Jeb," he added.

"Where is Jeb?"

"He rode west."

"This is Indian Territory, you know? You oughtn't to ride off alone." Kit began rubbing his saddle sore theatrically.

"I tolt you to put some wolf fat on that."

"I ain't puttin' wolf on me."

"Well, soon you ain't even gonna be able to ride a horse," Old Morg said. "I suppose you'll wanta sit up here on this wagon every day while *I* ride."

"No, I just wanta rest it," Kit maintained.

Old Morg said, "Well, I suppose I could ride out and see what I can find. Here, take the reins."

He handed them to Kit, and then got up and stepped over him, jumping down from the moving wagon – although moving, that is, at two miles an hour. Mostly they managed to do fifteen miles a day, moving not much faster than an entire herd of cattle would move, though sometimes if they pushed late into the evenings they could manage twenty.

They tended to push more now, now that they were in Indian Territory, although Kit had not yet seen a single Indian or even sign of an Indian, though word was the Indian Territory had long since been tamed. But the possibility of a raiding or war party was always a point of concern, although it was said to be further up north, Nebraska and Dakota and Montana, where the Indians were still a considerable problem. An Indian called Red Cloud, Old Morg had told him, had caused and was causing a lot of noise up there.

It shocked Kit to think that once Comanche Indians had been the scourge of Texas, and now there wasn't a one.

He saw Morg gallop past on Dandy, headed west. Soon he was alone on the wagon seat with Magdalena, who sat awkwardly in the silence.

Kit wracked his mind for something to say, becoming acutely aware that the length of time in which no one had spoken was unnatural.

"Why, it's a fine day, ain't it?" he decided to say.

"It's overcast," she said sullenly. "And it's likely going to rain tonight."

"Wuh-Well," Kit stuttered, "it's still a fine day, I reckon. And least *you* got the wagon."

"What's that suppose to mean?"

"Why, it ain't supposed to mean nothin'. I mean, it means you can be out of the rain, even if it does rain. Is what I meant," he added awkwardly.

"What do you want with me?" she asked, sighing.

"Why, I don't want anything," Kit said, shocked that she would ask. "What makes you think I want anything?"

She huffed sarcastically. She said, "Psh," but that was all.

"I mean, I want mainly to know if you're alright, that's all. I was worried that you was sick this mornin'."

That was true; he genuinely was – and it seemed strange to him it had just come and gone like that.

"Well, I'm fine," she said.

"Well, I'm glad to hear that."

"Just... just stop asking me all the time," she said. "Let me be."

"Have I... done somethin' wrong?" Kit asked worriedly. He was amazed with himself to be so brave as to even ask.

"No!" she said angrily. "Just–"

Suddenly there was a distant gunshot. Kit looked to the west, where it had come from.

"They must have got somethin'," he said excitedly. "No more beans tonight, I guess."

Kit didn't like to eat beans, because of the embarrassing noises they forced him to perform at night in his blankets. He was usually deathly scared Magdalena would hear them, so he forced them to remain inside him, which caused considerable discomfort and stomach pain.

Usually by morning he would be so full of gas he had to get up on his horse and go for a ride, before even getting any coffee in him, and let out the gas against his saddle, which Dandy didn't like none and seemed to find highly disrespectful, nickering indignantly at each posterior expulsion.

There was another echoing gunshot, which caused Kit to frown at the empty horizon to the west.

"Maybe they come across a herd," he remarked.

Magdalena had seen his frown and was frowning now as well. She began to feel afraid.

There were two distant pops of a pistol, and another crack from Jeb's rifle.

Kit stood in the wagon seat, still holding the reins.

"Magdalena, get behind one of the wagon wheels," he said.

What Kit saw terrified him. Old Morg and Jeb were coming at a gallop, whacking the sides of their horses with their rifles – but that wasn't what terrified him, as such. He could see long thin objects raining down from the sky above them.

Then he saw the Indian war party come over a rise in the land behind them, at least twenty strong, whooping and hollering. Some had rifles and were firing them.

Magdalena had not obeyed him and was staring in horror, frozen in her seat. Even Kit realized that the sight of the Indians must have terrified her even more than it did him, for she must surely have known that if the Indians managed to kill Old Morg and Jeb, and then Kit, she would most likely be taken again.

"Magda," he said out of the corner of his mouth. "Let's both get off this wagon seat right fast."

He stepped over her and jumped down onto the grass, holding both his hands out to her. She was still looking to the horizon, but glanced down at him and shook her head clear; this time she let him help her down, and followed him as he rushed around the back of the wagon. He reached in for a rifle scabbard, and pulled out the spare Winchester Old Morg had bought in a gun store in Dodge.

Magdalena began to climb up into the wagon.

"I wouldn't do that in a hurry," Kit said to her. "Injuns like to set wagons on fire. You're safer with me behind the wheel. Just stay with me."

Kit crouched behind the rear wheel and peered through the spokes. Magdalena crouched behind him, close behind him – but he had no time to enjoy her wilful company. It seemed just like a woman to want a man's company only when she needed him, and not when he needed her.

Kit saw that Jeb and Old Morg were closing the distance to the wagon now, but also that the Indian war party was closer to them, too. He and Jeb were hitting the sides of their horses frantically with their rifles, and Kit noticed a terrifying thing: Jeb had an arrow sticking out of the side of his thigh, one with bright yellow and red feathers at its end.

He saw another volley of arrows raining down on top of them. Some fell flat on the grass, others angled into the ground and stuck fast, quivering, and one landed straight in Apache's rump. The horse bucked and kicked its hind legs sideways in the air, as if it thought some kind of animal had suddenly caught up with it and given it a nip on the rump, and Morg was almost thrown, in which case the galloping Indians would have squashed him into the prairie and he would not have even needed a grave – they would have just had to pile him over with rocks.

He flew into the air when the horse bucked, his scrawny backside hovering for a moment over the saddle, still holding the reins in mid-air, and then he landed safely back in the saddle.

The horse had slowed from the buck and kick, and Jeb was several yards ahead of it, on Dandy. He and Morg must have swapped once Morg caught him up, for Morg favoured the spirited mount over the more docile Dandy.

The Indians were catching them up; some were now almost alongside Morg!

"They're going to take me away again!" Magdalena cried. "I know it, I just know it!"

"No they ain't!" Kit said. "If Morg and Jeb can make it to the wagon in time I reckon together we can scare 'em off!"

But this didn't seem to console her; she was crying frantically and clawing at Kit's shoulder.

"I'll die before I let them take you, Magda," he said. He loaded the Winchester forcefully and placed the barrel between one of the top spokes. "And if they take you and leave me alive I'll follow them to the ends of the earth, just like I done the first time. And I won't stop till I find you," he added. "And when I find you there'll be hell to pay for them that has you."

He fired a round, which startled Magdalena so that she jumped.

Kit opened and closed the trigger guard and a spent casing dropped into the dust, smoking.

But none of the mounted Indians in the war party seemed to be affected. It was as if they were bulletproof, for he was sure he had sighted one, and his horse, at that.

One was alongside Old Morg now, and Kit saw him start to climb his own horse. The Indian stood briefly and then launched himself off its back and into the air. He had to have performed the dangerous manoeuvre at about thirty miles an hour, at a full lope, and what was worse is that he landed perfectly on the back of Old Morg's horse.

Kit gasped, and even Magdalena, but they needn't have: Old Morg immediately let go of the reins with one hand, clenched his free fist and lashed backwards with the point of his elbow.

It caught the Indian in the eye and he flipped backwards off Apache's rump, sheering the jutting arrow off its rump, which caused it to buck and kick again. Its double hooves caught the airborne Indian in the stomach, and he was propelled straight into another horse's forelegs.

The horse braked with the Indian tangled in its front legs, tripped, and then rolled face first into the dirt. Its rider was thrown, and when he landed there was an explosion of red dust around him.

"Yes!" Kit hissed triumphantly, and fired another round.

He had aimed for an Indian trying to sidle up alongside Morg again, only this one was raising a lance, ready to pierce Morgan's side, but Kit hit his horse, right between the legs.

Suddenly it was as if the galloping horse hit an invisible wall. It stopped instantly, and the rider was thrown so far in the air with the lance held out in front of him it snapped sheer in two when he landed. He continued to skid and roll along in the red dust and dirt, and no sooner had he come to a stop than the mounted Indian war party mowed him down.

The ones in the vanguard seemed intent on catching up to Morg, since Jeb was far too far ahead.

"Can you fire a pistol!?" Kit shouted to Magdalena out of the corner of his mouth.

"I ain't never fired one," she cried, still in tears.

"Well someone's gonna hafta teach you," Kit said, handing her his pistol. "Just point and shoot, there's six shots."

She looked at the gun curiously. For a moment her attention shifted from her concern about being captured again, and she looked at Kit, now firing his rifle repeatedly through the wagon spokes. His face had a grim intensity, which she momentarily admired. It looked similar to the able-looking and determined cowboys she had seen herding cattle onto the train cars in Dodge City.

Crouched, she walked on her haunches around Kit and got down on her knees in the grass, holding the pistol out in both hands, aiming under the wagon.

She closed her eyes tight and turned her head away.

Kit glanced sideways momentarily and then did a wide-eyed double-take.

The pistol roared in her hands and a split second later a splintered hole appeared in the bottom of Old Morg's wagon.

Kit reached out quickly and lowered her pistol.

"On second thoughts, just hold on to it in case," he said.

He turned back and sighted down his rifle.

He hadn't hit anything, despite his continued firing. He was beginning to think the Indians themselves must having been wearing ghost shirts, which Old Morg had told him he had seen Pawnee and Cheyenne wearing on the reservation; he said some mad medicine man called Yellow Bird had made them believe they would all be bulletproof if they wore them. Old Morg had told Kit his Pawnee wife had made him wear one.

Kit saw Old Morg swing and then throw his rifle at another Indian who had ridden up alongside him. It merely bounced off his shoulder and spun off into the dust, to be trampled and crushed.

Jeb was only about half a minute from the wagon!

Kit shifted his focus and saw Old Morg draw his big Colt pistol; the problem was the Indian alongside him was drawing a pistol too.

The Indian pointed the pistol and fired; it happened so fast that in the time it took to blink Kit suddenly noticed that Apache was riderless.

"Morg!" he shouted, a part of him wanting to jump up and run for him.

Then he caught glimpse of something on the side of Apache's neck. Old Morg had ducked and slid sideways and was hiding behind the horse's neck, still holding the pistol in one hand and looking ahead towards the wagon, his furs rippling in the wind.

The Indian was still galloping alongside him, and Morg suddenly hung lower and fired his pistol under the horse's neck.

The Indian was blown sideways off his horse, taking his horse blanket with him and landing in the dirt to be trampled a split second later.

Jeb galloped the last few yards to the wagon and jumped down off his horse, landing so hard on the ground he turned his fall into a roll and rolled in under the wagon, crawling out in front of Kit and Magdalena on his hands and knees.

"Howdy, Jeb," Kit said, and fired. "When you said you was goin' hunting I didn't know it was Indians you was after."

"It weren't," Jeb said. "But I guess game is chancy. They was after the same deer we was."

Jeb poked his rifle through the other wheel and began to fire.

Kit added his own fire to Jeb's and saw Indians begin to slow their horses and turn back. An Indian blew back off his horse, as if suddenly lassoed from it, and Kit could swear it was he who had hit him.

Then another and another were blown from their horses – it seemed Kit's aim had suddenly improved. An Indian riding and hollering near Morg was even hit, and he suddenly slumped dead on the horse, and then slowly slid sideways off it, again taking his colourful horse blanket with him.

More Indians were reining in and turning back now, and finally Old Morg galloped up, bursts of dust exploding under Apache's hooves. He swung down from the horse and crawled in under the wagon hurriedly on his hands and knees.

"'I God, them Indians are riled up!" he said, turning around to fire himself. "Let's show 'em they're better off on the reservations, boys!"

He began to fire his big Colt, and enthused by his company both Jeb and Kit added to the gunfire. Even Magdalena raised the pistol again, squeezed her eyes shut and turned her head away and fired, kicking up a spurt of dust several yards away.

Both Dandy and Apache were standing by the mules on the other side, nickering on the spot nervously.

The remaining Indians were suddenly faced with a near impassable wall of steel, turning back and galloping off, but the bravest of them rode right up to the wagon, touched the side of the canvas and then quickly turned and spurred their horses' flanks wildly, galloping off and whooping and hollering triumphantly, as if to show them they were not afraid and had no fear of the death they dealt.

The last one to reach the wagon, however, took hold of one of the horses' bridles and rode away with it.

"Son of a bitch horse thief!" Old Morg shouted, standing up. "Lookit him!"

Kit pulled his rifle out from between the wheel spokes and ran around the wagon, stopping on the other side to shoulder the rifle and fire after him. But again it was as if he wore a ghost shirt. Kit decided, as a last measure, to take a shot at the horse under him, but unfortunately by this time he was too distant and although he fired he may as well not have.

He lowered the rifle disappointedly, although relieved the Indians were finally gone.

They stood in the near silence, listening to the aftermath. They could hear the distant pound of hooves, and the victory hollering.

"That son of a bitch took Dandy," Old Morg said behind Kit.

Kit whirled and saw Morg tying Apache to the rear wheel.

"They coulda at least took this here Indian lover," Old Morg said.

Kit saw that the horse had another arrow in it, this one jutting from its hind leg. It seemed righteous to Kit, that Apache had been shot at by Indians. Maybe it would change its evil temperament now.

"What was that all about?" Kit asked, flustered. Old Morg was getting ready to leave in a hurry.

"Jeb rode over a rise and ran right into them," Old Morg said. "It weren't exactly their fault. He's the one started firin' on them first. They was just sittin' there. Ain't that right, Jeb?"

Jeb looked at Kit guiltily.

"I thought they was goan scalp me," he said.

"Well, they may have," Old Morg admitted.

"They was lookin' at my haid awful strange."

"They probably never seen hair like that, or maybe they just never saw a black man afore."

"I could swear they was goan scalp me," Jeb maintained.

"Did they pull any knives?"

"Nope."

"Let's just skedaddle before they come back for your black hide. They do that, I'm apt to skin it for them myself. *Jesus*, but that was close!"

Kit put the rifle back in its scabbard in the wagon bed and took his pistol from Magdalena. He had to pry it from her fingers, she held onto it so tight.

"It's alright, they're gone," he said to her softly.

"What if they come back?"

"Then I 'spect we'll hand Jeb over and they'll leave us be."

Jeb was rubbing the strange short black carpet of curls on his head.

He said, "I could swear they was goan take my scalp, way they was lookin' at it."

"I coulda swear I saw an arrow in your leg earlier," Kit said to Jeb. Kit was sitting on the wagon seat and Jeb was in the saddle on the back of Apache, trotting alongside at a slow pace.

"Musta falled out," Jeb said, looking down at his thighs. He had a bloody handkerchief tied around one.

"I saw it fall out while you was off galloping," Old Morg observed. "You're one lucky negro. Lucky we didn't hafta push that on through."

They had pulled the arrow out of Apache's hind leg, which had made the horse buck and kick for a third time. Kit himself had risked it, since Magdalena had been watching; he had quickly stepped up to the horse and then ripped the arrow out and run – a good several yards, for that matter. The horse had kicked thin air and that had been the end of it, though a chunk of the horse had come out on the end of the arrow, but not a very big one.

Fortunately the arrows were neither poisoned nor barbed, since they had in fact intercepted a hunting party, and not a war one.

"They must of snuck away from one of the reservations," Old Morg pointed out. "It's time for the annual buffalo hunt – only there ain't none. I wonder what my wife is doing?" he added.

"Was you actually married?" Kit asked.

"In the Indian way, sure."

"What's the Indian way?"

"I admit it ain't graceful. You go in the tepee and the entire village sits outside and waits."

"For what?"

"For you to get married."

"Oh. You got any Injun kids then?" Kit asked.

"Not that I know of."

Kit wondered what that meant; if Old Morg left behind kids, those kids would probably grow up without a father, as Kit had, though at least they'd have a mother, even if she did only have one eye.

As Magdalena had called it, it rained towards sundown; not a heavy or alarming rain but wet enough to make even the mules look hangdog and miserable.

In the long run, Kit's horse swap with Jeb had backfired on him, since after the Indian brave had made off with Dandy, only one horse remained between them, and it was roundly considered to be Jeb's. Even Old Morg, who had been the one to pay for it, referred to it as "Jeb's Injun horse".

It didn't seem to give Jeb any trouble any more; the two had formed the mutual arrangement between each other that if Apache didn't bite, Jeb wouldn't kick, which seemed to be working.

Unfortunately, however, Kit could no longer join Jeb on his hunts and it came to be the task of Jeb alone to hunt. He went east that afternoon and came back with a prairie chicken and a jackrabbit, which they skinned and ate greedily, sucking the meat clean from every bone.

"I honestly thought my time was up this day," Old Morg said. The rain had let up, and even though a light drizzle fell, they managed to keep a fire going. "I never thought I'd see dinner time," he added.

"What if they come back?" Magdalena asked.

"We'll shoot, I guess, until they go away," he said simply, and chucked a bone aside.

Kit sat on the far side of the fire, away from Magdalena. He was gloomy and looked depressed. It was saddening to him that Magdalena's attitude had only changed briefly toward him, and then only during the Indian attack. He almost wished Indians *would* attack again, so that Magdalena would want him.

He decided to say, "I reckon they may."

"May what?" Old Morg said, raising an eye from his chicken leg.

"May come back."

"What, you think they're gonna bring back the horse and say sorry?"

"No," Kit said sheepishly.

"Then I see no reason for 'em to return. Did you hear them hollerin'? That was a victory holler, that was them lettin' us know they had us whipped."

"Did you see the way they come right up to the wagon and touched it?" Kit asked, looking around from face to face, eerily underlit by the flickering and sputtering fire. "I couldn't believe that," he added.

"I believed it," Jeb contributed. "Thought they was goan come right in after us unner the wagon. And take my scalp," he added.

"They was just playin' with us," Old Morg said. "Lettin' us know they had us beat."

"I can't believe the way they just rode up to touch the wagon and then rode off," Kit said. "In a hail of bullets, to boot."

"Well, an Injun's a funny animal."

"*Are* they animals?" Kit asked.

"Why, yes and no," Old Morg said authoritatively.

"Well, which one?" Kit asked, confused.

"There's a animal in Africa," Old Morg said. "It looks like a horse, it's the same size as a horse, it even has all the same bits as a horse's got, only thing different is its hide has black and white stripes. It's called a zebra."

"I saw me a zebra," Jeb said, "when I was jes a boy."

Kit perked up at this absurd image, a black and white striped horse.

Old Morg said, "Jeb knows it. It cannot be broke in. No matter how much you try, it won't take the saddle – won't even take a horse blanket. It's a completely different animal. I had a friend in Missouri had a brother went to South Africa and wrote him back, told him about the zebra."

"What's that got to do with Injuns?" Kit asked curiously.

"Well, you asked was they animals or not, and it's the best explanation I got. An Injun is like a zebra. It's a horse only it ain't a horse – it's a completely different animal. And you cannot saddle a zebra."

"You oughtn't to, either," he added. "I mean, think about it – what kind of man tries to saddle a zebra?"

Kit pondered the peculiar question most of the night, staring up from his blanket at a full moon, for Morg had not expanded upon his strange philosophy. Kit knew that Indians hunted when the moon was full, and it kept him up almost until light – mostly he was afraid that Magdalena might get stolen, for Indians were not only known to attack with whoops and hollers, but were also known to be expert sneak thieves. Old Morg had once told him that he had heard a story of a band of Indians make off with a cook's entire chuck wagon, the chuck wagon nowhere to be seen the next day, and that it was on account of the cook was hoarding several secret bottles of whiskey in it. None of the cow camp had apparently known about the whiskey bottles, but somehow the Indians had known. Kit distinctly recalled Morg mentioning that the hands had been mighty riled up come breakfast time.

Towards morning, while it was still dark, Kit got out of his blanket to relieve himself. Afterwards he dared to check on Magdalena, who, to his surprise, was wide awake.

"I didn't mean to scare you none," Kit whispered. "Just checking you was alright."

"Leave me alone," she whispered back. "Can't you see I'm just fine?"

"Why, only now that I've checked."

"Go away," she groaned.

Kit swallowed his pride and left her be, climbing back into his blankets. Finally, as the glow of the sun showed beneath the edge of the dark earth, he managed to get some sleep.

★ ★ ★

The next morning Magdalena vomited again, complaining of the same symptoms as before, which perplexed Kit no end.

While she was vomiting several yards from the wagon, Kit decided to ask Morg, "What's wrong with her?"

"I don't know exactly, Kit," he replied. "But I do have a nagging suspicion."

Kit was surprised to hear this.

"What's that then?" he asked.

"Well, let's just wait and see. Maybe it's some water she drank or something – although there oughtn't to be alkali in these creeks."

Once again Kit kept a close eye on her all day as they travelled across the dusty prairie, but again, just like before, she recovered and was fine.

They made good headway and didn't bump into any Indians.

"Two more days and I reckon we're to Doan's Store," Old Morg said in the afternoon. "And then we're to the Red."

The rest of the day was uneventful, and Kit was so tired by nightfall he turned in early.

The next morning, to Kit's relief, Magdalena was not sick at all, nor felt dizzy or nauseous.

That day they met a small band of cowboys herding a hundred horses or so, who were surprised by the sight of them. They bought some coffee and sugar from Morg, at which point they noticed Magdalena, which came as an even bigger surprise to them.

They had stopped the wagon and Magdalena did not climb out, sitting right back in the wagon instead. Kit got down to oversee the transaction going on at the back of the wagon, where two cowboys stood bartering with Morg.

He got there in time to hear one of them say to Morg, "Why, you sly old devil. Checky here, Mike. They're travellin' the country with a whorehouse on wheels. How much for a turn on the whore, old man? I got six men who'd pay four dollars apiece to lie with her. I would myself. We ain't seen womenfolk since San Antone."

"She ain't a whore!" Kit said defensively.

"That's right, she ain't," Old Morg said gently. "Calm down, Kit," he added.

"You take that back!" Kit said to the offensive cowboy.

"Watch the way you talk to me boy, or I'll box your ears!"

Kit launched himself at him, and was punched clean on the chin. He landed in the dirt, momentarily stunned, and before his eyes could clear a boot kicked a wave of sand into his face and caught him under the chin. He lay flat, blinking dust out of his eyes and listening to his head ring.

Kit heard a horse galloping up hastily and the next thing he knew Jeb had dismounted and was in between the two, pushing the man back.

"Get your hands off me, nigger!"

"That's right, get your hands off him!"

A shot rang out.

"Take your sugar and coffee and get back to your people," Kit heard Old Morg say. "Before I leave youse both for the coyotes."

The two men took one last look in at Magdalena, spat angrily in the dirt, and then unhitched their horses, mounted and rode off.

Old Morg and Jeb helped Kit back to his feet, and as he tried to put his jaw back into place he looked in at Magdalena. She looked frightened and on the verge of tears. Kit thought the only reason she hadn't gone further back into the wagon was because she couldn't.

"I'm sorry you had to hear that, Magda," he said.

But she didn't say anything, just stared at him. He looked down disappointedly and walked off, moving his jaw this way and that.

The next morning all was forgotten and Kit's spirits were up – were up, that is, until Magdalena shot out of the wagon and vomited into the grass again, which caused him considerable concern.

He wanted to walk up and put his hand on her back, but he no sooner took a single step toward her than she held out a hand and told him not to come any closer.

"What's *wrong* with her?" Kit asked Morg again. "Is she gonna die, Morg?"

"Son, you and I'll hafta have a little talk. We'll step aside and talk once we get to Doan's Store."

After vomiting Magdalena soon cleared up, and everyone boarded the wagon, even Jeb, and they rode along patiently, knowing that by midday they would finally arrive at Doan's Store, a landmark all had been looking forward to since the day they left for Texas.

Soon they saw the big, wide, muddy-brown Red River meandering across the horizon, and on their side of it, saw the small shacks and shanty buildings belonging to Doan's Store.

M uch throughout the journey Doan's Store had come to be a
landmark in Kit's mind, so much so that he had expected it
to be at least half the size of a city like Dodge, even though
the name of the place had given him cause for suspicion.

But when they rode up and stopped the wagon, it wasn't even half
as big as the town of Wagon Trail, or anywhere near as big as Farlow.
In fact, Doan's Store was just that: Doan's Store. Save for a few other
clapboard sheds and shacks offering items for trade or sale, and a hard-
ware store.

There were two wagons stopped outside it, and a big family of
homesteaders were in Doan's Store buying and coming out with ploughs
and spades and pickaxes – sod breakers. There were some young girls
among them, and mean-looking mothers – even a grandmother – and
Kit watched them milling about the two wagons with interest.

When they climbed down from the wagon seat, Kit saw that Magdalena
was already out of the wagon, stretching her legs and yawning. They had
pushed the mules hard since they set out that morning, wanting to make
Doan's Store before midday so that they could cross the river and be on
the other side by early afternoon.

Old Morg went off and interrupted a man who was scolding his
wife for some reason next to the other wagons, and began having a
conversation with him.

Meanwhile one of the mules tried to bite Kit on the wrist when he
wasn't paying attention, and he stepped aside. Magdalena was looking
fidgety.

"Are you alright?" Kit asked her, realizing too late that he should have found some way to rephrase the question.

"I need to go," she said bluntly.

It shocked Kit that she would just reveal that she needed to relieve herself like that, in front of Jeb and he. He flushed, but managed to keep it to just a light flush and not let his embarrassment become a full-blown red-cheeked display for all to see.

He looked around.

"Why, I think that there's an outhouse," he said. "You can use that."

He pointed at the little wooden shed with one door and a sod roof and she shot quickly for it. Kit wondered if she was feeling nauseous again, but didn't dare ask.

"Keep an eye on her, Jeb," he said. "I'm gonna go see what Morg's talkin' with them homesteaders about."

He walked over to the two wagons slowly, looking up at two young girls sitting up on the wagon and waiting for their journey to commence.

They were whispering to each other and giggling at him, which Kit rather liked actually – after Magdalena's constant dismissal of him, that is. He lifted his hat briefly and said, "Howdy, girls."

"You just leave my daughters be," a voice said.

Kit turned around and saw a big, heavily bearded man standing there holding a pitchfork.

"Why, I was just greeting them," Kit explained.

"I know what you was doin'. Go on, beat it."

Kit took one look at the rusty pitchfork and decided to do just that. He walked over to the other wagon, where Morg was talking to a thin, tall man in loose-fitting farming clothes.

He heard Morg say, "I'd be careful going through Indian Territory. We ran into a hunting party yesterday and there was a little altercation. You may come across some of the bodies," he added. "We had to kill a few. Almost got kilt ourselves."

"I thought the Indians was whupped," the thin, tall man said.

"So did we," Old Morg said. "So did we. They must of fled one of the reservations. You can always expect Indians to be around at the time of the annual buffalo hunt."

"Well, I'm mighty obliged for the warnin'," the man said.

"How'd you fare gettin' those wagons across?" Old Morg asked him, meaning across the Red, of course.

"We used a log raft. We left it there on the north bank if you want to use it to take your own across."

"Why, we'd much appreciate it."

That made Kit's day; he had not been looking forward to taking the wagon across the wide muddy Red, but now, thanks to the sod breakers and homesteaders, they were going to get to cross on a raft.

"You won't fit your mules on it," the man was saying to Morg, "but your wagon'll cross fine."

"Well, we much appreciate it."

"I hope we don't run into those Indians."

"I'm sure some soldiers will be after them soon enough," Morg assured him.

Old Morg saw Kit out of the corner of his eye and turned about.

"Why, Kit, you oughtn't to sneak up behine me like that. Or be eavesdroppin', for that matter."

"Why, I just didn't want to interrupt, is all," Kit explained.

"Jim, this here's my... my... well, he's sort of my son."

The tall, thin man – Jim, Old Morg had called him – held out a hand. He had a very hollow-looking and bony face.

Kit shook his hand, noting how rough and hard it was.

"Looks like he'd be good on the plough," Jim said.

"Oh, he's better with a knife. Used to be I hired him on to skin buffalo."

"Is that right? I hear they're all hunted out."

"There's the odd one, somewhere," Old Morg admitted. "Mostly it's just bones on the plains now," he added.

"That's a shame. When my ma and pa come west over the Oregon Trail they said there was so much buffalo they lit their campfires with their manure."

"Quite so," Morg said. "There's still plenty of buffalo chips out there, that's for sure."

"I know, there's bags of it in Doan's Store. I don't see why a man would pay for somethin' he can collect for free, but there they are."

"Well, I'd just as soon be going into that store myself. Nice talkin' to you, Jim. Wishin' you luck now."

"I make my own luck," Jim said grimly.

"Well then make it good luck. Come along, Kit," Morg said. "I think it's about time we had that chat."

They stepped into Doan's Store. It was full of the wagon party; men and women inspecting ploughs and spades and other obscure farming tools. There were bags of dry seed, some saddles hanging off the walls, reins and bits and even horseshoes.

Old Morg inspected a pickaxe and then a hammer.

"I ought really to buy these down by the Rio Grande," he said, "rather than have to cart them through Texas. I'm afraid I'll have to get you that gun when we reach San Antonio." He added, "It don't seem they've got none at Doan's Store, just a few rifles and carbines."

"What were we going to talk about?" Kit asked, more interested in that.

"Kit," Morg said, as he moved along the shelves inspecting the items, "that girl's been through somethin' terrible: first thing you gotta understand. I mean to say, those Indians performed the sex act with her."

This was such a shock to Kit his face turned pale. Why would Magdalena have done that with Indians? At the mere mention of "the sex act" he remembered the bare backside he had seen sticking out of the flaps of the tent on the outskirts of Farlow, and the milky-white female legs that had been open beneath it.

Old Morg saw his confusion and seemed to read his mind, for he added, "I mean against her will, of course. And I'm not sure how many. I just know Indians don't capture no white girl who's that age without doin' *some*thin' to her. At least not Indians who would associate with that rascal we hung."

"So that's why she's vomiting?" Kit asked, frowning.

"Well, yes and no."

Old Morg started passing Kit tins of beans.

Not more beans, Kit thought abysmally.

"Shouldn't we get peas?" he suggested.

"There ain't no peas. What kinda man tins peas?"

"Why, I don't know," Kit said.

"Might as well tin grass," Morg said. "Back to the girl. See, I reckon she's got mornin' sickness."

"What's that?" Kit asked.

"It's somethin' happens to a woman who's... who's..."

Kit was high confused, women proving to be as much a mystery as why the moon sometimes appeared full, other times like a scythe.

"I mean to say, Kit, that I reckon that girl may have an Injun baby in her."

Old Morg said no more. He grabbed up some beef jerky from a box and some hard tack, and Kit put the tins down on the hewn-wood counter, acting automatically but feeling miles away, so completely and utterly shocked was he.

Old Morg asked the owner, a large well-fed man with a big nose on him covered in burst capillaries, if he had any whiskey.

"I got two bottles left," he said. "Some boys trailing a horse herd up to Fort Sill bought the rest."

"I'll take 'em," Morg said, and the man hurriedly totted up the cost of the goods. "And a box of the Therapeutic Papers – I don't much like the look of the bushes in Texas, much less the feel."

Kit walked slowly out of the store, while Old Morg paid and the man placed the items into a sack, and stepped out into the sunlight.

Nothing in life seemed to go the way it was supposed to, he thought to himself. An Injun baby? Magdalena was going to have an Injun baby? It was too much to comprehend. Who would take care of it? Who would raise it and be its pa? What if it grew up and scalped all of them?

Did Magdalena even know herself?

He saw that one of the sod busters was waiting outside the outhouse, tapping his foot urgently. He was a youngish, broad-shouldered man with red hair and not much more of a facial hair growth than Kit himself.

Kit walked over to where Jeb stood. He was about to speak to him when he heard an impatient knock nearby, and then a burly voice saying, "What you doin' in there, mister? Readin' the newspaper what's there for wipin'? I didn't come all this way to Doan's to use no leaves!"

Kit frowned angrily and walked over to admonish him.

"Can't you see it's occupied?" he said. "Go do your business in the bushes like all the rest of us."

The way Kit saw it, outhouses were for the express and solitary use of women; always had been. A man had no business in an outhouse; ought to do his business in a hole in the ground.

"What's it to you, you skinny little runt?" the redhead said.

He began to pull on the door handle and it almost opened.

Kit threw a sucker punch, and socked him clean on the jaw. To Kit's surprise, the man went out like a lantern light, landing against the wooden door and sliding down it. The door was trying to open now, against the unconscious sod buster. Kit grabbed the handle and pulled, shifting the man out of the way. He fell over on his side in the dust and Magdalena stepped out over him.

She was shocked to see that Kit had punched him.

"Why did you do that?" she said, crouching down over the man.

Kit sucked at his red knuckles and said, "Why, I thought he was tryin' to... to... to interfere with you, Magda."

But she ignored him, helping the man, who was slowly coming to, to sit up against the door. He shook his head and blinked at Magdalena crouched before him. To Kit's surprise she was holding his cheeks in her hands.

Finally the man spoke. "Why, was it you was in there? I had no idea it was a lady was in there. Begging your pardon, ma'am."

"Magdalena."

He smiled at her, and then looked at Kit and a dark intention flashed across his face.

"Why, I oughta–"

"The outhouse is free now," Magdalena intercepted.

"Why, I can see that," he said to her. "I guess I'll use it."

He stepped into the outhouse and closed the door, and Magdalena flashed Kit an angry look of her own as she went back to the wagon.

"What'd I do wrong?" Kit asked Jeb.

"I reckon I doan rightly know," was his prompt reply.

The incident soon went out of Kit's mind, and he returned to the sickly feeling he had had before.

Old Morg finally came over to the wagon and dropped his goods in the back.

"Let's go cross that river," he said, looking off to the south where it lay.

They climbed up onto the wagon and Morg whipped the mules with the reins, and Kit never said a word – all the way to the river.

★ ★ ★

Kit had the unpleasant task of taking the mules across the Red; one of which unfortunately started to swim downriver and had to be collected a quarter of a mile down the bank.

Kit borrowed Apache from Jeb and when he returned with the wayward mule saw the crudely built raft floating out from the north bank with the wagon on top of it. Jeb and Old Morg were standing on the south bank and reeling it in with the long length of rope which Morg kept in the wagon for just such an occurrence. While the sod busters and homesteaders left the crude raft they had fashioned, they wouldn't likely have left a rope. Some men, as Kit knew, would not even waste a rope to hang a man, and would cut him down after and collect it, or at any rate if they left him there hanging it was begrudgingly.

The Red was wide and almost, as its name suggested, red. The mud of its bed and banks was thick and sticky and almost clay-like, adhering to everything it came into contact with.

From his vantage point on top of Apache, Kit saw Magdalena sitting on the wagon seat, very still. Kit didn't like that; the wagon didn't look any too secure sitting on that float, but finally when it bumped up against the bank and Old Morg and Jeb were covered in sweat, Magdalena stepped off onto the bank unharmed.

Kit had to go into the water on Apache and try to hold the raft still while Morg traced the mules and then pulled their harnesses to get them moving forward. The wagon slowly wheeled off the wooden platform.

Kit spurred the horse up the muddy bank and only realized he had let the raft float loose once he had dismounted.

It was floating off down river.

"Now that's just wasteful," Old Morg reprimanded him. "Someone else coulda used that raft."

That day they passed a number of sod houses and little isolated farm buildings. They bought some eggs and bacon from a middle-aged couple of sod busters, who invited them to stay the night if they wanted to. Old Morg declined but thanked them for their hospitality. In fact, originally they had even offered them the food for free, but Old Morg had declined their offer, saying, "We pay our way, ma'am."

Later in the day, Old Morg said to Kit, "Next stop's San Antonio, where I'm gonna look to buy land on the Rio Grand'."

"What about the lumber?" Kit asked him, though the real question on his mind was: What about Magdalena?

"What we can't find and use we'll order, unless there's a ranch for sale that we could buy. I hear there's a few dilapidated ones. Maybe we could fix 'em up and expand 'em."

"How long till we're in San Antonio?" Kit inquired.

"'Bout another month or so," Morg said.

Kit sighed depressively. Another month on the plains, and the dry dusty Texan plains at that.

"I hear Texas is full of outlaws," Old Morg mentioned.

"It is?"

"And Mexican bandits."

"That don't sound too good."

"Fortunately there's Fort Worth to the east and Fort Griffin straight south. Next river'll be the Trinity, by the way."

"Is the Rio Grande big?" Kid asked.

"Why, it's a wide river, but runs no higher than your calves. We don't have to cross it anyway, only later – we'll go into Mexico to catch us some livestock. I expect we'll have trouble with the Mexicans, but it's likely all Texas cattle anyway."

Kit was silent on the wagon seat for a while, thinking about Magdalena, and trying to imagine an Indian baby.

Later that afternoon there was an unexpected turn of events. Jeb came riding back to the wagon with another man riding shotgun with him. Kit just saw the man's arms at first, wrapped around Jeb's waist. Old Morg slowed the wagon and then reined in the mules.

"Looks like old Jeb's growed a pair of white arms," he said.

Jeb dismounted and helped the man down. The man wasn't wearing a hat, and he was bright red and had been blistered by the burning sun. He also wore a gun belt, though containing an empty holster. Although fairly young looking, he appeared to be going bald already, and what was left of his bright blond hair was sticking up nightmarishly.

The first thing he said is, "Dern rustlers jacked my horse, left me out here with nothin'. Even took my canteen."

"You're lucky old Jeb didn't think you was a deer and took a pop at you," Old Morg said. "You look thirsty, Mister..?"

"My name's Newcombe," he said. "Lynus Newcombe."

"Well, which is it I should call you, young fella? Lynus or Newcombe?"

"My friends call me Lucky Lynus. I'm from Fort Worth."

"Maybe from now on they'll just call you Lynus. What you doin' up here?"

Lynus Newcombe said, "I'm suppose to be meetin' an outfit in a few days at the Red River Station, on account of there's an Indian raiding party loose in Indian Territory. They already set fire to a sod shanty and kilt a mother and child. Child was one year old."

"I 'spect we done some of your work for you," Old Morg told him.

The man frowned. "How's that?"

"We felled some of those Injuns just about a week ago. Reckon we dropped about nine of 'em."

"Well, that don't much matter now. Would you boys much mind givin' me a lift back to Fort Worth?"

"We ain't goin' to Fort Worth," Morg said.

"Well, as near as, then."

"That I can do."

And so Kit had to budge up on the wagon seat and spend the day next to Lynus Newcombe. Old Morg offered him water from his canteen and he near emptied it, gasping for breath after glugging down near all of it in one go.

"Any idea where these horse thieves might be headed?" Old Morg asked.

"I think they cased me at Fort Worth, followed me out into the brush. They set upon me in my camp."

Jeb was riding alongside the wagon, trotting slowly to give Apache a rest.

Old Morg said to Lynus, "Whereabouts was this?"

"Oh, about ten or twelve miles due northwest from Worth."

"Jeb, whyn't you ride on and see if you can't spot their trail," Old Morg suggested. "We can't be havin' horse thieves out on the plains. They're apt to terrorize other innocent folk."

"How many riders was there?" Old Morg added.

Lynus Newcombe said, "Oh, about four – maybe five. Though I think it was five. Dirty-lookin' bunch."

"Go on, Jeb – you heard the man: four horses due northwest."

"That's really not necessary," Lynus said. "It was just one horse."

"Like I said, we can't be havin' horse thieves loose on the plains. Jeb..."

Jeb nodded and spurred Apache's flanks. Kit watched him disappear into the shimmering distance. He kept seeing what looked like creeks in the distance, but every time they wheeled closer they seemed to get further, or even dry up and disappear, a disappointment to Kit because he knew that if they came to a creek they would stop to water the horses and he might get a look at Magdalena.

Just as he was thinking that, there was a distinctly feminine sneeze from inside the wagon, which caused Lynus to start on the seat and turn back.

"Ye gods, I didn't know you had a girl in there," he said. "She near scared the Bejesus out of me."

Lynus said no more, but Kit became defensive and wary of him. He had a lively sparkle to him, as if he couldn't quite sit still on the wagon seat and wanted to climb down and explore the range, but was trying his best to sit still. Kit felt unnatural and not himself sitting next to him. He was conscious of how close his shoulder was to Lynus's, but couldn't quite work out why.

Towards dusk, they stopped the wagon and climbed down. Kit went to the back to collect some wood for the fire. Every time he or Morg spotted a good piece of firewood lying on the plains, Kit would jump down and go fetch it, handing it to Magdalena. It became so that he would look intently for the wood, just for the opportunity to jump down and deposit it and get to see Magdalena.

She handed Kit logs and broken branches of wood until both hands were full and he had to hold them in place with his chin.

"Why, thank you, Magda," he said, and carefully walked them over to the camp and dropped them, jumping back so they didn't bounce or roll onto his boots.

He had come to call Magdalena "Magda", finding it more appropriate – or, at least, it *felt* more appropriate – than "Lena", which also irked Kit to say since Magdalena had said her sister used to call her it.

As he set and started the fire, Kit wondered if he would ever tell Magdalena that he had accidentally killed her sister. He hadn't even told Morg. The only one who knew was Jeb, and, of course, Dwight and Lebold.

He missed those two, in a funny way, and thought their company would have enlivened the trip to Texas a good deal. He consoled himself, however, with the fact that next year he may very well be working with them.

That led to a grisly thought; by the same time next year Magdalena's baby – if she indeed *was* pregnant – would already be born. On the other hand, maybe the baby would be a key to Magdalena's heart; at any rate Kit was willing to try it as one. If Magdalena still didn't like him by then, he intended to win her over with his willingness to act as a father type.

All he would have to do is do what Morg had done for him, unless it turned out that the Indian child would teach *him*. Probably how to scalp a head.

He wondered what type of Indian baby it would be? An Apache? He hoped not, for all their sakes. If it was Apache or Comanche they were all done for, would wake up scalped. It'd probably even scalp the livestock.

That made Kit consider another question. He had assumed it was going to be a he, but what if it wasn't? What if it turned out to be a she-Apache? Kit felt he could play father to a he-baby, but didn't have a clue what would be entailed in raising a little Indian girl.

And what name would they give to it? Indians had funny names, so far as Kit knew. Names like Man Afraid Of His Horses, and Touch-The-Clouds, and Stands Looking Back, to name a few he had heard. It seemed that their names bespoke something of their characters, which further confused Kit, for what would you call the little anklebiter in the meantime, before it did something to be called after? Perhaps just that: Ankle Biter, or Whipper Snapper.

Lynus Newcombe sat in front of the fire cross-legged once Kit got it going, using matches Old Morg had gotten from Doan's Store, lighting them on the wagon boards.

Magdalena, Kit noticed, stayed in the wagon, which she wouldn't usually do; probably because of their new guest. But Kit was fine with that; he didn't want this Lynus fellow looking at her – she didn't like to be looked at, he of all people knew that.

While Old Morg was stabbing at a bean tin with his skinning knife there was the pound of approaching hooves in the distance, and to their amazement Apache trotted into camp...

Without a saddle or, more importantly, Jeb.

The Kelsey brothers were a bad bunch, and they knew it.

Four in all, they took great pride in the fact that their pappy, Benjamin Kelsey, had been something of an enterprising man, if you wanted to put it lightly. He had belonged to the first emigrant train ever to take wagons west from Independence, Missouri, over the Oregon Trail bound for California – even though they had to ditch the wagons halfway. Of course, there had been other Kelseys – relations, of course – and there always would be. Even then they had been called The Kelsey Clan, and been considered roughnecks and indeed pappy Ben had been in trouble with the law – the reason he went west in the first place.

That's how they got here, and the way they saw it they were carrying on the family tradition. Ma had been fifteen when she married Pappy, and was herself a tough sort, something the four Kelsey brothers took an even greater pride in. She had not only followed Pappy on the trail but brought along her one-year-old child, to boot.

That one-year-old child had died, as many emigrant youngsters did in those days, and after giving birth to the last Kelsey boy she herself had died of the pox. Pa, Dan had kilt with a shotgun – for goin' with another lady and tryin' to marry her.

There was Dan, Jake, Benny and Walton. Walton was the eldest and toughest of the Kelsey brothers, and he usually led the way.

They were rustlers, of course, and prided themselves with their ruthless and unforgiving natures. Jake liked to hang children, though didn't often get to do it, and when he did, Walt made him take them down after they was dead and bury 'em. He'd say a clan out on the plains hanging children was apt to attract a manhunt quicker than a war party of Apache Indians.

The Kelsey brothers had been in numerous Indian fights, had fought against the Yankees in the Civil War, rustled cattle, stolen horses, robbed stagecoaches and even sod houses and ranches.

Jake was as rowdy as a rabbit when it came to ladies, but preferred to rape them, so they did that too. Their favourite occupation, though, was stealing horses, but they hated to herd them. So what they'd do is steal 'em and sell them to the closest buyer they could come across, someone more willing to take them all the way to the railhead towns.

In fact, they had just stolen and sold over a hunnert horses, to an outfit headed north. They had stolen them from a cattle outfit further south, that they had spotted while they roamed the land looking for the next opportunity to steal and deal.

They had stopped at Fort Worth and drank and gambled the money they had gotten for the horses, and then made off. But Benny's horse had taken sick and they had to eat it.

That meant they were shy one horse, which is why they decided to turn on their unrelated accomplice in crime, Lynus Newcombe. None of them liked him anyway. They had just needed another man to herd the horses 'cause it happened that they were useless when it came to herding anything anywhere. Lynus had worked for a cow outfit some years ago but was fired for falling asleep during his night shift and losing a passel of cattle. He'd sworn to steal cattle and horses from the outfits ever since, and when they met him in Austin he had seemed a good choice for an accomplice, since they was headed out on a "treasure hunt", as Dan gleefully called them.

They had moved on from Fort Worth quickly, not only because they gambled, drank and whored away all the money they had gotten for the hundred horses, but also because they knew the herd down south would be coming up sooner or later, and might be looking for them, though they would be moving far slower, a lot harder as it was to herd cattle than horses. And a hell-load of cattle at that.

When they surveyed the herd from the distance, Dan had said,

"Why, that's gotta be more'n five thousand shitting cattle."

"I reckon it's more like four thousand," Jake had estimated.

"I reckon four thousand five hunnert," Benny had said.

But Walt had had the final say. "Dan's right," he said. "That's gotta be around five thou, and you know who that is?"

"Who who is?" Dan asked.

Walt said, "That trail boss – I recognize him. He's ahead of the point."

"Well, who the heck is it?" Benny said impatiently. "Tell us, Walt, who?"

"That's Florence Hightower, the rich cattle baron. Look at all them horses, a hunnert at least!"

They had been on a tree-studded hilltop, looking down over the valley, and those cattle were spread for miles upon miles – one of the largest herds ever to push north, had to be. They didn't come much bigger than that. The outfit had to have had about twenty hands, not counting the cook riding up on the chuck wagon.

"So, Lynus," Walt had said. "You reckon you can show us how to herd them horses out from under their noses?"

"No problem," Lynus had said. "I could herd ever one of them cattle out from under their stupid noses."

Originally they had had no intention of parting ways with Lynus, but then again they had not planned on Benny's horse taking sick the way it did, although it had tasted just fine.

It would otherwise have been an impersonal matter, taking his horse, but he kicked up such a fuss when Walt had turned a pistol on him and told him to get down from his horse, that Dan had suggested taking his canteen as well as his pistol, which he had – clumb down off his horse and took it.

Benny had suggested taking his boots as well, but Walt had said, "What're you gonna do with an extra pair of boots, put 'em on your hands?"

"Why, no," Benny had replied. "I just thought it would be funny, is all – Old Lynus barefoot on the range."

They had left him in the middle of the wastes, with indeed not much more to his name than his boots – they had even taken his hat. They had pushed west, in an attempt to get out of the way of the cattle herd in case it came, but Walt wasn't too worried. Five thousand cattle were liable to draw attention before any hand got anywhere near them. They pushed gently northwest and took things as they came.

The day after they left Lynus to die they came upon a sod house. There was a man just starting to work on building a sod shed, ploughing a square furrow in the earth, and when he saw them coming he stopped and leaned on his plough.

Then they saw his lady come out the sod shanty, holding a baby in her arms.

"Well whaddo we have here?" Walt said, and spat tobacco juice. "Dan and Benny, you go take care of the sod buster, but don't kill him. We need to see if he's hiding money somewheres. Jake and I'll have a holt of this little missy and the brat she shit out."

Dan and Benny skirted the sod house and rode their horses right up to the man with the plough. They both dismounted and Dan hit him straight on the head with his pistol. Benny picked up his plough and they got him back to his feet and walked him back to the house, leaving their horses to graze.

Meanwhile Walt and Jake had parted the baby from its mother and Walt was dangling it over a well, its little feet kicking out beneath it. This sight caused the woman to scream and cry frantically, until Jake took her inside and the screams changed their tone.

Jake liked to take his ladies that way.

Dangling the baby over the well, Walt said, "I'm gonna drop this baby on a count of ten if you don't go in that sod hole of yours and come back out with the money I know you got hid up in there."

The sod buster was trembling and had gone purple-white in the face.

"We ain't got no money," he said. "Why, all we got is what you see. A house made of mud."

"He has a point, Walt," Benny said. "These don't look like the richest of folk."

Walt pretended to drop the baby, opening his fingers and then catching it up again. It startled the sod buster so badly he jumped forward, as if perfectly willing to dive down the well after it if Walt really did drop the baby.

Soon Jake came out the sod house pushing the lady ahead of him. Her clothes were hanging half-off and the Kelseys had a good gander.

"You boys oughta have a turn on this whore," Jake said. "She's right feisty, puts up a fight."

He pushed her by the arm into her husband, who hugged at her.

"Oh, please don't drop my baby!" she cried. "Please!"

Walt said, "Well then you best tell your husband to fetch me some money."

The woman hesitated. "But we don't have any," she pleaded. "Bob and I live off the land, can't you see? We're soddies."

"Jake, get back in there and check see."

The baby started to cry dangling over the well, while crashes and bangs came from within the sod house.

Soon Jake stepped out.

"Why, they're tellin' the truth, Walt. There ain't nothin' in there but mud."

"God damn sod busters," Walt said, lowering the baby and stepping away from the well. "Let's go."

"What about our baby?" the sod buster's dishevelled wife cried.

Walt had walked it to his horse.

"I'm takin' it," he said.

"What we gonna do with a baby, Walt?" Dan asked.

"These soddies ain't gettin' away without payin' *some*thin'."

Walt handed it to Dan and mounted up, holding his hands out again for the child once he was in the saddle. Dan handed it up to him hesitantly, unsure of this new development.

"Mount up, let's go!" Walt shouted, and go they had.

As they rode north towards sunset, none of the Kelsey brothers could forget the sound of the child's screaming mother, but dared not challenge their elder brother.

Now it was nightfall and they were set around a fire, with the dern baby crying, lying on a saddle blanket next to Walt.

"Why'd you have to bring that dern baby?" Dan braved to ask – he couldn't stand the thing.

"Why, I took a liking to it," Walt said.

"A liking to it? All it's done since you took it off its mother is cry its eyes out – and shit its pants."

"It was a spur-of-moment type thing," Walt explained. "It was that or drop it down the well."

"Yeah, well, then you ought to dropped it down the well rather," Benny said, now that Dan had braved to broach the subject himself.

"How'd you like it if someone dropped *you* down a well when you was a kid?"

"I don't reckon I would have cared either way."

"When's Jake gonna get back?" Dan asked.

"He was just meant to go look for some firewood. Shoulda been back by now," Benny pointed out.

"He probably couldn't find any," Walt said.

Just then they heard the excited pound of hooves, which startled them. There was the creek of saddle leather and then Jake walked into the firelight, holding the bicep of a bloody and beaten-looking black man. Jake had a beaming smile on his face, but his brothers weren't too pleased by the sight.

"I don't see no firewood," Dan pointed out, his face expressionless.

"I didn't get any," Jake replied.

Walt said, "You go out to get wood, but you come back with a nigger."

"That ain't all I come back with, originally. I had his horse, but the dern thing bit me and runned off. I got his saddle, though. This nigger was tracking us," he added.

"Say what?" Walt said, standing up. The baby began to whine.

Dan and Jake stood, dusting their pants.

"You trackin' us, are you, nigger?" Dan said.

"What you trackin' us for, boy?" Walt asked.

The beaten black man looked down at the ground, miserably.

"Let's beat this black boy even blacker," Walt suggested.

The four brothers set into him, kicking and punching; backhanding and stomping once he was down. And didn't stop until he lay still.

"Tie him up," Walt said. "And stuff his mouth with a hanky."

Dan and Benny did so, putting him up against the bole of a tree. His nose looked broke, and he was bleeding heavily from it.

"Whyn't we put a hanky in that babe's mouth, too," Dan suggested hopefully.

"You leave little Jesse James, Jr. be," Walt said.

"Jesse James, Jr.?" Dan said. "Psh! Well this is a right sight; we got no firewood, no money, a baby and a nigger. I'm turnin' in early. Curse your hides and especially yours, Jake! You done ought to have left that nigger and brought some wood – and that baby ought to have gone down that well."

"I tolt you he was tracking us."

"Why would a nigger be tracking us?"

"Maybe he's a scout for that herd we stole them horses from."

"Hightower's maybe," Benny suggested.

"Well then they're gonna find themselves minus one scout," Walt said, lying down next to the baby and playing with its fingers. "Ain't that so, Jesse James, Jr.? You gonna be a outlaw, just like your pa, ain't you?"

★ ★ ★

That very same evening the Kelsey brothers' reign of terror came to an end.

They had not been able to sleep much, due mainly to the baby's constant cries, though all were trying, Dan occasionally cursing the baby and turning over to try see if he couldn't sleep better on his other side.

That was when the voices shouted out of the darkness.

"Everybody up on their getaway sticks!" one voice shouted. "Keep your hands in the air! Do it! Now!"

A young voice shouted, "There's three guns on you boys!"

The baby on the blanket began to scream as the men stood up out of their blankets sheepishly, looking tired and racoon-eyed.

"We tracked you boys by the sound of that baby alone," the first voice said – an old man's voice, it seemed to Walt. "Now don't nobody move," it continued. "There's a passel of us out here."

Old Morg and Kit stepped out of the darkness and into their camp.

"Howdy, boys," Old Morg said.

"Howdy, Jeb," Kit said, nodding at Jeb, who was looking at them wide-eyed from where he was tied at the base of the tree. He had heard a twig snap before anyone else, but had not expected the boys to have been the gunmen, though had expected gunmen of some sort.

Kit and Morg were both pointing rifles at them. To the four brothers' surprise, a third gunman stepped out of the darkness, holding a pistol in two hands – only it was a woman.

"What kinda outfit are you," Walt said, "got a gunwoman?"

"The last outfit you're ever gonna see," Morg said. "Kit, untie Jeb and give him my Colt. We're gonna have us a hanging party."

Kit stepped past the four men cautiously and bent over Jeb, pulling his skinning knife and cutting his hands free of their string restraints.

Jeb immediately pulled the hanky out from his mouth and gasped.

"You alright?" Kit asked, handing him Morg's Colt.

"Am now," Jeb said, standing stiffly. He had a big cut on his eyebrow that had bled down one side of his face.

"Jeb," Old Morg said. "Kit. Collect any weapons these men have lyin' around."

Kit and Jeb went about collecting their pistols and rifles.

"Maggie," Old Morg said, once Kit and Jeb had joined him again and had their guns trained on the four brothers, the guns they had collected piled at their feet, "how 'bout collecting up that cryin' baby?"

At first Magdalena was reluctant, wary of the four mean and desperate-looking men, but soon she gathered herself, let out a deep breath, and walked behind them, fetching up the crying baby in both hands.

She came back to them with it and Old Morg had a quick look.

"What you boys doin' with a baby like that?" he asked.

"Walt took it," Benny blurted.

"Shut up!" Walt shouted at him.

Morg said, "Well, it don't much matter. I'm sure a fine baby like that don't belong to you rascals. There's some nice trees right here, and we're gonna have us a hanging. Boys, I see these rustlers have all got lassos hangin' from their saddle horns, four ropes for four hangin's – let's get 'em ready. Jeb, tie their hands with any string you can find. They had string to tie you, now it's gonna tie them."

Jeb found more of the same string in a saddlebag and went from man to man, tying his hands behind his back. Each man's eyes were fast stuck to the guns Old Morg and Kit had trained on them.

Once Jeb had them all tied, Kit lowered his rifle and handed it back to Morg, intending to step forward and assist Jeb in tying the lasso ropes to the four separate tree limbs above, but as he lowered it, one of the Kelsey brothers suddenly turned and made a run for it – Benny.

Morg ran through the tied men and trained his rifle down into the darkness and after the crackling footsteps of the running outlaw. There was a big flash and a bang, and the next thing they could hear was the escapee's screaming.

"They dern shot me!" he was wailing. "I'm shot, boys! The bastards shot me in the back. I'm dyin'! I can see the pearly gates!"

"Any else of you boys wanta take to runnin'?" Old Morg asked them, waving his rifle under their noses. "That boy ain't escaped his hanging. Jeb, go fetch him. He's gonna hang with the rest of 'em."

It took near half an hour to get all four of the men mounted on their horses with the nooses over their necks. The one who had been shot in the back cried out as he was helped into the saddle, but Old Morg told him to quit his whining, he was worse than the baby.

Predictably, Walton Kelsey attempted to deny the noose, and it happened to be Jeb who was trying to put the noose over him, so...

When he resisted it, Old Morg said, "I wouldn't do that if I were you, sonny – the last man who did that hung from his jaw for about five minutes before anyone thought it might be a good idea to shoot him full of holes."

Finally all four men were mounted and noosed – a grisly sight in the milky moonlight. Crickets chirped in the bushes.

"Any last words, boys?" Old Morg asked them, drawing his big Colt now and pointing it to the sky.

Dan spat.

"Yes, no? Okay then."

"Wait!" Benny cried.

"What is it, young man?" Old Morg asked him impatiently.

"I only was doin' what my brothers tolt me to do."

"Shut up, you son of a bitch," Walt cried out.

"I'm afraid that don't change nothin'," Morg said. "Square it with the Almighty."

Morg raised his Colt straight up into the night sky and stood to one side of the horses.

He fired four times, four big flash-bangs ripping through the night, and the horses jerked out underneath them. They dropped, hung, jerked briefly, boot tips tapping and kicking, and then they hung still, within ten or fifteen seconds, Walt going last.

"See?" Old Morg said after. "That's how a man's suppose to hang. He ain't suppose to dance on the end of the rope like that Injun did – at least, he ain't meant to much."

In the eerie moonlight, as the dead men slowly swung back and forth under the tree from the four separate branches, they looked like some kind of strange, eerie fruit that grew there.

"Let's go catch up those horses," Old Morg suggested tiredly. "We hung four men and won four horses, and gained a baby – not bad for a night's work. Though I don't know about the baby," he added.

They caught the horses and were able to return to the wagon a lot faster than they left it, Old Morg riding with Magdalena on the back of his horse. Jeb had untied some of the men's hands and left them to hang still at their sides – an even more eerie sight – so that the baby, which didn't stop crying the whole ride back, could be secured to Kit's stomach.

They had left Lynus Newcombe to watch the wagon and the mules, and when they returned he was sitting on the wagon seat, the rifle Morg had left him lying across his lap. It was the same rifle Kit had used when the Indian war party had chased down Jeb and Morg, the one that had been in the rifle scabbard in the back of the wagon.

They had brought all of the hanging men's rifles and pistols, including their ammo. They were distributed over the fourth horse, which was riderless. Jeb's saddle with the bite mark Apache had put in it was also attached to this horse.

When they rode into camp Lynus stood on the wagon seat, and said, "Why, that's my horse!"

Kit thought he looked very uncertain of himself for a moment, standing there on the wagon seat, and he didn't even mention the baby, which surely should have surprised him. It sure was making enough noise against Kit's chest, down which it had copiously slobbered.

They dismounted.

"What about the Kelsey brothers?" Lynus asked urgently.

"Is that what they were called?" Morg said. "You never mentioned that. I didn't know you knew 'em."

"Why, yes – no. I mean, I didn't."

Morg looked at him curiously, and so did Kit, but they dismissed his odd behaviour. Maybe the man was skittish is all. He looked it.

All of them were exhausted, even after only the initial trek on foot, and dropped their saddles more or less where they stood, all except Lynus, who seemed both on edge and unnerved.

"It's all right," Kit said, undoing his bedroll and preparing to get into it. "They're all hangin' dead under a mesquite. Only their ghosts could come get you now."

Jeb had helped him to untie the baby and Magdalena had taken it, to all of their relief – even Morg's. She said goodnight to all and then climbed into the back of the wagon, and soon, within no time at all, the camp was full of snorts and snores. Even the baby slept soundly.

Lynus sat on the wagon seat with the rifle, breathing slowly.

★ ★ ★

"Why, Lynus's took off," Kit said the following morning.

"Well I'll be," Morg said, scratching himself. "I call that right ungrateful."

Kit saw that one of the four horses was gone, and a pistol and a rifle, though not the rifle the man had had last night, which had been left on the wagon seat.

"He stole a pistol and a rifle," Kit pointed out.

"Let's hope that was all he stole," Old Morg said, checking his saddlebags. "Wait a minute – one of my saddlebags is missing. That son of a bitch."

A panic spread through the camp, and items and foodstuffs were hastily checked for. Nothing was missing from out the back of the wagon, in which Magdalena had been sleeping with the baby, which Magdalena was now rocking gently in her arms – the two had taken an immediate liking to each other.

To Kit's surprise, both the rifle and pistol Lynus had taken had belonged to the pile of weapons they had brought back from the late Kelsey brothers, if that is who they had been. Kit recalled that Lynus had mentioned "Kelsey brothers".

"Somethin' ain't right with this," Kit remarked, to no one in particular. "He took a pistol and rifle from the pile we come back with, but there's still four rifles and pistols."

Old Morg was still searching frantically across the camp, lifting saddles and blankets. The morning's surprise had come immediately, and they had not yet retied their bedrolls, or even had breakfast.

"Kit," Morg said, "all the money's missing, all of it – ever last dime we had. That son of a bitch! We needed that money to start the ranch."

Jeb had mounted Apache and was searching for tracks. From having studied Dwight and Lebold, he had become quite adept at it.

Kit was in a panic, not knowing what to do. The saddlebag that had contained Morg's money was indeed missing, and with its absence came a terrible feeling.

Old Morg was now circling the camp looking for tracks too. "Careful, Jeb," he said. "You and that horse might trample the tracks."

Kit said, "I don't see why he left one perfectly good rifle, and chose to take one of the Kelseys'."

"You're slow to catch on, Kit," Old Morg remarked, inspecting the grass. "He must have been riding with the Kelseys and they double-crossed him, took his rifle and pistol and horse. Now he's took 'em back. Only he's lit out with every cent we have."

"Can I help in any way?" Magdalena asked politely.

"Sure can," Morg said. "Toss what you can see into the wagon and get up on that wagon seat with the 'snapper. I just found the son of a bitch's tracks."

Magdalena went about the camp, with the baby on her hip, lifting up the blankets and saddles and taking them to the back of the wagon, where she quickly deposited them.

Old Morg was crouched down a few yards in front of the mules, inspecting the ground.

"What is it, Morg?" Kit asked him. "Where's he headed?"

"He's gone south," he said. "Must be headed back to the forts, either Griffin or he's goin' back to Fort Worth. If this man escapes," he added, "we ain't gonna be startin' no ranch, that's for sure."

After tying the Kelsey horses, they set out in the wagon, Old Morg pushing the mules particularly hard – he didn't want to leave the wagon behind and ride ahead, for to do that he would have had to leave someone with it. After the Indian attack Magdalena had refused, and had even insisted on coming with them as they went after Jeb. Although Old Morg usually left any tracking or scouting to Jeb to do, he was as adept a tracker as any Indian himself, which had been fortunate since Jeb had been the one they were tracking. Nor had Old Morg wanted to leave an able man behind with the wagon, either Jeb or Kit, for he knew he might need them both if there was going to be any kind of confrontation with Lynus Newcombe.

They pushed steadily south, over the flat dusty plains, occasionally navigating the wagon around thick thickets of chaparral and mesquite, Jeb scouting only slightly ahead, keeping sight of Lynus Newcombe's track. So far he seemed to be headed directly south, as before, and Old Morg was becoming more confident that he was going to Fort Griffin.

"He probably thinks we bought that story that he was headed north, to join a posse and go after those Indians."

"How'd he know about 'em, then?" Kit asked Morg.

"I don't doubt he was tellin' the truth about comin' from Fort Worth," Old Morg admitted. "Someone probably telegraphed the fort while he was there and the word spread."

Magdalena was also sitting on the wagon seat, as usual sitting so that Old Morg was between them. She played with the baby's fingers and occasionally held it to one shoulder and patted its back. It was behaving remarkably well, Kit thought, given how stiflingly hot it was, although Magdalena was keeping it well watered, using Old Morg's canteen and watering it by dipping a finger into the canteen top and then placing it against its little lips.

The Kelsey horses were well behaved for that matter, too, tied as they were to the rear of the wagon and plodding along behind it, grabbing up the occasional edible clump of grass.

When they spotted the sod house in the distance and headed for it, to ask the owners if perhaps a man had stopped by, they were stunned by the coincidence. As soon as the distraught-looking woman came out of the door, she rushed to the side of the wagon and reached for the baby, which Magdalena handed down to her – a little disappointedly, Kit thought. She had sure grown fond of it, that was for sure.

Kit wondered if the news that she was pregnant would in fact please her then, and if he could have used it to his advantage, but on the other hand there was no knowing how she might react, since the child was Indian. Half-Indian, Old Morg had told Kit.

"I don't know how to ever thank you," the woman cried, tears in her eyes. "Please, please come in. What can I get you?"

Old Morg said, "That's mighty kind of you, ma'am, but we're after the last one of them rascals that took your baby, and he ain't gonna live to see this night. I give you my word on that."

Her husband said, "Did someone get those men?"

"They're right now in the hereafter," Old Morg assured him. "We sent them there last night with their own ropes."

"Ain't that good news, Janey?" he said to his wife.

"I'm just so happy. I thought I'd never see you again," she said to her little baby.

"Well, it's elevatin' to see a fine family reunion like this," Old Morg said. "Though we have to lit out, I'm afrait."

"Wishin' you good luck now," the husband said.

"Wish it to them that have it comin'," Old Morg said, and whipped the mules into motion.

Kit thought Magdalena looked solemn, after losing her little companion. She sat there on the wagon seat jolting up and down, looking mostly into her lap, though occasionally ahead.

The empty red plains of Texas could send a man mad, Kit knew. He felt a little mad himself. It was the sheer endlessness of it all, and utter dryness – one quickly came to wonder if any of it would ever end. Occasionally he heard Jeb's rifle firing, and saw spurts of dust kick up from the ground as he shot at the rattlesnakes in their path.

Then Kit noticed a peculiar sight. He had shifted his focus to the far horizon, a heat-obscured undulating red line that merged seamlessly into the perfect blue sky, the land's end shimmering as it joined the skyline. At first he thought it was just a mirage he saw, but then a tiny steer's head and horns rose out of it, also shimmering, and then another and another appeared, until hundreds and thousands began to appear all along the southern horizon, as if consuming the land with their dark, black bodies. At this distance, they looked no bigger than ticks. Ticks with horns.

"'I God," Kit said. "That's the biggest herd I ever seen. That's an even bigger herd than the one we saw in Wagon Trail. Ain't that right, Jeb?"

Jeb was standing in his stirrups just ahead and looking.

"I don't see no point man," Old Morg said, squinting. "Or flank riders," he added.

Jeb sat and immediately put spurs to his mount, galloping off to get a closer look.

Something wasn't right, Kit realized. Not only could they see no flank or point riders – or any men at all, for that matter – but a huge cloud of dust was rising at the horizon behind the herd, swirls and palls of it beginning to climb to the clouds.

The land was quickly becoming ever the more engulfed.

"Those cattle are movin' way too fast," Old Morg remarked.

Kit's heart missed a beat. Soon the herd filled the entire horizon from end to end, east to west, and the wagon was rolling head-on towards them. He realized they had made a grievous error, following the cattle trail directly instead of to the west or east of the wide, trampled highway. They had overlooked the possibility of encountering a herd this late in summer.

And this was no ordinary herd. Not only was it the largest herd they had ever seen, they had not even encountered a scout. A scout, as Lebold and Dwight had explained to Kit, rode far ahead of the herd, clearing the path of obstacles and looking for good bedding ground and crossings in a river. If he spotted a sod house, for instance, he would have to direct the herd from it.

But there had been no scout – not that they saw – and there was no point rider, either, nor flank riders, as Old Morg had pointed out.

It was as if the herd were driving itself, in one great big migratory movement – an impossibility, Kit knew.

But most worrying of all, was how fast the herd was coming towards them. They could hear the din now, the din of hundreds and thousands of hooves. Soon little rocks and stones began to vibrate on the ground beneath them, and the Kelsey horses started to rear and strain at their ropes, beginning to pull the wagon backwards against the forward-straining mules, who were also beginning to behave skittishly in their traces.

They saw Jeb galloping towards them in the distance, coming at a dead run, a long dust cloud billowing along the land behind him. He was riding fast, standing in his stirrups and spurring the horse wildly.

"Stampede!" he appeared to be shouting. "It's a stam*pede*!"

Kit's mouth hung open.

Magdalena's eyes flew wide on the wagon seat.

Old Morg stood slowly.

"I 'God, it is," he said.

The din was building now into a deafening roar of running hooves. An unstoppable wall of cattle was rushing towards them, a horn-topped army of deafening death and doom for all that lay in its wake.

Kit saw a coyote go slinking by the wagon, about twenty yards away, headed north as fast as its paws could take it. Then he saw other animals sprinting by, running and swerving for their very lives: an antelope, a deer, a little rabbit, two prairie dogs and even a wolf.

The mules, spooked at the sight of the predatory coyotes and wolves, began to rear and tug at the traces, squealing. They were being pulled backwards by the three big horses attached to the rear, and Morg made a fatal mistake. He whipped the mules to stop the wagon from being pulled back and they strained forward against the traces. Suddenly there was a cracking noise behind them, and then a crash as the wagon's back-board tore loose and plunked to the ground.

Kit immediately jumped down and rushed to the rear of the wagon, only to see the Kelsey horses hightailing it into the dusty distance, dragging the backboard along behind them. It scraped up a narrow wall of dust as it was dragged across the desert, which rose into the air, a wavering dust wall in their wake.

"We're done for!" Old Morg shouted.

Kit hardly even heard him over the roar of the oncoming herd. He ran back and climbed up onto the wagon seat to weigh their options.

He could see individual steers running ahead of the herd, the animals trying desperately to get out of the way of it. He saw one swerve suddenly to the left, and then the herd bowled into it and it was trampled. Where it went under the steers began jumping, as if over a low fence. Another swerved and was bucked into the air by the big lead bull it got in the way of; it landed on top of several others and caused a domino-like effect, several steers tripping and toppling and being trampled into the hard earth.

Kit spotted a speck on the far western side of the herd, a horseman attempting to head them off – at least there was some operation underway to stop the herd.

Jeb rode his horse right up to the straining mules and reined it in.

"Get on the back the horse!" he shouted.

But none of them made a move to, for it was not known who should have the privilege.

"Take the girl," Kit said.

But time was little and Magdalena was clutching onto the wagon seat desperately, her knuckles white from her tight hold. Apache was becoming skittish at the closeness of the herd, too, which didn't help matters. Jeb was struggling to keep him under control.

"Get on the back of him!" Kit shouted to her.

"No!" she cried. "I'm staying up here on the wagon!"

"It ain't safe!" Kit shouted. "They won't just go around it – they're gonna tear right through it!"

But she was shaking her head hysterically and holding onto the seat, tears beginning to roll down her cheeks. She seemed to think she was going to be safer up on the wagon.

Kit looked up and saw the solid barrier of the onrushing herd not more than thirty yards away, the wagon itself shaking and vibrating now, juddering across the trembling earth.

Kit made a last moment decision. "You get on the horse with Jeb, Morg. I'll stay with the girl. We'll huddle in the wagon!"

Morg gave him one last desperate look, and then, knowing there was no time to argue otherwise, stepped over them and jumped onto the back of Apache, who Jeb had waiting at the side of the wagon.

"Good luck to youse," Old Morg called.

"Just go!" Kit said.

Jeb touched his spurs to the horse and it burst into a northbound gallop.

"Magdalena, we gotta get down and get into the back of the wagon!"

She didn't respond, so he began to pull her fingers off the seat edge and then stepped over her, pulling her down forcibly. Finally, with the earth vibrating under her feet, she began to respond. They ran to the rear of the wagon and Kit helped her up, looking out around the side as he did.

The wall of rumbling cattle were not but five yards away.

'I God!

Kit braced himself and dived into the wagon bed, landing on top of Magdalena. She began to scream, a piercing shrill shriek that was soon drowned completely out as the cattle began to pass the wagon. The mules squealed and shrieked briefly in the traces, so loudly that they were heard even above the herd, but then they were suddenly cut short.

The herd opened up around the wagon like a flooding river flowing around a rock.

Cattle began to bash at the sides of the wagon bed, sending great big bone-jarring judders through the wood. The canvas began to tear and rip as the tips of the long white horns rushing by caught in it. One of the white horns stabbed straight through the canvas and cut the back of Kit's arm; it tore horizontally along, and then caught against one of the wooden bows – for a moment the wagon began to turn, pulled by the horn, and then the bow snapped and fell into the wagon bed – the steer was freed and its horn shot out and disappeared as it passed.

The canvas sheeting had drooped inwards above the broken bow.

There were continuous judders and crashes as steers bashed and shouldered into the sideboards. Two more bows broke, and an entire side of canvas tore as a large horn ripped through it, flapping up and open like a tent.

Kit could momentarily see the galloping rumps of the cattle through the back end of the wagon, swerving and veering past, but soon their hooves had kicked up so much red dust he and Magdalena could not see a thing. They held onto each other tightly, Magdalena's head buried in Kit's neck.

The wagon seemed to be steadily disintegrating around them.

Another bow blew, sending wooden splinters flying. More worryingly, the wagon was slowly turning, as more and more cattle bashed and scraped along its sideboards. Kit could feel the wagon bed shifting beneath them.

A steer must have run straight into one of the wheels as it angled out, because there was a terrific splintering crash, and then the wagon bed fell downwards at one of the rear corners. The bed dropped beneath them, and they slid towards the declivity.

Magdalena cried out, but her cry was cut short as the wagon was bashed brutally, again and again, so hard it was now turned completely sideways.

"It's gonna tip!" Kit screamed. "Hold on!"

A wall of cattle hit the exposed side of the wagon with a *boom* that was so loud it reminded Kit of dynamite in a cave. He felt the wagon bed lift right up beneath them, and begin to tip precariously. Even as it rose beneath them and began to tip he could feel more steers colliding into it and pushing with all their added might.

"*Whoa!*"

The wagon tipped over.

There was another great splintering crash as it landed on its side. Kit was thrown into the remaining arches of the bows, with such force they broke beneath him. Magdalena landed against him a split moment later, winding him, their heads colliding and cracking together hard.

Flying boxes and barrels landed down against them, unrolled blankets, loose ammo boxes, rifle stocks and pistol butts. A tin of beans hit Kit's head and drew blood.

Kit clutched Magdalena as the wagon broke apart around them. Shafts of dusty sunlight shone in through the tear holes in the canvas, flashing dark and light, light and dark, as the steers continued to stampede past them.

A pair of long, sharp horns suddenly smashed right through the wagon bed, almost puncturing one of Kit's calves. The horns were immediately pulled upon and torn out, and there was more bashing against the back of the bed as the battered wagon lay on its side.

Suddenly the bows collapsed with a dry crackle and caved in, and then the wagon bed, straining from all the steers colliding against it, overturned.

It crashed over on top of Kit and Magdalena, and they were trapped against the canvas and the bare earth.

The cattle began to leap and land on top of it, with great big whacks and booms, pounding across it with their hooves. Dust and sand poured in between the creaking and groaning boards, as if they were buried alive in a leaking coffin.

Kit steadied himself and held onto Magdalena, as hard as she held onto him, and waited to die. Surely the wagon bed would break right in above them from the weight of the sheer numbers of cattle pounding across it.

It seemed there was no end to the crossing cattle, they scraped and pounded across the boards endlessly, and Kit's head was ringing. He felt deafened by the continual bangs and blasts of the hoofbeats.

But eventually they *did* begin to slow, becoming less consistent, if no less loud, and then finally there was only the odd – though even more startling – bash of hooves over the overturned wagon bed above them.

Then there were no more, and the only thing Kit could hear was his own wheezing breath, his lungs tight in his chest from breathing in all the dust.

His ears rang and he could barely hear Magdalena's own strained and rasping airways.

Slowly, their breathing became more regular as the dust settled, though no less wheezy.

"We made it, Magda," Kit said, himself amazed by this fact, for they had come closer to death than ever before. "We're alive!"

He tried to turn under the wagon, but too many boxes and barrels and other items were against him. He could see light shining in through broken holes and gaps in the board, particularly from the gap in one end, where the horses had made off with the backboard.

Kit felt intense claustrophobia, but knew they were going to have to wait for help and he needed to calm his nerves. Panic, he knew, had a way of spreading as fast as a prairie fire.

He put a hand on Magdalena's head, the way Morg had at the hanging of God Dog, and slowly he brushed it, as much for his own comfort as hers.

"Shhh, Magda," he said. "Someone'll come and then we'll be out of here."

But they waited and no one came, and the broken and overturned wagon bed in which they found themselves stuck was slowly beginning to heat up like a Dutch oven.

"Shhh, Magda."

"Get your hands off my head, Kit," Magdalena said. "You're pullin' my hair."

"I'm Florence Hightower, and you gentlemen are lucky to be alive. I lost two men in that stampede."

When Old Morg and Jeb had seen the flank riders heading off the herd and trying to turn it and get the animals to mill, they had slowed the horse and turned back. They watched as the two riders successfully managed what seemed an impossibility. By heading off the cattle on the outskirts on one side, they managed to affect the entire herd, even those animals far too distant to be affected directly by their actions. They fired their pistols into the air as they headed them off, both riders with their lower faces covered with bandanas.

Soon the herd had slowed and been turned to the east, the more sluggish animals bringing up the rear and following, the riders whipping at them with their coils of rope to get them to turn to the east and join the milling herd.

The entire range appeared to be floating with dust from end to end. Occasionally the odd solitary animal went trotting by, lost and trying desperately to catch up with the rest of the herd.

Slowly they had trotted back, and then a figure had appeared from the dust, a large dust-covered man in riding chaps with a full beard. His hat had blown from his head and hung behind him by its string, his hair white with dust.

He slowed as he approached them and, noting that they were not a part of his outfit, had introduced himself and told them how lucky they had been to be alive.

The man who had introduced himself as Florence Hightower said, "You were the fellas with the wagon?"

"That was us," Old Morg said.

"Good thing you abandoned it when you did – there ain't much of it left. Don't know if you'll be able to repair it."

"There was a man and woman in it," Old Morg said, concerned.

"There were?"

Old Morg remained silent, looking worried.

Florence Hightower noticed this and said, "Maybe they're okay. I'll have some of my men ride back and check it."

"We'd be much obliged," Old Morg said.

While Florence Hightower explained that he was the trail boss for the N.U. Outfit, two riders came wandering out of the settling dust, both wearing bandanas over their airways.

They rode up and checked their horses.

"The herd's been stopped," one said. "The boys are rounding up the stragglers."

"Losses?" Florence Hightower asked impatiently.

The other cowman said, "We've counted twelve so far."

"I'm sure there's gonna be a dern sight more than that." Florence leaned over his horse and hawked and spat several times, ridding himself of the dust in his throat. "I want you two boys to ride back and look for the remains of a wagon. There's two people were in it when the herd hit."

"Yeah," the first who had spoken said, "lucky sons of bitches. We dug 'em both out of the wreckage."

"They're alive?" Old Morg said.

"A few bruises and cuts, and the lady's right shook up, but otherwise they seemed aright. Your mules are dead, though."

"The hell with my mules, thank the Lord Almighty," Old Morg said. "How do you like that, Jeb – they made it, 'I God!"

Florence said, "Good work, men. Now go on and help them boys round up the stragglers."

They spurred their horses and rode east through the hanging curtains of dust.

"What in hell spooked your herd like that?" Old Morg asked him. "I thought most stampedes happened at night."

"These animals were deliberately spooked," Florence said.

"By Indians?" Old Morg asked.

"Not by a damn sight. It was a man by the name of Lynus Newcombe. My scout ran into him and there was an altercation. He was shot, but he'll live."

"What about Lynus?" Morg asked.

"After he shot my scout he flanked the herd on the eastern side and tried to slip by it, and one of my flank riders saw him and tried to head him off. When he started firing the herd spooked, and both of them boys got trampled by cattle. I saw it."

"You found the bodies?"

"Not yet. Why're youse so interested?"

"He made off with a saddlebag belonging to me, containing all my worldly wealth."

"Well you're welcome to go look for him. He's back south somewhere, trampled clean into the earth, I'd imagine."

"We'll do that," Morg said sternly.

Florence said, "I'm after the boys he was ridin' with. They made off with a hundred horses belonging to me. It was Lynus helped them to herd 'em out under our noses. In fact, a partner of mine once hired him on a drive to Denver, but the man's ineptitude cost him a sizable loss of cattle."

"Much obliged for the information, Mister Hightower," Morg said. "We seen both your horses and by chance we happened to bump into the men who stole them, though I've a mind they sold 'em on to boys who were none the wiser."

"Well, if they have I'll find them up north, I expect. What about the Kelseys? I tell you, I intend to hang each one of those boys."

"Well then you'll have to hang 'em twice. We already spared you the hassle."

Florence Hightower was mighty surprised with that, but he seemed agitated by the fact that someone else had got to them first. He seemed a vengeful man.

"Well, that's good to know," he said grudgingly. "I guess I'll feel mighty safer at night knowing they ain't out there preyin' on my herd. Much obliged, gentlemen."

He placed his hat back on his head and tipped it to them. As he did, sand sifted out around the crown and added to the dust on his shoulders.

"I can't wait to get out of Texas," he said. He put spurs to his mount and galloped off.

Old Morg said, "Come on, Jeb. Let's go pick up the pieces."

★ ★ ★

They found Lynus Newcombe – or rather, what was left of him.

It was a sight Jeb would not forget, and even Old Morg wasn't going to forget it in a hurry.

Man was inseparable from horse. It was as if they were looking at a trampled minotaur. Lynus Newcombe had been mashed flat into his horse; vital organs had burst from them both, bones had been splintered and stuck out sharply, poking through bloody shreds of fabric and cloth. Hundreds of half-moon marks had been mashed into both flesh and hide everywhere, so hard and deep they had reached through to the mud beneath.

The blood of both man and horse had already dried, turning the ground around them into a bankclay-coloured mess. Flies buzzed about the big squashed muddle. Old Morg could just make out Lynus Newcombe's face, stomped flat, nostrils and eye sockets packed full of mud. He could see a crooked row of upper teeth and a bit of exposed facial bone. The horse's head was perhaps the most horrific of all the sights on display. It was flattened into the earth but the snout still protruded, the tongue hanging out at the end and what few teeth remained askew, one angled straight out directly below its snout.

"'I God," Old Morg said. "Is that my saddlebag?"

They had dismounted and were standing over the ungodly mess of man and horse, and both Old Morg and Jeb had to peel the saddlebag out of the mud and blood, hide and flesh. It had been completely flattened, but when Old Morg opened the flap on one of the saddlebags, his coins and notes were still more or less intact.

"Well, I guess all things considering I can't complain," he said. "I got my money back, and Kit and the girl are alive. And the scoundrel got what was comin' to him," he added.

There was another similar mess of man and horse nearby, although they decided not to go and have a close look at it. They saddled up and went looking for Kit and Magdalena instead.

They found them half a mile southwest of the dead minotaurs. Kit and Magdalena were afoot and were heading north, hoping to encounter Jeb and Morg along the trail. Most of the dust had settled now, although the air still had a dusty quality to it, which they could in fact taste at the back of their throats with every breath they took.

"Well, it looks like you two're takin' a walk in a park," Morg said merrily, he and Jeb dismounting.

Before Kit could speak Old Morg wrapped his hands around him and gave him a hug, something so unexpected Kit blushed bright red – Old Morg had never hugged him, not even in the old days; for that matter, *no* man ever had. No woman, either – although that still remained the case. He did not count Magdalena's death-clutch as much of a hug.

Morg gave Magdalena a hug as well and they set off back to the wagon, where the first thing they were drawn to inspect was the trampled mules. The animals were as dead as they were ever going to get.

"We're gonna hafta go back and catch those Kelsey horses," Morg said, examining the rest of the wreckage. "We'll have to proceed the rest of the way on horseback, I'm afraid. This wagon's done for."

Old Morg left them at the wagon and mounted Apache, informing them that he was going to find the horses and would be back. That would give them a mount each, Kit realized; even Magdalena.

"Can you ride a horse?" Kit asked her.

"I've ridden a pony," she said.

"Well a horse is just a... a big pony, I guess."

But when Old Morg returned trailing the Kelsey horses, he ordered them to go through the wagon and to pack two of them with as much of their possessions as they could, leaving the barrel of wolf fat behind – it had burst open, anyhow, and was leaking a white greasy mess – and a few wooden boxes and sacks. He had only managed to catch two of the Kelsey horses, and had bought another two from Florence Hightower's remuda, telling the cattleman that if he came across the third missing horse he could have it.

Once they had the horses packed, Kit helped Magdalena to mount behind Morg's saddle, which to his disappointment was still her preference, even after what they had just been through together.

Soon they were all mounted up and ready to continue the final leg of their journey.

"On to San Antonio!" Old Morg said, and spurred the Kelsey mare.

Kit followed with much less enthusiasm, though it was nice to have a horse under him again.

In total it had taken over three months to reach San Antonio, and when they finally rode into the busy, little, Spanish-influenced adobe town it was with a feeling of incomparable relief.

Kit felt somewhat as the cowboys must have felt, he thought, at the end of a long drive, the cattle finally stabled and the trek over, although the town was nothing like those towns at the end points of the drives, and sure looked to be no pleasure resort.

They tied their horses to the hitching rails outside a hotel, where Old Morg told them they were all going to get to stay for the night. Kit's mood skyrocketed, for to be able to stay overnight in a town after having spent so many nights under the open skies – and often rainy skies, at that – was an unforeseen if more-than-welcome turn of events. Even Magdalena seemed excited.

To top things off, Old Morg handed them each a ten dollar gold piece, warning them, however, that it was to be deducted from their future wages. Then Old Morg told them to go have a good time, while he paid for a boarding room in the hotel reception area and went to stable the horses for the night in a livery.

He asked the young man in the livery whom he might speak to regarding land acquisition, and the young man told him to see the local realtor, who had an office in San Antonio's busy main street, or to visit the Land Registry Office.

Meanwhile, Kit, Jeb and Magdalena wondered the town. The people here were much less flamboyantly dressed, which was a relief to Magdalena. They certainly did not see a single woman wearing mens' trousers.

419

Kit decided he was going to take a bath when he noticed a sign hanging over a barbershop, but Magdalena wanted to look in a dry goods store, so they split up, Jeb going off with Magdalena to keep a protective eye on her.

In a way it was a relief to be alone, and Kit went into the barber's and paid the man to use the big iron bath in back behind a wooden partition wall. A small man with some sort of growth defect filled the soapy lukewarm water in the bath with buckets of hot water that had just been boiled in a big steel pot on a stove.

The water scolded Kit as he poured it in, and he could feel gritty sand against his bare buttocks from the bath's previous occupants – which the owner assured him had not been more than three, the last one being a woman – but soon the warm bath was so soothing to lie back in Kit would happily have never left it.

He paid a little extra to use a coarse bar of soap, but made sure to pick the hair out of it before lathering up his armpits. He slid under the water several times, submerging himself and rinsing the soap from his hair, and he did not leave the bath until the water was almost completely cold, such was the experience.

The small man handed him a towel and he dried himself off and got changed.

But when he went to leave the barbershop he caught a glimpse of himself in the mirror, his hat in his hand, and decided to have a haircut too – all to impress Magdalena, of course. Perhaps she just wasn't seeing him clearly, and once she finally did would fall head over heels for him. The tall barber trimmed his hair into a neat, close cut and then asked him if he wanted to be shaved.

Kit agreed to a shave and was startled when he saw the barber sharpening his cutthroat on a whetstone. But the barber shaved him without nicking him once, Kit tense on the seat, and when he was finished Kit paid him and had a good look at himself in the mirror before putting his hat on and leaving.

He looked a sight better than he had, that was for sure. Surely Magdalena would be impressed by the way he looked now.

He remembered Lebold and Dwight fantasizing about buying new clothes and a hat as soon as they got into Dodge, after taking a bath and having a haircut – as Kit just had – but when he went looking for a new hat, the ones he found were way overpriced, and there were certainly no new clothes he could afford. The clothes on offer were nothing of the sort that had been available in Dodge City, anyway, most looking to be Mexican.

One day, he promised himself – next summer, in fact – when they completed their drive, he would buy himself a fine pair of new boots, without spurs, and a new hat and trousers. He would do everything the cowboy did, even drink whiskey – and maybe visit a whore. He no longer considered to follow the principles of Old Morg, and in fact resented them. He felt they had stunted his development, delayed his rise to manhood in some way, so that Magdalena found him unattractive, or at least unsuitable. He felt it had made him immature, and he wanted to eradicate that immaturity as soon as possible.

That thought stopped him in his tracks, and a defiant new thought popped into his head. There was a way to do that right now, if he wanted to. It started with liquor, easy enough to be had in any saloon, and ended with a whore.

After having been with the fat woman in Farlow, he felt that another turn with a whore – although a thinner one this time, mind – could be no worse.

He found a little saloon and went in, stepping up to the bar. Unlike Farlow or Dodge, the place was neither busy at this time of the morning nor particularly full. Though several sporting women were hanging around, looking hopeful. He asked for a glass of whiskey and when it arrived he dropped the whole thing down his throat, the way he had seen Old Morg and the boys do in Farlow, in the Hog's Head Saloon.

It burnt his throat so suddenly he burst into a coughing fit, and the bartender looked at him with amusement. He was a Mexican-looking man with a face of dark stubble and a small sombrero.

"Another?" he asked Kit.

"No, I think that'll do for now," Kit said in a strangled voice.

Soon a sporting woman had sidled up to him and was smiling at him.

"Care to buy a lady a drink?" she said.

Somehow the warm feeling the whiskey had given him made him feel less nervous, he noted – and now that the burning sensation had passed, another might be a good idea. The young sporting lady was thin-looking, though had a large pair of–

"Are you gonna buy the lady a drink or you forget your manners?" the bartender asked him, waiting with another shot glass and the whiskey bottle.

"Why, of course," Kit said hurriedly. "And I'll have another," he added firmly.

The bartender gave him an unimpressed look, and then filled the two glasses.

Kit downed the whole of it again, and found the burning sensation was not quite as bad the second time as it had been the first, though it still made him cough some.

When he lowered his glass he saw that the sporting girl was only sipping hers, and scolded himself for having forgotten his manners again. It seemed he was always forgetting them, and to make things worse, always remembering them just a moment too late.

A funny feeling slowly came over him, a warm sleepy haze that made him want to smile, although he didn't. All of a sudden it seemed he didn't much care if Magdalena didn't like him, for the woman before him was a beauty – although he hadn't thought so at first – and all he had to do to make her like him was pay her.

He asked the bartender for another drink, and even though the woman had not finished sipping her whiskey, the bartender put down a third glass and filled it. Kit wasn't having that and decided to drink it himself, after downing the other.

He was not sure at which point he ran out of money. He became aware only once he asked for another drink and the bartender poured it, and then he couldn't pay for it.

"What'm I going to do with this whiskey now?" the bartender asked, highly displeased.

"Uh... drink it?" Kit suggested sluggishly.

"Go on, get out of here! Your pathetic."

"Thanks a lot," the whore said sarcastically, and rolled her eyes as if Kit were a morbid idiot, which he felt he was.

Kit left the saloon feeling sorry for himself. He felt light-headed and his feet didn't seem to be as sturdy as they usually were. So this was what it was like to be drunk – it didn't seem all that. As he made his way back to the hotel he wished he had used his money to buy the whore, and not wasted it on whiskey. Though the one thing to be said for it was that it made him feel carefree and without worry.

He found Magdalena outside of the hotel, sitting on the steps with her hand in a bag of horehound candy.

"Why, howdy, Magdalena," he said.

She immediately noticed something was different about him.

"You've had your beard trimmed," she said.

He took off his hat.

"Oh, and your hair – it looks much better," she added.

"Really?"

"Yes – you looked like a hog."

"Oh."

For a moment there he thought she was going to be pleasant. He stumbled towards her, intending to take a seat on the steps next to her.

"Where's Jeb?" he asked bluntly, sitting down.

"He went with Morg to see about the land. You smell of whiskey," she added.

"Why, I don't see why. I ain't drunk none," he lied.

"You're drunk," she said.

"I, uh... am I?"

"Yes. You sound slurred."

He lay down, his legs still planted on the steps. It seemed he was indeed drunk, for he would not normally have tried to sleep on a hotel's stairs.

"You're embarrassing," he heard her say, and heard her get up and go into the hotel.

"I guess I am," he said to no one.

A strong feeling of self-pity came over him, though he wasn't quite sure why, exactly.

Magdalena was looking forward to having dinner under a roof for a change.

Old Morg had paid for her to have her own room, whilst he and Kit were sharing another and poor Jeb had to stay in a stall in the livery. On the other hand, he had always seemed to her to get along more with horses than with people, anyway.

The room was just delightful – that is, for a girl used to a mud roof and the jolting canvas-covered bows of a wagon. It had a bathtub in it and one of the hotel porters soon came and filled it with several buckets of boiled water for her, and she took her clothes off and washed herself and then lay back in the bath with her eyes closed.

It was a relief to be able to do her business and to be able to wash without fearing that someone might be looking – like Kit. That was the thing about the open range, it afforded one no privacy. She knew Kit had seen her that time in the river, just not how much of her he had seen.

She had left him and gone into the hotel after he had collapsed on the steps, drunk, of all things. She could not stand drunks, and neither had her ma ever been able to stand them. She had threatened to leave Pa once when he had gotten drunk, and he never drank again.

She had asked the little receptionist what room number she had been put in, and explained that she was with the old man in the furs and given her name. He had checked his little register and been pleased to inform her she was in room 4 and had given her the key.

After she dried herself she changed back into her green dress and went down into the small lobby where the reception desk was, inquiring if two men matching Morg and Kit's description had come down.

"They're in the drawing room, ma'am," the receptionist said. With the small navy blue hat and dusty tasselled blazer he wore, she thought he looked like a solider from the Civil War.

When she entered the drawing room the men were waiting by a fireplace with a big ornate mantelpiece. Kit seemed to have sobered up some, and she could see Jeb outside waiting by the hitch rail. They went out and found a saloon, where they were able to order a meal of beef and vegetables, potatoes and gravy. The proprietor, another Mexican, didn't seem to give a hoot if they were there with a black man, probably since everyone in the place seemed to be dark and foreign, though most were indeed Mexican.

"Well," Old Morg said, taking a sip of whiskey. "Our future awaits us."

Magdalena had finished her dinner and had placed her knife and fork across the plate. She smiled politely.

Old Morg said, "I bought a new wagon, and a tract of land near a town called Wishbone, within sight of the Rio Grande."

"Wow," Kit said, smiling.

"Best news is yet to come," Old Morg said. "The tract of land already had a few buildings on it, a springhouse and a small barn, plus some corrals and stables. There's also a saddle shed – though they all need fixin' up some."

"I can't wait to get to it," Kit said.

"Well, you're gonna hafta. We leave tomorrow morning, early, so enjoy San Antone while you can."

Magdalena decided she wanted to get an early night, wanting to make the most of the peace and quiet and privacy of her room, so excused herself, to Kit's disappointment.

"Well, son," Old Morg said as they watched her leave the saloon, "this is it. We've come to the end of our trails and to the beginning of another trail altogether. First thing we're gonna do is fix up those abodes. There's no well so I guess we're gonna hafta sink one in. And Wishbone's in walking distance, though I hear it's a dusty little town with only a few people in it. At least it's got a little saloon and a general store, a few houses. Can't be too bad."

"It sounds great," Kit said.

"Then once we've finished doin' her up, well I guess we'll wait out the winter and start rounding up the cattle in the spring."

That night Kit couldn't sleep very well, thinking about all the possibilities the future held. Old Morg's snoring kept him awake, too, though he doubted that he would have been able to sleep anyhow.

Somewhere, he knew, Magdalena was lying in a bed just like this one, only all alone. He wanted to go to her, and do the sex act with her – though it was not the same feeling he had for the whores. It was a physical pain he felt, deep inside himself. He wanted to do it only so he could get close to her, as close as a man could ever get to a woman.

When finally he did sleep, he dreamed that he lay next to her, and that she held him, and that she smiled at him.

If only real life could have been like the dream...

EPILOGUE

As the months passed two things came to define Kit's life: the building of the ranch and the repairing of the outbuildings, and the growing lump of Magdalena's belly.

Everyone had settled well on the tract of land Old Morg had seen fit to buy. Even if the town of Wishbone was a small, dusty little clapboard row of buildings with a few washing lines hanging out behind some of them, and even though it was the smallest town yet − scarcely even a town, in fact − it was nice to be able to take the wagon at the end of a hard working day and visit the saloon, play cards and drink.

Kit had come to drink often, developing a fondness for the warm feeling the whiskey would bring. Kit had also developed a strong friendship with Jeb Rawlins, the two of them working together night and day. Old Morg had ordered a load of lumber from San Antone and when it finally arrived they were able to replace the rotten planks on the shed and springhouse, and fix the corrals and pens, including the round enclosure for breaking the broncs.

When they had arrived, the main house, a small stone-walled building of Spanish style, had had no roof, but now they had been able to build one. Magdalena spent most of her time in the house, preparing the morning and evening meals.

After that Kit and Jeb had spent many back-aching and stifling hot days digging a well. There had been an incident as well, although only one. But all the same Kit had thought Jeb had been killed in it.

One afternoon while Jeb was down in the well and Kit was hauling up the wooden bucket full of rocks and dirt, the bottom had blown out, and the sharp rocks had showered down on Jeb. Fortunately, however, when Kit pulled him up, only his elbows and arms had been hit, and one shoulder and foot, and not his head. He had held his arms over it protectively and deflected the falling rocks from hitting his skull, but the rest of him wasn't a pretty sight and there had been a lot of blood.

He had not been able to work on the well for a week, and Kit had finally completed it himself. Magdalena had tended and looked after Jeb in the small stone-walled house with its makeshift sod roof. Inside the house was the room in which Kit and Jeb and Old Morg slept, three pallets down on the floor, and the separate room in which Magdalena stayed.

She had adjusted to life on the ranch slowly but happily, taking charge of the chores with a sense of responsibility and necessity. She had become even more happy once the well had been dug, for before it was completed she would have to walk down to the shallow, muddy waters of the Rio Grande, and collect it with a bucket, and although the river was not far, the bucket was heavy and pulled her to one side. When Kit could, he helped.

Occasionally other hands from other outfits on the border came to Wishbone to play cards and exchange stories, some coming all the way from Matagorda. Kit enjoyed drinking with them and hearing the heated stories of their mishaps and adventures on the drive. Some had even said that they might hire on if they had a herd ready in the spring of next year, and Kit looked forward to working with some – although not all – of them.

Some nights he rode down to the Rio Grande and patrolled along its borders, looking out across the wide river into Mexico, where they would ride next year to round up the cattle. He knew it would not be an easy task, and that they were apt to meet strong opposition at the hands of the Mexicans, but he was ready for it.

Old Morg spent a lot of his time in Wishbone; he had met an old widow lady there and he often visited her, even spending the night. The first time he had it had shocked them all, for the lady was elderly and it amazed Kit to think she was still up for the sex act. Though when Old

Morg returned he never said much, had not even told Kit her name, and seemed to want to keep it that way.

It always seemed there was work to do on the ranch, but as winter closed in and the ranch buildings and corrals were completed, it was only their upkeep that they tended to. They spent much of their time in town, in the warm saloon, although Magdalena only went into town to get things from the general store, taking the wagon, sometimes with Old Morg.

At night, as Kit slept with the knowledge that she was just across the small stone hall from him, asleep on the pallet in the other room, he thought about Magdalena so much it seemed the sun would come up before he could get himself to sleep. He thought mostly about that growing lump.

She had filled out around the face, and her appetite had increased considerably, which allowed them to remain silent about her condition the longer. No one, not even Old Morg, had yet been able to work up the nerve to tell her that she was pregnant, of which there was now no doubt.

Kit wondered who, in the end, would have to tell her, for the time would have to be soon – her belly was beginning to curve out unnaturally, and her back was arching like an Indian's bow, and one morning she had even asked *him*, of all people, if she was getting fat.

"Why, no, Magda," he had said. "You're thin as a post."

Mostly, at night, Kit thought about the on-hurtling future. Magdalena was going to give birth to a baby, a half-breed, and Kit would take the place, whether she wanted him to or not, of father to the child – or at least father *figure*. Old Morg, he figured, would be a sort of grandfather, and Jeb an uncle. That is how he saw it.

But that wasn't all the future held. They would begin working sincerely as the winter passed, rounding up the horses and steers, travelling into Mexico routinely to get them. They would begin amassing a herd, breaking broncs and hiring hands, a cook and chuck wagon for the drive, not to mention branding all the animals.

And then eventually the time would come to take the herd – up to

Nebraska, Old Morg had said. A near one-thousand-mile drive, if not more. And Old Morg had said he would set out with a herd of no less than three thousand five hundred, with twelve hands. The intention was to sell them in Ogallala, Nebraska, where there was still, in fact, considerable Indian presence, according to some.

He wondered what would become of Magda and her child amidst all of this. They could not stay, and would have to be brought along – that was only common sense. Morg would be on the drive, Jeb, possibly Dwight and Lebold – or at least Dwight. And new hands would be hired on…

It would be the adventure of his lifetime, full of danger and fraught with obstacles, Kit knew. But he intended to go through them all and get that herd to Nebraska.

Most of all, he intended to get Magdalena to love him by then.

No matter how much he tried she remained distant from him, did not love him as he loved her. He always tried to work within sight of her, to impress her in every way he knew how, but she never seemed to be impressed at all.

But he refused to give up.

He had an image of the future in his mind. It was of he, Kit Cope, standing outside the little stone-walled house in the light of a new dawn, staring out at the great Rio Grande, its banks covered from end to end in cattle – their cattle – and the hands were down there among them, working their shifts, holding the herd and singing to calm the cattle. He could see Jeb Rawlins in the corral, breaking in a new horse, and Old Morg standing outside with his hands through the rungs, watching and encouraging.

But most of all he could see Magdalena, her hand held tightly in his as she stood next to him; and then he saw the little Indian child with its own little hand in hers.

This is the future Kit Cope saw, and he intended to see it come to pass.

Afterword

Dear Reader,

I have struggled all my life to reach you, to be in a position whereby I may communicate my ideas to you, and *now*... here we are. I always wondered what I might say to you, once I got here, but now that I am here, I find myself somewhat... wordless – which is no good position to be in if you are a writer. For a point of discussion then, we should turn, rather, to you.

I hope you have enjoyed the exploits of young Kit Cope and his friends as much as I, for even if you have enjoyed them half as much, I have done this work justice – they are far from over, let me assure you; our next outing is presently well underway, and Kit and I and the various other characters that occupy my head think of you often, as always. To us, you are the meaning of our world – without you, our world has no meaning. It exists like an earth without a single pair of eyes to perceive it – and like all earths, it was created lovingly, in order that it may be perceived time and again, by all the generations to come; what a crime then, would it be, were no one to see it!

I have often pondered the idea of writer as demi-god to his own creations. Certainly my own characters have always seemed to step onto the page without any prior announcement. I have never been one of those writers to plot, for I believe the best writing – that is to say, the most magical – pours forth spontaneously, and that anyone, in truth, is capable of it. Yes, even you, dear reader. I would feel selfish not to share this fact with you. It was never shared with me, which is perhaps why it took me so long to come around to realizing it.

One day I read a smashing book, that turned me from a sullen teenage boy without direction into a proverbial armchair buccaneer; but when the joy of that book came to an inevitable end, I found myself wanting more of this rich and rewarding world full of endless possibilities – this world of the mind. It was only a small jump from this notion to my next idea, which was to sit down and write my own book. For a moment I battled the same thought I expect might cross your own mind at this point: yeah, but how can someone like *me* write a book, I'm not...

Fortunately, some either stubborn, or naive – or untainted – part of me, said, "Yes, but hang on a minute, the guy who wrote that smashing book you just read, is no different than you; just a guy, that is, with a pair of hands just like you, a head, and in it, a *mind*."

And with that attitude I sat down and wrote my first book, and it was hilarious – amateur, yes, but even my parents (my father, mostly) agreed it was hilarious; and although sceptical of this, the truth of it was confirmed to me the day my late grandfather, Harold Barrell, read it to my grandmother Toy, who was at the time just beginning to suffer from Alzheimer's disease. I remember leaving them the manuscript and hiding around the corner at the top of the stairs, listening as my grandfather began to read her the story. And every now and again I heard her laughing out loud, at all the places I had intended to be funny. I swear to this day, there is no memory that brings me more confirmation of the beauty of this craft, and my ability to perform it. I remember being so happy to hear her laugh and so anxious to see their reaction that I was sweating buckets.

All it took to write, it seems, was belief – or maybe denial; call it naivety, actually. I was too naive to think I couldn't do it; do, that is, what so many others were doing out there: *writing*.

I was sixteen when I wrote my first book – but that was not in fact my first foray into writing.

When I was about seven or eight years old, my grandfather Arthur Goodchild came to visit us in Mombasa, Kenya, where we lived at the time. And in a bold attempt to occupy me, he declared we were going to write a book together. I remember sitting curiously at the table with him, where he had a CNA tablet of lined paper and a pen waiting. We sat there and discussed what the story was going to be about – it was to be about three young boys who stowed away on their father's galleon when he left to sea, and a mutiny that occurred on board – and then he set to penning it. It was aptly named *Three At Sea*.

Although I did not begin penning novels at this age, I suppose I can consider it my first collaborative effort, and although it was not until age sixteen that I sat to write my first book, I still believe some sort of seed must have been planted. Perhaps, in retrospect, it was the very reason for my lack of self-doubt, since I had seen first-hand how a novel could be written: simply by sitting there and thinking about it, and then hunkering over the pen. The good old-fashioned *logical* way.

For I assure you, I am convinced it is only the self-doubt that prevents so many from discovering themselves, not in this life, but in the life of the mind. I think it was Steven Spielberg who said, "There are two different kinds of people, those who discover themselves in the world, and those who create a world to discover themselves in."

The fundamental difference, I suppose, is only initiative and belief. And perhaps it is only self-doubt that stands in the way of that initiative.

Oh – and another thing. You cannot sit down, new to this world, and expect to enter it with the solitary motive of making money. Money will come, one supposes, if the writing is good; and the writing will be good, I assure you, if you create lovingly. You have to love the words and the sentences, the paragraphs and chapters – the *smell* of the pages – and you have to absolutely adore even the worst of your creations, as one imagines God must (with possible exception of a few).

Indeed, you must see yourself as demi-god, for if you do not believe that your creations are real, well, then, they aren't – and nobody else will, either. In general, people only believe in what is real. Clever people, anyway. There are a good number of fools – and I suppose there always will be – who will believe in what isn't real. That's why we have things like Scientology and a lack of socialized medical care in even the most advanced countries today. The latter is most definitely irreal.

And so I return to my former notion: that of spontaneous creativity.

I believe that truly magical writing is done this way, and for the most part – aside from a few failed experiments – have written this way myself. Usually I will ponder an idea or outcome endlessly in my head, but will never write it down in the way of anything resembling a *plot* – I have the faith; for I saw my grandfather all those years ago put pen to paper and watched those magical words form and begin to make sense. And I have seen, time and again, characters like Old Morgan simply barge into a scene and nearly shoulder the main character out of the way, and little characters like Dim Bill open up a livery in my own imaginary town without my knowing it, and discovered their strange little quirks and traits.

Suffice it to say, that I have seen enough magic to *believe*.

Until next time, dear Reader, this is Alan Eltron Barrell, Kit Cope, Old Morg and Company, saying "So long for now." Perhaps we will have a longer chat *next* time.

Belgium, Flanders, February 4th, 2011

ABOUT THE AUTHOR

Alan Eltron Barrell was born in South Africa in 1983, where his great grandfather was once Senator. He wrote his first book when he was sixteen years old and has been writing ever since. He has lived in several countries around the world, including Kenya, England, Wales, Cyprus, Spain, and Belgium, and enjoys touring America on his various research expeditions. Here his real passion lies, for that phenomenal period of migratory movement that culminated in the great rip-roaring Wild West.

As a writer he has a passion for satire and understated humour, and says he developed a pretty good sense of humour the day he discovered his father's father's Godfather was made a pair of sandals by Mahatma Ghandi.